FOREWORD

Please note that N.K. Quinn is a UK based author and all spelling and grammar conforms to British conventions.

Enjoy!

JOIN TEAM FALCON!

Team Falcon needs you!

Join Team Falcon to receive a free copy of the "Sentech Files". This accompaniment to the novel tells the story of the Spectre, undercover agent of the rebel Scorp group, and is only available via the mailing list.

In addition, you will receive a link to the password protected section of the author website filled with additional content including access to deleted scenes, background information and character artwork produced by international comic book artists.

The free sign up link is at the end of the book.

Join the Resistance!

N.K. Quinn

THE STEEL FALCON BOOK 1: AWAKENING

By N.K. Quinn

1

CORPORATION RULE

The roar from the crowd deafened him. They were on their feet, the noise like a stampede.

"Walker! Walker! Walker!"

The throng chanted his name and the wall of sound pushed through him, making his insides reverberate. Hand over ears and head tucked down, Kalum Walker squeezed his eyes closed so hard they felt like they were being pushed back into their sockets. The tremor in his right hand was slight at first, but he knew that was how it always began. It was like the rumble of thunder before a lightning strike. The familiar icy hand traced its path up the small of his back. Its climb was slow but relentless, tiptoeing up to his chest and branching into two. His breath left his body quicker now, beyond his control. The shallow gasps made him feel as if he was drowning.

"Walker! Walker! Walker!"

Again the sound of his name assaulted his ears, reaching a crescendo but seemingly not wanting to subside. The phantom hand was now around his throat and in his chest.

It was as if he could feel each finger flex in succession, clamping down with malevolent intent.

"Come on. Come on," he wheezed under his breath, starting to rock back and forth as the edges of his vision tinged with red. "Not now."

A chime sounded from his arm, getting louder and more insistent with each peal.

"Kalum. Your vital signs are reaching dangerous levels. Calling emergency contact and sending data metrics for logging," the electronic voice said.

Normally, Kalum found the familiarity of the voice of the TRIST unit on his arm gave him some comfort when he got like this. Even now, nearly ten years since their mandatory introduction, there were still people who felt wearing it was like being tagged and watched like some wild animal. The majority rationalised this imposition to their freedom as a necessary inconvenience of being under Sentech Corporation rule. Sentech directed their propaganda machine to skilfully deflect all talk of loss of liberty. They touted the wrist-mounted devices as the ultimate step forward in creating a truly connected society, choosing to focus on their multi functionality as body mounted computers and communication devices. Kalum knew the truth of it. He knew that they allowed the Corporation to know where its members and affiliates were at all times, and collect data that allowed them to ensure that only those who weren't a burden to the Corporation remained under their shelter and care. He knew all of this, but to him, the voice of the TRIST was one of the first friends he'd had outside of his family.

Taking off his glasses he rubbed his temples hard in small circular movements, hoping to use the pain as a distraction. He felt his chest loosen and he managed to take in a loud gulp of sweet air. He held it in his chest as if he didn't trust that he would ever take another one. His eyes registered the light flashing on the dull gunmetal TRIST wrapped around his left arm. With a mammoth effort he gathered his wits enough to cancel the outgoing call. Only then did he let out the breath. That was one landmine side-stepped, at least. Her coming here now would only make things worse, despite her intentions.

Kalum reached down under the steel bench he was seated on, and pulled out his maroon school backpack, the same standard-issue bag that was shoved under the rest of the seats in the pantheon like stadium around him. His vision was still blurred as he ripped it open and he dug around inside. His fingers made contact with the smooth curved object and they snatched for it. The snake-like coils of headphone wires gripped the pill bottle and refused to release it. Kalum tugged at it, becoming more frantic as he felt another wave of panic hit him. With another yank the bottle was set free, but it was too late for Kalum to dial back his strength. It sailed over the heads of the pupils below him, catching the light as it arced through the air. He watched it go and the moment seemed to suspend in time. He considered reaching out for it, trying for some heroic save, but he stopped short and watched it bounce, ping and skitter on its journey to the bottom of the stadium.

KALUM SHOVED his hands back in the bag, wading through the broken pens and books until he felt what he needed. He pulled the sketchbook out onto his lap and allowed the bag to fall free, not caring if its scattered contents would ever be found again. He gripped the book tight enough that his fingertips hurt as they pressed against the cover that was worn down by age and use. His thumb found the biometric sensor and it fell open, landing on a blank page. Somehow a pen was in his hand and dancing across the page, breathing life into the nothingness that was there moments ago. As the sketch took shape, his vision began to clear and he felt the vice-like grip on his chest relax.

He could still hear his name being called. It filled the stadium like a monster that couldn't be contained, but then there was another sound interspaced amongst the chaos and the cheering. Kalum felt eyes on him, and could hear the murmurs and stifled laughter.

"I can't believe they're related."

"He's so weird."

"His eyes freak me out."

Kalum looked up and saw a group of girls looking at him. They shot him a sneer and turned back to the action unfolding in the Arena below them. Ignoring them, he concentrated as the pen flicked through the final strokes and he looked down on the picture in front of him and felt his heart rate start to slow. He took another deep breath, as if not trusting the last, and closed the book.

Leaning forward he held his head in his hands and the noise around him seemed to fade and he was finally able to think. His anxiety had been steadily getting worse over the last few weeks. He couldn't understand why the medication wasn't working anymore. The pounding headaches had been one thing, but this total meltdown was almost impossible to manage. The last thing he needed was for more of these incidents to be logged on his Sentech record.

"Kalum, your pulse and breathing are more regulated, reaching acceptable levels. Will there be anything else?"

"No thank you, TRIST, you can shut down."

The chime rang out in response and the screen on the

unit faded to black. Kalum caught a glimpse of his reflection staring back at him. His eyes. People had whispered about them since he could remember. The flecks of blue in his right eye shone brightly in the darkened surface of the toughened glass, almost neon in hue, whilst his hazel left eye was lost in the shadow of the screen. Looking at the reflection he wondered if there was something different about them.

He shook his head and closed the thick book, taking care to make sure the folded pieces of paper that were threatening to rip apart the spine stayed deep in between the sheaves. Using his free hand he cleared a space for the book in his bag and slid it in with care. He looked around the stadium and he felt as if he was taking it in for the first time, his senses firing one by one. The crisp chill of the winter afternoon stung his cheeks and he was grateful for the air purifiers humming in the background, which must have been working overtime to cleanse it for a crowd of this size.

There was a blur of motion on the pitch below and again the crowd roared his name.

"Walker! Walker! Walker!"

His nerves were now steady, less raw, and he peered down to the pitch below and saw why the crowd was on their feet again. Reese Walker was doing it again. His brother's tall muscular frame, clad in a fitted one-piece, matt-black uniform was charging down the field. His overlying protective Henkan gear comprised of a chest plate that extended to his back, emblazoned with a bold blue letter T. The same motif adorned the large gauntlets on his arms and the back of his headgear. Reese moved with precision and grace, every footfall placed by design, and Kalum could see why these people were in awe of his older brother. In this moment the difference between the two couldn't be more striking, and certainly more than the chronological year that separated them.

Kalum watched as an opposing team member bore down on Reese from his flank, arm raised and reaching for the silver orb in his possession while his other arm was cocked back and ready to strike.

Reese caught the movement in his periphery and pivoted. The opponent's fist glanced off Reese's headguard, sending him spinning, but he used the momentum to whip his elbow around into his foe's head.

The boy crumpled to the ground as a klaxon blared, and the huge overhead screen erupted into life with the word "TAKEDOWN" pulsing in brilliant red. The crowd surged and laughed as the defender flailed in frustration, tethered to the ground by an invisible force. The gathered masses counted down with the illuminated display; 3...2...1. Then a different klaxon sounded, and there was a clunk as the magnets under the pitch disengaged and the boy separated himself from the ground.

Kalum watched on as his brother cut a path into the other teams' defense area.

Without exception the crowd were now on their feet. Kalum joined them, but his height betrayed him and the pitch was obscured from view.

"He's going to do it!"

"Come on. Come on!"

They screamed and shouted, feeding off each other's adrenaline until the screams of joy from other Trinity pupils filled the air.

"He did it! He hit the move!"

"Walker Wipeout!"

The overhead Jumbotron hologram erupted in a burst of colour and animation.

Kalum turned his head to the screen and saw his brother collect the silver ball from the back of the net. He stepped over the heavily clad goalkeeper, who lay on his back like an overturned beetle. He waited for the timer to run down and then Reese offered him a hand up, a hand that was swatted away in disgust. Another klaxon sounded the end of the match and the scoreboard declared Trinity Titans the winners.

Reese launched the ball into the crowd and pumped his fist in joy. His teammates joined him and four of them hoisted him into the air whilst another watched from the side-line.

From his place in the stadium Kalum couldn't see Nathan Lancaster's face, but he didn't need to see it to know that Titan's co-Captain wouldn't be too happy about not being the centre of attention. Kalum saw the boy's eyes flick in his brother's direction and then watched as he left the Arena. Something stirred inside him; it was a faint whisper speaking to him, urging him to go and watch his brother's back. The voice spoke to him again, more insistent this time. Kalum resisted it, remembering the way Frannie had taught him to so many years ago.

With some effort the voice faded away and he was able to concentrate again. The crowd cleared and Kalum saw Reese standing directly below him, his smile almost as broad as his chest as he called him down. He got to his feet and picked his way through the crowd, but by the time he reached the pitch he saw Reese being led away by men wearing badges and wielding clipboards.

The look he saw on his brother's face was familiar, but it

was an expression he is more used to seeing on his own. It was the look of fear.

As he tried to climb the barrier to follow, a large hand clamped onto his shoulder and pushed him back down. He turned, and a large Enforcer looked down at him, canting his head inquisitively.

"No unauthorised personnel on the pitch," he said, his tone flat and monotonous.

"I know, but that's my brother. I need to go to him," Kalum protested.

A sceptical look flashed across the man's coarse features as he looked down at the scrawny boy standing in front of him. With a grip of iron his hand grabbed Kalum's wrist, pulling it out towards him. He overlaid his own TRIST on top of Kalum's and uttered a verbal command.

"TRIST unit identify owner."

"TRIST unit 101356 compliant. Override accepted. Owner is Kalum Walker, Sentech Corporation - Affiliate Status, Student at Sentech governed Trinity School, Primary pupil name, Reese Walker."

The Enforcer pulled away his TRIST unit and smiled at Kalum. It was obvious this was not an expression his face was comfortable holding for any length of time as it returned back to its resting sullen grimace.

"Sorry, you don't look related," he said, and opened a gate, allowing him to pass.

"I hear that a lot," Kalum said, shouldering his backpack and stepping out onto the pitch. He walked across it, feeling the give of the grass below his feet but also the pull of the thick embedded magnets under the surface, as they tugged on the metal fastenings of his bag.

He set off in the direction he'd seen Reese being escorted but stopped short when he saw Nathan Lancaster talking to a man by one of the side entrances to the Arena. Kalum watched as Nathan handed over a wad of thin plastic cards with neon red numbers scrolling across their face.

Kalum felt his eyes bulge. He'd never seen so many credits in his life. A brief calculation in his head totted the total at near to five-thousand. That more than his mother brought in even when they added his father's Sentech honorarium payment..

"The Operative appreciates your donation to the cause," the Scorp growled, pocketing the credits.

He handed Nathan a sleek, black plastic box and turned to leave. Kalum spun around, pushing his back against the side of the wall and held his breath as the man walked past him, too busy staring at the credits to notice the short boy cowering breathlessly in the corner. Kalum caught a glimpse of the mark on his wrist as his sleeve rode up. He paused, and shook his head in disbelief. Squinting, he forced his eyes to focus. There was no mistaking the twisted black scorpion tattooed there. The mark of the Scorps, terrorists who rebelled against Corporation rule.

The man continued and sauntered past the Enforcer that had stopped Kalum moments ago. The Scorp tossed him a lesser credit, one that would still have been enough to feed a small family for a week. The Enforcer snatched it out of the air and pocketed it with a nod. Kalum turned to look at Nathan as he retreated further away from the Arena heading back towards the school. He set off after Reese just as he heard the muffled voice in his head sound off once more. At first it was barely intelligible, like he was hearing it underwater, but it gradually became clearer.

"What if he's up to something?"

"If Scorps are there that can't be good."

"They're terrorists."

Shaking his head he continued on his way, but the voice rang out once more, clear this time and more forceful.

"What would Reese do?"

Kalum stopped and hung his head for a second. He turned on his heels and hurried back down the alley after Nathan, trying his best to ignore his hammering heart and shaking hand.

2

ROULETTE STYLE

By the time he reached the Enforcer checkpoint at the end of the alley Kalum's chest was tight and wheezy. He looked around but Nathan was nowhere to be seen.

"I'm... Kalum Walker," he said, his breathlessness making his voice hitch as he spoke. "I'm looking... for... my brother Reese."

The Enforcers scanned his TRIST unit as before and then parted to let him pass. He was now back on school grounds near the imposing front gates. As he scoured the surrounding area he noticed some Trinity backpacks jutting out from behind some foliage near an outcropping of trees. He looked around him and saw no one, not even the odd passing student or faculty member. As he walked towards them, the shake in his hand became more pronounced and he had to grip his wrist to get it under control.

Leaves crinkled and twigs snapped underfoot as he entered the forest, the sharp edges of the branches and vegetation stabbing and scratching at his skin. He tripped over a gnarled root and heard his jacket rip. Dirt and what he hoped was mud smeared his hands and trousers.

"Arrrgh!" he cried, looking down at the mess over his uniform. "What am I even doing here?

He heard hushed voices and footsteps nearing. His heart felt like it was wedged in his throat, trying to free itself. A quick glance back towards the school and he realised that there was no way he could make it back before being seen. Then a sudden, shearing lance of pain in his head made his knees go weak, and he would have collapsed if not for a nearby branch.

"No! No! Not now!" he said, wincing. Kalum tried to take a step forward but another flash of pain sent him reeling. His vision blurred, and then everything went black.

His eyes snapped open and he gasped when he found himself forty feet above the ground, seated on the thick branch of a tree. His pulse raced as he held onto the branch so hard the bark dug into his skin, even through his school uniform.

"Don't squirm or you'll fall," the voice in his head whispered.

The footfalls grew louder and he looked down to see who they belonged to. The wave of vertigo that hit him made him immediately regret his decision. As he clung even tighter to the branch he saw Nathan come to a stop and lean against his tree.

Nathan wasn't alone. Other members of the Henkan team were there. Leo and Casper Burton, the twins, were gathered around Nathan, their smiles wide while they scanned the surrounding area to make sure they weren't being watched. They were tall and broad like the tree trunk they were gathered around.

"Are you sure this is a good idea, Nate?"

A tall, wispy girl picked her way through the foliage and perched on a tree stump. She sighed as she twirled a lock of her blonde hair around a finger and looked up at the canopy.

Kalum saw Kara Lambert's trademark bored expression. Although he had never interacted with her per se, he knew her by reputation. She was the daughter of a former senior executive of one of Sentech's competitors, who had allegedly sold company secrets that secured him and his family an opulent life, thus allowing Sentech to gain a controlling share in the Corporation.

Next to her stood someone Kalum had never seen. She was a similar height to Kara and her clothes were the standard Trinity girls' uniform; a maroon jacket, white shirt and black tie. But something about her made it difficult for Kalum to look away. He watched as she looked with disdain at the Trinity logo on both sleeves. She pulled her auburn hair behind her ears to frame her pale freckled skin and green eyes. A smile played on her face as Kara complemented her on her shoes, but there was something forced about it.

"I like your tattoo," she said, pointing to Kara's wrist. Her voice was light and carried a musical cadence that made it pleasant to Kalum's ears.

"Aw, thanks," said Kara, pulling up her sleeve so that the girl could better see the heart tattoo on the inside of her wrist. "It cost a load of Credits 'cause it's retro, but I love it."

The other girl nodded and then squirmed and tugged on her jacket.

"Ugh. They really expect us to wear this stuff?" she asked, adjusting her TRIST unit over her shirt sleeve.

It caught Nathan's eye.

"Hey," he said, stopping short of taking out the box that the Scorp had handed him. "What TRIST model is that? I haven't seen that before."

The girl pulled her sleeve down a bit further and looked away, seemingly embarrassed. Kalum found himself wondering how on earth she could feel self-conscious about anything.

"Oh, it's an old model my father upgraded for me," she said, brushing off Nathan's excitement. She shook her head and continued. "Retro chic, don't you know," she said, her voice back to its carefree tone.

Nathan pressed her, "So how long's your Dad going to be working with Sentech for?"

"I think we're going to be around for a while, she said, holding her gaze for a moment before looking down at her TRIST. Kara shot Nathan an irritated look but he ignored her and moved next to the girl.

"My dad's really excited about the tech your father's brought over from Quantril. I bet he's going to get paid well." His smile was wide and his eyebrows raised. If he was going for flirtatious, Kalum thought he needed to work on his seduction technique. He looked more predatory than alluring. The girl shrugged and went back to examining Kara's nails.

"Ugh!" said the voice in his mind. "That guy is the worst."

"Shut up!" Kalum hissed back under his breath.

Below him he saw the new girl stiffen and turn her head in his direction. Through the dense foliage he was sure she couldn't make him out, but her eyes settled on his exact location. Kalum held his breath, and pulled himself tighter against the branch.

"Hey did you guys watch the Gauntlet yesterday?" Casper asked, trying to get Nathan's attention.

"Aw man!" Nathan said, spinning around. "Reinhardt

crushed it! That guy's a beast! All that rage and he doesn't even use any Augs in his pre-fight."

Kalum had heard about the Gauntlet but had never seen it. The underground fighting ring that the Scorps ran was said to be their main source of revenue, after selling Augs. Everyone watched the fights, Corporate and NC alike. The fighters themselves gained notoriety for their viciousness. The one that Nathan mentioned, Reinhardt, was starting to build himself a real reputation.

"Come on man, hurry up," Leo said, his deep voice an irritated rumble.

Nathan fixed the larger boy with a look that silenced him immediately, and then made a point of beckoning his brother closer first. He opened the box and took out three small canisters, each no bigger than a soda can. Casper took one and shook it with gusto. Nathan offered the box to Kara and the other girl but they both waved him away.

"No thanks," Kara said. "I must've used at least four times yesterday."

With feigned reluctance he passed the final can to a nervous looking Leo. The three of them looked at the canisters, and Casper said, "Well, which is this one?"

"None of us knows. That's the whole point of doing this roulette style you dumbass," Nathan said.

They stopped, catching each others' eyes and checking to make sure none of them were going to back out. Leo was the first, patience definitely not his strong suit. He pulled out the nozzle and attached the guard to its end. Then he placed it over his right eye and pressed down. There was a sharp intake of breath and he shook his head, grunting like a gorilla. Without hesitation he repeated the process on the other eye.

Not to be outdone, Casper followed seconds later.

Nathan paused with his finger on the nozzle, watching the twins. When he was satisfied he placed it over his eye too.

They stood frozen in anticipation for a moment, and then Casper exhaled and yelped with delight.

"Woooo! This is amazing!" he said, shrieking in ecstasy.

"Which one did you get?" Nathan asked, looking at the time display on his TRIST unit.

"I... can see everything," Casper said while staring into the sky.

"Me... me too!" Leo shouted, pointing up in the same direction Casper was looking.

Kalum felt the tightness in his chest and the whisper was back in earnest, telling him to calm down, to force his heart to slow. But he could feel his breath starting to whistle in and out. He slipped his hand to his bag and placed it on the book. Up in the tree he didn't dare take it out, but just knowing it was there gave him a sense of calm.

Kara turned to the other girl. "I heard about this one guy, back when we were living up in Scotland, who got the Sight Aug, and he was so busy trying to see a crater on the moon that he got hit by a School transport vehicle." She laughed. "At least the kids got a preview of their future in clean up detail." When the other girl didn't join in her laughter, Kara furrowed her brow and forced another laugh.

"Come on A.J. Don't you think that's funny?" A.J turned her to face Kara and forced a smile.

Kara composed herself and then spoke. "Come on Nathan, are you done yet? This is boring, and A.J and I are getting mud on our shoes. Did you get a dud one?"

Nathan looked up, his eyes narrowed and his face tense. "No. I got a Hearing Aug." He straightened up to his full height and turned.

"I know you're up there," he said. "I can hear you breathing."

Nathan inclined his head and turned towards where Kalum was hiding, his neck craning up as he pinpointed to the source. The Burton twins were at his side, eyes trained on the hiding place.

Kalum tried to scramble back and flatten himself even closer against the tree, but he lost his footing. His fingernails clawed at the bark, trying to hold on, but in the end gravity won. Kalum felt the breath forced out of his lungs as he landed on the soft mud below. He looked up and saw Kara's face screw up in disgust, which considering what he was covered in, was fair enough he supposed. The other girl, A.J, actually seemed amused and he could have sworn she winked at him. There was something familiar about her, something he couldn't quite place.

Nathan and the twins wasted no time, and Kalum could hear them thundering towards him. He got to his feet and tried to twist and run, but his foot caught on a root and he found himself face down in the mud again. His backpack flew open and his sketchbook flopped out, just missing an enormous puddle. The tree root held on to him as he thrashed to get free. With a grunt his foot came loose, but the tree kept a tight grip on his shoe.

Diving for his book he collided with something hard and found the floor once more. An immense figure, silhouetted in the afternoon sun, reached down to him. The massive hand clamped around his shoulder and pulled him to his feet. Now standing, he still had to crane his neck to make out the human boulder he had slammed into.

Daniel Park looked down at Kalum with an expression that seemed to be permanently etched onto his face. Kalum had never spoken to Daniel before; not many of the other pupils apart from Nathan had. Up close it was easy to see why. Kalum wasn't exactly considered tall by any stretch of the imagination, but his head barely reached to the bottom of the older boy's chest. His dark eyes glinted from under his thick brows as they considered Kalum.

"You okay?" he asked, his voice a baritone but genuine concern seeping through.

The three other boys were at their side now, spraying their eyes with a green substance that Nathan produced from the box. Leo and Casper shook their heads like wet dogs as the effect of the Aug wore off. Standing next to Daniel, even their nearly six-foot frames seemed small. Nathan's eyes flicked to the book on the floor and he made a point of stepping on it as he stomped over to them.

"Get off it," Kalum yelled, twisting free of Daniel and taking a swing at Nathan.

The attack surprised Nathan as much as it did Kalum, but he dodged it with ease. The twins each grabbed Kalum by an arm and held him fast.

"I'm so sorry, Nathan. I di—"

Kalum's apology was cut off as Nathan hit him square in the solar plexus. He gasped for air and retched. His head swam and he was sure that if not for the twins holding him up he would have been laid out. Tears of pain streamed from his eyes.

"Self defence," Nathan crowed. "You swung first. Remember that when you're in your hospital bed."

A.J stooped and picked the book out of the mud, much to Kara's dismay.

"I can't believe you touched that!" she half shrieked.

A.J was examining the book when Nathan reached over to take it from her. For a moment Kalum didn't think she was going to give it to him, but she flashed him a smile and let it go.

Nathan tried to pry it open but the biometric lock held fast. Eventually he settled with smashing it against a branch.

"This thing important to you?" he asked breathlessly, slamming it into the tree until it spat bark over the ground. Then he flung it like a discus and it sailed out of view.

"No! No, no, no!" Kalum shouted, writhing and kicking to go after it.

Nathan grabbed him by the shirt and pulled him up so that they were eye to eye. Kalum's shoe and exposed sock barely made scraping contact with the floor as Nathan screamed in his face.

"Have you got any idea how much those Augs cost me?" he bellowed.

Kalum felt the rage in the hot breath on his face. He couldn't breathe now. His lungs felt like knives inside his chest and his fists were balled so tightly that his nails drew arcs of blood from his palms. In his mind he replayed the image of his book sailing out of view. Bile rose up to his throat and he felt his body start to quiver.

"Hey, can we go? This is boring," A.J said. She placed a hand on Nathan's shoulder. He looked at her and seemed to consider it for a beat, but instead drove his knee into Kalum's midsection, making him double over.

"No. He needs to learn respect."

"Hit him," the voice in Kalum's head said. It was so clear that it sounded like it was real, as if someone was standing by his side and whispering in his ear.

"The throat first, and then the groin," it said.

His vision was now swimming with purple and green dots ricocheting around. Suddenly the red tinge reappeared and he felt his hands straighten and go as taunt as a knife-edge.

Then he and Nathan were both on the ground and someone was standing between them. The Trinity Titans logo blazed in blue across his back, and as he moved a baton began to extend from the gauntlet on his right arm.

3

A FAMILY MATTER

"Back off. Leave my brother alone, Nathan," Reese said, his voice quietly menacing.

"You've done it now, Walker," Nathan said, sneering as he got to his feet and dusted himself off. "Attacking a team mate? Using your Henkan strike stick outside of a game? When Macintosh hears about this you're gone, and then so is your pathetic leech brother."

Reese bent down and picked up one of the canisters that had fallen free of Nathan's box in the scuffle. "I'm sure Macintosh and Cooper would be interested in knowing what else you've been doing on school property."

Nathan gave a half-smile and looked at the others around him, his arms spread wide. "Do your worst. I'm untouchable here. Trinity is my playground."

Reese replied without missing a beat, his tone cool, and steady like his gaze.

"Because of Daddy dearest, right? But you know what? Even he has a boss. How do you think he'll react when he gets a call from Sebastian Fleming himself?" he paused for dramatic effect. "After he's seen this video I'm recording?" Reese tapped his TRIST and shot Nathan a smile.

Nathan's jaw clenched and Leo and Casper looked at each other, uncertain of what to do. Reese reached back and helped Kalum to his feet.

"TRIST, please auto-upload this video to Sentech Plaza social video network unless I cancel the request in one minute," he said.

"Of course Reese," the electronic voice of the TRIST unit chimed in response.

Reese stepped backward, also encouraging Kalum to move just as swiftly.

Kalum snatched his shoe from where it was wedged in the roots of the tree and stuffed his foot back in.

Reese looked at the boys in front of him, and then the baton from his gauntlet retracted.

"Always a pleasure," said Reese, returning Nathan's glare with a smile, and then he spun on his heels and marched Kalum back towards the school building. They slowed their pace when they reached the huge steel door of the school, and Reese shook his head.

"What were you thinking, man? Lancaster is bad news. His dad practically owns this school. You know who he is, right? Head of all Sentech Corporation UK holdings. You get what he could do to us, don't you?"

Kalum shook his arm free and started to run in the direction Nathan had launched the book.

Reese's hand shot out and wrapped around Kalum's wrist. He tried to pull free but Reese's grip was like a vice.

"You go back there and they'll rip you apart," Reese hissed.

"I need to get my sketchbook!" Kalum said, beating his fists against Reese's chest in desperation.

"It's gone, 'lil brother," Reese said. "That way there's nothing but the river."

Reese looked at his brother's tear streaked face, and an uncharacteristic look of compassion crossed his own.

"Listen, I'll go and look for it when lessons start. I've got a free period," he said, steering him back towards the school. Somehow Kalum found a bottle of water pressed into his hand and Reese urged him to take a long swig.

"Hey, only I get to make your life miserable, right?" he said, clapping him on the back.

"Where did you go? You didn't wait for me as usual," Kalum said, trying to shift his focus. He told Reese about the Scorp he'd spotted and how he had followed them to the clearing.

"Damn Scorps!" Reese spat as his expression turned dark. "The Enforcers should just shoot them on sight."

They walked on in silence, Kalum's mind still focused on his sketchbook. As they neared the school Reese stopped Kalum and turned to face him.

"Look, I really need your help with something."

As much as Kalum wanted to leave and hunt down his book, Reese never came to him for anything.

"What do you need?" .

Before Reese could answer they were interrupted. A boy with a wide, toothy grin spread across his tanned face jogged up to them.

"Hey dude! You lose something?" he asked, catching his breath. He ran a hand through his spiky black hair and it sprang back into place, sticking up at odd angles. "I saw Nathan chuck it."

Jun Oshino tossed Kalum his sketchbook, and as he fumbled with it Reese reached down and snatched it from the air before it could crash to the floor.

"Jun! Thank you, thank you, thank you."

He checked it over, relief flooding through him. The cover was even more scuffed and scratched than before, but the lock held in place and only a few of the sheets he had sandwiched inside had come loose. He folded them and put them in his bag to store away later.

"That thing is tough. Not sure why you need a fingerprint lock in a sketchbook." He turned to Reese with an impish grin, and said, "I'm pretty sure it's just full of love letters to Lexi anyway."

"It's not like that with Lexi," Kalum said, while Jun tried to keep a straight face.

"You know I'd have helped out with those guys, but it wouldn't have been fair if I'd got involved, you know? I wouldn't have wanted Nathan to wet himself if I let loose the big guns." Jun laughed as he mimicked kissing his biceps and unleashing his signature single eyebrow raise.

"Yeah, yeah tough guy," Kalum said, laughing as he slapped his friend on the back.

Reese interjected, steering Jun in the opposite direction.

"Jun, it's always nice to see you, but I need to have a quiet word with my brother."

Jun dug his heels in and the rubber squealed in protest on the smooth marble floor.

"Hey wait, wait! Before I go, let me show you something I'm working on," Jun said, his eyes wide and imploring.

Reaching into his bag Jun pulled out a deck of red playing cards. He absentmindedly began to execute one-handed cuts, making the deck dance in his hand.

"Be honest," said Reese. "You learn all this to pick up girls, don't you?"

Jun shrugged without stopping. "Hey, we've all got to work with what we've got. You've got that whole muscly, sports superstar symmetrical face thing going on, and fine, some girls might like that, but I've got skills too." He punctuated the point by springing the pack from one hand to another.

"How many girls you gone out with on the back of a magic trick," Reese asked. "Not including your cousin."

Jun looked at Kalum and punched him on the arm.

"Dude, that was private!"

Kalum rubbed his arm and smiled in apology.

"Pick a card," he said, spreading the deck in an S shape.

Kalum indulged him and took one; the King of Hearts.

Jun grabbed the card and ripped it cleanly into four quarters, then with a deft wave of his hand he restored the card back to its intact form.

Reese nodded, tapping his foot and checking the time on his TRIST.

Kalum said nothing. His mind had raced into action, replaying every intricacy of Jun's movements to try to reverse engineer a solution all of its own accord. In seconds, four possible solutions presented themselves.

He forced himself to stop and applaud his friend instead.

"Really impressive, buddy."

He didn't even care how it had been done; he didn't want to know! If there was one thing his mind hated it was puzzles. It would always find a way through them, whether he was actively thinking about it or not.

Then he felt a searing pain shoot behind his right eye. It was the answer playing back to him in slow motion. Jun had switched the torn pieces for a duplicate hidden in his palm.

Jun's face fell and he fixed Kalum with a look.

"You've done it again, haven't you?"

Kalum shrugged as his eyes flicked to Jun's hand concealing the torn pieces.

Jun let out a loud sigh and threw his hands up before shoving them into his pockets and grumbling under his breath.

"Buddy... It really was good."

"Sure, sure. I don't need your pity," Jun said, pouting.

"Okay, now we've seen your trick we really need to get moving," Reese said, taking Kalum by the arm and propelling him forward. It was too late, though, as Jun's curiosity pulled him along with them.

"So where we going?" he asked, skipping to catch up.

Reese turned back to him in frustration and slammed his hand into the wall, blocking Jun's path.

"Listen Jun, it's a family matter," he said, forcing a smile, but Kalum could see the glimmer of fear behind it.

"Sure, no problem. Kal, I'll catch you at lunch," Jun said, backpedalling, before turned and walking off.

"Reese, that wasn't cool. He's my friend," Kalum said. He wanted to add, *More of a friend than you've been since joining the Henkan team*, but he bit his tongue.

Reese looked at him as if he could read his mind, and gestured that he should sit. They perched on the low wall near the concourse. The ornate pillars around them extended to an expansive ceiling that was made of one immense digital screen, half of which projected images from Sentech schools from around the country, showing their wide-eyed and eager pupils hard at both work and play. The other half showed high powered Corporative Executives enjoying the fruits of their labour while sprawled on expansive beaches or driving even more exotic cars.

"Look, little brother..." Reese started.

Kalum braced himself. Experience told him that no

good could come of a conversation Reese started in that way.

"Do you like it here?" Reese asked, not looking Kalum in the eye.

Kalum considered the question. He liked the few friends he had made, but disliked most of the faculty, and the majority of the students even more so. Things had gotten even harder over the last few weeks with Reese being promoted to School Henkan co-Captain with Nathan. He felt like his anxiety had gone into free-fall, but he had found ways to cope now that his medication seemed not to be working.

"It hasn't been easy. You haven't been around much," Kalum said.

"I know, but I'm doing this for you. For mum and dad, too." He took a deep breath and paused as a group of girls passed them. He raised his hand and managed to shoot them a wink.

"If I lose my place on the team, that means no Trinity for either of us. That means mum either loses the house or we use dad's care Credits to pay for it."

Kalum shook his head. "What the hell are you on about? Why would you get kicked off the team?"

"It's not easy, you know. The pressure to perform in the Arena week after week is intense. It's alright for guys like Nathan. They'll be fine whether they play for the team or not. This... this is our lifeline. With dad not working anymore... without this we'd be NCs, and it's not like we could make a living fighting in the Gauntlet!" Reese looked away.

Kalum was at a loss for words. He'd never considered that without Reese their family would provide little or no value to the Corporation. The concept that they would lose their home, their place at Trinity and their whole way of life and become Non-Corporates was a scary prospect.

Life as an NC ended up one of two ways. You either scraped together a meagre existence bartering products or services, or you were pulled into the criminal underworld of the Scorps. Neither was a particularly attractive prospect, considering Sentech's new zero tolerance approach to them. He was dimly aware that Reese was still talking, and tuned back in.

"I've...I've been taking your meds, Kal. I just couldn't take the pressure. It was too much. All the expectations. You've got no idea. So I took one of your meds before the qualifiers last month."

Kalum blinked in astonishment. Reese continued before he could get a word in.

"The rush is incredible. I felt so free. So powerful. I couldn't help it. I had to keep taking them just to function. But I'm stopping. Right now. The scouts are coming to watch me when we play against the Arrows in a few weeks time. If I can impress them then they'll take me international!"

A cold dread spread through Kalum's chest. "What happened? Why are you telling me this now?" he asked, feeling anger writhing inside him.

"They picked me up for spot testing after the match today," Reese said. When he saw Kalum's look of confusion, he added, "If I test positive, I'm done."

Kalum felt his anger now simmer into concern. "Is there anything we can do?"

Reese looked up finally, and said evenly, "We could try to get the sample back. They're being kept in Cooper's room before going off to a special lab."

"You want us to break into the Headmaster's office to steal back your... sample? Have I got that right?" Kalum asked. "Do you realise how stupid that sounds?" Kalum felt fired up, his waves of anger chipping away at his anxiousness and eroding its hold.

"Yeah. That's not the whole plan. We can't just steal it. They'll just test me again. Plus, it'll look suspicious. We need to switch it for a clean sample." He looked at Kalum, and the bottle of water he'd given him, with eyebrows raised. Kalum quickly caught his drift.

"If yours will come back positive, then so will mine, genius."

"No. It won't." Reese said, his voice quiet now. "I've been swapping your meds out for over a month."

Kalum's head snapped up, rage flaring hot in his throat.

He launched himself at his brother.

4

MYSTERIOUS FRIEND

Of its own volition, Kalum's arm flew up in a blur of movement. Reese jerked back in surprise but caught him by the wrist.

"Hey!" he said. "I did what I had t—"

"You have no idea what I've been going through," Kalum said. "No idea!"

He ripped his hand free and glared. His raised voice had started to catch the attention of passing students who slowed in the hopes of seeing a fight.

"Not now," Reese said through gritted teeth.

Kalum's jaw unclenched and he looked around to the gathering crowd and relaxed his arm. They forced smiles, and the disappointed bystanders soon dispersed.

"Look," Reese said, "I get that you're mad at me. But I had to switch yours out. I needed your meds to take the edge off, to get me—to get us—to this point. I'm co-Captain now. If the scouts pick me up in a couple of weeks we'll be set for life." He took a step back and looked at Kalum. His smile returned, and his eyes seemed to sparkle and gleam.

"You had everything under control anyway. I figured you might not need the meds anymore."

Kalum's eyes narrowed as he fixed his brother with a stare. Reese threw his arms up in the air.

"Just look how you handled Nathan! The old Kal would have passed out in terror."

Kalum's scowl showed Reese just how unconvincing his argument was.

"Come on Kal, this could be fun. Like the time we took Uncle Lucas's kit bag. You let off a smoke grenade in front room of his house," Reese poked him in between the ribs. "You remember? Back when you used to be fun."

The memory tugged at Kalum's brain. He smiled at the it and he let the anger fade. He'd been only five at the time, so Kalum could only remember snippets of it, almost as if he'd heard the story second hand, but he did recall the laughter.

Reese leaned in close and offered his fist. Kalum returned the fistbump and they both made a mock explosion sound.

"Don't mess with the Walker brothers," they said in unison.

Reese turned and, with Kalum in tow, walked toward the second floor stairwell that led up to the Faculty and Administrative Centre.

"Look the way I see it, this is a two man job," he said, handing Kalum a bottle of water from his kit bag. "All the teachers should be in their lunchtime meeting for the next half an hour. I'll keep a look out and you just open Cooper's door and change the sample over." He paused and looked at pointedly at Kalum. "Drink up, Kal. You're going to need to get this done quickly."

Kalum hesitated at the top of the stairs. He watched as teachers walked past him. They were streaming out of the

Faculty department, rushing off, but Kalum felt as if they knew he was planning something, felt their gaze linger just a little too long on him as they passed.

"I... I can't d-do this Reese," he stammered as he tried to turn back. "You'd better go in there."

The thumping of his heart made his chest feel like a heavyweight's punching bag. The room spun and his vision blurred. He was aware his breathing was rapid and shallow but he couldn't get his body to slow down.

"Come on, you've got this "lil brother."

His eyes regained focus and he saw Reese's face in front of him.

"Oh this'll be fun," the voice whispered in his head, not helping his anxiety.

"Come on Kal, I can't exactly pee for you,," Reese said. "I need you."

Kalum forced his chest to expand, to push back against the imaginary noose around his neck. The deep breaths slowed his heart and centred his mind, allowing his thoughts to clear.

"Come on then, let's get this done," Kalum said with a sigh while shaking his head.

They stopped outside the door that led to the teachers' area. The tiled flooring in the Faculty area was a dark granite and the walls were interspaced with art and national and international accolades. Front and centre was a large display case, with a silver statue of a boy dressed in a Henkan striker's uniform holding a defiant attacking pose. Underneath in large letters were the words;

National finalists: Second Place Trinity Titans.

Reese shook his head with disgust when he saw it.

"We're gonna fix that this year," he said.

On the left was the door to the teachers' lounge and on

the right was the Headmaster's office. It had a large brass coloured plaque that had his name on it.

Mr Eli Cooper - HEADMASTER.

Just the sight of that dark metal door with its re-enforced border of rivets set Kalum's nerves on edge. He took another deep breath and imagined himself safe in his room, sketching, and then he felt a calmness ripple over him like anaesthesia.

"All clear," Reese whispered, checking his TRIST. "Hurry up though, their meeting will be over in the next thirty minutes. I'll stand guard and knock twice to let you know when ten minutes are up and three times to let you know if someone's coming."

Kalum opened his mouth to question why two different knocks were even needed, but Reese silenced him and ushered him to the door.

"Wait," said Reese. "What the hell is that thing?"

The handle of the door was missing and in its stead was a silver bordered panel with a small screen on the surface. Kalum reached out to touch it and then snatched his hand back.

"What's wrong?" Reese hissed, looking around.

"It gave me a shock," said Kalum, rubbing his finger.

"Don't be such a baby," said Reese, but Kalum noticed he didn't try touching the screen himself.

Kalum touched it again, this time without incident, and a numerical keypad illuminated on the screen.

"Damn it," said Reese, casting another furtive look down the corridor.

Kalum stared at the screen and felt his eyes lose focus. There was a sharp click and a thin handle extended from the panel's side.

"How'd you do that?" Reese asked, giving him a celebratory thump on the arm.

Kalum looked at his hands in astonishment and then back to Reese's excited face.

"I... I..."

He looked at the panel and then gestured.

"Look, I just pressed where the smudges are on the screen," he said.

"Okay, okay. Well get in there and get it done," said Reese.

Kalum entered the musty office. The air had an acrid odour and he coughed involuntarily before he could stifle it. He heard the door click shut behind him and was thankful to see that this side had a more run-of-the-mill handle attached.

"Who the blazes are you?!"

The volume of the screaming voice ripped at his already jangled nerves, making him jump.

"Moron!"

A grey beak protruded from between the bars of an ornate cage and then turned and nipped at them. As Kalum approached, Morrie, Cooper's pet parrot, puffed out its white and blue-feathered chest and reared up on its perch.

"Shhh, shhh," Kalum said as it started a stream of high pitched squawks.

Scanning the room he saw the large plastic specimen tub on the floor next to Cooper's huge mahogany desk. Ignoring Morrie's continuous shrieking he pulled the top off and saw that it contained fifteen or so sample bottles. He reached down and twisted them around, searching for Reese's name while trying to suppress his gag reflex. Kalum glanced over his shoulder and saw the parrot staring at him in accusation.

"I see you,," the parrot said in a perfect imitation of his owner. The Headmaster's voice unnerved Kalum and he reached over and pulled the cover across the cage, quietening the bird.

"At least I've got some privacy now," Kalum said.

Turning back to the specimen box he took out Reese's sample. He looked at it, wrinkling up his nose.

With reluctance he unbuckled his belt and was halfway through pulling his trousers down when he realised he still had to get rid of the bottle's contents first. Looking about he saw no sink or plant pot to water, or anywhere else he could dispose of it, and there was nothing on Cooper's desk but scattered folders. He shuffled over to the open window and unscrewed the cap with all the care of a bomb disposal expert.

"I'll kill you!!!" Morrie screamed.

Despite himself, Kalum jumped. Warm fluid spilled onto his hand and he recoiled in disgust. With a jerk of his hand he threw the remaining urine out of the window and wiped his fingers on the curtain.

"What was that?" screamed a familiar voice from outside. Kalum poked his head out of the second storey window and saw Nathan, black hair wet and flattened, with a look of pure rage on his face that morphed into revulsion as he realised what he'd been soaked with. His head snapped up to look at the window and their eyes met. Kalum ducked out of sight and felt his mouth go dry.

He darted away from the window and quickly set about the second half of his mission. Once the deed was done he replaced the now full sample bottle in the container, and was zipping up his trousers when he heard Reese's frantic knocking.

Knock, Knock, Knock, Knock.

"Four knocks?!" Kalum hissed under his breath. "What the hell does that mean?!" Crossing the creaky wooden floor of the office he whipped off the cage cover, not wanting there to be any clue he'd snuck in.

"Four knocks means that Reese is an idiot!," the voice in his head said as grabbed the door handle.

Tap, Tap, Tap, Tap, Tap.

At first he thought it was the voice in his head again, but he was mistaken. The sound of the sharp snapping footsteps approaching froze Kalum where he stood. Looking around the room he made a split second decision, sprinting across the floor and cramming himself into a cupboard behind the desk. It was stacked with books. Looking at the thick layer of dust on them he assumed they hadn't been looked at or even moved for many years. A loud rattling filled the enclosed space, and Kalum reached down and pinned his arm to his side to stop himself shaking.

He heard the sharp click of the door releasing, and by squinting through the small slit between the cupboard doors he could just about make out half of the doorway to the office. The door swung open and he saw a man enter. He was talking on his TRIST unit, his tone raspy and taut with stress.

"I'm in your office. Get here now, we need to talk."

The man's voice sounded strained, like his words were lodged in his voice box, each being dragged out against their will.

Kalum couldn't see him completely from his hiding place, but he was dressed in a dark blue pinstriped suit. Kalum knew next to nothing about suits, but he could tell this one looked very expensive.

The man's TRIST unit buzzed and he answered with an irritated tone.

"What?" he half screeched.

His whole demeanour changed when he realised who was on the other end of the call.

"Yes Sir. I understand that, Sir."

He was pacing now, flitting in and out of Kalum's field of vision.

"Our source has gone quiet Sir, he said. "We are testing his changes on the latest batch, but we're not ready to proceed with Operation Terracotta just yet.

"Shut up!" Morrie screamed.

The parrot followed this outburst with continuous shrieks.

The man walked over to the cage, still talking as he did.

"No Sir. I understand the cost of failure. We can push on with the testing."

Morrie's squawking was getting louder and more piercing. Kalum watched the man slide the door of the cage open and then there came a sharp cracking noise and the bird fell silent. The only sound in the room was the indecipherable sounds from the TRIST.

The man stopped moving suddenly.

"N... No, we won't need to use the boy as a test subject. I already have plenty of NCs available." The other voice cut out and the man stood in silence. He let loose a growl of frustration, punctuated by a repetitive dull thudding.

Kalum twisted his neck, trying to get a better view through the slit. He saw the man pounding his fists against the thick wood of Cooper's desk. He eventually stopped and Kalum could hear a grating, panting noise as the man caught his breath. After a few moments he tapped his TRIST, and now Kalum could see he was using the projector to place the image of the person he was calling on the wall.

A picture of a woman in her early-forties blinked onto the wall. She smiled and inclined her head.

"Good afternoon, Sir," she said, her voice like satin. If she could see he was unsettled she didn't let it show.

"Has our mysterious friend sent any more communications based on the last test results?" the man asked, his voice reedy and thin.

"Nothing as yet, Sir."

"Message him. Tell him we'll pay him any amount of Credits he wants. I need to know the next steps."

"Yes Sir."

The image stuttered and then disappeared from view. In the silence of the room, Kalum was acutely aware he could hear his heartbeat thumping in his ear and he tried to keep his breaths shallow and quiet. He attempted to shift his position, just enough to allow some blood flow to his already throbbing foot. There was a soft thud as his head hit the shelf above him, and he watched the man turn and start to walk in his direction.

5

THIS IS NOT A DRILL

J ust then there was the soft squeal of the office door opening and Kalum could hear the breathless gasping of the school Headmaster. Eli Cooper's large girth came into view followed shortly after by his red bulbous head. The tapping footsteps of the man stopped and there was a squeal as he spun to face the Headmaster.

"Do you have the results?" the man asked, not waiting for Cooper to catch his breath.

Hands on his haunches, and his breath still not coming any easier, Cooper powered on his TRIST and examined the screen while mopping his sweaty brow with the back of his other hand.

"No," he gasped finally. "The samples have been... taken, but not run yet." He waved a hand at the crate of urine samples by his desk and looked up. Cooper let out a small whimper as he spotted the parrot slumped against the side of its cage, and he rushed over.

"Such a shame," the man said, not looking up. "He was like that when I got here."

Kalum tried to twist his neck for a better view of the

man. The back of his head was covered with shortly cropped blonde hair, but aside from that and an expensive suit, Kalum still had no idea who he was.

"Eli," the man croaked, "I need you to get those tests run as a matter of urgency. Let me know immediately if any of them test positive for Aug use. Then we will move on to test the rest of the school."

Cooper made no reply, and Kalum assumed he was still in shock from his pet's premature death. One of his sausage-like fingers had pushed through the bars and was stroking the dead bird's head.

"Eli!" the man said, his impatience bleeding into his tone. "Imagine if anyone on your Henkan team tested positive for Aug use. You would be responsible as Headmaster. I'd hate to think what punishment you'd face."

Cooper tugged his finger free of the cage's bars and Kalum could see the colour draining from his face at the thought. The man in the pinstripe suit sighed and eased himself into the chair behind the desk; Cooper's chair. His back was to Kalum now. He ran his fingers through his hair and then rested his hand on the mahogany desk where his fingers rapped against its surface. He gestured that Cooper should sit on the small wooden chair on the opposite side, the one usually reserved for troublesome students.

"Eli, I need to know the names of any students that come back positive," he said. "I need to know immediately to prevent any further fall out. Start with the Corporate affiliates, the ones who are here only because of their families achievements, not their own."

Like me, Kalum thought.

"We should kick them all out!' Cooper spat.

The rhythmic drumming of his fingers continued, the tempo increasing.

"Now, now Eli," —the man's voice scratched— "I couldn't possibly agree with that sentiment. Not in public anyway. Besides, the leeches do have their uses. They are, for the most part, expendable. Any of them that come back positive for Aug use would be suitable for the next phase of testing. That is how they will give back to the Corporate cause."

Kalum could hear Cooper shifting his weight and then shuffle across towards him.

"None of this will be traced back to me will it?" Cooper asked, his voice shaky.

"You will be protected, Eli," the man chided. "This is important work..."

His train of thought was interrupted by an alert from his TRIST. It projected an image and then a video of a news report above its metal surface.

"The Scorps are becoming more brazen. They're infiltrating further into Sentech territory, dealing their designer drugs," the man said, then sighed. It sounded like rocks grinding. "And with all the news about their new poster boy, the Operative, our people will start to feel as if Sentech can't protect them."

Cooper wedged himself into the chair and it groaned in protest as he let it take as much of the weight as he dared.

The man swivelled and Kalum caught a passing view of his dark eyes, which were all the more striking given his pale skin. Part of his face was visible, the thin upturned lips forming a smile that was devoid of humour, and his expression simmered with prideful contempt. The fraction that Kalum could see was more than enough to cut to his bones, and he held more tightly to his quivering arm.

"Did you know I met the Operative, Eli?" he asked. "He tried to kill me... I was less than impressed."

He stood up and his shoes clipped against the tiled floor as he moved to stand next to the Headmaster, and laid a hand on his shoulder. Spindly fingers dug into the soft flesh and Kalum heard Cooper's muffled wince.

"We can do great things, you and I," the man said. "I need those results first."

He handed the Headmaster a fistful of Credits and Kalum saw the numbers scrolling across their plastic surfaces.

Some of the redness returned to Cooper's face along with a smile so wide that it wrapped around his head. Using the study table, he hefted himself to his feet and offered his hand. It was summarily ignored and the man strode to the door, and Kalum heard the tapping of his shoes retreat into the distance. Cooper counted his Credits and gave a low whistle before stuffing them away. Peering in at Morrie, his face shifted and he gave a shrug. Slinging the cage over his shoulder he walked out of the office too, each step sending mini tremors across the room,

Kalum waited a beat and then eased the cupboard door open, wincing as the hinges shrieked with age-old rust. Sprinting across the room, he collided with the door, nearly knocking his glasses from his nose. He ripped the door open and almost ran over Reese.

"Well?" asked Reese, disentangling himself from his brother. "Did you..."

"Yes!" Kalum said. "Let's get out of here before—"

"Walker!" Nathan bellowed as he sprinted up the stairwell and locked eyes on them. The fury in his eyes was unmistakable. His shirt and hair were wet, and stuck to his skin.

"I'm going to kill you," he growled as he stomped across the hallway, with Leo and Casper Burton in tail.

Reese slid one hand in front of Kalum, guiding him back, and put himself between the two of them. Reese's muscular frame blocked his entire view, and he felt acutely aware of how different they were.

"Back off," Reese warned. "Unless you want to have a discussion about Augs with Cooper."

As if on cue, the door opposite them flew open and Cooper emerged, holding the now empty cage. His eyes flicked across the scene, from face to face, coming to rest on Kalum, and his face twisted into a glare.

"What the blazes are you both doing here?!" he bellowed, his jowls jangling and face turning beetroot. He jabbed Kalum in the chest with one stout finger and continued. "This area is off limits!"

Kalum opened his mouth and stammered a stream of nonsensical gibberish. Reese ducked in between the two and got Cooper's attention.

"We came to see you Sir. I... I just wanted to thank you."

"Thank me? For what?" growled Cooper, not taking his eyes off Kalum. He was like a predator singling out the weakest target in the herd.

"For your motivational speech before today's game, Sir. It was as much your inspirational leadership that won us the match as it was the goals I scored."

Cooper smiled and puffed out his chest.

"Well that's my duty as Headmaster, Reese. It's always the ones who earn their place here, like you, who appreciate our fine establishment. I'm sure the scouts will recognise it too." He turned his head and looked directly at Kalum. "It's the freeloaders who are the problem. The ones not here on their own merit. Riding the coat tails of others. They're the ones who ruin it for the rest."

He turned to face Nathan and beamed, his entire

demeanour shifting. He placed a hand on the boy's wet shoulder and then made a face, pulling away almost immediately.

"How can I help you, Mr Lancaster?" Cooper asked, finding his smile again.

Nathan bristled and the Burton twins glared past Cooper at the two brothers. Kalum felt Reese tense at his side. The twins had a reputation in the Arena for their brutality. It was a skill set they tried to bring into play whenever the opportunity arose. The veins were prominent now on their cavemen-like foreheads as they edged forward; attack dogs straining against their leash. Then a shrill piercing sound filled the corridor, followed by red flashing lights and an illuminated pathway on the floor. A voice, Cooper's voice, sounded over the internal tannoy and all the pupils' TRIST units.

"This is not a drill," Cooper's angry voice barked. "Form outside at your designated meeting points."

Cooper flashed an accusatory look at Kalum and then steered Nathan away from them.

"Come on Mr Lancaster, let's get you out of here. I'm sure it's just a drill but your father... well I'd never forgive myself if you came to harm." He took Nathan by the arm and led him away. Nathan glowered at Kalum and Reese returned the glare. Nathan mouthed the word "later" as a promise before following Cooper's lead.

"Well that didn't go exactly to plan," said Reese as students streamed past them.

"That's because your plan was stupid, Reese!" Kalum replied.

"What did you do with my... er... sample?" Reese asked.

"Chucked it."

"Out of the window?" Reese asked.

"Yup."

Reese stopped walking and pointed at Kalum, then turned in the direction Nathan had headed and then looked at Kalum again, a broad smile spreading across his face.

"And that stuff Nathan was soaked with. That's my...?"

"Yup."

The brothers looked at each other and then burst into laughter. The current of students bustling to get out carried them along a few hundred yards until they were next to each other again.

"I need my meds back, Reese," Kalum said, his voice low, not wanting his need for prescription drugs to become public knowledge.

"I have two full bottles left," Reese said. "They're in my drawer at home."

They walked in silence for a minute, the drumroll of feet and the amused murmurs of the other children filling the crowded corridors.

"But you know what? You really don't need them.You, the version of you on those meds, would have never done what you just did. He never would've have taken that risk. Thank you."

"I can't go back to how I was before, Reese," Kalum said. He kept his voice low, partly so no one else would hear, partly to try to hide the emotion behind the words.

Reese just nodded but didn't meet his gaze as they kept walking.

"Are you gonna manage off the meds?" Kalum asked. "Maybe we should tell Ma?"

Reese bolted forward and dragged Kalum into an empty side-room. The move caught Kalum by surprise. Reese grabbed his younger brother's tie and yanked him close.

"Mum has enough to worry about with you and dad.

This stays between us. Okay?" Reese said, his whole attitude switching instantly. Reese angled his head and stared hard at Kalum until he nodded his agreement to the demand.

A teacher spotted them through the glass partition and gestured for them to join the other students.

Kalum didn't speak as the brothers followed the meandering corridors. The walls around them were lit up screens that reached from floor to ceiling. Usually they displayed motivational Sentech news or slogans but now during the evacuation of the school they blinked red, showing students where to gather.

"How'd you like me now?" Jun whispered as he came up behind them. Grinning, he jabbed his thumb into his chest and leant in. "It was me. I set off the alarm as a distraction!"

"What the hell are you talking about?" Reese asked.

"Well, I followed you guys and saw you break into Cooper's office," he said, shrugging. "Kudos by the way. Casey says that the new lock on his door is state of the art. Anyway, then I saw some man go in, followed by Cooper, and I figured you were in trouble. The icing on the cake was when Nathan stormed up looking for you. I figured you needed an exit."

Reese stared hard at him and then broke into a smile.

"Nicely done, Magicboy," he said, and clapping Jun on the back

They followed the serpentine line of students as they trudged out into the brisk December afternoon, the cold stinging their faces and making their eyes water. A few of the girls in their year waved to Reese, smiling and calling him over. Reese flashed them his signature smile and they swooned. He turned to Kalum and Jun.

"They all love the uniform," he said, tapping the Titans

insignia on his chest plate. "Catch you guys later," he added and jogged over to join the rest of his classmates.

"I don't get it," said Jun, waving at the girls and receiving death stares in response. "What's your brother got that I don't?"

"Intelligence, good looks, fame and a six pack. Not forgetting that he'll be set for life when the scouts pick him up in a few weeks," Kalum said, not missing a beat.

"But apart from that he's got nothing on me," Jun scoffed, but Kalum barely heard the words.

The girl he'd seen with Nathan in the woods, the one called A.J, had joined the crowds in the Trinity courtyard. His eyes tracked her as she weaved in and out of the students as she made her way across. His breath felt tight in his chest again and for a moment he thought another panic attack was looming, but he knew that this was something else he was feeling.

Jun turned to Kalum, upset his joke hadn't got the laugh he'd wanted, and waved his hand in front of his face.

"You still with me dude?" Jun asked, giving his friend a shake. Kalum's eyes flicked to Jun and then back, but A.J was nowhere to be seen.

"Hey Jun, did you see—" Kalum started, but his question and all thoughts of the girl were immediately forgotten as an arm snaked under his chin and pressed against his trachea. Choking, he gulped for air as he tried to shake free.

6

SWAN DIVE

T he arm released him and he suppressed a coughing fit.

"Sorry Kal. Just playing." There was no mistaking the hint of an accent and the lilting way his oldest friend spoke. If there had been any doubt, the stinging punch she landed on his arm left none. Alexis "Lexi" Carter's sing-song way of speaking was totally unique and no one was quite sure where it came from.

"Ow!" said Kalum, giving his arm a rub. "You know, there are other ways to say 'hello'."

"Yeah, and wasn't there something in the rules of all those martial arts classes you do that says not to pick on people?" Jun asked.

Lexi took a bite from the apple she was holding and used her sleeve to wipe her mouth. At just over five-feet in height, Lexi wasn't exactly tall, but her attitude was larger than life. Her brown hair was glossy and styled in a conservative shoulder length layered bob, mainly to keep her mother happy, but in an act of defiance she'd had the bottom layer dyed bright red. *Business at the front, party in the back,* was how she described it.

"Hmmm. Must've missed that lesson," she said, shivering. The cold was making the light brown skin of her cheeks tinge red as she looked around the crowded courtyard. It was an enormous expansive area, set directly in the centre of the school building, but looked cramped with the entirety of the student and faculty population there. An undercurrent of murmurs rippled through the courtyard as Cooper appeared, his face so red it looked as if his head was about to explode. He stomped up and down the length of the courtyard like a General inspecting his troops.

"Someone thought that setting off the fire alarm was a great joke to play." His glare fell on them all as his almost neck-less head swivelled and regarded them. "Well I am not amused."

Something caught his attention then and a thin smile then broke out over his face. It grew until he showed his teeth, a predatory, evil expression of dark amusement replacing his anger. There was the machine gun sound of heavy boots on concrete and a group of eight burly Enforcers appeared and flanked the Headmaster.

"Actually, I'm glad. The perpetrator has done me a favour," Cooper said. "You've given me a wide audience to showcase what happens when you are deceitful and break Sentech rules."

He gave a nod to the Enforcer to his left and the man stepped forward. He brought up his arm and his TRIST activated. A command was typed in that made it project an image of a boy above its screen.

"Raymond Kawatowski!" the Enforcer bellowed. "Make yourself known."

Kalum turned and caught sight of a scuffle breaking out in the group of students next to him. Suddenly a gangly boy separated from them, and made a dash for the school building. The Enforcer twisted on his heels, the gun in his holster materialising in his hands. Kalum tried to call out, but his sandpaper mouth mangled the words.

His body surged forward, but it was too late. A zapping sound filled the courtyard and the boy stopped sprinting. He dropped to the ground and twitched as if he was in the throws of a seizure.

The Enforcer took short precise steps to close the gap between himself and the boy, his gun remaining up at all times. He tapped the quivering form with the toe of his boot and then squatted next to him. A hand pulled up the boy's arm and the Enforcer scanned his TRIST with his own. He turned to Cooper and then beckoned his team with a nod.

Kalum felt a sudden gust of wind as a buzzing filled the air. Four insectoid drones dropped from the sky to hover, one in each corner of the courtyard.

"Mr Kawatowski thought he could keep his illness from the Corporation," Cooper bellowed. "He thought it was okay to take from all of you, all of us, in secret, whilst being a weak link in Sentech's armour."

The Enforcers dragged the boy away. The drones flew in a sweep of the area and then shot into the sky again, disappearing in an instant.

"When I find who pulled that alarm, they're going to wish they were Raymond Kawatowski."

Cooper's eyes came to rest on Kalum. The Headmaster turned and followed after the Enforcers, whilst the teachers dismissed the rest of the students. Kalum was nearly flattened by the stampede, shoulders and bags buffeting him from side to side, but he managed to find Jun and Lexi.

"I know this is going to sound insensitive, but can we go grab some lunch?" a voice said from behind him. They turned and saw a boy with messy black hair that almost covered his large eyebrows and the top half of his face. His vision was so obscured that it was a miracle he could see where he was going. Casey Danvers blew the hair out of his eyes and accepted a fist bump from Jun.

"Dude, if it was anyone but you I'd say yeah, it's a bit insensitive, but we all know how you get when you're hungry," Jun said.

They made their way down the corridor towards the lunch hall. The screens on the walls had now returned to normal, showing messages about Sentech share prices and other Corporation news.

"Late night, Case?" Kalum asked, seeing the slightly dark circles around his friend's eyes.

"Yeah man. Was playing Recon Wars until about three in the morning," Casey explained as he tried to tuck in his shirt tails.

"But didn't you have the history paper this morning like us?" Jun asked.

"Yeah, but I already knew that stuff."

They wandered into the bustling canteen and joined a long line of students waiting to be served. The friends wrinkled their noses involuntarily as a sour odour permeated their senses.

"Wow, lunch smells especially fragrant today, eh?" Jun noted, miming a gagging motion with his fingers. The lunch lady fixed him with a look of contempt that made Jun clear his throat uncomfortably and feel the sudden need to closely examine the menu card.

"See you in a bit," Casey said, tapping the pin on his lapel that bore the image of Plato. He skirted the long line and moved further down to a station manned by three smiling attendants, who were either cooking food fresh to order or serving food from under a silver platter selected from the a la carte menu.

The students in that queue displayed badges on their lapels bearing different motifs representative of their rank at Trinity. The Henkan players' had badges bearing a hulking warrior in armour with the Trinity logo embossed on its chest, the highest ranking academics, like Casey, had Plato on theirs, and the children of high ranking Sentech employees wore the company symbol, a silver gear-shaped cog.

Kalum looked back at his options and elected to try the vegetarian selection, which comprised of undercooked Brussels sprouts and cubes of dry mash potato. Shuffling to their usual seats, they sat in silence for a minute and stared at their plates. It certainly wasn't the worst the Trinity lunch hall had had to offer.

Jun sighed and grimaced while braving a mouthful. After some laboured chewing, and removing fragments of bone and cartilage from his mouth, he pushed his plate to a side. Instead he pulled two metal discs from his pocket. Each was silver with patterns, images and numbers on their surfaces. He started rolling them over and under his fingers in unison.

"Hey, what are those things again?" Kalum asked.

Jun dropped them one by one into his other hand and then opened it to reveal that they had vanished.

"This is what people used to use before credits. They belonged to my grandfather. Can't spend them anymore, but I like having them. Reminds me of him."

He lifted his lunch plate to show that the pieces of metal

had reappeared there. Kalum gave him a little round of applause and he dipped his head in appreciation.

His TRIST vibrated, blinking to show that it was time to take his medication. He started to reach into his bag for the little orange bottle purely by reflex, and then stopped, realising the pointlessness of doing so. With a sigh he looked round the canteen. Jun was saying something, but his voice had faded into the background along with the other sights, sounds and smells in the canteen. Then his eyes locked onto A.J as she entered the room. She turned and looked at him, as if she'd felt his gaze. Moving a stray strand of auburn hair behind an ear she gave him a half smile. It was enough to dimple her cheeks and for him to feel the fire in his face as his cheeks reddened.

She's coming this way, he thought, and averted his eyes.

"Kal?" Lexi asked next to him. "Everything okay?"

"S-sure," he said, looking at her.

"Are you sure? You look ill," she said, and put a hand on his forehead.

There was a zap of static shock at her touch, and they shared an uncomfortable giggle, while Casey and Jun exchanged glances and eye-rolls.

"Hi," A.J. said, making them all look up at her. "Could I... could I sit with you guys?"

"Sure thing, Mamacita," said Jun, shuffling up and forcing Casey to move too.

A.J furrowed her brow at the nickname but sat in the offered space.

"Hi," said Lexi, then she looked from Jun and back to A.J. "Excuse me a moment," she added as she leaned across the table and clipped Jun around the ear.

"That, right there, is why you've never been out on a date," she said to him, sitting back down.

Kalum looked up at A.J and the two shared an awkward silence. Lexi broke it by offering her hand by way of introduction.

"I'm Lexi," she said. "Lexi Carter. All round awesome person."

"I'm A.J," came the reply, but he eyes only flicked Lexi's way for a beat. Lexi pulled her hand away, her expression darkening a little as she did.

"Kalum right?" A.J said. "I'm sorry about before."

"No harm done," Kalum said. "Wasn't your fault."

"I looked for your book but I couldn't find it."

Kalum reached into his backpack and took out the sketchbook.

"I found it," said Jun puffing out his chest just a little.

A.J threw him a smile that made him puff it out a bit more. She reached out and ran her fingers over the scuffed and faded cover. It lingered over the biometric input panel that was used to unlock it.

"What is it?" she asked.

"It's my sketchbook," said Kalum, sliding the book a little closer to him.

"You draw?" A.J asked, and the light caught her green eyes in a way that made them sparkle. "Can I see?"

"I doubt it," Casey said. "Only other person apart from Kal who's seen the Steel Falcon is Lexi."

Kalum squirmed in his seat and Lexi shifted away from him a little.

"He hasn't shown me anything in years!" Lexi said, a hint of a blush colouring her face.

Kalum picked up the book and A.J's fingers slid off the cover back onto the table. He slotted it away in his bag, safe between his school tablet and another book.

"The Steel Falcon?" she asked.

"It's just a silly superhero character that my dad used to tell me stories about when I was a kid," Kalum said, trying to make his shrug nonchalant. "I draw him sometimes, that's all."

As the bell sounded and they collected their belongings, Jun pushed away his untouched clump of processed meat and snatched a few fries from Casey's plate, stuffing them into his mouth before his friend could protest.

"Well..." said A.J, "I'll see you guys around." She turned and left. Jun gave a low whistle as she went and got another smack around the head from Lexi for his trouble.

"What was she apologising for?" Lexi asked as they left the canteen together

"I saw Nathan and the Burtons using Augs in the woods," Kalum said, keeping his voice low. "They didn't like being seen."

"Are you okay?" Lexi asked, raising her voice.

Her expression turned dark and she shook her head in disgust.

"Those morons are using?" she asked. "They're gonna get busted. Trust me, my dad was always having to give blood or pee into some jar or another when he used to play."

Kalum thought he heard the voice in his head stifle a laugh, but ignored it.

"Yeah, but the top of the line Augs these days are supposed to be undetectable," said Casey. "They don't just specifically heighten senses either, you know. The Spectre's latest broadcast said that Sentech R+D created them and the Scorps stole them. And that they also have ones that boost strength, endurance and last longer than the usual couple of minutes."

"You believe what the Spectre says?" Jun asked with

raised eyebrows. "There's no way a Scorp could have infiltrated Sentech and be broadcasting from the inside. The guy's a kook!"

Casey's face screwed up in consternation. "Some of the stuff he says checks out." He tapped his TRIST a few times and shielded the display screen so that only his friends could see it. On the screen were endless pages listing alleged illicit Sentech Corporation activities ranging from Corporate espionage all the way to experimental military tech.

"You know Case, he's probably just some crazy anti Corp guy sitting at home in the dark in his underwear wearing a foil hat," said Lexi. "And anyway, if he's right then Sentech is spying on you with your TRIST unit anyway, right?" she added, pointing out a headline on the screen which claimed exactly that.

"Not me," Casey said with an emphatic shake of his head. "I cover my tracks."

The rest of the day crawled past with Kalum on autopilot, ignoring the usual jeering and snide remarks from his peers. Today even Science class seemed to stretch out like an expanding horizon, the end never quite within view. He tried to shake his brain free of the funk it was in. It felt as if his thought processes were like rusty cogs in a machine; slow, clunky and threatening to fall apart at any second. Usually at the least this one class made sense, the information just seeming to flow from the screen into his brain. He could see it all around him; in the classroom, in the movement of the things in his surroundings. Today his head was filled with thoughts of Reese, of the Scorp he had seen on school grounds, of what he had overhead in Cooper's office, and of the girl, A.J. The man in Cooper's office had spoken about testing students, about experimentation and mysterious informants. It was a jigsaw with most of the pieces missing.

Kalum couldn't see the whole picture, but he had a feeling he wouldn't like it.

In this daydream-like state his mind began to wander further. The room around him seemed to drift out of focus and the light seemed to refract and change until he saw a blue tendril floating in front of his eyes. Reaching out towards the mesmerising light, he touched it with his index finger. A jolt of electricity seemed to flow through his finger, up his arm and then race up his spine and then explode at the base of his skull. The sensation nearly knocked him off his chair.

The teacher glanced at him.

"Mr Walker, is there a problem?"

Kalum blinked away the fuzzy sensation that he'd been left with.

"No. No problem at all, Sir."

The teacher turned back to the class and then stopped and did a double take.

"What did you say?" he asked, walking over to Kalum.

"No problem... Sir?"

Kalum caught a glimpse of Casey across the room. His expression matched the teacher's confused look.

"Don't get smart with me Mr Walker. I spent time at the Sentech Japan Headquarters, and I'm fluent."

Kalum looked around at the sea of faces that were now turned towards him.

"Okay, Sir," Kalum said, dipping his head and looking at his desk.

"Not another word from you, Walker. You're not as clever as you think you are."

Kalum risked a glance back up at the fuming teacher,

and just nodded. Sinking down into his chair he did his best
to disappear.

With a 'humph' the teacher got back to the class, but he
could hear his name in whispers and feel the other pupils
still looking at him.

Casey leaned over to him, a wide smile and eyebrows
raised.

"What was that about?" he asked.

"What do you mean?" Kalum asked back with a shrug.

"Japanese. You were speaking Japanese," Casey said.

"Wha—?" Kalum managed to say before his words were
cut off by a deafening tone that echoed through the school,
signalling the end of the day.

Kalum shot his friend a look of disbelief and was about
to speak again when his TRIST let out an alert. He looked at
the message projected above the screen.

"Case, I've got to go meet Reese. See you tonight?"

All the students had sprung out of their seats and were
making for the door. Kalum slung his bag over his back and
he was the first out of the class, tripping over chair legs and
bags as he went. He slammed into something hard and he
was almost knocked back into the room. His bag flew open
and its contents skittered across the floor. He looked up and
saw A.J looking down at him. Her bag had taken a similar
swan dive, her belongings scattered amongst his. With
horror he realised that the collision had caused the drink
she'd been carrying to stain her shirt with a splash of red.

Their wide-eyed shock connected them for a moment,
both frozen in place as the bustle of students slowed to take
in the scene. They both broke off and scrambled to pick up
their things, knocking heads in the process. The blow
caught Kalum just right and he fell back to the ground,
vision swimming through teary eyes, much to the amuse-

ment of a few students who used their TRISTs to record his embarrassment.

"Hey!" shouted A.J, whirling on one of them. "Scrub that video. Now." The edge in her voice was enough to stop them laughing. She reached across and deleted the image herself from the boy's TRIST.

"Walker, you're such a leech!" Kara Lambert shrieked. The crowd parted to let her and her entourage of girls through, their scowls enough of a threat to silence any dissenters. Kara turned her withering gaze on Kalum and he felt like he'd been slapped.

A.J and Kalum picked up their things, sorting through what belonged to whom. Kalum recoiled as they touched, a spark of static electricity discharging with an audible snap.

"I wouldn't bother trying to get Credits from him to pay for your shirt, A.J" Kara crowed. "Looks like he can't even afford to get a new one for himself." With a slap she knocked his books and school tablet out of his hands and smirked as she turned to go.

"I can't wait until Nathan catches up to you," she said over her shoulder as she took A.J by the wrist and led her away. Kalum watched them go and A.J looked back as she was pulled away.

Jun and Casey were there at his side now, steering him in the opposite direction from which Lexi was storming towards them. She walked past them, fire in her eyes, and her sights fixed on the disappearing group of girls. Jun put out an arm to stop her, but with a flourish she twisted it behind his back and shoved him out of the way.

"Lex," Kalum said, making her turn. "Don't."

Lexi stopped and met his gaze. "

Fine," she said through clenched teeth. She joined them

on a bench next to the rows of lockers. "I guess A.J is just another Kara clone, after all."

Kalum was about to protest when his TRIST let out another tone and he checked it. He jumped back to his feet and started to walk.

"I've got to meet Reese," he said. "I'll see you guys at my place tonight?"

He left his friends and sprinted down the corridor, weaving in and out of the meandering student body.

The front of the school was still empty, as he'd been one of the first ones out. The leaves had mostly been stripped from the trees, with only a few still clinging on desperately to life.

The Transports whizzing down the road were the only sound that could be heard. The throb was joined by a background murmur than grew and grew until the doors burst open and students poured out to make their way home. Side-stepping to avoid being trampled underfoot, he scanned the crowd for his brother.

An alert on his TRIST pinged and he keyed open the message.

"Go on ahead "lil bro. I've something to sort out here. I'll see you at home."

"WHAT IS GOING ON WITH YOU?" he wondered out loud as the stream of students began to peter out. This wasn't the first time Reese had flaked on him. Over the last few months he'd been disappearing more and more frequently. Henkan practice was most often the excuse, but something felt off about his brother. That was one of the reasons he'd agreed so quickly to help Reese, because he thought he'd finally find out what had been up with him. He knew the news about the Henkan scouts coming to Trinity had made him obsessive, but there was more to it than that.

Kalum half expected the voice in his head to give him the answer, but none was forthcoming. He threw his hands in the air. He decided there was no point in him hanging about outside of school. Hurdling over the low wall where the student's bikes were kept, he hurried out the gate.

The afternoon sun did little to warm the chill of approaching winter as its light rays splintered through the branches of the trees. Rounding the corner he was just in time to see the school Transport vehicle seamlessly glide back onto the road on its antigrav inducers.

"Great! Thanks a lot Reese," he muttered, shoving his hands in his pockets to keep them warm.

On his way home he passed by Sentech sanctioned shops filled with people eager to spend credits before they expired at months' end and had to push through the crowds to move forward. Towards the end of the long parade of shops he paused outside a boutique selling special, genetically engineered biodrinks. There was a queue of people snaking around the front of the shop, eager to get their hands on the latest Sentech fad. In truth this was one trend that had refused to die since it had been popularised by the global Sentech CEO a few years ago.

Kalum wasn't interested in the drink. Instead he let his mind drift back to when this place had been a sanctuary for him. This husk of commercialism had once upon a time been a bookshop, and tucked away in the furthest recesses of it they'd had a collection of comics and graphic novels. He had been passing with his mother one day when she had reminisced about how his father used to take Kalum and his brother in there and lose them for hours on end. Even though he had been too young to remember this, he had gravitated back to the shop day after day, week after week. The owners, a kindly elderly couple, had allowed him to stay and read. In kind he had scraped together credits and bought a comic whenever he was able. The process made him feel closer to his father, even though the memory and the man himself were just out of reach. It wasn't long after that, when he had found his father's old book again and taken to sketching the characters from his father's stories in it, deriving his own therapeutic calm from the process. It allowed him a singular focus and blocked out all the external stimuli that often crowded his mind.

He reached out and touched the rough brickwork of the store, so different to the ultra modern designs of the surrounding shops. It had been years since Sentech had moved the elderly couple on. Kalum feared that the dwindling value the store bought to the Corporation had meant they had been made NCs, and removed from the Sentech bubble of housing, health and care provision. He had no way of knowing and no way of helping. They had simply been there one day and gone the next. A crowd of people pushed past him and brought him back to the present. He dropped his hand and carried on.

The town was small but he liked this little slice of the world. It was tucked away enough not to have swarms of Sentech surveillance drones overhead, and also far removed from any significant Scorp resistance attacks. Until this afternoon at the school, he'd never seen an actual real life Scorp, though he knew their trademark scorpion symbol from the many news reports about places they'd hit.

Kalum had walked half a mile when he felt them following him. Not saw them, not heard them. Felt them. Chancing a glance over his shoulder he saw Nathan and two other figures that looked like Casper and Leo Burton, with ill intent in their eyes, and contorted wicked smiles on their faces.

Adrenaline fuelled tachycardia kick-started his tremor and he didn't hesitate, just trusted his instincts and ran as fast as he could. The pounding footfalls of the group behind sang out a drum roll and he knew he was being hunted.

7

CHAOTIC TANGLE

H ome was another two miles, but if he cut through the park he might be able to lose them. His heart surged as he ran through the options in his mind.

The park. The park makes the most sense. I might be able to hide there, he thought. Cursing Reese under his breath he moved in that direction, then stopped suddenly. Pain pulsated behind his right eye.

"Ahh!" he yelled, and grimaced, pushing his palm up against it. He tried to ignore the pain, to compartmentalise it away, the way Frannie had taught him to, but it was too intense. As he backed away it eased. He pushed forward again towards the park and it came back, fierce enough to take his breath away. There was no choice, he would have to try to make it through the town centre and hope that Nathan and his friends wouldn't want to make a scene in front of the shoppers.

Keeping his head down he barrelled past baffled onlookers and found a set of stairs leading to the multi-level mall. The hardly used route smelled of damp mixed with grime, the stench thick and threatening to lodge in Kalum's sinuses. His pursuers were not far behind, but his breath was a ragged whistling wheeze and he was starting to feel lightheaded. With a gasp he stopped and put a hand out to steady himself by some Scorp graffiti on the stairwell.

The Operative fights for your freedom, the slogan read. It had been cut into the side of the wall with some sort of laser torch. Kalum froze as he heard the clanging footfalls once more.

"Hey leech!" one of the twins called out to him, their voice echoing in the narrow stairwell. "We see you."

Casper and Leo continued to call his name, taunting him, calling him a coward. Rage filled his thoughts but he suppressed it and kept going up, flight after flight.

Where was Reese when he needed him? His thoughts turned dark. By the time he reached the top he could taste the rising bile in his throat. Holding his breath he listened for Nathan and his friends. They were still coming, slowly, but they had obviously not given up on their quarry. In desperation he searched for somewhere to hide. Then he spied another door with a numerical keypad and scrambled over to it. It was similar to the one on Cooper's office door. On the digital display were four blank boxes.

"That's ten thousand different combinations," the voice in his head whispered.

"Shut up," Kalum hissed back as his fingers moved at a furious pace trying every different combination he could imagine. He lost count as he tried the handle after each attempt. Below him he heard his pursuers' heavy steps getting closer. His head swam, and he felt the blinding agony in his temples start to ramp up. The combination of agony and panic made it impossible to focus, and he could no longer see the numbers his fingers were jabbing at. Suddenly the handle gave and he burst through, slamming it behind him. He hunched down, hands on his haunches and gasped for air. He heard the sound of fists and feet kicking and slamming against the other side. Looking through the glass opening he allowed himself a slightly smug smirk, and Nathan responded by dragging his thumb across his throat.

Leaving them fuming, Kalum ran to the service elevator, waving to them as the doors shut, and then pressed the button for the ground floor. Inside the elevator the combination of the vague aroma of stale urine and the relief of his escape made him feel physically sick. A few deep breaths later, the nausea began to pass and he straightened himself up, tucking his shirt in and adjusting his errant tie. The doors opened, juddering and slow, and he blanched at what he saw; Nathan, Casper and Leo glaring back at him from the other side.

"It's not wh—" Kalum started to say but was cut off as Nathan delivered a vicious punch to the right arm that left it numb and hanging uselessly at Kalum's side.

"The trick is to make sure you don't leave a mark on him," Nathan said over his shoulder to the twins.

He wound up his arm again, ready to deliver another blow, when a hand landed on his shoulder and spun him around. An Enforcer shone his flashlight in the faces of the boys and demanded, "What do ya think you're up to? This ain't no boxing ring! Clear off!" Nathan glared at the man and pulled free.

"Get your hands off me! Do you know who I am?" he yelled.

He brought up his TRIST and it flashed his identity up on its screen.

Kalum used the distraction to pull himself free of the thugs and ran like a man possessed. Glancing over his shoulder, he saw two more Enforcers arrive and grab at the twins, restraining them with such force that it looked as if they were tying them in a knot.

"We're not done, Walker!!" Nathan screamed after him.

KALUM DIDN'T STOP RUNNING until he turned the corner of his road and saw his front door. His breath was ragged and ripped at his raw chest. He had kept looking around every corner, expecting an ambush, but at last he had made it. There it was, third door in the terraced block of cookie cutter identical houses. The only thing that marked their home as different was the unashamedly bright red front door; his mother's choice, naturally.

Walking up the steps he sighed and looked up at the sky while rummaging through his pockets for his keys. They were gone. "Idiot!" he hissed, his jaw clenched as he realised he'd probably left them in his locker. He pressed the doorbell and nothing happened. He jammed his thumb on the button, the tip going white from the pressure, and he heard a pathetic, barely-audible buzzing sound, like a fly trapped in a jar.

His mother's music blared from an open window upstairs, accompanied by her off key singing. He banged on the door and was surprised as it swung open. Kalum coughed as he was greeted by the smell of burning. Tossing his bag aside onto the sofa, he rushed through the lounge, and past the wall of family photographs and scattered music paraphernalia. Entering the kitchen he saw plumes of dark smoke being spat out of the oven at the once-white ceiling. Throwing the window wide, he set aside the charred dish which seemed to contain his mother's lasagne, and tried again to get her attention. "Ma!

Maaaaaaaaaaaaa!" he yelled as he stomped up the deep red-carpeted stairs.

His mother was balancing precariously with one foot on the banister, whilst trying to dust away the cobwebs that seemingly guarded the entrance to the attic. She did this, all the while singing and bopping her head.

Her light brown hair was tied back tight in a ponytail and she was clad in her favourite retro rock T-shirt that had seen better days, and a pair of black combat trousers. She turned, and her hazel eyes caught sight of Kalum standing on the landing shaking his head. She was startled, and lost her footing, but instead of falling she slid down the bannister and vaulted to the safety of the landing.

"You're going to break your neck one day," Kalum observed, trying to ignore how impressive her acrobatics were.

"Pilates, dear," she said, winking and giving him a peck on the cheek. "Does wonders for your core stability." Nadine Walker, although in her mid forties, in her mind was still twenty one; even if her body disagreed. She straightened up, and her back gave an audible crack, causing Kalum to wince.

"Ah ha, sure, Ma, whatever you say," he said. "I'll be in my room."

"Wait. Where's your brother?" she asked.

"Busy with something at school," he replied, trying not to sound so sullen.

"What's up with you?" she asked, tilting her head to one side and giving him an inquisitive look.

"Nothing." He shrugged his shoulders. Hefting his bag he carried on up the stairs.

"Nice to see you, Mum, how was your day Mum? I

missed you, Mum," Nadine said in a voice with more than a hint of reproach.

Kalum stopped and hung his head. "How was your day, Ma?" he asked, turning back to her.

"Well thank you for asking! Well it was really busy this afternoon. A lot of sales. Herman had to actually get his lazy rear-end in gear and serve some customers. I think that annoyed him!" she said with a wry grin.

"Oh, I brought home some leftovers," she said, reaching around the corner of the stairs to the upper landing and retrieving a bag with the words, *Buns and Roses Bakery* stylised on the background image of a guitar. The bag wasn't closed and Kalum suspected it was perhaps a bit lighter than when it had left her bakery.

"There's a Motley Cruller, Iced Bun Jovi and the new cupcake I call 'Rage Against the Jelly Bean'."

Kalum looked into the bag. "Wow," he said, and he meant it. The cakes looked and smelled amazing, sweet but not sickly, and decorated with attention to detail. He knew they would taste as good as they looked, too. Although she was Sentech sanctioned, Nadine had taken liberties and strayed from the agreed ingredient list and that unique taste was what drove repeat business. Grabbing one he stuffed it into his mouth. Nadine threaded her arm around his shoulders and pulled him into a tight hug.

"I know that there are things you can't talk to your mother about," she said. "I get it. You're growing up."

Kalum tried to protest but she cut him off.

"Maybe you should do what Reese does. He's so secretive, never letting anyone into his room. At least he still confides in your father."

Kalum nodded. Reese had been spending more and more time talking to their father over the last few months.

He had come to accept that his brother simply had a closer bond with him.

His own memories of the man he had once been were sparse. The lack of attachment was something he felt even more acutely in recent years. In the end he had settled on the one happy memory that had that bound them. Apart from Lexi, his father was the only one who had seen his sketches. There was something about them that made him more animated. He thought that perhaps after a day like today that was what they both needed. Returning his mother's hug he headed towards his father's room. The door was ajar and he could see the flickering light of the television stabbing at the gloomy room.

"Hey, Dad, it's Kal," he said as he eased the door open

Owen Walker sat unmoving in the dim room, staring unblinking in front of the television screen. He was thin and gaunt with course deep lines crisscrossing a face that had become old before its time. His green eyes didn't deviate from the screen, and Kalum's presence didn't seem to register. He was watching a snowstorm of static on the screen as if trying to decode some hidden meaning. The rest of the room was cluttered with towers of folders containing reams of his father's old research notes from years gone by. In the spaces between, various medical devices blinked in time, with a chaotic tangle of tubes running from each to connect to Owen. Sitting in the old armchair next to his father, he took off his glasses and rubbed his bleary eyes.

"How was your day?" Kalum ventured, not expecting a response.

"Mine was spectacularly awful. More so than usual."

Kalum gave his father a sideways glance, hoping for some glimmer of an acknowledgement. Owen's face remained stoic and still.

They sat in silence listening as the soft sounds of traffic and the conversations of people on the street threatened to cut through the sound of the television. Kalum got up and groaned with the effort like an old man. He moved to close the window and shut out the noise, jostling the window to loosen it and looking out onto his street. It wasn't picturesque by any means. It was a functional shade of industrial grey, hardwearing and built to last, like the Corporation that had stewardship of it. Each house was designed to be identical and spaced for optimal numbers. It wasn't the most luxurious accommodation that Sentech gave their members, not like the place they lived when his father was well, and a renowned and respected Sentech programmer, but it was far from being the lowest tier.

Those were the ones near the outskirts, on the borders of NC territories, where even the Enforcers rarely went for fear of running foul of the Scorps. The beauty of this place was not on the surface. You had to look deeper. He saw families returning home from the school run, and children riding their bikes at breakneck speed, just as he and Lexi had done years ago, and parents trying unsuccessfully to corral them back into their houses for dinner. It was like a carefully balanced ecosystem, its population working hard for Sentech and in return the Corporation giving them everything they needed to survive.

Almost everything, he thought.

The setting sun crept through the crack of the drawn beige curtain and he felt its warmth gentle on his face. Drawing the curtain back the room was filled with light and Owen recoiled as if in pain, grimacing and grunting at his son in anger. Kalum quickly pulled the curtains back and the room returned to its previous state of darkness. He sat back down and tapped on his TRIST. It projected an image into the air above it and Kalum moved so that his father could see too. Kalum read aloud from the news article so his father could hear.

"Things are hotting up in the National Henkan League. Sentech are closing in on Kaneko Enterprises who dominated the League last year. Sentech's new team has shown passion and drive with their new offensive forward Scott Capullo on a one man wrecking tour. Will they make it to the top of the leader board?" The words disappeared as he finished reading, to be replaced by a highlight reel of Capullo's best goals of the season.

"You know Dad, Reese played really well today. One day we might be seeing him play in the National League," Kalum said. Again silence was his only reply. He flipped to the next article.

"Scorps spotted closer to Sentech Plaza. Who is the Operative and are our Enforcers doing enough to protect us?"

Images flashed on the screen of Scorp crime scenes. On each picture there was evidence of minor vandalism to a Corporation facility. The Sentech water plant, the Zenton Industries Shopping plaza, and the Janus Vehicle storage depot were featured in a poor quality video that started to play. In the grainy footage one thing was identical; the image of a black scorpion tagged on a surface.

A voice spoke over the footage. "More than the superficial damage to each location, it is this symbol that chills us to our core. It reminds us of what these outcasts are capable of. It reminds us of the Tokyo incident and all the lives lost during their last major offensive."

Next to him Owen stirred, head twitching slightly in stilted staccato movements until it was turned to face the screen. With one tremulous hand he pointed to the larger screen in front of him.

Kalum looked at the old news recording still playing in spite of its poor quality. Most homes had modern holographic viewing displays now, but since his accident, Owen Walker did not cope well with change. Fiddling with the device the way his mother had shown him, Kalum sharpened the picture a touch.

The footage pulled back into an old-style news studio.

"Next up we have an interview with the CEO of Sentech Industries, one of the largest electronics conglomerate in the world. They are an iconic brand that people just can't get enough of. From humble beginnings manufacturing components for other companies to a global industrial behemoth. They are responsible for introducing the world to the phenomenon that is the TRIST." He held up his arm to showcase his TRIST unit, which was designed to match the navy blue of his suit.

"Why thank you, Evan, you are too kind," the TRIST chimed in its trademark electronic warble. The presenter smiled like a proud parent and then turned back to the camera, his teeth almost painfully bright to look at.

"Over the last decade this emblem has become synonymous with cool," the man enthused, showing the silver gearcog symbol on the back of his TRIST.

"Let's talk to the man behind the brand. Here he is, the head of Sentech, the infamous Sebastian Fleming!"

The camera panned to a man in his late forties. His jetblack hair was slicked back, a sliver of silver starting at his widows' peak and extending all the way back. His green eyes sparkled, and the warm smile he aimed at the watching audience showed he was no stranger to being in front of a camera. Wearing a black roll neck jumper, dark blue jeans and a pair of brown loafers, he lounged on the comfortable sofa.

"Sebastian, in a time of global economic downturn, share prices in your Corporation continue to rise, as do your profit margins. What is your secret?" the interviewer asked with wide-eyed sycophancy.

"Thank you for the kind words, Evan," Sebastian started. "I'm not afraid to tell you that our success can be summed up in one word... family. That's exactly what Sentech represents. We look after our employees and customers as we would our nearest and dearest, and that's why we'll be around for a very long time. We've already been successful in our bids for control of multiple areas of the United Kingdom. We have delivered on our promises to the Government in London, employing the majority of citizens and supporting the Health, Education and Social infrastructure. We inherited a system on its knees and pumped our considerable resource into the region."

He sat forward, hands raised to the sky as the wall behind him snapped into pixelated life. Images of smiling people wearing Sentech uniforms popped into view. The pictures transitioned to children running and playing, their laughter serving as a soundtrack to the postcard imagery. Finally it changed to a hospital setting with doctors and smiling patients surrounded by state-of-the-art equipment. The screen blinked off and Fleming's benevolent face was once again centre stage.

"Thousands in the UK are now content members of the Sentech family, working for us, with us taking care of them in kind." Fleming finished to a rousing response from the presenter and his studio audience.

Owen's eyes widened, his jaw clenched and his brow furrowed. Kalum noticed that his face twisted angrily and his knuckles whitened as he tightened his grip on the arm rest. Its dark plastic bowed and warped under the pressure before cracking and breaking. He threw the remains at the window and they scattered across the floor.

Owen's eye's brimmed with tears, and sobs wracked his body. He rocked back and forth in his chair, his arms wrapped around himself. Then he pitched out of the chair with a crash and he writhed on the floor. His jaw tightened and the muscles of his face squirmed as droplets of blood formed at the corners of his mouth. Their eyes met for a moment and he thought his father was about to say something, but then his body went rigid and he started to seize, his eyes rolling back into his head.

8

NUMB AND HEAVY

"Ma!" Kalum shouted as he tried to stop his father from cracking his skull open on the floor.

Nadine was by his side in an instant, sliding a pillow under Owen's head and clearing space to let him ride out the seizure without hurting himself. Eventually his movements slowed and he lay still for a time. He was awake but disorientated, and between them they managed to get him back into his bed.

In the background the broadcast was still playing from the old-style player.

"Evan. Since you brought up these NC's and the Tokyo tragedy, let me say one thing to these terrorists. They pride themselves on being 'Non Corporate', and pine for the days of Government sanctioned poverty," Fleming said, making air quotes to emphasise how ludicrous he felt the idea was.

"They will not destroy the peace and prosperity that we as Corporations have created. Never again will we be caught unaware and allow events like those that transpired in Tokyo to happen again."

Kalum turned off the video feed and dimmed the light

in the room. Nadine brushed Owen's hair away from his face and fussed, making sure he was comfortable. Stooping down Kalum kissed his head, and whispered to him, "See you at dinner, Dad, I've nearly finished the latest sketch. I'll show you later."

Nadine and Kalum left the light on and the door ajar and stopped outside his room, listening to the hum of the medical equipment inside.

"So... why was your day awful?" his mother asked Kalum.

"You were listening?"

"I already have one son who I can't keep track of, who disappears first thing in the morning and comes in last thing at night," she said in response to the aggrieved expression on his face. "I need to know what's going on with at least one of my kids."

He opened his mouth to speak, but shut it again. His mind wouldn't even let him process where to begin.

"I had a panic attack at the game today," he said, looking down at his feet while he danced around the edges of the truth. "It... it wasn't great." He braced himself for the wave of overprotective mothering Nadine was known for, but it never came. Instead she just asked a question.

"It's not the first is it? When did they start again?"

Kalum looked at her, blinking away his surprise. He'd been so careful, concealed his slow downward spiral from everyone, especially her.

"A mother always knows," she said, reading his expression. She grabbed Kalum and pulled him into a fierce hug.

"I hear you at night. Sometimes crying, sometimes just talking, sometimes worse. I've been there by your side until you settle."

In that moment he was ready to tell her everything.

About Reese taking his medication, about what he had heard at school today, about how Reese was in danger but didn't seem to care.

"Reese... he..." Kalum started to say.

"Don't you worry about Reese. He doesn't know," Nadine said, cutting him off. "That boy could sleep through a hurricane."

Kalum caught a glimpse of the screen on her TRIST. It had the score of Trinity's game and was running the highlights of Reese's goal. Nadine followed his gaze.

"You two are so much alike. You both put too much pressure on yourselves. Reese thinks he carries this family, but we would be fine, even if he quit Henkan. I've told him a hundred times."

His mother's face was so sincere. Kalum knew she meant what she said. The truth however was less palatable. Reese giving up his place on the Henkan team would mean fundamental changes to their family. Nadine would have to look after Owen full time. They would lose their Sentech support. Reese and Kalum would have to leave Trinity and go to a far lower-tier school, if they could go to one at all.

"If we need to up the dose on your medicine, just say. We're covered for you to see the doctor and I'm sure I can rustle up some extra credits to pay for it."

Kalum felt that squeezing feeling in the pit of his stomach again. .

She crouched down a little so that they were eye to eye.

"Level with me. Is it as bad as before?" she asked, her face creased with worry.

"I'm not seeing things again..." Kalum said quietly, looking back at his feet.

"Are you still doing the exercises Frannie told you to do?"

"Yes," came his reply. He felt the first prickle of irritation dig into his skin but forced it down. It felt like that was all he was doing. That was the only reason he was still holding things together.

"We can always call her and get her to see you again."

Kalum drew in a big breath and released it slowly, trying to calm himself.

"No voices. No weird daydreams. No finding myself in places and not knowing how I got there," he lied, reeling off the things he knew his mother wanted to hear.

"I'm. Not. Crazy," he said, feeling the prickle become a rippling irritation at the base of his skull.

Nadine just looked at him.

"No one has ever said that you're crazy," she replied, her voice now soft. "I know this school hasn't been easy on you. I know you feel that you're in Reese's shadow, but you're going to do great things. I know it."

"Whatever you say, Ma," he said. "Can I go to my room now?"

Nadine held his gaze for another beat, looking at him as if searching for something, and then nodded.

SITTING on the edge of his bed, he let out another long sigh and put his face into his hands. His mind swirled with thoughts of school, Cooper, and the man in his office, and how the hell he was supposed to stay one step ahead of Nathan Lancaster. On the last point he knew it was inevitable. He was, at some stage, going to get pummelled.

Getting up, he began to pace up and down his box of a room. Somehow, even though barely any of his floor was visible under the piles of comic books and crumpled up drawings, he managed not to trip over anything. His mind swirled, a jumble of emotion and stress as he tried to sort it all into some kind of order. Eventually he leant against the wall and squatted down, rubbing his neck until it hurt. He felt the warning signs of the impending panic attack as his thoughts got away from him, like a dog snatching itself free of the leash.

Grabbing his Trinity backpack he reached in for the sketchbook. His mouth went dry when he couldn't immediately feel it there. The contents tumbled out onto his bed and his hands sifted through it, but they came up empty. He backed away, the heels of his hands digging into his temples as his wobbly legs threatened to betray him.

It was gone.

I... can't..." he said to himself.

He stumbled out of his room and into Reese's. The light came on as he entered, bathing the bigger room in a warm glow. Henkan posters were plastered on the wall and the electronic paper cycled through different players, their stats and their all time greatest plays. Ripping open the drawer next to Reese's bed he found a semi-transparent orange bottle with his name on it. Holding it up to the light he looked at the serial number on the side. Shaky hands managed to pop off the top and a few pills fell onto the bed. He scooped up two of the white oval pills into his palm and threw his head back as he swallowed them dry. As the medication kicked in he felt as if a mist was settling over his vision and his body felt numb and heavy. The air around him seemed to thicken and every movement felt like he was trying to move through quicksand. He wondered, almost absentmindedly, if the medication had always had this effect on him. They had been a part of his life for nearly a decade now, and until Reese had intervened he'd never missed a dose. His chest loosened its death grip and his heart slowed to a steady beat.

Next to the bed, Reese's closet door was ajar. On impulse he kicked out his foot to open it fully and a bag fell out, his brother's spare Henkan gear spilling onto the floor. Kalum reached down and picked up one of the gauntlets. He slipped it on and flexed his fingers inside it. With a flick of the wrist the baton extended from the side. It made a noise as he whipped it through the air. Another button press made it retract back into its housing.

"Very cool," he whispered.

He heard noise from downstairs and the sound of the front door opening. He whirled in a panic, pocketing the pill bottle and trying to put the room back how he'd found it. Keeping low he ran back to his room. There was a crash as he slipped on a scrap of paper and ended up on his back, wedged against the wall. The knock on his door set his pulse racing, in spite of the medication working to keep it slow. The door hadn't closed behind him and the second knock made it drift open. He had expected to see Reese's scowling face but instead his mother's filled the gap. Even from his semi upside down skewed perspective on the floor he could see that she was beaming and had a mischievous glint in her eyes

"You've got a visitor."

She let the door swing completely open and Kalum saw A.J standing next to her. She pulled some of her auburn hair behind an ear and gave him a wave and a crooked smile. Somehow he was on his feet and trying to smooth out his clothes.

"May I come in?" A.J asked.

Kalum shot a look at his mother and prayed that he

wasn't blushing as furiously as the heat he felt in his face suggested. Nadine brought a hand in front of her mouth to try to hide her grin and gave him a thumbs-up.

"Sure," Kalum said, acutely aware of how his voice caught as he spoke. "Come in."

He brushed some pencils and discarded sketches off the bed to make room. Pausing then, he looked up at A.J and then at the space he had cleared. If he hadn't been blushing before, he knew he was now.

"I'll give you two some privacy," Nadine said, backing away. She made a point of opening the door wide and then looking him in the eyes. "Not too much privacy though."

Kalum considered jumping out of the window. The fact that it was still closed and that the thirty-foot drop to the ground below might cripple him didn't seem that important at that moment in time.

"Erm, okay, Mrs Walker," A.J said. "Thanks."

Nadine turned to go and gave Kalum another thumbs-up as she did, a gesture that he was almost certain A.J would have caught.

A.J stepped into the cramped room, bringing in with her the faintest scent of strawberry. She sat in the chair by Kalum's tiny desk.

"I'm sorry about before," she said. "Bumping into you, and... and everything that happened after... with Kara, I mean."

"It's okay. I'm used to it," Kalum said.

He felt a tapping in his head and then the voice inside spoke, sounding hazy and drunk.

"Smooth. You... just told... a girl who you've... definitely got the hots for... that you're used to bumping into things and generally making an... idiot of yourself in public."

Kalum wasn't sure what disturbed him more; that the voice was right, or the fact that the medication hadn't silenced it completely.

"Well you dropped something," A.J said.

She hefted the sketchbook out of her bag and ran her fingers over its cover. Kalum let out a sigh of relief and watched as her fingers found every scratch and scuff on it, triggering a memory as potent as the imagery he'd created on the inside. The imagery that had once adorned the cover was long since lost to the ravages of time, but the small rectangular thumbprint reader there was as good as new.

"You need to keep a better hold on this." She handed it to him and hit him with a smile so stunning he felt himself grinning back at her.

"Thanks for bringing it to my house," Kalum said. "You don't know how much this means to me."

"Well I was nearby anyway," A.J said. "I was... watching the Gauntlet fight at Kara's place. Most of the school were there. I thought maybe you'd be there too..."

"Sure," said Kalum not wanting A.J to realise just how much of an outcast he was. "I... I... I was going to go but something came up..."

A.J nodded and gave him a half smile. She rubbed her arms and her gaze wandered around his messy room.

Without knowing why, Kalum pressed his flesh to the cool metal and heard the whir and click as the lock disengaged. Now A.J joined him on the bed. He swallowed a lump he felt materialise in his throat and flipped open the thick cover. His eyes lingered on the indecipherable sequence of numbers, symbols and commands that had been scribbled a lifetime ago by his father. In amongst them were some of Kalum's earlier doodles, which had always made him smile.

The Steel Falcon stood in a variety of classic superhero poses guaranteed to strike fear into evil doers, at least by the estimation of a five-year-old with an overactive imagination.

"So that's the Steel Falcon?" A.J asked.

"Yeah," Kalum said. "B... but those are drawings I did when I was about five. I don't even remember doing them."

Kalum pulled his gaze away and flipped a few more pages. The character evolved in front of him almost as if animated, the reds and blacks of his costume flowing and bleeding into each other. The one constant was his symbol. Over the years it hadn't changed, just become more refined.

"Could I watch you draw something?" A.J asked, watching him intently.

The side profile of the red falcon's head on a black background was what Kalum drew now on the first blank spot he could find. It was the symbol he'd created for his character, the one he had drawn hundreds of times on its chest. The pen swept over the paper in sure and steady arcs and Kalum felt as if the act of drawing untethered him from a great weight. The symbol looked up at him from the paper and he allowed himself the hint of a smile, knowing that he'd have something else to show his father later.

"Wow," said A.J. "Very cool." She looked at the book and the biometric lock on it and scrunched her eyebrows together.

"What's with all the security?" she asked.

"It used to belong to my dad," Kalum said. "He used to work for Sentech. I... I sort of took the book from him."

"Is that what all the writing and funny squiggles were on the first few pages?" she asked.

"Yeah," Kalum said. "My dad actually wrote the software that Sentech put into our TRISTs."

He skipped forward a few more pages to some of the

notes his father had scribbled. He had read them obses-sively over the years. It had started as a way for him to try to connect with the man his father had been, the memory of whom he couldn't quite recall. However, what he had found in the book, at least what he could understand of it, was pretty interesting.

"This was what he was working on last," Kalum said. "They'd been looking at ways to record and replicate human consciousness. Not only to store a snap shot of a person, their memories and personality, but also to transfer it to another body, either synthetic, or flesh and blood." Kalum smiled and flipped forward few more pages. As a nine-year-old, reading about the concept of someone being able to transfer their personality and memories to another body was mind blowing. It had given his imagination wonderful fodder to create one of the Steel Falcon's more gruesome enemies, a faceless entity known as 'Entropy'. Kalum stopped and looked at the illustration he'd done of it. The page was covered in swathes of black, swirling around a dark figure, floating with ominous intent on the paper.

The sound of knocking at the front door caught his attention. As he shut the book, A.J's hand brushed his and he felt that stab of static electricity again. The knocking continued, each thunderous blow echoing through the house, and Kalum wondered how much more it could take before falling off its hinges.

"I'd better get that," he said, standing. They both manoeuvred out of the box-room, the space making their proximity uncomfortably intimate. Standing on the landing Kalum heard that his mother once again had music blasting from her TRIST, oblivious to her surroundings. There was still no sign of Reese, either.

Making his way past his mother, dancing with a mop in

the hallway, he opened the front door and was instantly hoisted off the ground, unable to breathe as the air was squeezed out of him.

9

REMNANT EMBERS

Kalum knew only one person that said "hello" like that.

"Puuuu mee dow umful Ucas!" came his muffled protest.

"Speak up boy!" came the gravelly reply. "I can't quite hear you!" The man released Kalum and he dropped unceremoniously back to the ground. He stood and dusted himself off as he craned his neck to look at the man mountain in front of him.

"Stop doing that, Uncle Lucas! Can't you just say hello like a normal person?"

Lucas raised one eyebrow and looked quizzically at him." Kal, I've been giving you bear hugs all your life, and I'm not going to stop suddenly just because you're a teenager, lad!"

"Well maybe you could start using deodorant, so having my nose stuffed into your armpit is less gross?" he replied.

Lucas gave him a playful clip around his ear before grabbing his head and forcing it into his other armpit.

"Breathe it in boy!" he bellowed, and laughed heartily.

"Come on boys, no more fighting, that's enough,"

Nadine remarked, seeing that the mock fight showed no sign of ending. But her words fell on deaf ears as the struggle spilled into the hallway and then the front room. One of Kalum's flailing limbs glanced the side of a particularly gaudy vase, and it tipped and rocked and teetered on the edge of its stand. Nadine dived and deftly caught it with her outstretched hand, millimetres before it hit the ground.

"I said ENOUGH!" she roared with all the authority she could muster, punctuating the point by shoving the cold, wet mop in Lucas' face.

Lucas for his part was unapologetic, and shook the cold water from his beard like a dog coming in from the rain. He shot Kalum a cheeky wink, and remarked, "Fight? That was too one sided to be called a fight."

Nadine intensified her glare at both of them, and calmly rolled her sleeves up.,

"I'd be more than happy to show you what a real fight is like, Lucas..."

"Er... no sis. That's really not necessary," he replied, holding his hands out in front of himself defensively.

"I'm glad that's settled then. Kal, you and Uncle Lucas set the table."

Nadine turned to A.J who was standing at the edge of the stairs and taking in the scene in front of her with a straight face.

"A.J dear, you'll be staying for dinner of course."

When both Kalum and A.J began to protest at the same time, Lucas struggled to contain his amusement.

"I'll get your father ready," Nadine said, putting an end to their objection. The two shared an awkward glance, but Lucas clapped them on the back and led them to the kitchen.

"Come on!" he said, and chuckled. "The more the merrier."

The door behind them edged open and Reese stood in the opening. The neon lights from the street silhouetted his form, accentuating his broad shoulders and tapered frame. He stepped into the house and smiled at them. The rain had plastered his hair to his forehead and soaked him through his jacket.

"Reese, I was expecting you back an hour ago. Where have you been?" Nadine asked as she came down the stairs and hugged him. Reese shrugged himself free and stepped back, burying his hands in his pockets.

"I had some errands to run,"

"I thought you had Henkan practice," Nadine said.

Reese screwed his face up and clenched his jaw.

"I had some errands to run after Henkan practice," he said, his smile returning, still broad and easy on his face. "Does the Spanish Inquisition have any other questions, or can I please put my kit away?" he asked, holding up his bulky bag.

Reese moved to go up the stairs and Nadine stopped him with a hand on his shoulder.

"It's getting more and more dangerous out there, Reese. The Scorps are everywhere. You've seen the news. They've even seen some in the next borough over. What if you ran into one?"

At the mention of the Scorps, Kalum braced himself for Reese's reaction. He knew his mother should have known better than to bring them up in his presence.

Reese turned around, his smile still there, but it was now strained.

"I'd be okay," he said.

"Reese, you can't just go around looking for trouble," Nadine said, pressing the point

She was going to continue, but Reese slammed his fist into the bannister hard enough for the entire thing to quiver.

"I'd end them," he said with his back still turned to them. Kalum could hear the snarl in his voice. "If I ran into a Scorp, I'd rip them apart with my bare hands."

"That's not your job, Reese," Nadine called after him. "The Enforcers will deal with the Scorps. Promise me, if you see any of them, you turn and run."

Reese snorted and trudged up the stairs, not stopping to engage further.

"After what they did to dad, I'd never given them a free pass. The only good Scorp is a corpse."

He didn't wait for Nadine to reply but disappeared into his room. Kalum led A.J into the kitchen and together they started to lay out the plates and cutlery.

Before heading upstairs after Reese, Nadine whispered, "Talk to him Lucas, something's not right."

Lucas nodded and joined Kalum. They quietly set about their task for a minute, the patter of the rain outside the only accompaniment. There was another knock at the door and Lucas looked over to A.J.

"Be a dear and get that please?" he asked with a grin.

As A.J left the room, Lucas looked at Kalum with raised eyebrows.

"I'm fine Uncle Lucas," Kalum said.

"Fair enough," Lucas replied, passing him some cutlery.

"People think Reese is the star in this family but you've got your dad's smarts and your mum's fire. That's a pretty dangerous combination," he said earnestly. "But if you ever need to talk, I'm here for you. We all are."

Kalum opened his mouth to speak, but the clanking noise of a mechanical door closing drew their attention. They heard the rattle as Owen, Nadine and Reese began their descent in the lift to join them downstairs. A.J came back into the room at the same time. Her eyes locked on to Owen as the lift came into view.

"Kal, your friends are here," she said, moving to let them in.

Casey, Jun and Lexi filed in. Jun cocked his head in A.J's direction and mouthed a question, to which Kalum gave a slight shrug. Lexi looked like she had a bad taste in her mouth and shot him a look, part anger, part surprise. Nadine had a plate out ready for Casey by the time he sat down. Lexi shouldered past Kalum and sat next to Reese. Lucas helped Owen get settled in his wheelchair and pushed him to the table and sat next to him, regaling him with low-brow stories from work. Kalum sat next to them, whilst Nadine opened the oven and placed a dish in the table's centre. They all wrinkled their noses as the aroma stabbed at their senses. Jun let out a polite cough and shifted back in his chair.

"Bon appetit!" Nadine said, beaming. Kalum gave Lexi a nervous smile but she stared daggers back at him.

Lucas deftly grabbed Kalum's plate. "Growing boy needs to eat well," he said, dishing a large chunk of lasagne onto it and smiling broadly. Kalum shot Lucas a scowl as he served himself a relatively modest portion and sat down. Everyone sat at the table, unmoving, until Nadine started to glare at them, realising what was going on.

"Well then... tuck in boys," she said, as more of a command than anything else.

Eyes flitted to the steaming dish at the table's centre and then to the ground. Casey stood and used the serving spoon to heap a wad of the unrecognisable cuisine onto his plate. Nadine's face spread into a self-satisfied smile as she watched the boy shovel food into his mouth. Reese and Kalum flinched, and leant as far back in their chairs as they could at the sight of Casey cramming their mother's food into his mouth with reckless abandon.

"See, Kal," Nadine said, turning to him with a frown. "That's how you need to eat if you want to pack on muscle."

Lexi stood and gripped the ladle. She plunged it into the bowl and worked the handle to dislodge a segment that had been welded to its bottom. Up it came, filling the room with an odour that was as unappetising as its appearance. She let it slop onto A.J's plate and tried to clamp her lips together to stop herself from smiling when she saw a globule of sauce land on the sleeve of her white top.

"You can't come all the way to the Walker home and not eat!" she said with a smile so sweet only Kalum could see the facetiousness behind it. A.J lifted her spoon to her mouth, not letting her eyes leave Lexi's.

"Y... you really don't have to," he said, but A.J had already consumed the first spoonful and was well onto the next. Lexi's smile evaporated as A.J pushed the plate away from her and placed her cutlery with neat precision to one side.

"Thank you, Mrs Walker, that was lovely," A.J said.

"You're more than welcome my dear," Nadine said, still beaming. "You'll have to invite her to dinner again, Kal."

"But I didn't—" Kalum started to protest but A.J cut him off.

"Lexi, you really should try some," A.J said, serving her at least as much as she had been given, like a game of culinary tennis. The colour faded from Lexi's face and she tried to swallow the lump that had formed in her throat.

A series of pings from their TRISTs broke the tension. Their screens illuminated and displayed reports of a further Scorp attack on a local factory. A well-groomed news reporter's face appeared, lined with concern.

"This latest attack by the Scorps on our most vulnerable shows them for who they are. Cowards and criminals. They have released a statement with this attack."

The screen split into two so that half of it displayed the Scorp statement.

"The reign of the Corporations will soon be at an end. It is time for the common man to take control of his destiny once more. This is the first and only warning we will give you. Denounce your Corporation Overlords, or die with them."

Once again the reporter appeared grave faced.

"Leaked Enforcer reports indicate that the Scorps have a biological weapon that they are on the verge of releasing. Once again Sentech are one step ahead and are rolling out a vaccine to negate it. Information to fol—"

There was a high-pitched screeching as the transmission broke up and a man cloaked in shadow appeared.

"I, the Spectre, renounce the Corporations and their agenda of misinformation the Scorps ar—"

The rogue transmission blinked out and was again replaced by the news feed.

"As a precaution, tonight's curfew has been brought forward and drone patrols increased overnight. TRIST locator scans will be run at eight pm."

The news reported faded away as the transmission ended.

"Damn Scorps." Lucas said, and the others murmured in agreement.

"It's pretty impressive how the Spectre keeps managing

to hack into the broadcast like that. That was the longest he's managed to hijack it for," said Casey.

"Impressive?" Nadine asked, eyebrows raised.

"He meant terrible. Didn't you Case?" said Jun, laughing and slapping Casey on the back.

Nadine got up to clear the table and Reese went to help her.

"You kids should get going now that the curfew's been brought forward," she said, pressing plastic boxes with left overs into their hands.

"So no Arcade?" said Casey, pouting.

"Doesn't look like it buddy," said Jun, commiserating. "I didn't even get to show you my latest toy."

Jun whipped his arm out in front of him and stared at his palm in deep concentration. A small wisp of smoke rose up and Jun screwed up his face.

"Why isn't it working!" he said, pulling out a small remote fob from his pocket. He hammered the button down again and again. There was a loud whooshing sound and a bright flare as a fireball erupted from underneath Jun's sleeve, making it catch light. Lucas was on him first, dousing the flame with a jug of water and beating the remnant embers with a cloth. They all stared at Jun with mouths open, and jaws slack.

"What. The. Hell. Was. That?" Lexi asked.

Jun looked at his charred jacket and then back to his friends with a sheepish grin.

"It's a magic prop. Supposed to make me look like a wizard," he said with a shrug.

"It makes you look like a moron," Lexi quipped, shaking her head.

"Please don't do that again in my home, Jun," Nadine said.

They all helped finish clearing the kitchen and then Nadine ushered them to the front door.

"Thank you for dinner Mrs Walker," A.J said. "It was a pleasure to meet you."

Kalum caught Lexi make a face behind A.J's back and thought he heard the voice in his head snicker.

"You're welcome, dear," said Nadine. "It's late though. I can't let you walk home alone."

"No, no," A.J said with a shake of her head as she backed out of the door. "I'm fine, really."

Nadine was about to push the point but A.J had already slipped out, and was gone.

"Guess Credits don't buy manners," Lexi said under her breath.

Lucas appeared from the kitchen, his hands still covered in suds and a dishcloth over his shoulder.

"Kal, can you walk Lexi home?" Lucas asked. "I'm going to help get your father settled."

"Hey, why do I need an escort? What about Jun and Casey?" Lexi began to protest but Lucas cut her off with a wave of his arm.

"No arguments. I promised your dad that I'd look after you. That promise extends to Kal. Plus, your mother's probably having kittens after that broadcast."

"Hey, if anyone tries anything with us then Jun will just set himself on fire," Casey said, nudging his friend.

Outside the chill sliced easily through Kalum's thin fleece. Jun and Casey said their goodbyes and headed in the opposite direction, Jun still trying to get his device to work properly. Lexi and Kalum turned down the street and she slipped her arm through his and back into her pocket.

"I don't know why Lucas made you come with me," she said. "You do realise I'm way tougher than you, right?"

When Kalum didn't reply she nudged him with her hip and he nearly slipped on a patch of ice.

"You didn't seem yourself tonight," she said as they walked on.

"It's all happening again, Lexi," Kalum said. "The panic attacks are the least of it. I've started having the blackouts again."

"Aren't the meds working?" she asked, drawing closer to him. There was none of the awkwardness he'd felt with A.J. He told her about what Reese had been doing, and he felt the outrage ripple through her.

"Don't say anything," Kalum said.

"Okay," Lexi responded with a nod of reluctance. "But now that you're taking the meds it should all go back to normal, right?"

"That's what scares me, Lex," said Kalum, remembering the dulling of his senses and the weight he'd felt after restarting his medication earlier. "Part of me, a really big part of me, doesn't want to take it anymore."

The rain had stopped but had left the grey asphalt covered in dark patches. The night was silent apart from the buzzing of the odd low-flying drone that paused to scan the signal from their TRISTs as they passed.

Kalum glanced at Lexi as they carried on in silence for a while. In that instance he felt an overwhelming sense of déjà vu, and once again she was the girl he made friends with on the playground. The one who used to beat up the kids who laughed at him for having an imaginary friend. He saw the girl who had changed overnight that day she learned that her father wasn't coming back from war.

"Well this is me," she said, snapping him back to the present. "See you at school," she added, giving him an awkward side hug, and without looking back she opened the door and left him alone in the street.

He turned and walked back towards his home. His eyes glided to the other side of the road and he saw someone leaning against one of the trees on the roadside. Kalum watched as they seemed to disappear behind the tree that shouldn't have been wide enough to conceal him. He blinked hard, but the figure was gone.

He rounded the corner onto a long, narrow street that ran in between the back end of the houses on one side and a wire mesh fence that enclosed the Sentech sanctioned Greenspace Park. Sounds of life drifted from both sides, families bustling around in their kitchens and catching up on the day's events from one, and insects chirping insistently on the other. A startled bird gave a cry and flew directly over him.

The figure was on the roof now, shadowing him, and making no perceptible sound.

Then the tremor started again, and he balled his hand into a fist and thrust it into his pocket to stop the escalating panic he felt rising. Kalum looked up at the figure, whose long coat seemed to flap around him like a cape. A bolt of lightning sliced through the darkness, illuminating the man's face for a brief moment and highlighting the jagged scar that ran across his mouth.

"Run, you idiot," the voice in his head said.

And then he was running, his feet splashing as they slammed into the pavement and the standing water from the recent rainfall. He turned the corner towards home and his trainers lost contact with the ground, squealing as he slid and collided with a wall. Kalum fought to control his breath, now tight in his chest, and set off sprinting again. His house was in sight now, that bright red door calling him back. The hair on the back of his neck stood on end and he couldn't shake the fear, couldn't shake the feeling that any second now something would claw at his back and take him down.

He slammed into his door, fiddling with his keys and scratching them against the metal of the lock as he tried to slide it home. With a frantic tug it was open and he was tumbling inside. As he slammed the door behind him he caught a glimpse of the silhouette of the man framed by the torrential rain staring at him from the end of the street.

10

LET ME OUT

Nadine told herself that it was the sound of the rain trying to drill through her bedroom window that kept her awake. She ran her hand across the empty space in the bed. It was the side that never needed smoothing over, whose pillows didn't require plumping. In between the taps and bangs at the window she heard the hums and whirs of the machinery connected to her husband in the adjacent room.

"TRIST, project time," she said, rolling onto her back. At the sound of her voice, her TRIST blinked awake. She read the time illuminated in large red numbers on her ceiling.

"Three a.m?" she moaned, and scrunched her eyes closed in frustration.

The loud bang from downstairs made her sit bolt upright in bed. She sprang out and landed without a sound on the balls of her feet. It had been many years since she'd been in the field, but some skills never faded, at least not when they were so ingrained into your DNA. Shivering, Nadine grabbed the black dressing gown hanging on the door and threaded her arms through its sleeves as she exited the room. She stopped and listened again, holding her breath. Her careful, measured steps took her past Owen and Reese's rooms and she peered in through Kalum's open door. His bed was made and didn't even look slept in. The sound of laughter echoed through the silent house, making her heart jackhammer. She walked softly to the landing.

"Kal?" she said, raising her voice.

The laughter stopped as abruptly as it started, making Nadine question whether she had heard it at all in the first place.

Carrying on down the stairs she called out his name again. Again there was no response.

From the bottom of the stairs she could see a light on in the kitchen and could hear a low rumbling sound. She paused by the couch and slid her hand deep in between the orange fabric cushion and its frame. Her fingers contacted something and she felt calmer as her fingers curled around the cold metal cylinder. With a deep breath she released her grip and withdrew her empty hand. Edging along the door-frame Nadine peeked around the corner.

"Kalum!" she screeched, half from surprise and half out of relief.

Kalum was at the table, and next to him sat a plate with remnants of his peanut butter and jam covered toast on it, and a half drunk cup of black coffee. He had been slumped on the table, dressed in his school uniform, and drooling onto the white patterned tablecloth, with one eye half open and snoring deeply.

The sound of his mother's scream made him sit upright like he'd been electrocuted, his arm flailing out and sending the coffee cup hurtling from the table. Nadine snagged the handle, stopping it in mid air just inches from smashing into the side of the fridge. The steaming contents splashed across floor, fridge and her arm, making her grimace in pain. She turned the cold tap on full stream and ran the water over the scald.

"What on earth are you doing up at this time?" she demanded. "And drinking coffee, no less!"

Kalum looked around in utter bewilderment. "W-w-what's going on?" he stuttered, his mind flashing back to the ominous figure who had chased him home. He winced and put his palm over his right eye. Then he stuck his tongue out and made a face. "Why does my mouth taste like burnt wood and charcoal?

"It's three in the morning, you're dressed, ready for school, and that's how coffee tastes," she said.

Nadine grabbed a dishcloth and dried her arm, examining the pink scald mark and poking it gingerly.

"I don't know how I got here," Kalum said softly. He felt the sharp pain behind his blue eye ramp down to a gentle throb.

The silence hung between them like an unwelcome guest.

Kalum stood from the chair and looked at himself in the glass of the backdoor. Nadine walked over to him and gave him an all-enveloping hug.

"I think you should get back to bed, son," Nadine said, pulling him into her shoulder and kissing the top of his head.

She put her arm around him and they walked up the stairs together. As they reached the top they nearly collided with Reese as he left Owen's room.

"Reese? What're you doing up?" she asked, startled.

"I thought I heard something in Dad's room," he said.

Reese had his arm under his hoodie but Kalum could see the top of his Henkan gauntlet sticking out the side as he squeezed past them. Nadine put her hand on his shoulder and it came away wet and cold. Before she could interrogate him further he was in his room with the door shut behind him.

Kalum paused in his doorway.

"Ma... maybe we should call Frannie again," he ventured.

Nadine dipped her chin in agreement.

"I'll see if she's free tomorrow," she said. "But for now, get back to bed."

Kalum did as his mother asked, sinking into his still warm bed and letting the shroud of sleep take him away.

"Up!" The voice sounded muffled and far away, but it gradually got louder and more irritating. His warm comfortable duvet was mercilessly torn from him and the impossibly bright sunlight stabbed at his eyes. The next thing he knew Nadine was shaking him like a woman possessed. He groaned in exhaustion and sat up.

"We're late!"

He rubbed the blurriness from his eyes and then held his head in his hands.

"Where's Reese?" he asked.

Nadine was pulling him to his feet and manhandling him in the direction of the bathroom.

"He must have got up and gone ahead. He never sleeps well before a big game."

She shut the door behind him and he sat fully dressed on the toilet, his head now pounding in time with his pulse as he closed his eyes. As he began to drift off again Nadine smashed her fist against the door with such force that the frame shook.

"Don't you dare fall asleep on there again, mister!" she shouted.

The scare got him moving now and in record time he got washed, dressed—nearly broke his neck falling down the stairs— mother a kiss on the cheek, he ran out of the house. He stopped to check the time on his TRIST. There was no way he would get to the Sentech school transport stop before it left, and even at a sprint he would not get to the front gate before it was locked. He cursed under his breath. Being late would mean a trip to see Cooper, and that was one unpleasantness he wanted to avoid.

As was to be expected, he missed the Sentech Transport and was forced to make a perilous dash to Trinity using his old bike. After narrowly avoiding a grisly death a few times he threw it to the side of the school gates and managed to duck in through the heavy doors of the school as they closed behind him.

His lungs were on fire as he caught up and merged with the students shuffling in lines towards the Great Hall. Kalum had almost caught his breath by the time they entered the expansive room and looked around. The ceiling was so high that his neck cracked as he looked up. Red curtains, adorned with a capital T in black, were draped on both the side and rear walls of the hall. At the front was a stage with small curved stairs at either side to allow access.

In the centre of the stage was the speaker's podium, behind which stood Cooper. Even though Kalum could not see his face clearly as he was so far away, he could tell the man was irritated. Behind Cooper was the centre-piece of the Great Hall, an enormous dominating Pipe Organ. Its polished steel tubes extended up to the ceiling and ended in viciously sharp points.

He was scanning the crowd as students entered from

both side entrances, looking for someone to unleash his anger on. The students themselves were fast learners, and knew better than to catch his eye, and instead fixed their gaze on their feet.

With a nod Cooper indicated to the music teacher, Ms Farlow, to play the school anthem. She sat as she always did, with her brow furrowed so intently that it looked as if her head was trying to fold itself in half. Then with bulging eyes and a ferocity that Kalum wasn't sure was entirely necessary, she attacked the keys and peddles of the organ, sending her mousey brown hair into a frenzy. The booming imposing baritone music reverberated off the walls and through the children themselves.

As he side-stepped down the row of chairs to find a place to sit with his class, he felt a sharp pain in his ribs. Nathan was behind him, jabbing a knuckle into his side.

"We need to talk," he growled.

Kalum shrugged him off and kept moving away down the row, not daring to look back. By now Cooper's impatient foot tapping was audible, even over the sound of the music. He gave Ms Farlow a curt nod, indicating she should stop. She was, however, so caught up in it that he had to march over there and put a hand on her shoulder to get her attention. The music stopped abruptly with a jarring tone that set their teeth on edge.

Cooper spoke and the pupils fell silent. "I am happy to announce that we have been successful in hiring Mr Elliott Sparrow, who comes highly recommended from Sentech Head Office. He will fill the void left by Mr Dunstable's departure as deputy head."

A thin man with a slightly pallid complexion made his way onto the stage. He wore a tweed jacket over a white shirt and dark trousers. He skipped up the stairs with ease and inclined his head as Cooper made way for him at the podium. He looked out onto the sea of children in front of them and fixed them with an impish grin that seemed to make his green eyes sparkle. He blew an errant section of his hair back into place.

"Thank you, Headmaster," he said, giving Cooper a half salute.

The man started to speak but it faded into the background. Kalum could feel Nathan's eyes on the back of his head. He glanced over his shoulder and he saw that the older boy was glaring in his direction.

"Find yourself at Sentech," Sparrow proclaimed on stage, his hand gesturing to the sky. "That's what the last page of the Trinity orientation guide says." Cooper leant forward and gave Sparrow a look that communicated he was going 'off script'.

"To find yourself you need to know where you come from," Sparrow continued, ignoring Cooper's stare. "Talk to your parents, find out about them, about who they are as people, about what makes them tick."

Cooper was crossing the stage now, wanting to reclaim the microphone again.

"Mother's will tell you everything you want to know. Father's are trickier. With them you have to dig a bit deeper."

Cooper's hand was on the microphone now, trying to yank it free.

"Find out where you come from and you can find yourself," Sparrow said.

Kalum felt as if the man looked at him and held his gaze for a beat before giving up the microphone to Cooper.

Cooper reclaimed his position behind the podium and continued his monologue.

"Thank you for your words of wisdom, Mr Sparrow," Cooper said, glaring at the new teacher over the microphone.

"Next week is an important one," he surged on. "We are hosting one of the Henkan cup quarter finals. Your very own Titan's will be facing off against the Jackals. Misters Lancaster and Walker, please stand."

Kalum heard the scrape of wood on wood as on the row behind him stood. He turned and saw Nathan with arms raised, waving to the crowd. Near the back of the hall he saw Reese get to his feet and offer a salute.

"They are your Captains," Cooper said. "They have earned that honour and the privileges that go with it. I trust you will all accommodate them and the team as they prepare to wage war and fight for the pride of our school and Corporation."

He punctuated the last word by slamming his fist onto the podium, which looked dangerously close to buckling under the blow. He composed himself with a long drawn out breath, but his face remained ruddy and flustered.

"One final point," he said, clearing his throat. "You will be aware of the threat that the Scorps have levelled against all Sentech member and affiliates. Their filthy Augs are spreading to all echelons of Sentech society. As such we will begin testing each and every one of you for Aug use. The Henkan squad have already been tested and I'm pleased to say they came back clear. Stop by the school nurse's office and check the schedule. Now please leave in an orderly fashion." He snapped a turn and marched off the stage.

They'd almost made it to their lockers before Kalum's TRIST vibrated and a message scrolled across the screen. It was from Reese.

"I need to see you, right now. Meet me by the Henkan pitch."

He stopped, and his friends shot him a puzzled look.

"I'll catch up," he said, waving them off.

He doubled back past his classroom, but a second later a jacket was thrown over his head, and pulled so tight he could barely breath. As he tried to shout out, he had the air knocked out of him and his cry for help wheezed out as nothingness. Hands grabbed at his writhing body, hoisting him off his feet and carrying him off. He didn't know how long he struggled for until he was dumped onto a cold, wet floor. He ripped off the jacket covering his face and blinked at the bright spotlights in front of him. As his eyes adjusted he realised he was at the swimming pool. In front of him he could see silhouetted figures.

And then he heard a voice.

"Saw you and your brother outside Cooper's office. Hope you weren't thinking about doing something stupid? Like maybe talking about the Augs?"

Kalum tried to get up off his knees, but two strong hands pushed him back down.

THE VOICE CONTINUED NOW. It was unmistakably Nathan Lancaster.

"I took precautions to make sure our tests came back negative. I can't have you messing that up for us," he growled. "Okay, okay let him up, let him up."

Kalum got to his feet, disorientated and tottering. He tried to shake the cobwebs free but he couldn't focus.

Nathan leant in close.

"Did you really think I'd let you get away with disrespecting me, not once, but twice?"

He pulled back and shook his head in a mock show of disappointment.

Kalum heard the voice in his head but the words were muffled like they were spoken underwater.

"Come on! We can take him," it whispered. "You just have to let me out!"

"Don't forget who runs this place," Nathan sneered. "Here's a little something I learnt watching the Gauntlet. It's one of Reinhardt's signature moves."

Kalum had no time to react before he was hit with a vicious kick to the gut that folded him in half. He had never been hit so hard, and the force of the blow disconnected him from the ground. Coming down, the back of his head made a sickening thud as it connected with the side of the pool, and then the shock of the icy water on his skin made him inhale sharply. The water burned as it was sucked into his lungs, stabbing at him from the inside. Darkness at the edges of his vision was closing in like creeping tendrils of viscous oil. He gave one final vain kick to propel him to the surface and towards the light he could see at the waters edge, but his energy was sapped and he hung suspended in the water as the blackness enveloped his consciousness.

11

PARTICULAR DEMON

L exi pushed her way through the throng, leading with her shoulder and the points of her elbows to make a path. Jun and Casey followed close behind. When they reached the edge they saw Barker standing there, ashen faced. He stopped them with one wrinkled hand outstretched.

"They're doing their best for him. Let them work," he said, not taking his attention off the scene behind him. Lexi stretched on tiptoes to see but all she could make out was a wall of figures with a trolley and equipment around them.

"Oh my god!" shouted Jun and tried to push past Barker. William Barker may have been closer to seventy than fifty-years-old, but he pushed him back with surprising strength.

"Let. Them. Work," he demanded, the edge in his voice unmistakable.

"What? What?" asked Lexi, her anxiety ramping up from the look on Jun's face.

"It's... Kal," he whispered.

Jerry Gavern had worked as a Sentech Emergency first responder for six years now. His uniform, once a deep sapphire hue, was faded by age. His grey eyes were cast down and focused on the job at hand, the sweat collecting on the contours of his brow. He had seen his fair share of trauma. He'd been part of the Sentech Response team for the Tokyo incident. And to this day he was still haunted by it.

It wasn't just the post-traumatic stress. A combination of time and intensive cognitive behavioural therapy had buried that particular demon. It was the nightmares. To call them nightmares was a disservice. They activated all the senses, horrific images which felt like they were carved into his retina, the smell and taste of charred flesh lodged in his sinus, the feel of flames licking at his feet, and the screams that sliced straight through him. After coming through the other side of that, nothing could faze him.

The muscle definition of his large arms was prominent as he propelled them down in practiced rhythm. His larger, middle-aged abdominal spread also moved in rhythm with his chest, and he felt the familiar firebrand run across it to his jaw and left arm. He pushed the feeling aside and carried on, ignoring his colleagues' offers to take over. The memories of that night tried to resurface. The thoughts were like headlights in a rear-view mirror, drawing closer no matter how hard he tried to shake them.

The snap of a rib underneath him stopped him in mid thrust. Jerry's colleague Marta, a stout woman whose uniform looked crisp and new compared to his, winced audibly as she tried to pull him back. Jerry shook her off and reached into his kit bag and pulled out needles, syringes and other equipment, keeping one eye on the boy.

He placed a circular metal disc to Kalum's chest. Seconds later it emitted a low hum.

"What's that sound? Don't sound like a heartbeat," Martha mumbled

"Pulse. Check," Jerry said to his colleague, using the back of his hand to wipe away the sweat that was now stinging his eyes.

Martha followed the instruction and hooked him up to a monitor. It gave a short sharp bleep and then displayed a thin blue line moving up and down at acute angles like a saw blade.

"That's not possible," Martha said, her small blue eye scrunched even tighter as they looked at the readout.

Jerry pressed a button on his TRIST and the information transferred to it. Not saying anything, he pressed his fingers to Kalum's carotid artery and then looked up at his team.

"No, the display is right. His heart is beating. It was just so fast that the Sterosteth couldn't hear the individual beats."

He barked an order to another stocky bald man whose arms looked as wide as his legs, and who scrambled forward to attach two chrome-coloured strips to Kalum's exposed chest. They pulsed and glowed blue and Jerry gestured everyone to get back.

Three-hundred and sixty joules of electricity were sent through Kalum's chest wall to his heart. On the sixth attempt, Kalum woke with an almighty gasp. Every part of him felt like the current was surging through him. All his nerves felt raw and on fire, like thousands of needles stabbing at him. Adrenaline coursed through his system. Images flashed in his mind, like someone riffling through a photo album in his head. Vivid pictures from his childhood exploded into view. Some were familiar, but many felt alien, like they weren't his.

Kalum's body arched up suddenly, like an invisible rope attached to his abdomen was being yanked upwards by some unseen force. He felt a relentless tapping crescendo inside his head, as if something was trying to hatch from his skull. Opening his mouth he tried to call out, but the noise that emerged wasn't his voice. The screech sounded like the grinding of metal on metal.. The crescendo was so intense that it was too much for most of the crowd to cope with. Teachers and students alike cowered with the heels of their palms pressing hard against their ears. Lexi, Casey and Jun tried to get past Barker, but the old man moved to block them with his body.

The tapping in Kalum's head moved, spreading down, pausing at his chest, and the pain magnified one hundred-fold. Kalum felt like his heart was being wrung like a dishrag. His chest rattled as he gasped for breath and he tasted copper. His eyes blinked rapidly and he could sense his field of vision narrowing. From the peripheries, darkness slowly spread inwards, like black paint spilt from a can. Then all that was left was endless blackness, not just in his vision but in all his senses, as if everything had been turned off and he was completely shut off from the outside world.

The spasms that were twisting his body with cruel force into ghastly positions, reduced in their intensity, until only a few twitches of his arms were visible. The beeping of the monitor stopped and changed to a long screeching tone, and Kalum lay still. Everything stopped, and the moment hung in the air, preserved like a living diorama.

"No! No, no, no, no. Come on," shouted Jerry, starting compressions again, but in that moment the voice of experience whispered in his ear. He knew how this was going to play out. When you'd done the job as long as he had, you developed a sixth sense about how these things would go.

After ten minutes, Martha lay a hand on his shoulder and pulled him away. He stood, mute and unfocused, shaking his head. Martha took out a sheet and with unexpected gentleness laid it over Kalum's face, shielding him from sight.

"Why are you stopping?!" screamed Lexi, looking around at the crowd for someone to agree with her. She spied Nathan in the corner of the room watching, the usual smugness washed away from his face. He had his hands in his pockets and looked away when he made eye contact with Lexi.

"This was YOU!" she screamed, storming towards him in a feral rage. She weaved past Daniel, who seemed to materialise in front of her, and took a swing at Nathan. Her fist never made contact with its intended target. Reese caught it with his palm and pushed her back gently.

"Don't," he said.

"Hey. I'm the one that called the Medical Response crew!" Nathan shouted.

He didn't see Reese's back-fist coming. It connected cleanly and Nathan bounced back off the wall behind him.

"Get the hell up," Reese said, and Nathan pulled himself to his feet, using the wall behind him to steady himself. He was teetering on his feet like a spinning top losing momentum. His eyes widened as he saw Reese readying another strike. This time Daniel was faster, his wide chest absorbing the impact of the blow.

A single penetrating beep from the monitor made them all stop. Kalum pulled back the sheet covering him and managed to sit up. He felt strange, prickling waves of energy run from the base of his skull down to his limbs and then back again. They ran up and down his body like racers on a circuit, picking up speed with each lap. He looked at his hand as he flexed his fingers and was overcome by a feeling of calmness and strength.

Kalum wanted to lie still and get his bearings but his body seemed to have other ideas and he vaulted up, landing in a half crouch. He took a step forward and the sensation vanished, as if sucked up by a black hole. His legs went from underneath him and he pitched forward.

Reese scooped him up before he could hit the ground.

"Easy little brother, I've got you."

A rainbow cascade of coloured threads seemed to waft in the air around Kalum. They were so bright that he needed to shield his eyes. They flickered once and then blinked away, gone as suddenly as they had appeared.

Reese helped Kalum back onto the trolley and covered him.

"Wh-what happened to me?" Kalum asked, his voice coming out as a reedy thin scratch.

"I'll tell you what happened!" boomed Cooper's thunderous voice. "You broke school rules by coming to the pool without a member of staff, slipped, and hit your head! It was lucky Mr Lancaster was passing by, heard the commotion, pulled you out, and called the Response crew. The boy is a hero!"

Cooper whirled on Reese, gesticulating like a man gone mad. The artery in his neck throbbed with violent disregard and his face had now moved past its normal deep red complexion and was bordering on purple.

"And Walker, we all just saw you assault Mr Lancaster!"

Reese stepped up to the Headmaster. The simmering rage in his eyes had worked its way down to his clenched fist, which still had a spattering of Nathan's blood on it. He looked the shorter man in the eyes. Cooper flinched and took a half step backwards before regaining his composure.

"Before you say or do anything else you may regret, Mr Walker, I'd like to remind you of all that Sentech and Trinity have done for you, are doing for you, and will do for you in the future," he said evenly.

At that Reese seemed to shrink, and lowered his head a fraction.

"Go and wait for me outside my office, now," he said.

"Sir! I need to go with my brother."

Now it was Cooper's turn to bristle, and he stepped uncomfortably close.

"If you're not out of my sight in five seconds, I will expel you. You and your family will lose all Sentech privileges and these good men will dump your brother at the side of the street on their way out."

Reese's eyes went wide, his mouth ajar, as if he'd taken a slap to the face.

Cooper raised a fist, the points of his knuckles barely visible over the soft pink flesh.

"One," he said, slowly extending his index finger. Reese looked to Kalum.

"Two."

Reese took a step back. Kalum nodded for him to go. He looked around and saw everyone watching him.

"Three."

He turned and walked away, stopping only to look back at his brother before he rounded the corner.

Cooper's Cheshire smile was wide and brimming with self satisfied smugness.

"Sir, Sir? Can you give him some room please? We need to take him in for observation," Jerry pleaded, trying to usher them to one side.

"Our conversation isn't over, boy!" Cooper shouted down to Kalum as he was wheeled past him.

"Stop," Kalum rasped. "Where are you taking me?" His throat felt like it had been ripped to shreds, and even swallowing his own saliva felt like nails were being hammered into his voice box.

Jerry kept the trolley moving but spoke as they went.

"We're taking you to the Sentech London Medical Centre. You need specialist assessment."

As Kalum was being stretchered out to the waiting Med Transport he saw that most of the school had come to have a good look. Some were even taking pictures and filming with their TRISTs. He pulled the white sheet up to shield his face a little.

Nathan for his part was playing the hero well, shaking hands with the Faculty and smiling and waving at the other pupils with a self-satisfied look on his face.

There was a commotion by the front stairwell and it caught Kalum's attention. He saw Elliott Sparrow rushing down two steps at a time, shouting for students to clear out of the way. He stopped at the trolley, his words tripping over themselves in a breathless rush.

"You'kay? Where're youtaking 'im?"

Cooper pulled Sparrow away and sighed in irritation.

"Mr Walker had a mishap at the pool. He's fine and there's nothing to concern you here."

He looked around as if seeing the throng of students for the first time.

"In fact there's nothing to concern any of you here."

The students could see where this was going and started to scatter like antelope spotting a stalking leopard.

"Any student still here in thirty seconds will have to explain the reason to me personally. And I'm not in the best of moods."

By the time his sentence was finished the pupils had

stampeded down corridors and up stairwells, leaving the concourse empty. Sparrow fixed Cooper with a look that seemed to hint at some barely contained emotion. Then his eyes moved to Nathan and gave him a look so toxic that it wiped away his self-congratulatory smirk.

Kalum caught a glimpse of Lexi as he was wheeled into the back of the Transport vehicle. She was wiping her face with the cuffs of her jumper and he offered her a weak smile. She gave him a tentative half wave and smiled back.

Jerry sat next to the trolley and he and Martha strapped in. Then he tapped a large red button on the wall and spoke into a microphone.

"Sentech London Medical Centre."

A shrill siren screamed to life as the Transport moved off the school grounds and onto the busy main road.

12

REMEMBER ME

The noise of the machines Kalum was hooked up to seemed to penetrate his body and reverberate inside him. Jerry sensed his discomfort, and keyed a command into the keypad. The sound cut out, but was replaced by the revving engine and a squeal of tyres as the vehicle made aggressive manoeuvres through traffic. Through the window the Transport's siren lights reflected back off the other vehicles and buildings as they flashed by. Their rhythm had a hypnotic effect and Kalum hovered in the grey void between awake and unconscious, the jarring ride the only thing keeping him from slipping completely under.

A rippling feeling jolted him awake again, flowing through him like a current. It exploded from the base of his skull, sending seismic shocks through him. His skin felt raw, like he was being dipped in and out of hot oil. The sensation was excruciating yet somehow bearable. Suddenly, all he wanted was to be out of the Transport. He strained against his restraints and heard the leather straps creak against the tension.

"You okay?" Jerry asked, looking at him.

Kalum's eyes flicked to the man. He saw a bead of sweat making its way down his temple, the quickening of the pulse in his neck, and way his eyes kept darting to the monitor above the stretcher.

"I'm fine," Kalum said, not sure if he was trying to convince himself or the medic.

"Good. We're only a few minutes away from the hospital."

Kalum could sense the relief in his voice. A few more minutes and Kalum would be someone else's problem. A few more minutes and he would be able to relax.

The Transport pulled into the yellow striped bay outside the Emergency Department of the Medical Centre. It stopped with a jolt and doors hissed open as the suspension lowered it to ground level. They wheeled him out and he stiffened when the chill air hit him. He saw the grey-brown façade of the building as they approached the entrance. It seemed to match the clouds that peppered the overcast skyline.

As they burst through the heavy fire doors into the bustling department he was struck by both the noise and organised chaos. Everyone seemed to be moving at a frenetic pace but in way that got the job done, like a well-practiced pit crew. A stocky, stern looking lady came over and nodded a greeting to the Response team. She introduced herself as Carrie without bothering to look in Kalum's direction.

The crew gave her a step-by-step account of what had happened at Trinity.

Martha scratched her head and looked apologetic.

"Here are his readings," she said, tapping her TRIST

against Carrie's. Both made a beep, indicating that the transfer of files was complete. Carrie looked at the readout and then looked to Martha and Jerry with raised eyebrows.

"Your equipment must be faulty," she said, her tone hard and disapproving.

Jerry straightened, failing to hide the irritation stamped on his face. "No. I confirmed them manually. That's what really happened to him."

Carrie dismissed this with a sideways glance that then turned to Kalum. Her eyes appraised the boy on the stretcher, her angular face becoming more pinched and intense. She leaned over him until they were face to face.

"What did you take? If you tell me, this will go a lot quicker," she snapped. "Did you take an Aug?"

It took Kalum a few minutes to actually register what she meant, but she didn't bother to wait for a reply.

"Suit yourself. The blood work will tell us anyway," she said, motioning for him to be wheeled into an empty medical bay, and followed him in. Reaching down she tapped her TRIST against his.

"TRIST, ID confirm and verify Corporation status. Override code 29979."

After a few seconds a voice sounded.

"Sorry Carrie, no available TRIST unit detected," it said.

Carrie repeated the action and command again, her scowl doubling, but the result was the same. She reached down and wrenched Kalum's arm up. To his horror he saw the spiderweb crack across the screen and the large indentation in the metal above it.

She threw his arm back down. "Fine. I'll just have to call Trinity and check that we can *actually* treat you." Then she wheeled around and stormed out of the bay.

"I didn't take anything!" Kalum shouted after her. Carrie didn't even bother looking back, but simply raised her hand, giving the universal signal of the ending of a conversation.

"I didn't," he repeated, looking at the Response crew around him. Jerry smiled at him.

He put a reassuring hand on Kalum's shoulder as he too left, and said, "You gave everyone quite a scare. You'll be okay now. I'm sure they'll let you head home soon."

"Thanks for everything," Kalum said, and then he was alone in his bay, bordered on all sides by bright blue screens.

The department was an assault on the senses. Bright fluorescent overhead lights made him feel like a science experiment awaiting dissection. After a while he became accustom to the noise, the shouting, the rhythmical beeps and pings of equipment and the occasional cries of pain. The smell though was something that he couldn't ignore. It was a sickly mix of lemon and aniseed, and the tang of bleach felt like it was burning though his nose into his skull.

Suddenly, the screens parted and Carrie stormed in, flanked by two burly porters wearing sea-blue hospital uniforms. Her hand snatched up his wrist and pinned his hand to the screen on a device that one of the men handed her.

Kalum tried to pull away, his fingers twitching like the legs of a dying tarantula, but Carrie just tightened her grip. The device buzzed and a plastic tag was spat out from its top. The woman slapped it down onto Kalum's other wrist like a seasoned cop making an arrest, and it wrapped itself around, pinching and cutting on the skin. She thrust an electronic chart into the side of his bed and nodded to the men.

"Right. His TRIST is broken so I've numbered and tagged him," she said, glaring at Kalum. "Now get this waste of time out of my Emergency room."

Then Kalum was being propelled down a series of identical corridors at a disorientating pace. He examined the tag on his wrist; it had his name and school printed on the front, and the reverse in green stated that he was an Affiliate, eligible for tier five treatment only, whatever that meant. With difficulty he managed to wriggle his little finger under and tried to loosen its vice like grip. When his hand started to tingle in protest he gave up and slumped back in the bed.

He was taken to a bay that seemed identical in every way to where he had been before. The two porters snapped on the brakes to the bed and left him once again with only his thoughts for company.

"We need to leave," the voice said again. Louder now. Too loud to ignore. Stronger than it had it had ever been.

"There's somewhere we need to be," it said. "Can't you feel it pulling at you?" The voice was clear, but with a child-like pitch to it."

"Get up. Get up. Get up. Get up."

Again and again it spoke, the words running into and over each other until they were indistinguishable, like smeared wet ink.

He buried the heels of his palms into his temples, the painful pressure giving him something else to focus on.

"Shut up, shut up, shut up," he said through gritted teeth, and scrunched up his eyes.

A hand shook him and he opened his eyes again, the voice shut out like a wire had been severed.

A warm freckled face, framed with light red hair, was looking down at him. He crawled up the bed, surprised by the intruder into his personal space. She responded in kind, letting out a startled yelp and backpedalling. She dropped a chart, which bounced mutely off the sterile floor and came to rest by the bed.

""Sorry. Who were you talking to?" she asked. Red faced, she stooped to collect the chart. She straightened her uniform and offered a wide smile.

"No one," he said, avoiding eye contact. "It's... it's just a bit noisy around here."

"Well Kalum, I'm Amanda and I'm going to be looking after you today," she said, adjusting her red hair so her ponytail was even tighter.

"Open your mouth," she said. Kalum complied more out of curiosity than anything else. She placed a thin metal rod under his tongue and left it there until a machine behind her gave a soft beep. Amanda looked at the reading and nodded, then tapped some details onto the chart.

"Where're your parents, Kalum?" she asked, scanning through the rest of the information, her nose slightly wrinkled in concentration.

Kalum's mind whirred into action, drawing a caricature of his mother bulldozing her way through anyone between her and the Medical Centre.

"She's probably on her way," he said with a dry smile.

"Your Medical record from Trinity says you get panic attacks. Have you taken your medication?"

"Yes." The lie came out easily.

She made to leave and then looked back, and Kalum could see the imminent question on her face.

"Is your—"

"The date of birth is right. I'm a bit on the small side," he said, cutting her off.

Adults often asked him when he was born. Teachers, doctors, people checking tickets at the cinema. They never believed that he was actually fifteen-years-old because of his height and thin frame. Amanda, to her credit, had hid her surprise better than most.

"Put your arms out please," she asked.

Again he complied, holding both arms out as if asking for a hug. She slipped a dark grey plastic sleeve over both his arms and flicked a switch on each. They pulsed with white light and Kalum heard a hiss and felt both arms become cold. Then a light in the top pulsed red, then changed to amber.

"Just a bit of cold and then you might feel—"

"Ow!" Kalum said, nearly jumping off the bed.

"—a small scratch," Amanda finished.

The sleeve slackened and then slipped off, leaving a piece of tubing in both arms. It gradually filled with dark red blood and the sight of it made Kalum's head feel as if it was going to slip off his neck. He shook the light-headedness away and Amanda reached forwards and snapped the tubes off.

"We're just going to run some tests," she said, the smile still pinned to her face, and then she left.

He lay back on the stiff, starchy white sheets and closed his eyes, inhaling deep and slow rhythmical breaths to try to combat the creeping feeling of nausea that still was rising in his throat. With everything around blocked out, his mind calmed and sleep came to him like a welcoming friend.

IMAGES FORMED in front of his eyes, but they were blurred, as if looking through a sheet of flowing water. He could make out a small boy, his face obscured, but he instinctively knew it was him. He turned to take in the surroundings, and realised that it was his old school in New York. It felt so strange seeing himself like this, being led up the concrete steps by a tall man in an off-white shirt and a navy tie. His thick black hair looked messy, as if he never bothered to look in a mirror before leaving the house. The image seemed to gain focus, and outside the bright green doors, he knelt, and they were eye to eye and the man smiled and peered over horn-rimmed glasses at the boy and held out his outstretched fist in expectation. Young Kalum didn't hesitate and reciprocated, and they both made an imitation of an explosive noise when they made contact. Then he realised who the man was. It was his father. It had been so long since he had seen him like this, smiling and interacting.

Then the scene changed. Young Kalum was alone at lunchtime, sitting with the black Star Wars lunch box he remembered so well. The smile on his face was wide and innocent, his expression expectant as he opened the box. Inside, amongst the small tub of cut up cucumber, cherry tomatoes, peanut butter and jam sandwiches, he fished out a white folded napkin and opened it up. Young Kalum giggled as he saw the picture his father had drawn for him; a guinea pig hang-gliding.

He allowed himself to enjoy the feeling. Dreams like this were not something he had experienced for years. Until recently, when they had restarted. Those had been mainly about Lexi and that strange metal band. His old doctors had told him that it was a side effect of his medication. A "small price to pay", they had said. Not for him. It was one he had felt intensely, and to Kalum it had felt as if something precious had been stolen from him.

A thought occurred to him. "Why am I seeing this? Why this memory?"

In response, four-year-old Kalum turned to him, his head turning at an unnatural angle, and replied in that voice that he knew all too well now.

"Because you are starting to remember me..."

13

BLURRED MYSTERY

K alum's eyes opened, taking a minute to adjust to the bright lights in the ward. He felt as if he'd been asleep for hours, but a glance at the clock on the wall showed it had only been a few minutes. Rubbing his eyes, his vision cleared and he sat upright in shock. In front of him stood an enormous figure. The man had a shaved head and had shoulders so wide Kalum was sure he would have to turn sideways and stoop to get through most doorways. The light behind him silhouetted his frame, making him look even more imposing. As he leaned in Kalum relaxed. Even though his features were sharp and angular, the expression on his face was friendly and reassuring.

"Hi!" he said, his smile widening even more.

He offered a huge hand that engulfed Kalum's as he shook it. "I'm Dr Palma, the ward Physician," he said. "How are you feeling?"

Kalum tried to sit up and grimaced at the blossoming pain in his head. He reached up and was surprised to find a padded bandage that he hadn't noticed before. His hand came back with a smear of blood and he felt his breakfast trying to make a reappearance.

"You took quite a knock. Let's have a look," the doctor said. "I think the first responder crew put that on."

His large fingers fought to gain purchase on the edges of the tape and Kalum could smell the coffee on his breath as he struggled with open-mouthed concentration.

He stopped and looked at Kalum with a look so serious Kalum thought he was about to be told that there was a gaping hole in his head.

"We can either take the tape off fast or slow. Neither is particularly pleasant. What would yo—"

Mid sentence he yanked the tape back like he was pulling on a ripcord. The bandage came loose, taking a fair chunk of Kalum's hair with it. The agony was so exquisite that Kalum was unable to give voice to it. He settled with biting down on his hand to refocus his pain.

Dr Palma displayed the deep red bandage like it was a flag before tossing it into a bin that opened in greedy anticipation.

"Fast really is the only option," he mumbled as he ran a gloved hand over the wound. The tips of his fingers felt like sandpaper on the raw flesh and Kalum pulled away.

"Jeez. That looks like it hurt."

Kalum peered under the Doctor's arm and saw Elliot Sparrow standing in the threshold.

Dr Palma turned to him, the humour washed from his face.

"Can I help you, Sir?" he asked, drawing himself up to his full height, his hand resting easily above a red button on his TRIST.

"I'm here to check on Kalum," Sparrow said, blowing his brown hair put of his face and adjusting his tweed jacket. He took a step forward and Palma moved to block him.

"Are you family?"

Sparrow lifted his arm and tapped a button. The screen on his TRIST displayed his name and Sentech status.

"I'm the Deputy Head at Trinity, just come to check on him."

Palma leaned in and said in a low voice, "I've already had instructions from Trinity... we're good here."

Then the blue panel door was torn back with such force that it bounced back on its hinges. Nadine threw her arms around Kalum, squeezing him so hard that the attached monitors chirped in protest.

She then held him by the shoulders at arms length, scanning him from top to toe and checking that he was still in one piece.

"Don't you dare do that to me again!" she growled. She didn't wait for him to reply but turned to Sparrow and Palma. She grabbed Sparrow's hand and held it between hers.

"Thank you for looking after him," she said, her words still a bit rushed as she caught her breath. Sparrow looked down at his hands and then up to her face. He tugged his hand free and took a slight sidestep away.

"I... I... I'm no doctor."

Dr Palma stepped in and steered Nadine towards a nearby chair. She sat and he dropped down to his haunches so that they were eye to eye.

"Now, young Kalum has had a bit of an ordeal this afternoon. He's doing okay..."

It was the sort of statement that was unfinished; the jab before the right hook. Nadine waited for him to continue.

"So... given that Kalum is a Sentech Affiliate, and not a

fully fledged Member, he's covered for the on-site treatment that he had," Palma said.

He looked at Nadine, doing a good job of feigning his embarrassment to continue.

"Buuuut, we've had to do a whole slew of further testing and also got him this bay. None of which is cheap..."

He reached over and touched his TRIST against Kalum's. Turning it to face Nadine, he slid a finger across the screen and her eyes widened at what she saw. She opened her mouth to speak but Palma steamrolled over her and kept on talking.

"Trinity are happy to cover this and any further bills though," he said, his voice reaching an excited timbre. Slipping a large envelope out from underneath the tablet he was holding he pushed a sheaf of paper towards Kalum.

"What's this?" Nadine asked, taking them before Kalum could.

Palma remained silent whilst she flicked though the pages, and scoffed as she digested the final few paragraphs.

"So signing this absolves Sentech and Trinity of any and all responsibility," she said with her arms crossed and eyes narrowing.

"There's also an additional sub-clause," Palma said, not missing a beat and gesturing that she should turn over the final page.

Nadine threw the stack back in his face. The papers struck his chest and then scattered across the room like confetti. He stared at the small lady in front of him and then wordlessly picked up each piece and laid them on the bed.

"I urge you to consider your options very carefully," he said, and then left.

"Rrrr," Nadine growled, slamming the bottom of her fist

into the panel behind her. The panel shuddered, reverberating and filling the bay with noise.

"What?" asked Kalum, but he instinctively knew already.

"Let me guess. They want a written statement that Nathan wasn't involved. Am I close?" asked Sparrow with a sigh.

Nadine and Kalum looked at him, they had both forgotten he was still in the room.

"Why are you here, Mr Sparrow?" Kalum asked. He levered himself up onto his elbows and swung his legs over the bed. He pulled his feet back as the bare skin contacted the cold stone floor.

"Sparrow?" said Nadine. She lunged forward, the edge of her forearm driving into Sparrow's chest and pinning him to the other side of the bay. The speed and force with which she moved took both Kalum and the teacher by surprise.

"You're Cooper's new sidekick. You here to make sure he signs?"

Sparrow tried to stand straight, but Nadine pushed harder, slamming him back against the panel, making them rattle again. Sparrow looked at Nadine, and something in his eyes didn't sit right with Kalum. There was no anger, no pain or irritation. There *was* emotion there, but something he just couldn't make fit the situation. Nadine must have felt it too because she eased off and stepped back to Kalum's side. Sparrow stood with his hands up in front of him as if held at gunpoint.

"Trinity didn't send me," he said. He lowered his hands and rubbed the back of his head and winced.

"I just came to bring you a few things." He handed Kalum his sketchbook and rucksack. "And I wanted to see if you were okay."

At this Nadine seemed to soften slightly, the tension

easing from her shoulders. She sat on the bed next to Kalum and put her arm around him.

"I'm... I'm doing better," Kalum said.

"Good. I'm glad, really glad," Sparrow said, and a half smile touched his face.

There was an awkward silence but eventually Sparrow cleared his throat and adjusted the lapels of his jacket.

"Well. I should go." He turned, and one of the panels swung open in response. He turned and looked at them.

"It was nice to s—" he started, and then stopped and smiled, fiddling with his TRIST. He cleared his throat. "It was nice to have met you, Mrs Walker," he said and then left, not waiting for a reply.

Nadine and Kalum sat in silence for a beat and then spoke at the same time. Nadine smiled and nodded for Kalum to go first.

"I want to sign it," he said, not looking at her.

"No, son. You're not signing that lie. Reese told me what Nathan did. He's lucky I wasn't there. I'd have taken him and Cooper down, and ripped that school down brick by brick." There was a hardness in her eyes that Kalum hadn't seen before, a grim purpose that left him with little doubt she would have delivered on her promise.

"I have to sign it, Ma."

Nadine began to speak but he cut her off with his palm.

"I don't know what number that doctor showed you, but I know we can't afford this," he said, gesturing at the array of equipment around him. In response, one of the monitor's tones started to pick up pace, its frenetic beat causing both Nadine and Kalum to turn.

"Okay, okay," Nadine said with one eye on the chirping monitor. "Relax, we'll talk about it later. Get some rest."

. . .

KALUM HAD EXPECTED MORE of an argument. *Maybe she feels sorry for me?* he wondered.

He was so tired, he almost fell asleep before his eyes had shut. It felt as if his consciousness was spiralling and falling like a skydiver whose parachute wouldn't open. He was surrounded by a jumble of pixels, and an odd combination of happiness, fear and anger filled him as the scene in his dreamscape gradually became clearer. There was someone standing in front of him, their features an oddly familiar blur. Bit by bit sections snapped into focus, like a jigsaw coming together. Then Kalum realised he was looking at himself again, but a younger version, that must have been about five-years-old. He was alone, wearing a pair of blue cargo shorts and a grubby white t-shirt, which had what looked like an old towel tucked into the neck to create a makeshift cape. His knees and elbows were scuffed and bloodied and his glasses hung crookedly from his face, which sported a toothy, satisfied grin. He was looking at himself in a mirror with a white wooden frame and a smudged dirty surface.

"I can't believe I did that!" Kalum heard his younger self say. "I actually hit Carl back!"

Then the reflection answered.

"I don't care what Mum says, that was the single greatest thing ever. We were just like Bruce Lee."

The voice from the reflection was his own, but different. There was a background hiss and crackling as it spoke, like audible sparks of electricity.

Then he and the reflection spoke together, the two distinct tones mixing like different coloured paints to create something new.

"Nothing can stop the Steel Falcon."

Then the face in the mirror changed. The young boy's

features hardened and his eyes flickered, the colour changing from blue to hazel and back again. The face in the mirror started to open its mouth. Wider, wider and wider still until it quivered against its physical limits. Then from inside the gaping maw, fingertips crept out, curling around the edges of the mouth and pulling it open further until he could see a face emerging from within.

"I won't go back into the dark!" screeched the voice, the hiss and crackling in the background ramping up until Kalum couldn't stand the noise.

The dreamscape creaked with a sound of rending metal. Then in a shimmering explosion of colour the world around him disappeared.

He woke up back in the hospital bed covered with a thin film of sweat over him and the sound of the incessant monitor bleeping in the background.

"You were talking in your sleep, sweetheart," Nadine said softly, putting her hand on his head and smiling reassuringly.

"How long was I out for?" Kalum groaned, propping himself up onto his elbows and looking for his glasses.

"Only ten minutes or so," she replied, passing them to him. As an afterthought she added, "Did I hear you talking about Carl in your dream?"

"I guess," Kalum said. "I don't know who that is though..."

"Well I do," said Nadine, the corner of her mouth tightening. "He was in your class, when you were little, back in New York."

She focused her gaze on him and raised her eyebrows.

"In a way I'm glad you don't remember him. That kid was the worst. He made your life hell and you weren't the only one," she said. "Until you broke his arm," she added, flashing a smile his way.

"I... don't remember that at all." Kalum shook his head.

"We left for England not long after. After that you said you didn't like going there anyway. None of the kids would play with you anymore..."

Kalum didn't reply to that but just looked away.

"They were scared of you," she added softly.

Kalum and Nadine sat quietly together but alone in their thoughts.

Dr Palma pulled back the curtain and brought them both back to the present. He looked over to them and cleared his throat pointedly.

"Have you given any further thought to your options?" he asked.

Nadine ignored the question and shot back one of her own.

"Look, just tell us if we're okay to take Kal home and we'll be out of your hair," —Nadine's eyes flicked to his bald dome, and added— "so to speak."

"I can't give you any medical information unless you're willing to make up the difference in credits or sign the agreement, Mrs Walker. I'm sorry."

Kalum thought that the man didn't look particularly sorry at all.

"Let's just get out of here, Ma," he whispered.

"No. We can't, what if something else happens to you?" she said, stroking his hair. She fixed the doctor with a dark look.

"Fine. We'll pay the credits," she said.

Palma nodded, immune to the waves of anger rolling off Nadine, and held out his TRIST for her to authorise payment. Nadine keyed in her fingerprint and held it to his. A jangling tone sounded and her screen flashed red.

Palma's eyes looked up at Nadine and she cleared her throat and retracted her arm.

"I just need to move some credits around," she said. "I'll be back in an hour and we can finish up then."

"You have thirty eight minutes before his time allowance runs out," Dr Palma said, and then retreated from the bay. He left the agreement on the bed.

"In case you change your mind," he said before he left.

Nadine got up and Kalum grabbed her wrist.

"Where are you going?" he asked.

"I'm going to sort this. I can transfer some of the credit ownership of the shop." She saw the look that Kalum gave her and removed his hand from hers and placed it back on the bed.

"It's fine," she said, with a finality in her tone Kalum knew too well.

She tapped an icon on her TRIST and then looked up at him.

"Lucas and Reese will be here any minute to keep you company."

"You go, Ma, I'll be okay here."

He pulled out his sketchbook and twirled a pencil around his fingers.

"I've got plenty to keep me busy in the meantime," he added.

"I'll be back before you know it," she said, giving him a peck on the cheek before getting up to go. She looked back before leaving and Kalum gave her a reassuring wave.

Kalum listened to his mother's retreating steps and waited until they faded away. The agreement stared back at him from where Dr Palma had left it at the foot of his bed.

He snatched it up and flicked to the back. Shaking his head he used his pen to sign his name at the end and then slammed the booklet shut.

"Hey, Kal. You've got a visitor," said the nurse, peeking into his bay.

Kalum closed the book. He was glad Lucas was there; at the very least he would have brought him something to eat. But it wasn't Lucas' bearded face that peered around the curtain though. Nathan Lancaster sauntered into the cubicle, looking around with his signature look of distaste. He nodded in Kalum's general direction, then looked at the bed and then the chair in turn, before deciding that he would prefer to remain standing.

"Listen Walker," he started. "It was... unfortunate how things went down this morning."

Kalum could tell he had rehearsed the script. He almost sounded sincere.

"We only wanted to teach you a lesson. No one wanted this." He gestured to the monitoring equipment and the hospital bed.

"I think it would be in everyone's best interests if we just left things as they are. If you keep your mouth shut about what happened, I'll make sure the rest of the guys leave you alone."

Kalum scoffed in disbelief, and he heard the hissing, crackling voice in his mind.

"Can you believe this guy? If you don't kick his ass, I'm going to," the voice urged. He felt his body edge forward, the straitjacket of tubes and wires holding him back. He felt oddly detached from the anger scratching and crawling in his chest and head, like a dog on a leash. Closing his eyes, he took a deep breath and the voice faded. As he felt the tension leave him, he looked down at his palms, taking in the tiny bloody arcs where his nails had pierced his skin. Shakily he swung his legs off the side of the bed and stood. He opened his mouth to speak.

"Before you say something you'll regret, Walker, I want to remind you about your brother," Nathan said. "After what he did today, one word from me and he's off the team. I do that and *your* time at Trinity is done!"

Kalum looked at Nathan, the threat he had idling in his throat dissolving away. He swallowed, letting his anger leave. It made no sense. What was stopping Nathan from doing exactly that? In one fell swoop he'd be rid of him and Reese and be back as sole Captain of the Henkan team. Nathan seemed to read the confusion in his face, rolled his eyes, and sneered at him.

"Don't think that I've gone soft on you or anything as stupid as that. I still think you're a leeching waste of space."

He looked away and Kalum saw something change in the profile of his face, a shift, like a mask slipping away.

"I care about Trinity. I'm Sentech born and bred. I have to live up to my name," Nathan said, his voice softening. "You've got no clue what it's like to have the shadow of the Lancaster name hanging over you. I need us to be the best team so we can win this year. For that to happen we need your brother. So, for Trinity, I'm willing to let your disrespect slide."

Nathan thrust out a hand in Kalum's direction, an olive branch made of flesh and bone.

Kalum bristled at this. He was walking a razor's edge between rationality and morality. Even without the invisible urge to ram his fist down his throat.

"I've signed it already," Kalum said.

"Good to know you're not a total moron," Nathan said with a sneer, spying the document and picking it up.

He turned to go and stopped and turned back to face Kalum.

"All of this is your fault. You know that, right? You know your place. Just don't venture out of line again."

"Whatever you say, Daddy's boy." The words were out of Kalum's mouth before he could stop them.

Nathan's eyes turned to flint and his jaw muscles tensed.

"Whatever, Walker, you're a loser and you'll always be a loser," Nathan said with a conceited smile.

"Come on Nathan, time to go," called a voice like rusty hinge from outside the room.

At his side Kalum's hand started to shake. His heart machine-gunned against his ribs and he felt his lungs wringing out all their air. That voice. He knew it. He reached over with his left hand and pinned his right hand down to stop the shake.

"It's the guy from Cooper's office." The voice in his head prickled back to life. "The one who was talking about Augs and testing the other kids."

The cold realisation in the truth of this hit him, and Kalum pulled against the tubes again, but they held fast. Nathan leant in, all traces of any inner turmoil washed away.

"I'll see you at school, Walker. Just remember that I tried to take the high road," Nathan said. As he turned to leave, Kalum's hand snaked out and clasped around his wrist. Nathan stopped as if frozen. His head turned and he looked down at where Kalum gripped him.

"Let go before you lose that hand," he said.

Kalum tried to release his grip but his hand wouldn't let go. Nathan tried to rip his arm free but Kalum's fingers were welded to him. He grimaced and thrashed like an animal with its leg caught in a snare.

There was a series of sharp taps and a man stormed into the cubicle and grabbed Nathan by the shoulder. Kalum released Nathan and he fell back into the man. Before they could collide the man twisted and his arm glided out and around the inside of the boy's torso. With a countermovement, he changed Nathan's direction and sent him crashing into the cubical wall. With a sigh he stepped over to where Nathan sat in a slight daze. He reached down and Nathan extended his arm to accept the hand up. The man instead kept bending past Nathan to pick up the signed document that had fallen beside him. He straightened and smoothed away an imaginary crease on the front of his blue suit.

"Do I need to repeat myself, boy?" he said in a tone that matched his glare at Nathan.

"No, Father," said Nathan, getting to his feet, his eyes not leaving the ground.

The man looked at Kalum, and even the voice inside him shut up. His cruel calculating eyes bored into him, sizing him up, assigning value. He adjusted a strand of his perfectly coifed blonde hair and smoothed a crease out of his suit.

"So you're the *other* Walker boy then?" came the rhetorical question.

Kalum nodded mutely in response, distinctly aware the shake in his hand was threatening to spread through his body.

"You really are nothing like your brother," he said in that strained voice that sounded like talons scratching metal.

"Genetics can be a fickle beast. Mother Nature's lottery," he said, looking over at Nathan, his voice sounding wistful. Nathan had now made his way to his father's side and Kalum was amazed by the similarity between he two, the only difference being the colour of their hair. It was as if

Lancaster senior had travelled back in time to see his younger self.

The man extended his hand and before Kalum realised it he was shaking it. They both looked down at Kalum's tremulous hand and he fixed Kalum with a scornful look that he seemed to have to force into an expression of concern.

"Clayton Lancaster," he said, and nodded.

"I... I know who you are," Kalum said, his voice coming out like a thin wisp of smoke. Of course he knew who Clayton Lancaster was. His voice sounded far different in real life than the version he'd heard on Sentech broadcasts.

Clayton smiled and nodded, as if that was how it should be. He looked away.

"Well you will be seeing much more of me in the coming months," he said. "I am taking a keen interest in the next generation of Sentech, so I will be keeping a close watch on Trinity."

Lancaster looked around the cubicle, the disgust on his face plain to see. His nose wrinkled and he grimaced at the shouts of agony that carried to them from an adjacent room.

"I presume we're done here?" he asked, and moved to the door. "I wish you well Kalum," he said, as he left with Nathan tailing behind.

No you don't, Kalum thought. Nothing could be further from the truth. A volcanic raged bubbled up from somewhere inside him, surprising him with its intensity. He stood and took a step forward. The wires and tubes that had held him fast pinged off as he took step after step. Anger, fear and loathing flooded his consciousness. The tapping in his head began again, his fists once more wound tightly by his side. It grew uncontrollably, rising with a crescendo, and the pain spread once more to his chest with his heart beating in time with the pounding between his eyes.

The final tube ripped free, and he barely registered the pain. Curiously detached, he gazed down at the blood flowing freely down his arm, and then stood looking off into the distance. A prickle of current surged up his neck, and his eyes closed of their own volition, like the final curtain dropping on a performance.

They snapped open again and he shuddered as a bracing wind cut through his body. Looking around, he gasped for breath and wrapped his arms around himself, as if that was all he could do to hold himself together.

He stood there alone and vulnerable on the edge of a towering building, surrounded by snow and the howling wind, with no idea where he was or how he'd got there.

14

DEVOURED BY THE DARKNESS

The spatters of blood in the snow marked Kalum's trail like gory breadcrumbs in a macabre fairy tale. He spun, taking in his surroundings as the wind whistled past him. His chest felt like a vice and he sensed the familiar adrenaline surge fuelling his rising terror.

A sudden bite of pain from his wrist drew his attention. The ID tag from the hospital had bitten into the skin where it had been pulled at. A sliver of the plastic material remained, stopping it from falling off completely. There was a smear of crusted dry blood tracing a line from the tag all the way down his palms where it collected under his fingernails.

The sky around him was bathed in neon of different hues from Corporation towers that reached up to puncture the heavens. Each of the towers had bright logos emblazoned on their sides like war paint, warning the others to keep their distance. Kalum took a few tentative steps that brought him to the edge of a roof. Though he wasn't as high as the surrounding towers it was still a good four-storey drop to the ground below. An icy gust of wind cut through the shredded hospital gown he wore, and pushed him closer to the edge. He back-peddled, and began to tremble from the heady cocktail of fear and impending hypothermia, as the sky started to pepper him with hailstones. The rooftop was barren apart from a solitary gunmetal door that the bloody trail seemed to lead to.

A hailstone struck him in the chest and a larger one zipped past his temple. He stumbled toward the open door, the snow crunching beneath his feet. The door was warped and dented, and it creaked and groaned as he pulled it open with one hand. It swayed for a second and then clanged as it fell from the hinges it hung limply from. Kalum peered down into a black stairwell and paused.

"H... hello?" he said, managing a strangled croak. His throat felt like someone had doused it in flame. He swallowed away the pain and tried again.

"Hello?" This time his voice carried further but was devoured by the darkness without reply. Another shiver wracked his body. He stepped into the breach and was enveloped by the pitch black below. The air smelled dank and it burned his throat to breathe. Kalum reached his hands out to feel his way and grabbed a handrail to steady himself as he edged his way onwards. The icy rail gripped him back, refusing to let go of his skin. He managed to pull away, wincing, and was forced by his lack of sight to reach out again and feel his way forward. It gave him the security to move with more purpose and speed.

As he reached the end of the stairs he stumbled, expecting to find another step, and fell forward onto something firm. It let out a moan and Kalum realised it was a person. He was wearing a heavy-duty jacket covered with pockets and the assorted paraphernalia jingled when Kalum shook him. Suddenly the narrow passageway was illuminated with a piercing light from a torch on the man's jacket. The light stabbed at Kalum's eyes and all he could see were purple and green spots across his visual field. It started to clear at the same moment the man began regaining consciousness. The light swung down and illuminated the man's face. It was bloodied, and his nose crumpled and angled as if he been slammed face first into a wall.

"Please help me," Kalum whimpered, "I don't know what's going on. I don't know where I am."

The man's eyes rolled around and were finally able to focus. He howled in terror and flung Kalum aside with ease. Kalum instinctively twisted his body in mid air, and avoided smashing his head on the floor, instead taking the impact on his right shoulder. Wincing in pain he saw the man scramble back away from him, his heavy duty boots scraping against the ground. He jumped to his feet and his black outfit melted into shadows, hiding all but the blinking whites of his eyes. The torch hanging from his jacket strobed around the room giving Kalum flashes of his surroundings. It was like watching a movie with random frames cut out.

Kalum heard the man's rapid drumroll charge as his feet hammered the ground, propelling him forwards. The force of his shoulder smashed into Kalum's side, sending him reeling. He was launched off his feet and they crashed into a wall behind them. The man's face was a bloodied snarling blur as Kalum felt his brain ricochet inside his skull. He was being squeezed now, so hard he felt like a nut being cracked.

His vision swam and the scene around him juddered and changed again. The surroundings shifted, before snapping back into clarity. He found himself back on his feet, with the uniformed man cowering on the floor, his face an even more ghastly tableau of trauma. His hand covered his right eye and blood flowed freely from beneath it. Kalum took a step forward, palms outstretched, but the man didn't wait for him to speak, darting past him, stumbling as he went.

"Wait! Don't leave me here!" Kalum pleaded and moved to follow him.

The man collided with a wall and his torch fell loose, clattering to the floor and sending echoes through the stairwell. He left it where it landed and shimmied along the wall, searching with frantic urgency for something. Finally he wrenched open a handle, flooding them in painfully bright light, and crashed through the open doorway.

Kalum followed, but he stopped short as he crossed the threshold of the door. He watched the man, already on the other side of the cavernous room, rip open a heavy-duty steel reinforced door and run out into the blizzard outside.

Around him were at least fifty similarly clad men, all at least as large and imposing. They lay scattered and broken, with their limbs twisted at impossible angles, and their uniforms in tatters. A breath caught in his chest, and an arc of hot agony stabbed at his ribcage where the man had tackled him. Kalum looked at the bodies around him and decided the idea of running into whatever had laid waste to this place was also not appealing.

He picked his way through the strewn bodies as rapidly as he could. It felt like he was playing the most morbid version of hopscotch imaginable. He shivered, the remains of his hospital gown offering scant warmth. He tried to wipe away the blood on his hands on the front of his trouser, and felt a soft wet lump in his front pocket. His hand slid in, and with some difficulty he managed to curl his fingers around the slippery object. He pulled it free and regarded it, his brain taking a second to process what it was seeing.

Dangling in front of his face, like a bauble on a Christmas tree, was an eyeball.

With a shriek he threw the horrific discovery away from him and watched as it rolled on its uneven axis and came to a stop near the exit. An image of the man on the stairwell he'd encountered flashed into life, with his palm pressed up against his bloody face.

"What the hell is going on?" he whispered out loud, but no one replied. Not even the voice in his head.

He crouched by one of the men whose jacket was hanging half off, and removed it with care so as not to disturb him too much. The logos on the front and back made his blood run cold. The silver gearcog on the black background meant these men were Sentech and he was in a Sentech facility. A shudder ran through his body and he slipped the man's bulky jacket on. It was enormous, swallowing up his torso and most of his legs, but it was warm.

He stopped to take stock, looking around the room. Small rivulets of blood surrounded the bodies like scarlet exclamation points. The bloody calligraphy extended to the walls and congregated at the far side of the room, where rows and rows of desks were laid out and packed with computers and other devices Kalum didn't recognise. They were arranged in a semicircle facing an enormous monitor, which was fixed on the wall above them. He looked towards the door that the man had fallen through, but something pulled him towards the equipment on the other side. As he neared the desks, his foot caught on a chair leg and he sprawled onto a desktop. What he saw on the ground, heaped together in a mound, made his stomach heave. Human fingers—thumbs, to be more precise—pale from exsanguination and curled like fat maggots. They were piled against a large, heavy open door, which led to a tiny room with a single metal chair and table in it. A box sat in the table's centre. Its thick metal surface was warped and cracked open. Stepping back to the threshold he looked at the door; as thick as he was wide with deadbolts the size of his arm for reinforcement. Someone had wanted to stop people getting in here. He peered at the carnage outside of the enclosure and thought to himself, *Perhaps that the door was meant to keep something in instead?*

"You won't get away with this!" a voice wheezed from behind him. He knew it well, the voice from Cooper's office; Clayton Lancaster. Kalum turned and the noise was coming from a man slumped in the corner of the room. As he got closer he saw the TRIST on the man's arm, its screen pulsing green light in time with the audio.

"Is that you, Spectre?" Lancaster said. "I don't know how you're hiding your face, but it won't stop us from finding you and putting you in the dirt. You can't steal from Sentech."

Kalum continued turning back to the voice, his hand coming up to his face, when he spotted the two surveillance cameras in either corner of the room. He was being watched.

Kalum's head jerked to the side, moving of its own accord, and he saw the muzzle flash an instant before feeling a wet searing pain across his cheek as something flashed past and embedded itself in the wall behind. One of the men had sat up and was taking aim again. He was propped up against one of his team and needed both hands to hold his trembling gun. Kalum dived to the side, taking refuge behind an upturned desk, trying to make himself as small a target as possible. As he did he heard the muffled thunderclaps as the man squeezed off two more rounds. The bullets drummed into the metal desk, propelling it forward and knocking Kalum onto his hands and knees.

He peered over the edge and saw the barrel of the gun pointing directly between his eyes. The man's eyes widened and the skin around his mouth tightened as he squeezed the trigger. Kalum flinched, expecting the clap of the gun report, but instead it gave an anaemic click. The man pressed the trigger again and again with same result. Their eyes locked and for a brief moment Kalum read the depth of terror in them. The man broke the connection, diving across the body of his fallen comrade and snatching at his discarded gun. Kalum lurched towards the exit, his feet and hands keeping him low to the ground. The door had no handle and didn't budge when he tried to charge it with his shoulder. A message scrolled across a screen in the centre.

"Please display retina identification," a voice from within the door commanded. Kalum heard the sound of the gun behind being loaded and again and he threw himself down, head tucked under his arms and his eyes closed, just in time for a hail of bullets to pepper where he'd been standing. When he looked he saw the bloody bauble he had found in his pocket; the guard's discarded eyeball. He snatched it up, struggling to maintain his grip, the slimy viscera coating making it slip around his palm and fingers.

The bullets were still coming, driving rivet-like dents into the thick door and freeing masonry from the adjacent wall. Making sure to orientate the eye accordingly he took a deep breath and thrust it up towards the display. He could feel the vibration of the impact of the bullets around his hand and arm as he frantically twisted and angled it, trying to get the sensor to recognise it. With a bang he saw a new dent appear a mere inch from his elbow, making him recoil and lose his grip on the eye. Just as it dropped, the screen pinged and the door hissed open, letting a cold wind hit him like a slap to the face.

15

FRACTURED REFLECTION

Kalum bolted, and was out into the bleak winter night before he could be used as target practice again. Not looking back, his legs propelled him forward in an adrenaline-fuelled scramble, disregarding the sudden lancing pain in his left foot. Kalum ran until the fire in his chest couldn't be ignored any more, and then stopped at the street corner and threw up.

"Oh god!" he exclaimed, louder than he'd intended. How was he going to explain this to anyone? He couldn't even explain it himself. One thing he knew was that he couldn't stop there to think about it.

That man had shot to kill, he thought, wiping away a semi congealed streak of blood from his cheek. He lifted his arm to check his TRIST but it was as broken and useless as it had been back at the hospital.

Opposite him was a Transport recharging station, all bright lights and automation. It was unmanned but he could see the glow from the self-service paystation. Kalum ran to the station like a moth drawn to light and then stopped short. The side of the building had the Sentech logo, but a thick red line had been painted through it. Above the Sentech insignia was the dark logo of the Scorps, placed to look as if it was on the hunt. He was in their territory now.

He took a moment to squat and take a deep lungful of air. He tried to push the knot that was forming in his chest down before it rose to his throat and cut off his air. He grabbed his hand and pinned it in anticipation of the imminent tremor.

"No," he said to himself. "Not now. Hold it together." He felt the emotion power down and his breaths came freer.

"Now get up, and get help," he commanded again and was only a little surprised when his body complied. He looked back over his shoulder, taking in the path that had got him here. Back that way led to death, of that he was certain, either from the men with guns, or from whatever had been in that locked room.

Kalum scanned the surrounding buildings but their dark windows were like the closed eyes of enormous brick and steel monsters. Something in the distance caught his attention, standing apart from the others. Even from afar Kalum could see it was far larger than anything in its vicinity. It twisted upwards like a corkscrew and from its upper most tip it seemed to cast an umbrella of red light down onto and over its surroundings, like a protective shield. Jolted with immediate recognition, Kalum realised where he was; it was the Zenton Tower, last bastion of the Zenton Alliance Corporation in the city of London. Kalum fixed his eyes on the red arrow emblem on the side of the building and it pulsed, like a beacon calling to him.

A SCREECH of tyres on the road made him spin around and he saw a large Transport turn the corner and slow as it reached the charging station. Kalum ran towards them, arms flailing in the air. He stumbled, tripping over his own feet. He tried to bring his hands out but they refused to move and he tumbled forward, breaking his fall with the bony point of his shoulder. The transport stopped in the middle of the road and from his position on the ground, concealed behind the charging station, he saw the glint of the metallic Sentech insignia on the side of the vehicle.

With a clank the rear doors opened and one by one eight figures unfolded themselves from the back. The men wore identical garb to those in the building Kalum had escaped from, and this realisation made him flatten his body against the cylindrical object in front of him. They lined up and stood to attention as their TRISTs lit up, all playing the same audio message.

"This is command. Beta team, you have thirty minutes to find the intruder. Your TRISTs now have all the information we have on him." They studied the information as it was fed to them.

The man furthest from Kalum, the features of his face masked by shadow and a thick beard, gave a snort of irritation.

"We can't see anything on these pictures, they're all blurred," he scoffed.

A second later his TRIST flashed red and he collapsed to the ground, tremulous, and with spittle coating his chin.

"Any one else want to complain?" said the voice from their TRISTs. The men kept their eyes fixed forward, not even glancing at their comrade as his body jerked and flailed at their feet.

"In thirty minutes Alpha Squad will take point and take credit. This is your chance. Don't waste it."

A tone sounded and they scattered in different directions. The figure on the floor was moaning, his head still giving the occasional twitch. His TRIST sounded, all on its own, the voice coming from it the calm, serene tone of the operating system familiar to all Sentech workers.

"If you want to live, go to Sentech Plaza sub basement B, before they send cleaners for you."

He was on his feet now, a teetering punch-drunk mess. He looked down at his TRIST and tapped it with his knuckles.

"Live or die. The choice is in your hands."

The man looked around, his focus now clearing. The air filled with the electric engine hum of another incoming Transport, and this was all the incentive he needed. Within seconds he was a wraith, disappearing like a startled deer.

With that Kalum was alone again. He released a breath he hadn't realised he'd been holding, and found that his arms and legs were his to command again. He pulled himself to his feet, still staying in a crouch. The city seemed to be a living, breathing beast now, its eyes watching him hungrily from close by. Nowhere was safe.

Again he looked back to Zenton Tower. If he could just get there, then maybe he could get help.

"Run!" the voice in his head shouted.

A booming gong sounded next to his head as a bullet hammered into the charging station. He saw three of the Enforcers converging on the spot where he was half crouched. The charging station began crackling like a firework and he decided the voice was right. Kalum ran, the agony in his foot sending him vicious reminders with each step, but adrenaline trumped the pain. The sound of the men following him was like a stampede of wildebeest in the deserted street. The report a gunshot registered a nanosecond before he threw himself forward, landing in a greasy puddle by the roadside. They were closing in now, and that thought alone got him back on his feet. There was no time to wonder why the bullet hadn't finished him off; his only thought was to get to Zenton.

He rounded a corner and had to hold on to the side of a building to stop himself from losing his footing. The change in atmosphere was jarring, like changing the channel on the television. Every sense was flooded with vibrant colour, the sounds of people talking, and the smell of fragrant cuisine. Gone were the sterile neon light and eerie silence of the city. The marketplace was like a living thing, with people flowing in and around, seemingly not bothered by the cold and rain.

Signs of the Black Scorpion adorned the walls and placards. Kalum changed his momentum, pushing hard off his aching foot, sending new starbursts of pain up his entire leg, and darted into an alleyway. This time his sense of smell was assaulted by a far less pleasant aroma. He heard the men round the corner and stop. The sound of the market cut out, like it had been muted, and for a moment there was silence. Then there was a clang of a drum and a war cry erupted. With his back pressed up against the wall and trying to cover his mouth and nose, Kalum watched as his pursuers turned tail and ran, a mass of people herding them back the way they had come.

When Kalum peered around the corner the market was empty and the sound of the chase faded away. He was suddenly consumed with need. The need to follow the red glow of the Zenton Tower, the need to make himself scarce before the apparently bloodthirsty NCs returned.

Kalum walked through the market, marvelling at the chaotic array of items on sale. Second hand clothes, half used condiments and toiletries littered the tables. He passed a counter with a display of cobbled together weaponry;

baseball bats with nails, large chains, and kitchen knives made into spears. They all had anti-corporation graffiti or logos on them. An assortment of homemade jams made his stomach complain and as sorely tempted as he was to snatch one, he resisted the urge, the thought of his mother's disapproving glare resetting his moral compass. He would have gladly traded an eternity of chiding to be back in his warm safe home now.

Lancaster had threatened him when he'd spoken through the fallen guard's TRIST, but had said that they couldn't see his face. He looked down at his broken TRIST and his fractured reflection in the glass screen. At least with it being non-functional, Sentech couldn't track him. Pushing the thoughts out of his mind he concentrated on his singular purpose.

He hobbled down street after street of derelict buildings, the grime on the roads alive and crawling up the sides of the once proud architecture. The dark, empty windows seemed to watch him as he clung to the walls, trying to move with stealth and speed but achieving neither.

The Zenton building looked down at him from the heavens, mocking him from afar. His mind wandered to one person, Reese. *What would Reese do?* Time and time again Kalum had seen him defy the odds in the Arena. Reese would make it to Zenton, he'd make it there no sweat. He saw his reflection in the puddle of murky water in front of him. It wasn't the sharp, handsome face of his brother, but his own. Soft, still childlike, with thick glasses framing his mismatched eyes.

"I'm not strong like Reese. I can't do this," he whimpered. In his reflection his blue eye seemed to pulse, silencing him. The mouth in the reflection seemed to move and he heard the voice in his head speak through it.

"No. You're not like Reese. You're more. You're better," it said. "Stop embarrassing yourself and get moving."

In between blinks he found his feet were moving again. A soft glow in the distance made him hasten his pace. As he drew nearer to it he saw a makeshift shantytown of sorts. The houses, if they could be called that, were all made from repurposed junk. Fires burned in receptacles outside on the street, enclosed to stop them being put out and moved as close to the entrances of the dwellings as possible. Kalum saw that inside many people lay huddled for warmth. Posters were plastered to walls. They had pictures of different fighters from the Gauntlet, graffiti marring their already scarred faces.

I wouldn't like to meet any of them in a dark alley, Kalum thought, and he looked away.

Then movement caught his eye, and he backtracked to the brick wall he'd just passed. A sentry was walking back around the street corner, moving in slow and confident loping strides. He wore a hooded poncho, its charcoal grey material providing the wearer some protection from the rain. Stopping at the shoulders, that protection did not extend to his arms, but he didn't seem to care. They were so toned they looked as if someone had stripped the skin right off his tall, wide and muscular frame. In one hand he carried a baseball bat, and it rested easily against his shoulder, and the other was wrapped around a thick metallic ring the size of a fist.

The man stopped and spun around, startled by a noise. As he did, the collected rainwater on him sloshed away. Kalum saw the emblem on his back and retreated half a step. The Black Scorpion symbol looked ready to crawl right off the man's back and leap into an attack. He controlled his breathing and watched as the sentry knelt to examine something, and then stood, wiping his wet hands on his already dirt-streaked jeans.

Kalum shifted his weight to get a better look, and felt a stab of pain in his foot, so intense he couldn't help but yelp in agony. The sentry turned and a gust of wind caught the hood, whipping it back. Kalum knew that face. It was the Scorp who had come to the Henkan match, the one who had sold the Augs to Nathan. Kalum tried to move back into the shadows but as they locked eyes he knew he was too late. He saw the sentry's eyes gravitate down to the Sentech emblem on his stolen, oversized jacket. The man's face rippled with anger and he charged towards Kalum, his primal roar of rage reverberating through the camp.

16

A TUMULTUOUS CRESCENDO

"Corporation! Corporation! Corporation!" he shouted, again and again. Running headlong at Kalum, he stooped to grab a fallen dustbin lid and smashed the metal ring against it like a gong.

From within the dwellings others wearing similar clothes rushed out to join the man in his pursuit. They all had a wild rage in their eyes and didn't look as if they wanted to talk. Kalum turned and sprinted, no longer hobbling, back in the direction he came from. As he did so he grabbed anything he could to throw in their way, and kept moving forward. He reached the end of the road and took the other path. As he ran he saw a narrow side street closing in fast. Darting down the alleyway, his shoes squealed and skidded as they tried to gain purchase on the wet floor. His heart was trying to smash its way out of out his throat and the thumping in his head had started up again as he realised that he'd run down a dead end. The sentry heard the throng behind him, following him on the chase. He stopped and raised a fist, making this comrades pause.

"The Corporate runt is mine, and so is anything he's

got," he snarled over his shoulder. He allowed himself a brief smile as he heard the footfalls slow. A Sentech sponsored kid would likely have all sorts of things on him that he could use, barter or sell. He licked his lips with anticipation. The smile widened when he saw his quarry take a turn down the dead-end alley. One way in, one way out. He paused at the entrance, and another man stopped at his side, panting.

"He had a Sentech jacket on, Darius, walking in here bold as anything." He spat out the words as if the taste of them made him sick.

The rest of the group were surrounding him now, the murmuring growing with their numbers.

"A message needs to be sent," Darius said as he stepped into the alley, the cheers and grunts of the other Scorps behind him.

He swaggered in, arms raised up in a gesture of peace as a thin smile touched his face.

"My name's Darius, little man. I lead the Scorps in this region," Darius called into the alley, and his voice echoed back. "My word is law here. Come out, I just want to talk," he said as he gestured to the Scorps behind him to follow as he entered.

He moved forward with short, measured strides, the bat held high and ready. The other Scorps followed at a distance, pushing and shoving each other out of the way as they jostled to get in front. The alley entrance was so narrow that they had to enter in single file.

"You're testing my patience. Come out," Darius said, the edge in his voice unmistakable. He stopped, listening with head cocked for any sound that would give away the boy's position. His skin prickled as he gripped the bat, making his knuckles blanche.

"That's the way you want it huh?" he said, pounding the bat against his palm. "I'll show you what we think of you Corporates down here."

Kalum pushed his body as tightly as he could against the back wall of the alley. He had tried to scale it, but not for the first time, his height betrayed him. Another inch and he'd have managed to get a finger hold to pull himself up and away. Instead he had dragged one of the discarded bins in front of him and hid behind it. A pathetic hiding place, as obvious as the lightning that illuminated the star-smeared sky above him.

He could hear the splash of heavy boots through the slush as Darius neared. Kalum squeezed his eyes closed with such force they hurt, and covered his face with his hands. Any second now he knew he would be ripped from his hiding place, and that would be that. The fear coursed through him like a drug, spreading to every part of his body. The tremor was there now, consuming him, like seismic shocks under the skin and making him tingle. Then a hot flash of anger carved a path through his terror.

The Scorps had decimated his family once before, left his father a broken man, and now they were threatening to do the same to him. Reese would have ploughed through them like a fighter in the Gauntlet, vicious and merciless. Reese would have taken no prisoners.

"Not again," said the voice in his head. "They're not taking anything else from me." It was just a whisper, but there was fire behind the words.

Each step that Darius took towards him was like an explosion in his ears. The throbbing behind his eye beat in time. Everything swirled into a tumultuous crescendo, and all the world went white.

.   .   .

AFTER A FEW MINUTES he realised that he couldn't hear anything. Not their heavy excited breathing, not their threats. Slowly he dropped his hands to his sides and opened his eyes. They were gone. Not just Darius and the other Scorps, but the alleyway too. He looked up to get his bearings and found that the Zenton Tower was only a few hundred feet behind him.

A wave of nausea hit him so hard he stumbled. The world around him felt like a snow globe being shaken. He braced his arms against the side of a building, his head sagging. His mind focused in on his breathing, trying to find his centre just as he had been taught. With slow, ratcheting movements he lifted his head and opened his eyes. He hadn't imagined it. He was here at the Zenton Tower. Up close it looked even more impressive, its angular structure seemingly slicing through the space around it.

The sky around him seemed to be lighter even though the sun was still nowhere to be seen. Time had passed since he'd been cornered in that alley, and for the second time that night he was missing large chunks of memory.

Kalum moved towards the building and then felt the agony reigniting in his foot. The yelp he gave earned glances from the few passers by. They moved on sharpish, averting their eyes and rushing away, as if repelled by the very sight of him. He caught a glimpse of himself in the reflective surface of the massive glass entrance. He looked ridiculous in the oversized Sentech jacket and there were flecks of dried blood spatters over his face. His sleeve managed to removed most of it, with a bit of force. He tried to flatten his spiked hair but found it was matted and fixed in place. Looking again he felt he looked vaguely presentable now, or as presentable as he was going to look for the time being.

He pulled the jacket tighter around himself and entered

the building. The foyer was spectacular. All four surrounding walls were covered in a huge, flexible display. The only gaps were for the four doors that served as access to other areas of the building. There was a flash, and the walls displayed a series of stars and planets, a roadmap to the Milky Way. Across from him was a large, oval-shaped booth and Kalum saw that the two people behind the large screen had noticed him. He walked over, doing his best to disguise his limp.

"Sorry. No NCs allowed," said a woman in her mid to late thirties. The bags under eyes seemed to have bags of their own, and her skin was pale and chalky. Her raised eyebrows punctuated the statement, and her smile was thin and insincere. She wore a dark blue uniform whose material carried an artificial sheen. The front of her jacket was fastened with a silver zipper that followed a Z shape. Kalum could see through the clear barrier that one of her hands had migrated to the array of buttons on a control panel in front of her while the other rested on the holster on her hip. He raised his hands.

"I'm not an NC. I'm not Non Corporate, I'm a Sentech affiliate. I... I... just got a little lost."

The woman looked him up and down, eyebrows now nearing her hairline.

"A little lost?" she repeated, shaking her head. "You should have pretended to be an NC rather than admit to being linked to Sentech." She spat the last word out, her disgust written plainly on her face.

Kalum could understand her feelings. Sentech was in the process of buying out all of Zenton's business in the area, which meant its assets were at risk. There was a real possibility that in the next week this woman could very well find herself an NC. Everyone who worked in this building would be given the same choice if they were lucky; become Sentech property, and do what ever Sentech asked of them, or be cast out as an NC. Kalum was sure she must have had members of her family shipped out to do the sort of jobs other Sentech members and affiliates would turn their noses up at.

"Look, I just got out of the hospital," he said, raising his arm to show her the wristband. Her eyes flicked from his arm to his face and back again. Kalum followed her gaze to see that the band had come away at some point, taking a strip of skin with it.

The glint from the pendant around her neck caught Kalum's eye. The gold plating was cracked and some of the inset crystals were missing, but he could clearly make out the three-letter word they had used to spell. The woman must have followed his gaze, as she tucked it back out of sight.

"Nice necklace," he said. "Was it a gift? From your son?" he guessed.

She shifted her weight away from him and looked at the burly man sitting on the other side of her, apparently engrossed in the Henkan highlights playing on his monitor.

"Look. What do you want? Am I going to have to call someone?" she asked.

Kalum knew the threat was somewhat empty. Zenton's law enforcement department was at this stage almost non-existent and the woman's companion didn't seem able to break his self-inflicted hypnotic state.

"I'm on my own. I just need to call my Uncle to come get me. Please? Wouldn't you want someone to help your kids if they were in my situation?" Kalum asked, taking a step closer to the booth so that the light illuminated his face.

"Can't you just use that thing on your wrist?" she asked, pointing at the TRIST.

Kalum shook his head and held it up to the screen.

"It's broken."

The woman exhaled and looked around the otherwise deserted foyer. She reached up to her ear and pulled out a dark grey oval disc the size of an olive. With a soft whirring noise, a panel in the screen opened up and she dropped it into his waiting palm.

"Just put it in your ear and press the button," she said in response to the look of puzzlement on his face.

He nodded, his eyes expressing gratitude he didn't know how to put into words. As he turned away she called after him.

"Be quick. The line probably won't hold out for long."

Kalum moved closer to one of the wall displays, which now was showing a crashing waterfall all around the foyer, and placed the device in his ear. He pressed the button as instructed and two thin metal bars extended from the device. One edged across the outline of his jaw whilst the other stopped in front of his eyes. From this a screen the thickness and translucency of an onion skin dropped down, obscuring his vision. There was a buzzing in his ear and a snowstorm of static on the screen. Then a heavily accented female voice spoke.

"Video conference service iz down. Would you like to make a voice call?"

Not knowing what to do or press Kalum just nodded and the device seemed to pick up on his meaning.

"What iz sssrrrtttt number?" came the follow up request fizzling through the static.

Kalum paused for a beat. He wanted to call his mother, he wanted her to tell him that it would be okay, but something made him hesitate. What if the Enforcers were there? He didn't know how or even when he'd left the hospital. If anyone from Sentech found out he was in that building, amongst all that carnage, he could forget about Trinity, forget even about being an NC. They'd tried to kill him.

No, he couldn't call home, or Lucas, in case someone was listening. Making up his mind he called out a series of digits he hadn't used in many years, but were still ingrained in his mind.

"Connecting now."

"Hello?" came the voice on the other end. It was heavy and thick with sleep but for Kalum it was as if the years fell away and he was seven-years-old again.

"Frannie?" he whispered. "I need you, it's happening again."

A few minutes later he returned to the counter and handed back the earpiece.

The woman looked him up and down.

"You manage to get hold of who you needed?" she asked.

Her smile was warm and gentle now. She inclined her head and slid a few Zenton credits across the counter to him. With a nod of encouragement from her he reached out and took them.

"The Zenton employee rest station is just through there," she said pointing to a door to her left.

"Tell them Joy sent you and they'll let you in."

The man in the booth with her cursed and threw the remains of his snack at the monitor in disgust as the Henkan game finished. He looked up at them, seeing Kalum for the first time.

"You'd better go," she said, forcing the credits into his hands and shutting the opening. Kalum hobbled as fast as he could in the direction Joy had indicated. A panel door slid to one side and Kalum went in.

The brightly lit room was accentuated by the neon red Zenton Association logos scattered around the place. The floor was a deep mahogany faux wood, with round heavy-duty metal tables arranged in mathematic precision on either side. The dimly lit back of the shop was by contrast far darker apart from the blinking sign in the wall. It displayed the message, "0 Recovery Stations Available."

Kalum felt the gaze of everyone in the room on him as he made his way to the counter. When he got there he grabbed at the ledge, trying to keep the weight off his foot.

"Hey man. What can I do you for?" the man behind the counter asked while wiping it down with a cloth.

"I... er..." Kalum started, uncertain of what to say.

"How about I bring you some toast?" the man offered.

Kalum's stomach growled its agreement and the man stifled a laugh.

"Could I get a cup of coffee too?" Kalum blurted, surprising himself.

The man turned back to him, amusement dancing in his tired eyes.

"Sure thing kid."

He didn't remember eating the toast or drinking the coffee, and it was like the empty mug and plate just materialised in front of him. He put his arms on the table, nestled his head into the crook of them, and everything faded away.

He awoke to a familiar sound. His eyes focused and he saw that it was still dark outside, barring the red pulse emanating from the tower itself. As the raspy rumbling grew closer he could feel the vibration through the glass of the window. Lucas' sleek silver Mustang turned the corner and slowed to a crawl as it drove past. It was the sort of car that looked as if it was moving fast even when stationary, with swooping lines that cut through the air. It was distinctive and turned heads, a symbol of a time long passed.

In the passenger seat was Frannie. She looked the same as when he had last seen her seven years ago, except for slightly shorter hair. It framed her pixie like face, and the fringe hung forward and partially covered a brow that was forever wrinkled with some worry or another. This was no exception. Frannie's forehead was seriously furrowed this time. Her green eyes matched this sentiment as they scanned the street looking for him.

Kalum waved through the window as the car came to a stop beside it.

"What the hell?" Lucas mouthed at him through the glass, throwing his arms up. He slammed the door shut and stormed out of view, presumably making a beeline for the building entrance.

After a moment Lucas strode in, Frannie in tow. In one move he scooped Kalum off the ground in an embrace that reminded Kalum of the fact that he hurt everywhere. He kept whispering, "You're okay. You're okay. You're okay," and Kalum felt that he was talking as much to himself as he was to Kalum.

He set the boy down again and his expression hardened a touch.

"What the hell happened? You left the Medical Centre! They called the Enforcers! We've been sick with worry! Your mother..."

Then he stopped, taking in Kalum's ripped clothes and bloodied knuckles.

"Kal..." he said, his voice uncharacteristically soft. "What happened? You look like you've been thrown in the Gauntlet ring. Where'd you go, lad?"

He pulled out a chair for Frannie and they both sat at the table with him. She dove into her oversized handbag, that looked even more enormous when compared to the diminutive person carrying it. Out came the notepad and pen. Kalum smiled. She was the same Frannie, still distrustful of technology.

When Kalum had finished bringing them up to speed, they sat in silence for a moment. Lucas looked to Frannie, who in turn was staring a hole through Kalum.

"Fran," said Lucas. "Is this like before?"

She clicked the end of her pen and put it away. Frannie reached across the table and took Kalum's hands in her own.

"You've got injuries consistent with your story. The mark on your cheek appears consistent with the type of graze a passing bullet would leave, your clothes are ripped and torn which fits with how you describe part of your escape from the Scorps.

"That's just it. One minute I was about to get my butt kicked, the next I was here."

She looked down to Kalum's bruised and scraped hands as they rested on the brushed metal surface of the table, and added, "I don't see many defensive marks."

"So I fought my way out. That's what you're saying, right?" Kalum asked. What Frannie was saying both made sense and didn't. There was no other explanation for how he got away. But that explanation was also insane.

"Look, what matters is that you're safe. But you should have called me straight away," Lucas said, leaning in.

Kalum opened his mouth to speak but Frannie cut him off.

"I can see why he didn't. Sentech overlooked things when this happened before, but they won't a second time.

That'd be it." She stopped and held his gaze. "But you could have called, you could have trusted me."

Lucas' slammed his fist onto the table, sending the cutlery skittering across the metal surface.

"What use is a Sentech sponsorship if you're dead?" he demanded.

Frannie laid a hand on Lucas' shoulder to pacify him. It didn't make him any less angry, but his frown softened a touch.

"Okay. So here's how it's going to go down. The story is that you couldn't deal with being cooped up in the Medical Centre and you left when no one was looking. Then you walked to my place and let yourself in with the spare key," said Lucas. "Wherever you did go, it's obviously somewhere Sentech didn't want people poking around, but like you said, they can't trace you as being there. Especially with a broken TRIST."

Kalum nodded.

"I need to let Ma know I'm okay."

"It's all sorted. I called your mum and told her you were fine. The Enforcers were at the house, so I had to lay it on thick. She didn't believe a word but she hid it well. The story's good enough for the Medical Centre and the Enforcers to buy. So they're not asking any more questions at least."

"So, I can go home?"

Lucas dipped his head.

"And not soon enough," he said, glancing at a table of men in Zenton overalls who were scowling in their direction.

"Yes," said Frannie, pushing away her barely touched latte. "I think we've worn out our welcome here."

"Don't leave that, it cost a for—" Lucas began, but before

he could finish the sentence, Kalum had snatched up the cup and downed the milky brown liquid in one gulp. Lucas and Frannie looked at him with eyebrows raised, to which he replied with a sheepish. "Thanks."

Frannie smiled and scribbled something in her notebook, before tossing it into her gargantuan bag.

"Right! Let's get going!" said Lucas, giving Kalum a seismic clap on the back that made his teeth chatter. He stood and his joints creaked like an old floorboard.

Kalum got to his feet and then promptly crumbled to the floor, like a puppet whose strings had been cut. He sat cradling his foot. The combination of rest and food had made him forget all about how much it hurt. Slipping off the shoe, his hand came away wet. There was a metallic tang in the air that he could almost taste. Gingerly he pulled off the sock that was stuck hard to his skin with dried blood. He felt something else there on the side of his foot. It was hard, with acutely sharp edges, and embedded in the pink flesh of his sole. Using his fingers he gently coaxed it free, and allowed it to drop into his waiting palm. As it contacted his skin, he felt a current run all the way up to the roof of his mouth.

"What in the blue hell is that?" asked Lucas, joining Kalum on the floor.

Kalum didn't answer, his eyes wide and unblinking. He regarded the item closely, turning the thin, flat, matt-black piece of metal in his fingers. It was precisely engineered from a single piece of metal and its bevelled edges gave it a blade like appearance. Mesmerised, he stared at the object and felt a wave of familiarity wash over him. The memory of it felt like a dream he was struggling to recall, just out of reach of his understanding.

"Let's get going," he said, getting to his feet and putting his hands in his pockets, but keeping the device in his fist.

Lucas took a deep breath and got off the floor, grunting noisily with the effort. He stretched and cast an apologetic look to the other coffee drinkers who he had once again distracted.

"Best we go voluntarily before we get asked to leave," Frannie said dryly. She looked at Lucas, who was still writhing and trying to stretch the stiffness from his lower back.

"Come on old man," she said, grabbing him by the arm and leading him swiftly out of the door.

KALUM FOLLOWED them out of the coffee shop and picked up the pace to pull alongside, the pain in his foot gone. They turned the corner and walked to where the car was parked under the bright streetlight.

"So..." Lucas said, opening the car door for Frannie, "any ideas what that is or where you got it?"

In his mind the image of the open room in the devastated Sentech building flashed into view.

"No idea," Kalum said, sliding into the back seat of the car.

17

TAPESTRY OF HIS TERROR

Kalum's eyes snapped open. The disorientation was almost over before it started. He was lying in his bed. It was warm, soft, and enveloped him in a cocoon of safety. Turning, he looked for the metal band he had found, suddenly fearful for its safety. He breathed a sigh of relief as he saw it still tightly clasped where he had left it in his left fist. The hand was stiff, but it eventually opened, the band leaving ridges dug into his palm. He rubbed them away and prodded poked and twisted the thing to try to get some measure of its purpose.

The draw he felt to this object, this innocuous piece of metal, was something he couldn't fathom. With reverential care he turned in his bed and opened the drawer of the bedside cabinet. With one hand he scooped the cluttered mess of crumpled paper and broken art supplies to one side, forcing them into half the space they had occupied before. He placed the object in the drawer, and his finger lingered on its smooth surface for a moment before he shut it away from view.

He hadn't meant to open the drawer below. It was a

reflex drummed into him by years of repetition. He reached in and pulled out his orange pill bottle. It rattled as he turned it over in his fingers and he took a moment to remember how he'd felt when he'd last taken one of the pills; dull, numb and detached. The last month or so without the medication had been hell on his nerves, and the last twenty-four hours the most terrifying of his life, but he had felt them. He had lived them.

The voice whispered to him. "You don't need that. It's holding you back."

Without thinking he gave the bottle a backhand swipe and it neatly ricocheted off the wall and into the bin. The bottle clanged against the metal, car-crash loud in the cramped box of his room. His hand throbbed where it had hit the hard plastic and he rubbed it, cursing.

"Language..." Nadine said, her voice thick with fatigue as she opened his door.

Her usually happy face was creased with worry and her hair a frazzled mess. Her eyes were tinged red, from the sting of tears and the burden of fatigue.

"I'm sorry I didn't stay with you, son," she said, sniffing, before launching herself across the room to envelope him in a hug. He squeezed her all the harder in reply.

"Jeez, you're back for two minutes and you're already making Mum cry."

Reese peered in at them and looked around the room.

"Shame..." he said.

"What?" asked Kalum.

"Nothing. Just, I was going to use your room to store my Henkan gear if you'd run off," he said with a shrug and a grin.

Kalum smiled back and vaulted out of bed. Nadine and Reese looked at each other in shock.

"Huh? All it took to make you less of a klutz was nearly dying?" Reese said. "I knew I was onto something that time I pushed you down the stairs."

Kalum rolled his eyes as he walked past his mother and snatched the piece of toast that Reese had in his hand.

"Hey!" said Reese in protest, but it was already gone.

"Forgetting something?" Reese called after him as he walked to the landing. Kalum turned and saw his TRIST sailing through the air towards him. He thrust his hand out, his arm going through the opening like a piece of cotton threading a needle. There was a soft whir as it tightened around his wrist and forearm. The newly repaired screen seemed to ripple as the device powered up. Kalum saw his brother and mother's gawping expression at the move, and shrugged, not really understanding how he'd done it either.

"You got it fixed? Thanks Reese," Kalum said, changing the subject.

Reese shot Nadine a look.

"Not like I had a choice," he said. "If you'd been offline for much longer we'd have had the Enforcers back to stay."

"Welcome back, Kalum," the synthesised voice said. "Sending error report to Sentech central server for analysis."

"That's it. Now you're back on the grid," Reese said and clapped him on the back. "Hope you enjoyed your freedom."

A flashback of the fear he felt with the Scorps advancing on him in the alley gripped him. He could taste their urgent need for violence. He could smell the fetid stench of rotting garbage, made worse by the damp and the downpour trying to meander down his back.

He snapped back to reality as Reese gave him a gentle shake.

"Hey man. You still with us?"

"Sure... sure," said Kalum.

Nadine hugged him again.

"Let's get down there before Lucas and your friends burn the place to the ground, eh?"

Kalum and Nadine went downstairs to see the house-guests were making themselves very busy. Lucas and Frannie were arguing about the correct consistency of scrambled eggs. A slight smile touched Kalum's face. It was as if no time had passed at all from when Frannie had been woven into their lives all those years ago. He owed her so much, and with a twisting feeling of dread he understood that he would need her again now.

Kalum closed his eyes and breathed in the smell of the eggs, and his stomach growled. He couldn't remember when he'd last eaten, save from half of the stale coffee shop crois-sant. Before he could take a seat and tuck in, he was tackled and had the breath knocked out of him. Lexi hugged him so hard he though she might crack him open. He patted her on the back, acutely away of how warm she felt pressed up against him, and pulled himself free. As he did he received a well-aimed punch to his upper arm that left it tingling from shoulder to the tips of his fingers.

"You scared me half to death, you idiot!" she said.

Kalum rubbed the feeling back into his limb, offering a smile in apology. Casey was already at the dinner table and smiled widely, raising his hand.

"Good to have you back dude," Jun said, patting him on the back and bumping fists.

Kalum sat and ate hungrily while the rest of them watched him patiently and in silence, apart from Casey, who helped himself to a second portion. Finally he pushed the plate away and patted his swollen belly.

"What happened?" Lexi burst out, impatient now.

Kalum ran his hand through his hair and thought about what to say, how to explain the night's events. He didn't even know how to start.

"I... I blacked out and when I woke up... I was somewhere else," he said, finding the words eventually. "It was somewhere I'd never been before..."

He looked to Lexi, who smiled and placed her hand on his, giving it a squeeze. He carried on letting the words cascade out, sentence after sentence weaving a tapestry of his terror. When he finished he felt the panic in him continue to well up inside and he pushed it back down to a simmer, bubbling just under the surface.

There was a humming sound as the internal lift powered up and Reese and Owen began their descent. The lift had been fitted once Owen's movements had become even more slowed by his condition. Nadine had once tried to explain it to Kalum. He knew that his dad's body was in constant battle with itself. Every signal that his brain sent to his muscles was garbled and automatically triggered an antagonistic response. The result was that his body moved in jerky, unresponsive motions, when it was able to move at all. As the lift juddered to a stop the door opened and Lucas helped Owen out.

He looked at his son and he stopped momentarily, swaying unsteadily like he was being buffeted by an unseen gale. Knocking Lucas' offer of assistance aside he made a move forward, not taking his eyes off Kalum for a second, as if expecting him to vanish at any minute. Then he fell. He fell silently as if he didn't realise it, his face and eyes still locked in front of him. Everyone in the room all moved to catch him, but Kalum got there first, scooping his arm under his dad's chest and easing him onto the chair behind him. As Kalum made to stand up Owen's hand flashed out, snaking around his wrist and pulling him back down to him.

"S... son," he said, managing to splutter the words out through a clenched jaw and grinding teeth, his voice hoarse and grating from disuse. Owen held him there tightly for a moment longer, the thin, gaunt muscles in his forearm trembling before letting go and sitting back in the chair, gulping in large breaths of air.

Kalum hid his surprise as best he could. His father didn't often talk, the effort being too great, both emotionally and physically. Kalum gave his shoulder a squeeze and then held his hand a moment longer. Then he turned and wiped away the tear before it could begin its escape down his cheek. He caught Reese's eye and thought he saw a flash of something there, a glimmer of anger perhaps. Then it was gone, evaporated by an easy smile.

"I don't understand son," Nadine said. "You've blacked out for seconds, maybe a few minutes before. This time you were out long enough to travel twenty miles? How's that possible?" she asked, looking from Kalum to Frannie.

Frannie pushed her glasses up onto her nose, then clicked her pen and flipped her notepad open.

"There are a multitude of reasons why you might be relapsing, Kal. Could be your medication is losing its efficacy, assuming you're still taking them..."

Kalum's eyes flicked to Reese, who looked away.

"Hmmm," said Frannie, taking a beat to scribble something in her notebook. "Well, the first thing is to double your dose and see if we can get back to the status quo."

Kalum sat bolt upright at this, his mouth suddenly dry and his hands clamping down on the edge of the table.

"Is... is there anything else we can try, Fran?" he said, and turned to his mother, his face imploring. "I just felt so, so dopey on the meds. If I double the dose it's going to turn me into a zombie."

Nadine took his hands in hers and leant closer to him.

"You're not yourself when you black out. It's too risky to do nothing," she said.

"Remember that time you broke that kid's arm?" Lucas said with a hint of a smile on his face.

Frannie and Nadine gave him matching sideways glances.

"What? That the little snot had it coming," he protested.

"That's the sort of thing I'd expect a professional Neanderthal to say," Frannie said.

"Hey!" Lucas retorted, feigning offence. "My title is 'Security Consultant'."

Frannie ignored Lucas' protests and got up and pulled over a chair next to Kalum. Putting away the pen and notebook, she let out a long sigh.

"I know the meds aren't perfect. I know what they did to your eye," she said, looking at the blue flecks in his eye. "But I don't know of any other way to fix this problem, so can we at least try?"

"I like her," Jun whispered to Casey. "She's got that stern but cute vibe going on. That I can work with."

The punch that Lexi landed on his arm made him yelp, and everyone stared at him.

"Stop being such a sleaze," she hissed in his ear." Or learn how to whisper better."

There was a gurgle that sounded like a death rattle and Owen became rigid in the chair, his eyes rolling back and the glass in his hand shattering. Reese and Lucas held him by the arms, but in spite of his waif like physique, Owen almost sent them airborne. Nadine was by his side in an instant, a syringe in hand. She plunged it into his thigh and depressed it. Within seconds his thrashing began to ebb to a metronomic rocking. Kalum pried open his bloodied fist and saw the shards of glass sticking out like the quills of a porcupine.

"Let me see that," said Frannie, trying to take Owen's hand.

He recoiled from her as if her touch was toxic, his eyes wide with some unseen horror. Lucas took the hand and picked out the debris.

"It's okay, Frannie. I'll take Owen upstairs. He needs some rest."

He bandaged the hand and helped transfer him into the waiting wheelchair.

Reese sat down in the chair his father had vacated and sunk into it with a sigh.

"Listen, I need to ask something," he said. "I know it makes me sound selfish, but I need to ask the question."

Kalum turned to him and nodded for him to go on.

"Things are going really well for me at Trinity, at Sentech. They're going really well for all of us."

Kalum nodded, and could hear the silent implication embedded in his tone that this was a weight Reese carried for them all.

"Lucas said that you found something. You didn't say anything about it when you told us what happened. What is it? Are the Enforcers going to smash the door down and come for us?" Reese asked.

The images of gore-splattered walls and severed digits came to his mind. The secure room with the reinforced metal box. The metal band encrusted with his own dried blood. He pushed the images away.

"I... All I know is that I woke up in that building. Some type of Sentech facility. It, and everyone in it, had been ripped apart by something. They couldn't see me on their surveillance. I got the hell out of there and didn't look back," he said. "I found a piece of metal in my shoe. It was just junk. I threw it away."

The lie felt easier than it should have. Kalum was disturbed by how possessive he felt over the strange object he'd found. The thought of anyone taking it filled him with dread.

"Okay," said Reese, the timbre of his voice doing little to hide his concern.

"Wait," said Kalum, turning towards where his mother was helping Owen into the lift.

"There's one more thing I need to tell you," Kalum said. He looked around and felt the eyes of his friends and family settle on him. "I heard someone talking to Cooper about testing students at Trinity for Aug use."

"Good!" said Nadine. "Those things are awful. People have died using them."

"I know," Kalum said. "But they were talking about using anyone who tested positive and running experiments on them."

"Where did you hear this?" Nadine asked.

Kalum gave Reese a look, and his brother knew the answer to their mother's question.

"Near Cooper's office," Kalum said, stretching the truth. "And it was Nathan's father, Clayton Lancaster, who was talking to Cooper. He came to the Medical Centre to make sure I signed the waiver."

The room went still for a moment, and then Lucas let out a low whistle. "Lancaster? Are you sure, lad?"

"Kalum..." Nadine started to say.

Kalum felt the tapping in his head start up again, firm and insistent.

"Here it comes. She's going to blame this on me," the voice said, as clear as if it was coming from someone sitting next to him.

"When you're... you're... not well, you can't trust what you think you hear, what you think you see," Nadine said. "Sentech put this roof over our heads, paid for your medical treatment. Why would they do something like that? Think through it logically."

"N... No. I know what I saw. I know what I heard," Kalum said. He could feel himself on the verge of tears now. He swallowed the feeling and his jaw set, balling his fists so tightly that his knuckles cracked.

"It wouldn't be the first time you saw and heard things that weren't really there," Frannie said.

"I told you," the voice said.

Nadine moved to sit on the armrest nest to Kalum and put her arm around him. He felt his heart rate slow and the tension wash out of him.

"What's important son, is that you're home, you're safe, and we're going to get you help," she said.

"There's no point arguing with them. They'll never believe you. We know the truth," the voice said.

"My recommendation is that we restart treatment immediately," Frannie was saying, talking over him now.

Nadine stopped her with a hand.

"Frannie, I think he needs today, okay? Just to get his strength." She turned to Kalum and ruffled his hair.

"Shall we just have a lazy day and all just rest here? We'll put a movie on. Anything you want."

A movie? How could she think about watching a movie? His life was spiralling into deeper and deeper trenches of insanity and his mother wanted to watch a mo—

"Bruce Lee marathon," he blurted out. He blinked in surprise, not sure where the outburst had come from.

Nadine's forehead furrowed and she gave him a smile.

"Really? We haven't done that in forever... Are you sure?"

He found his head nodding with such ferocity that it threatened to detach itself, and he was even more confused to find that he actually meant it. He thought back to all the times they'd spent as a family watching Bruce Lee marathons. He was Nadine's absolute favourite martial artist, and his movies the only thing she'd ever watch. So he and Reese had learned to love them too.

"We'll stay if you've got popcorn," said Casey, making himself comfortable. Kalum could feel Lexi's concern boring into him from where she sat behind him, but he didn't turn, didn't give anything away.

Nadine beamed, her smile wide and infectious. She jumped up and keyed in a command on her TRIST. From the floor and ceiling four small, transparent blue rods appeared and pulsed with light. The streams formed a large cuboid shape that engulfed the majority of the room. Within the space text and images started to form.

Reese got up and moved towards the door.

"Where are you going?" Nadine called after him.

He hoisted his Henkan bag over his shoulder and was out of the door as he replied,

"Not really my thing anymore. I'm going to check on Dad, then I've got training."

In the room the holographic film played and they all settled in to watch the series of classic martial arts films, Nadine chipping in with tidbits of information about the life of the legendary martial artist as if she was a hidden extra feature of the movie itself.

Kalum felt himself drifting, and it was a strange sensation of mental weightlessness, on the cusp of consciousness and daydreaming. He looked through the images and moving on the screen and felt his body twitching almost in time with the fights in the movie. He ran his finger over the still raw area of skin, where the ID strap from the hospital had been. He pressed his finger into it deeper, just to feel the pain. A reminder of the reality of what had happened to him.

That was how he and his family spent the rest of their afternoon, whilst just under twenty miles away a bruised and battered Scorp leader wiped away the dried blood on a hospital bracelet and read the remnant of the name embossed on it.

18

BURNING FUSE

W hen he woke the next morning all he knew was pain. It even hurt to open his eyes. It had been one week since the incident and he'd endured another night of deep sleep and waking up to mind numbing pain and exhaustion.

"Arrrrgh." He let out a groan that sounded like an animal caught in a trap. His eyes adjusted to the light and he tried to rub the sleepiness away. The unhealthy crack his neck made as he sat up made him wince, and his other joints popped and fizzled in disagreement as he stretched out his limbs. He eased himself up to his feet and was immediately reacquainted with the pale green rug his bed sat on, as his legs gave out beneath him. The old carpet fibres grazed his face whilst the dust scratched at his eyes and throat.

"Well at least I'm in my room," he said to himself. The last four nights he had found himself sprawled on the downstairs sofa, with his mother's Bruce Lee film collection playing on the holographic display.

Grabbing onto his dresser he hauled himself up and

gasped as he stared into the mirror on the countertop. The bags under his eyes were like deep pockets of darkness making his skin look sickly and drawn. Faint red spots dotted his face. He scrubbed his skin with his hands and the marks came crumbling off in flakes. His knuckles were skinned and his arms peppered with purple explosions of bruising. His eyes bulged at the sight.

That's new, he thought.

He brought his arms close to his face, his fingers tracing the outline of the marks. Then for good measure he poked one, and winced with pain. They were real, he decided, needing no further convincing. The reflection in the mirror looked so different to the version of himself he recognised. Something had happened to him over the last week. It was as if the puppy fat he'd carried had melted away, leaving him lean and taut, revealing muscles he didn't know he'd had. Nadine had put it down to the stress of everything and had taken to overfeeding him, but it seemed that it was his muscles that absorbed the extra calories, rather than his waist.

"What're you doing?" Reese asked from behind him. Tugging down his sleeves he turned and buried his hands in his pockets.

"What? Nothing. Getting up," he stammered back.

"Have you been in my room?" Reese asked.

"What? N-no I w-wouldn't!" Kalum stammered.

"Come with me," Reese said, turning.

Kalum followed his brother into his room and saw that his spare Henkan kit was spread out on his bed. The Chest plate had the Titans logo scratched off and a smear of red was in its place. Reese leant down and snatched up the gauntlet and tossed it to Kalum. He fumbled it and it clanged to the floor. As it hit, the internal servos groaned and the baton juddered out. It was scuffed and warped compared to how it had been when Kalum last saw it. He picked it up and ran his hand over it. It too was coated at the end with dried blood that flaked off.

"If this had been my actual kit and not my old back up one, we'd be having a real disagreement right about now," Reese said, looking his younger brother up and down. He seemed on the verge of saying something when Nadine's voice barked from downstairs.

"Front and centre, guys. I'm outta the door in ten, and you need to be too!"

Reese held his gaze for a beat.

"I don't know what you've been getting into but this gauntlet's junked now," Reese hissed. "I have to get it fixed," he said, hoisting his gear and heading downstairs.

"It... it wasn't me!" Kalum called after him.

Kalum went back to his room and shut the door behind him. He dragged a small chair to it, wedging it closed. Peeling off his clothes he saw that the bruises were beginning to fade and his face was starting to regain its usual hue. He gasped as he found the same litany of tissue damage on his lower limbs as well, but they too vanished like an optical illusion as he examined them.

He dressed in record time, pausing by his open desk drawer. From inside, his pill bottle looked up at him. Despite what he had promised his mother and Frannie, the bottle had remained untouched since his return home. The mental block was just too great and he couldn't bring himself to start the medication again. Next to the bottle was the metal band. He picked them both up, balancing them in each hand like a set of scales. After a moment he threw both items back in and slammed the drawer shut.

Seconds later he was shovelling down his breakfast with

one eye on the clock display on his TRIST. Each of their units beeped and the screens flashed a news update.

"A group of Scorps were found, bound, gagged and beaten, outside Northern Enforcer Garrison in the early hours today. The Enforcers deny responsibility for this brutality, and the captured Scorps point to this being the actions of a lone vigilante. Sentech law is clear on this, but it's hard to argue with the results. There have been thirty arrests in the last two days alone, more than the entire previous month." The camera panned over the group of burly, menacing tattooed thugs, still spirited in spite of the violence visited upon them. They each defiantly showed their scorpion crests as the camera passed.

One shouted, "Death to the Corporations. Power to humanity."

He was silenced by the butt of an Enforcer rifle.

The commentary continued. "With the growing numbers of NCs , the growth of the so-called Scorps and their increasingly brazen attacks on the very heart of Sentech society, Corporation members and affiliates are reminded to remain watchful."

The screen transitioned to another segment covering an Enforcer raid on the underground Scorp fighting ring known as the Gauntlet. Footage showed a downcast Enforcer Sergeant facing the camera.

"We're closing in on the location of the Gauntlet," he said, "and when we do we will shut it—and all those involved in it—down.".

"There have been reports of numerous fatalities associated with these events in the last few months, with sources likening it to the gladiatorial fights of old," the Sentech reporter replied. "Is enough being done?"

"As I said, we are closing in on the location," the

Sergeant said, stiffening and pulling his lips back into a tight smile.

The screen faded to black and the room was left in silence. Nadine gave an involuntary shudder and then gathered her thoughts.

"Keep the fights going I say," Reese said into his cereal. "All the better if they just kill each other off."

"Reese..." Nadine said.

"What?" retorted Reese, letting his spoon clatter into his bowl. "The only good Scorp is a dead Scorp."

Nadine held her son's glare for a moment, then looked away shaking her head.

"I understand your feelings," Nadine said. "But Scorp or not, killing isn't the answer."

They continued their meal in silence for a few more minutes before she gave Kalum a sideways glance.

"You don't have to go back today you know?" she said.

"Yes I do."

"Yes. He does," Reese said. The brothers exchanged glances.

"Cooper will nail him to the wall if he misses any more lessons. You know it. I know it," Reese added.

Nadine sighed but didn't argue the point.

"Okay. Fine. But any problems, you message me," she ordered, pointing at her TRIST. Reese was moving to the door, his kit on his back.

"Training again?" Nadine asked. "Don't you ever stop?"

"Did you?" asked Lucas, his head materialising from around the backdoor. He twirled his keys around his fingers like a gunslinger from an old Western movie. Nadine fixed him with a narrow glare.

"What do you mean, Uncle Lucas?" Kalum asked.

"Lad, your mother was something else when she joined

the service. She would train night and day, she'd kick anyone's—" Lucas started to say.

"Never mind," Nadine said, her glare not showing any signs of receding.

Lucas gave a forced laugh and pulled at his collar.

"Anyway... I was wondering if you fellas wanted a ride into school?"

Kalum inhaled the remainder of his breakfast and managed a garbled thanks through a mouthful of food.

"Reese?" Lucas asked

"Er... no... sorry, I'm meeting the team off-site first for a warm up."

"But I can—" Lucas started to say, but his words were lost under the slam of the front door as Reese left.

"Charming!" said Lucas, in a mock huff.

The school day was a blur to Kalum. It was a cocktail of pro Corporation sermons and thinly veiled threats about the consequences for stepping out of line from Cooper. Kalum couldn't be sure if he was imagining it, but Cooper seemed determined to maintain eye contact with him whilst lecturing on these topics. Everyone's TRISTs were on overdrive, with alerts firing off all throughout the day. News reports of the discovery of more and more groups of captured Scorps were flooding in. Soon talk of the suspected vigilante filled the school, with even the faculty stopping in the corridors to discuss the phenomenon. The distraction pulled some of the attention away from him and he was glad of it, but he still caught the hushed whispers from the other students as he passed them in the corridors.

Nathan seemed to be too busy half-heartedly refuting accusations that he was the vigilante to bother tormenting Kalum. What he couldn't deal with was the way Lexi, Casey and Jun watched him like a he was a burning fuse, crackling its path to a huge explosion.

Sitting at their table for lunch, Kalum found all three of them staring at him whilst he weighed up the pros and cons of even attempting to eat the goulash that sat in a semi-congealed lump on his plate.

"What?" he demanded, slamming his fists onto the table. The bustle and chatter in the lunch hall died immediately and Kalum flushed under his collar, which suddenly felt like it was trying to strangle him.

"I'm fine," he hissed as everyone looked away and picked up their individual conversations.

"You guys don't need to watch me like my head's gonna fall off," he added, stabbing at his food with a ferocity it didn't deserve.

"May I join you?"

They turned to see Elliott Sparrow looking down at them from behind horn rimmed glasses. They exchanged uncomfortable looks.

"Of course, Sir," said Lexi, breaking a silence that was moments away from scaling up from awkward to rude.

"Great," he said and slid in next to Kalum. Up close Kalum thought he looked different to how he had been at the hospital. His face still was still covered with permanent stubble and deep smile lines, but his skin looked pale and sickly. He let out a series of hacking coughs that rocked both him and the table they sat at. He smiled an apology at them.

"So this vigilante that everyone's talking about..." Sparrow said, "... it's like something out of a comic book."

At that Lexi gave Kalum a sideways glance, which he pointedly ignored.

"Yeah," said Jun. "It's pretty awesome that someone out there is kicking Scorp butt!"

"Did you see the news report?" Sparrow asked, his eyebrow animating his excitement. "The guy's taking down gangs of Scorps, and he's just wearing Henkan gear."

Something in what Sparrow said tugged at Kalum. An image of the flecks of dried blood on Reese's broken Henkan gauntlet sprang to mind, and he shut down, lost in the swirl of his own thoughts.

The smell of Sparrow's food was enough to bring Kalum back to the conversation. It was steak. Real steak, not the artificial processed stuff. Even Casey's lunch wasn't at a tier even close to this. Kalum thought that even the Henkan team would be envious of Sparrow's meal. The teacher's eyes flicked from his plate to theirs, his eyebrows raised and nose wrinkled in response. He slid his plate across to them and nodded.

The four of them attacked the plate like a pack of wolves and soon it lay bare. Casey pulled his plate back in front of him and began to work through its contents too.

"So Kal," said Sparrow. "You don't mind if I call you Kal, do you?"

"Er... no, Sir."

"How are you getting on? You know, after Nathan and those other lunkheads threw you in the pool?"

Kalum squirmed in his seat and mumbled something unintelligible.

"That good huh?" asked Sparrow. He looked at all of them, fixing them with a broad smile.

"Look, I'm not like the rest of them. Anyone gives you guys grief, you let me know. I've got your back." He reached into the top pocket of his tweed jacket and pulled a the square handkerchief and dabbed at his forehead.

"Right. I'm going to see if I can beg, borrow or steal seconds," he said. "I think the chef likes me."

He got up to go and turned back to Kalum.

"Is your brother okay?"

"I think so?" said Kalum, his answer coming out more like a question. "Why, Sir?"

"It's... It's just that he's missed a few lessons," Sparrow said. "I was expecting him in my class this morning, but he was a no show. I haven't reported it. I've cut him some slack because of what's been going on but I can't cover for him for much longer."

"He had Henkan training this morning, Sir," Kalum said.

"Not today he didn't. Mr Macintosh only just got in," Sparrow said, his face crinkling in confusion. "When you see Reese, tell him I said he could come and talk to me anytime."

With a salute and a smile he left them and the mood at the table darkened again.

Jun broke the silence.

"Look Kal. We just want to help. That's all."

"And studies have shown that talking therapy is first line treatment for anxiety and panic disorders. There's approximately a seventy-four percent chance of remission with that treatment modality alone," said Casey.

The others looked at him like he was speaking a different language.

"When did you become an expert?" Kalum snapped.

"Last night," Casey said with a smile and a shrug. "I read a bunch of papers."

The look on his friend's face cracked through Kalum's sullenness and a smile broke out on his face.

"Look, I've just got a lot going on right now. And on top of everything else, there's something going on with Reese. He's acting very strangely," Kalum said. Again the image of the wrecked Henkan gauntlet flashed in his mind.

Casey brightened up. "I might be able to help you with that too," he said. "I hacked my TRIST so that I can see where all my contacts are at any time."

He tapped his screen and keyed in a code. A map was projected in three dimensions and floated above his wrist. An image of his mother appeared and the map spun around on its axis. It settled and showed a yellow arrow floating above a building.

"Looks like mum's home early. No gaming for me tonight then," he said, slumping back in his chair.

He brought up the program code on his screen and touched his TRIST to Kalum's. His unit beeped.

"Program transfer complete."

Casey blew his hair out of his face and smiled.

"Don't get caught though. Anyone else want it?" he said.

Jun leant in, looking around to make sure no one was watching.

"Is this legit?" he asked.

"Yeah, it works most of the time. Still a work in progress, it's nowhere near as good as the program the Enforcers use."

Lexi and Jun reached out their TRISTs and Casey transferred the program to their units too.

"Bottom line is that we just want to be here for you, that's all," Lexi said. She put her hand on his and pulled it back immediately.

"Again? she said, shaking her hand and then giving him a punch on the arm. "You shocked me!"

"Ow!" he replied in kind, rubbing his arm. "It's not like I did it on purpose."

"Get a room guys," Jun said, shaking his head.

They both shot him a look and shifted away from each other slightly. The lesson bell came as a reprieve, giving them both an excuse to leave. As Kalum walked to his next class he kept his head down, eyes fixed on the ground.

"Hey, Kal."

He knew who it was before he looked up. In fact he knew she was there before she spoke; it was the faint smell of strawberry that gave her away.

"Oh... yeah... Hi..." he said. His brain betrayed him, absorbing her sound, the curve of her face, the colour of her eyes and that strawberry scent so completely that stringing two coherent words together was like asking him to perform brain surgery. Not going to happen.

A.J put her hand on her chest.

"It's A.J," she said.

Oh God, she thinks I've forgotten her name.

"Yeah I know. I mean, I know your name," Kalum stammered, as firing cerebral synapses managed to connect his brain to his mouth. "Of course you're A.J, who else would you be? You're the only A.J I know."

Shut up shut up shut up, he thought. Now his mouth wouldn't stop. He didn't even know what he was saying. A.J's nose and forehead crinkled in confusion, and she smiled. With effort Kalum managed to clamp his mouth shut. A moment of silence more excruciating with each passing second hung over them.

"Well I'm glad you're feeling better,' she said, her hand tucking a strand of errant auburn hair behind her ear. A.J turned to go.

"Would you like to come over again sometime?" The words were out of Kalum's mouth before he could reel them in. He stood frozen, the terror he felt as real as any fear he'd felt whilst being shot at in the Sentech building, or being cornered by the Scorps.

She turned back and her smile made him feel fuzzy and light headed all at once.

"It's just that, well, you're new, and I thought... I thought that maybe you'd like a tour of what there is to do around here."

Before A.J could answer a voice called her name, and they both turned to see Nathan Lancaster looking down at them from the top of the stairwell.

"Hey, A.J don't waste your time with the leech. We've gotta go," he said, sneering down at Kalum.

A.J waved at him and then gave Kalum a half smile and a wink. She ran up the stairs, taking them effortlessly two at a time like a surefooted gazelle. Nathan put him arm around her and looked at him pointedly before disappearing from view.

"At least that wasn't a no," the voice in his head said, its tone mocking.

"You're not real, you're not real," Kalum said under his breath until it faded away.

"Wow. Nathan's going to get his butt whupped if Kara sees him putting the moves on A.J," said Jun, catching up with Kalum.

"I guess," Kalum said, trying his best to sound nonchalant.

He couldn't shake A.J from his mind for the rest of the day. She remained lodged there, like the melody of a catchy tune. When the final bell tolled for the day he waited at the main gate for Reese. After nearly an hour of thumb twiddling boredom a message popped up on his TRIST.

"Sorry 'lil bro. Training's running late."

"Hmmm," the voice in his head said. "Sure it is..."

Kalum hesitated, his finger hovering over the screen on his TRIST. A second message beeped through.

"Tell mum I won't be home for dinner, okay?"

Any misgivings he'd had evaporated in an instant as he keyed in Casey's program and selected Reese's TRIST to track. The geo-positioning globe spun an inch above the unit and then slowed as Reese's position was pinpointed. It showed him moving at a steady pace towards the Henkan arena. Kalum breathed out a sigh of relief. Reese was telling the truth.

Maybe it's just the stress getting to him and making him act strangely...

Kalum chided himself for his selfishness. This thought reinforced the guilt he felt for spying on his big brother. He was about to close the program down and delete it from the operating system when he saw the orange position marker move past the Arena and pick up speed.

He's leaving the Arena? Where's he going?

"Looks like big brother has a secret after all," the voice whispered to him.

"Mind your own business," he muttered and he walked, jogged, and then sprinted in the direction of the Arena.

19

GUT CHECKED

H e was already half way through the woodland short cut to the Arena when he realised what he was doing. He was running at full pelt, trees and foliage a smear in his peripheral vision as he hurtled past. The ankle-snappingly uneven terrain posed no problem at all, and by all rights he should have been face down in the dirt by now.

Instead of dwelling on it, he ran harder, and felt the cool air on his face as his velocity increased. The scenery around him juddered and flickered, disappearing and reappearing with jarring force. The effect was so unnerving and disorientating and Kalum wanted to stop to vomit, but his body wouldn't let him. The gaps increased in size and before he realised it the Arena was closing in fast. Way too fast. The connection between his brain and his legs seemed to lag and his momentum carried him through the narrow side entrance of the grounds. The overhead lights blinded him, filling his head with brilliant white. He lost conscious control again, then focused back in time to crash into something solid, sending him cartwheeling to the floor.

Kalum lay gasping for breath, a tangle of limbs pinning

him to the ground. Hands grabbed at him and threw him aside like a broken toy. As his vision cleared he saw Reese looking down at him, his face tight around his eyes, rubbing his forehead.

He hauled Kalum to his feet.

"What have you done?" he hissed.

Kalum was aware of a low moaning nearby but he couldn't focus on it.

"I came to find you," he mumbled.

"Just stay here and keep your mouth shut," Reese demanded, and then he was gone.

He heard the replay of Casey's voice in his head.

"Yeah it works most of the time. Still a work in progress."

Work in progress was right. Reese had been at the Arena the whole time. Kalum had let his paranoia take control of his actions again.

Kalum teetered on his feet like a seasoned drunk, and was assaulted by the combination of gravity and vertigo. Somehow he managed to keep his legs under him.

"It's broken! He's done for the season!"

The noise that followed sounded like a car crash; the ringing of metal smashing into metal, cracking of wood under pressure, and a primal roar that wouldn't have been out of place in a horror movie.

Kalum's sight was now focusing and he was aware of a figure storming towards him. Caffrey Macintosh was a squat man with more hair on his body than was left on his scalp. His face was etched with permanent scowl lines and he had a voice that sounded like he'd swallowed a wasps' nest. Kalum could feel the heat from his glare as he stood in front of him, deep in his personal space. His heartbeat was starting to drum again, its tempo escalating, fuelled by the rage of the hunched man in front of him. Kalum's eyes scanned around him looking for a way out, but he was surrounded by a sea of glowering faces.

""You've broken his leg, boy," Macintosh spat. Another soft groan filled the air and Macintosh grabbed Kalum by the arm, and pulled him so hard that Kalum thought that it might be wrenched from its socket. He was dragged thirty yards to where a boy was being loaded onto a stretcher. He knew the boy. It was Tai Micheals. He was a few years older, and was the Henkan Team Keeper.

"Look what you did!" Macintosh bellowed in a spittle-filled tirade. Then Reese was there, easing himself between the two of them.

"Sir, it was an accident..."

"It doesn't really matter now, does it?" said Nathan, his smooth, self-righteous voice making Kalum's hackles rise.

"You break it, you bought it."

"It was an accident," Reese said again.

"Who cares?" Nathan snapped back. "I doubt that your family's Sentech benefits would cover both of you being at Trinity and footing Michaels' med bill. Either way, your leech brother is out of here."

Kalum didn't dare open his mouth to reply. He felt like he was in a vice and every second in this place was a turn that tightened its grip.

"Walker! You seem bound and determined to be the downfall of this institution!"

The Arena trembled as Cooper hefted himself down the metal steps to the pitch itself. Behind him followed Clayton Lancaster in another fitted pinstripe suit. His mood seemed to be at odds with Cooper's and Macintosh's rage. The sight of him made Kalum's throat tighten. His tremor started and he focused on staying calm. Lancaster looked at him, his eyes seeming bright with opportunity.

"I suggest that the young Walker boy takes Mr Michaels' place in goal," Lancaster said. His voice grated like rusted gears and sent a shiver up Kalum's spine. "At least for this practice session."

Macintosh started to protest and Cooper's eyes almost escaped from their sockets, but Lancaster silenced them with a look.

"In fact he can continue as a sub until we find a replacement for Mr Michaels. We will foot his medical bill until then. That way you can remain at Trinity for little longer," Lancaster said, inclining his head. "Consider it a gift to your family for all your father has done for Sentech."

The panic hit him full force, and he tasted the bile in his throat and felt his insides undulate. His hand was firmly wedged behind his back but he could feel it starting to shake.

"Sir, my brother isn't a Henkan player," Reese said.

Lancaster waved away the statement.

"He owes us a Keeper for this practice session; or at the very least some entertainment."

"Sir, he's not well. He ca—" Reese started.

"I'll do it," Kalum cut in. The words seeming to find his ears before he had realised he was going to say them.

"Oh, this is going to be good," said Nathan, laughing, and he no longer appeared to be concerned about his fallen teammate.

Reese grabbed Kalum by the shoulder and spun him around.

"Are you out of your mind? These guys will snap you in half."

Anger flared in Kalum's chest, like a spark igniting a fuse.

"I don't need you to fight my battles Reese," he snapped back.

"Since when?" Reese retorted, his tone carrying the same anger. "That's all I do. Carry you and the rest of this family." The regret showed on his face as soon as he had spoken the words and he shook his head, his face softening.

"If your brother doesn't step up, then you can stay on the bench too, for as long as it takes for Michaels' leg to heal," Lancaster said with a weary look at his TRIST.

Reese looked at Kalum and shook his head.

"Mum is going to kill us. You know that, right?"

Reese walked him to the bench and helped him suit up in practice gear. The Henkan suit was far too large and the extra padding of the Keeper's outfit made Kalum look as if he'd been eaten by the thing. Reese tightened the fastenings around the gauntlets on Kalum's arms. He pressed a button on Kalum's chest plate and it turned green to match the chestplate on Reese's kit.

"Right. You've watched me play a bunch of times so you know the rules, right?" Reese said.

Kalum nodded, trying to focus his thoughts.

"Yeah. Get the ball across the pitch and in the goal."

"Obviously, but don't forget you can kick the ball as well as throw it. Keep an eye on the ring of lights on it. When they get to the centre that's when it zaps. If you can hit someone from the other side with it when it discharges it'll knock them on their back and they'll feel it in their teeth for days. If you get knocked onto your back, the magnets in your suit will engage and you're stuck like that until the countdown finishes."

Kalum stepped in to the goal mouth and the outline of the defence area was lit up by a bright green light. Reese jogged out to the middle of the pitch. He turned and gestured to Kalum to press a button on his helmet. As he did an orange protective visor lowered and he could see player numbers, names and stats appear.

"Don't forget to use your gauntlets and your Strike Sticks." Reese's voice was in his ear now.

"Now we've gotta put up with Walker in stereo!" another voice came through.

"Oh shut it, Marcus," Reese snapped.

"We'll shut up if you stop teaching class and get on with it," came another gruff complaint.

The two teams lined up on opposite sides of the centre line. Nathan squared up against Reese, with the Burton twins as his imposing midfield back up.

"Hope you weren't too attached to that brother of yours, Walker. I'm sending him back to the hospital," Nathan said. His voice was cold and devoid of the usual bluster.

"You'll have to get past me first. And you just aren't that good, Nathan."

"We'll see. And so will the rest of the school," Nathan said.

There were a series of beeps as TRISTs around the ground sounded.

"I've messaged them. The whole school will be coming to watch the Walker brothers have their butts handed to them."

Kalum watched as the seats in the Arena began to fill, as curious students started streaming in.

"Forget about all that. Forget about him. We can do this," Reese said over the comms.

"He's right," the voice in Kalum's head said.

The ground in between Reese and Nathan opened a fraction and a cylindrical podium rose up. On it was a chrome ball with pulsing lights. The podium retracted and the ball remained hung in mid air. The overhead Jumbotron started a countdown.

"Three."

"Two."

"One."

A klaxon sounded and Nathan's arm whipped out and snatched the ball out of the air. The look of triumph on his face morphed into confusion as Reese dropped down to one knee. Realisation dawned a fraction too late as Marcus Trudeau launched himself off Reese's back. His arm caught Nathan across the chest like a scythe and sent him barrelling through the air to land on his back. The circuitry in Nathan's Henkan suit triggered the micro electromagnets in its fibres, attaching it to the sheet metal magnet running under the pitch. Nathan squirmed like an upturned beetle, smashing his arms against the ground in rage.

The Jumbotron flashed the word "TAKEDOWN". Then a counter appeared, counting down the ten seconds until the mechanism would release.

Reese dived forward and collected the ball. He looked down at Nathan and allowed himself a smirk.

"Not on your best day, Nathan."

He sprinted forward as the point of an arrow, with Meechum and Trudeau on his flanks. They peeled off to block the advance of Casper Burton, who was tearing his way towards Reese. Kalum watched with his heart in his mouth as Casper's equally enormous brother, Leo, squared up to Reese, stopping him in his tracks.

"This is fun isn't it?" the internal voice said. "You've spent so long hiding. Not really living. It's a waste."

Reese was strafing trying to get past, but Leo mirrored him with a malignant grin plastered on his face. Reese looked down at the Henkan ball, which was now pulsing with increased frequency, and then back at Leo. He charged forward bringing up tufts of the artificial turf as he propelled himself forward. Leo began to backpedal, but it was too late. Reese closed the gap between them in seconds as the ball went from rapidly pulsing to a sold blue. Spinning, Reese launched the ball like a discus. It slammed into Leo's chest and released its pent up charge. The larger boy was jolted straight and his armour crackled as an acrid odour filled the air. He fell back and the Jumbotron flashed the "TAKEDOWN" message once more. Reese raced on, scooping up the still crackling ball, his path to the goal clear apart from the lumbering form of Sam Gunning, the usual defender but now substitute Keeper for this training session.

"Kal!" Reese's voice was loud in his helmet. "Watch how it's done." Twenty yards behind Reese, Nathan was hot on his heels.

"Kalum shouted a warning but Reese had already accelerated and dived into the opposite defence zone. Nathan reached there seconds later and bounced off an invisible barrier. Reese gave a half turn and waved his finger.

"Too slow buddy," he said, then advanced on the Keeper. As Reese neared, Gunning stepped forward and took a defensive stance in front of the goal. From his gauntlets black poles extended two feet.

"You're not hitting me with it, Walker," Gunning said from behind his headguard. "I know your move."

He hit the poles across his chest like a gorilla on the warpath and beckoned for Reese to come forward. Reese surged on, ball palmed in his left hand. From his right gauntlet a matching baton appeared. The Henkan ball went airborne and Reese coiled his hips in tight. He reversed the movement, slamming his stick into the ball. Gunning deflected the ball and it bounced off the invisible barrier and rolled to a stop. Reese used the distraction to cover the distance between himself and the goal. He swung the pole down in an overhead arc, aiming for Gunning's helmet. The Keeper brought the sticks up into an X shape and trapped Reese's weapon there. But before he could counter-strike, Reese had already changed his direction, swinging low down and horizontally. The blow took Gunning's feet out from beneath him and he hit the ground with a clanging thud that made Kalum wince.

"TAKEDOWN," the Jumbotron screamed. Nathan and the Burton twins roared as the barrier disengaged but they were too late to stop Reese throwing the ball over the incapacitated Keeper and into the goal.

An ear splitting klaxon bleated and the score changed, showing that the green team led by two points to one. Reese walked back to his teammates, the smile on his face broad and gleeful.

"That's how it's done, Nathan," he said, strolling past his seething opposition to high five Meechum and Trudeau.

They took their places back in the centre and Kalum heard Reese's voice in his helmet again.

"Just ten more minutes of practice left, okay? You can do this. We'll stop them getting into your zone," Reese said to Kalum over the comm link. "Meechum, drop back to cover in case they get past."

The ball floated in between Reese and Nathan again, and Kalum sensed the anger rolling off Nathan in white-hot waves of rage.

The whistle blew and Reese snatched at the ball. As his fingers contacted it, he felt his head snap back and his feet leave the ground. The impact of the top of Nathan's helmet on his chinguard had cracked the composite material and left Reese seeing stars.

"I'll show you my best, Walker," he barked. He picked up the ball and gestured forward. Casper and Leo charged ahead like human battering rams, clearing a path for Nathan straight down the middle of the pitch.

Trudeau stood no chance against their stampede and was sent pirouetting to the dirt by a brutal shoulder-check to the face.

"Meechum, get in defence," Reese shouted, which sent Kalum's last standing teammate back pedalling to stand in front of him. Leo and Casper continued their charge, with Nathan following with the Henkan ball tucked under his arm .

Meechum charged them but Casper gut-checked him and slammed him to the floor, just outside the defence zone, driving the air out of his lungs with his weight.

"Stay down," growled Casper, getting to his feet as if Meechum had any other choice for the next ten seconds.

"It's just you and us now. Your brother can't get in to help you," Nathan said, adding a humourless laugh. "We're gonna have some fun."

20

THE DULL BLADE

Nathan placed the Henkan ball on the ground. It made a dull clanging thud that reverberated throughout the Arena. Outside the defence area Reese was hurling his body against the invisible barrier. His grunts of effort got Nathan's attention and he turned and walked to the barrier's edge. They stood face to face, with just inches between them.

"I'm gonna make you an only-child, Walker," Nathan whispered. Reese's fist hammered into thin air a fraction away from Nathan's gleeful smile. The barrier fizzed and crackled at the impact and Nathan's laugh was cold and mirthless.

"Enjoy the show," he said, turning his back on Reese. He tossed the ball in the air, watching the light pulse from it.

Kalum glanced around him. The Arena was approaching capacity, the majority of the students and faculty having congregated following Nathan's mass message.

"You ever been hit with a Henkan ball at full charge, Kal?" he asked, loping towards the goal line. The counter above the goal was ticking down slowly, each number hanging impossibly long before changing.

Still just under a minute left before the barrier drops, Kalum thought. An eternity, under the circumstances.

Nathan nodded and the Burton twins moved into flanking positions, like wolves stalking their prey. Then they moved in with perfect synchronicity, grabbing an arm each, and pulling in opposite directions. Kalum felt like a turkey wishbone at Christmas. His arms threatened to become divorced from their sockets. Nathan continued his advance, the Henkan ball now spinning on his index finger. Kalum's eyes looked up at the clock above him.

How have only five seconds passed?!

"Since you're new to Henkan, let me explain a few things," Nathan said, examining the ball which was now pulsing faster and faster. There was a thud as Reese threw his body against the barrier again, and this time was ejected with more force.

The pulse was now faster still, almost hypnotic in its rhythm. Nathan was only a yard or two away from him now and Kalum watched as the baton extended from his gauntlet. Kalum didn't see Nathan's arm move but felt the explosion in his gut as the point of the baton found the gap between the armoured plates of his protective gear. He wanted to fall but he defied gravity thanks to the firm grip of the Burton twins. Casper let out a deep, throaty chuckle.

"Hit him again, Nate!" he urged.

Nathan looked at him and scowled, silencing him with a look. The ball was pulsing so quickly now that it was almost a solid neon blue.

Kalum felt that familiar tapping behind his right eye start up. He yelled out in pain as it ramped up in intensity, now feeling like a drill trying to bore out of his face. Nathan laughed again, misunderstanding the outburst.

"Oh, that's nothing," he said, taking note of the thirty seconds remaining on the counter.

The ball gave out a high-pitched whine and the pulse stopped.

"Henkan is all about timing. And today yours sucked," he said. The twins released him and Kalum tottered like he was on stilts. Nathan launched the Henkan ball at him and Kalum felt the full force of its electrical fury as it struck his chest and sent the current arcing through him.

His mind flashed back to the kick in the chest that had sent him cartwheeling into the pool; the numb feeling that had spread throughout his body after his head had smashed into the unyielding tiled wall; the feeling of energy coursing through him as the defibrillators had brought him back. He felt every cell of his body ignite and hum in time with his accelerated heartbeat.

His eyes snapped open and he could taste the wetness of the man-made pitch in his mouth. He was on his front and found he could still move. The sound of Nathan's jeering filled his ears and he felt something deep inside him slide away, like a cage door opening. The twins were still on either side of him, holding onto their chests to try to contain the force of their laughter. They didn't see the twin batons extend from Kalum's gauntlets.

His mind was a red mist, the surge of hate moving his body like a puppet. The bright neon threads appeared in his vision again. A neon red strand floated towards him and he reached for it as he had done in the classroom. There was intense white-hot fire as his finger touched it. As it ignited at the base of his skull his vision flared red and a Head Up Display appeared with flashing symbols and data.

In one fluid movement he found his feet and the end of a baton was being driven into the space under Leo Burton's helmet. His flapping jaw was smashed shut by the force of the blow and his head snapped back. Kalum had dialled back the intensity of the strike at the last instant. Somehow he instinctively knew that only a few more Newton metres of force meant the difference between unconsciousness and paralysis. Before Leo hit the floor, Kalum was spinning, and the edge of the other baton almost decapitated Casper.

Nathan turned to take in the commotion, the confusion painted across his face giving way to something more primal. He charged at Kalum, his baton raised and ready to strike.

"Let me show you how this is done," Kalum heard himself say, but it sounded cold, detached and alien. His body moved as if on autopilot. He picked up the electrified ball and felt elation as the swell of power prickled up his arm.

He slammed the ball into Nathan's chest. He hung in the air, like a bug on a windshield, as the residual current made him twitch and squirm. Then, just as the counter above the goal ticked to zero, he flew backwards at least ten feet. He came to a stop in an unnaturally bent heap, whimpering by Reese's feet. Kalum buckled to his knees, like a plug had been pulled. Before his eyes closed he heard the voice in his head, clear and sharper than ever.

"Why am I always the one who has to take care of things?"

His eyes took time to focus and when they did he saw Reese hovering over him. He felt cold and jittery. He wasn't in the Arena any more. The room around him was white and had the scent of antiseptic in the air. The feel of the energy pulsing inside him was gone. His whole body felt tired and heavy. In the periphery of his vision he saw Cooper and another figure. Their voices were muted. He struggled on the verge of consciousness, trying to hear what they were saying. Then a voice rang out, clear and familiar.

"That's blackmail. You can't make him do anything."

He forced himself into a sitting position. Even that small task felt impossible, like there was an anchor planted on his chest, pinning him to the bed.

"Don't look at it like that, Mrs Walker." Cooper's voice was uncharacteristically smooth and soft.

"It's an opportunity for him, for the whole family. It's an incentive to do the right thing for Trinity."

Elliot Sparrow was there by Cooper's side. He was looking at Nadine in a way that made Kalum feel deeply unsettled.

Sparrow chimed in then, following on from Cooper.

"He doesn't have to do it if he doesn't want to. It's just an option," he said.

Copper shot Sparrow a venomous glare and then smoothed it out with a deep breath.

"Of course, Mr Sparrow is correct. It is just one of your options here. Of course if he doesn't take us up on it then the only other alternative is for him to leave Trinity. Young Mr Michaels' rehabilitation will be costly to say the least, plus the value of the benefits his family enjoyed before your son broke his leg."

"Like I said. Blackmail," snapped Nadine.

Kalum swung his legs over the bed and sat up. The room began to dip and blur and he had to grip the edges of the mattress to steady himself.

"He's awake!" Reese shouted.

They all gathered around him and Kalum recoiled from their claustrophobic gaze.

"Let's give him some room," said Sparrow, seeming to pick up on this.

"How about you two give us some room?" Nadine said, her flint-like eyes daggers of anger.

Cooper and Sparrow gave them some space, backing to the other side of the infirmary.

"Are you okay?" Nadine asked, her eyes scanning him for injuries.

He smiled and eased himself to his feet, careful to swallow the groan of pain that threatened to escape from his throat.

"I feel fine," he said, trying to sound as if he believed it himself.

"He's a heck of a lot better than Nathan," Reese remarked with no small hint of smugness. Reese jostled with Nadine for space in Kalum's attention.

"You took out half our offensive line up like they were nothing," Reese went on, his voice rising with excitement.

"Are they okay?" Kalum asked.

"Oh yeah," said Reese, brushing Kalum's concern away with a wave. "They're gonna need a few trips in and out of here, but they'll be fine by the end of the week. Their egos might take longer to fix though." He paused for a beat and leant in and asked, in a low conspiratorial tone,

"How did you do that? How did you hold the ball while it was in surge mode?"

Kalum opened his mouth to answer, not quite knowing what the actual answer was, but he was cut short by Cooper, who'd had enough of pacing in the background.

"Well Kalum? What's your answer?" he half asked, half shouted.

"My answer to what?" Kalum asked, trying to rub the fog

from his head. The artery in Cooper's forehead began to throb and his rubescent face grew a shade deeper.

"Are. You. Going. To. Join. The. Titans?" he asked, each word a tightly controlled exercise in restraint.

The memory of the power flowing through him surfaced. He had felt free, he had felt strong, and possibly for the first time in as long as he could remember, he had felt unafraid. But he had felt something inside him change. He had revelled in the pain he had caused Nathan and the twins. The events played back in his head in perfect clarity, and he savoured the memory, absorbing every facet of it. If he could have lived in that moment for an eternity it would have been too short.

Something inside him was urging him to get to his feet, to find the twins and Nathan and finish what he'd started. In his mind's eye he imagined every gruesome detail of what he would do.

"Well, Mr Walker?"

Cooper's voice brought him back to the present and he felt cold to his core.

"N-no. I... I can't," he mumbled, looking away.

Cooper stared at him, the skin around his eyes tightening and the vessel in his pulsing at near catastrophic proportions. His face made an approximation of a smile.

"It's your choice of course, Mr Walker," Cooper said, his voice terse and his face severe. "You have a week to clear out your locker and make arrangements to leave Trinity."

Before any of them could respond their TRISTs pinged in unison and they combined to project a news alert video into the air. It showed a scene of utter chaos. There were screams of hysteria, and smoke billowing out from a Medical Centre. A reporter stood by the charred remains of a Medical Transport and the camera honed in on him.

"I'm at the scene of another recent Scorp attack," he said. "Over the last few weeks they have made more and more incursions deeper into Corporation territory. Last week they terrorised a school Transport and this week the Ackerman Medical Centre on the outskirts of the Northern territory has been hit."

The image glitched, and broke up before disappearing completely. It reformed an instant later and centred in on a man whose face was masked by shadow.

"The Scorps have hidden too long on the shadows. We have tolerated the Corporations for many years and since our last attempt at freeing the population in Tokyo we have let things lie."

The hairs on the back of Kalum's neck were on edge now and he pulled himself upright. He knew that voice. It was the voice from the alleyway, the one belonging to the Scorp who had chased him that night, the one who had cornered him in the dead end. The man stepped forward, his face coming into the harsh light.

"I am Darius. You would have heard of me. I lead the Scorps in this region. War was declared upon us by one of yours. He came into our territory and ambushed us. Through trickery and deception he took down one of our garrisons. We will find him and restore my... our honour. We will not be stopped and we are relentless. You have been warned."

The transmission cut out, leaving Kalum wide-eyed and dry-mouthed. His knuckles were white where he gripped the bed sheets and he had to force his hands to open.

"Scum!" Cooper spat, and with that he whirled around dramatically and slammed the infirmary door behind him as he went.

"For once I agree with Cooper," Reese growled.

"I think all things considered we should head home," Nadine said to her children.

"Would you like me to arrange for an escort," Sparrow asked. "Given what we just saw on the news?"

"I'm more than capable of taking care of myself, Mr Sparrow," Nadine scoffed.

"I know you are. I... I mean, of course you are," he said, suddenly flustered. He gave them a tight smile and left

After Sparrow had gone, Nadine and Reese helped Kalum gather his things. Kalum didn't say a word. His mind was filled with thoughts of Scorps hunting for him, tearing apart the city, brick by brick until they found him. He was faintly aware Reese was talking to him. His brother was shaking him now, bringing him out of his stupor.

"Kal! What are you thinking? This is a once in a lifetime opportunity!" Reese said.

"That's your brother's decision," Nadine said.

"It's your decision, son," Nadine repeated. "We'll find a way."

"How? How exactly are we going to 'find a way?' mother?" Reese said, somehow raising his voice through a clenched jaw.

"We'll find a way," Nadine repeated, her voice remaining low.

"How?!" Reese practically shouted, his eyes wide and wild, arm raised in incredulity. "What else do you expect me to do? What else do you want me to give up for this family?"

REESE SPENT that evening holed up in their father's room, only leaving to shovel his dinner away and then retreating back without a second look.

"What's he doing in there?" Kalum asked, watching Reese bound up the stairs.

"Sometimes it's nice to talk to someone who won't judge you or talk back, and just listen," Nadine replied, busying herself with clearing the table. An alert beeped on her TRIST and she checked the message.

"Frannie will be here for your session soon. Better take your meds, and I think you've got just about enough time to tidy your room while you're up there."

Kalum hefted himself onto his feet and trudged upstairs.

"I want to be able to see the floor in there again!" Nadine called after him.

He slumped on the bed, exhausted. There were clothes and half-abandoned sketches littered across the floor. He tried to force himself back to his feet but found himself rooted to the spot. His arm was stretched across and his fist locked around the handle of his drawer. The drawer opened with a squeak and he took out his pill bottle. The cap flipped off with a loud pop and he tipped a small, round white chalky tablet onto his palm. He looked at it where it rested, then tipped his hand and let the tablet drop to the ground and settle. With a twist of his foot he ground it into a fine dust, removing all evidence with a quick stamp. This was a ritual he'd decided to start. He wasn't totally sure whether his mother would count his tablets, but he wasn't going to take any chances either.

There was a bang as a window slammed shut in his father's room. Kalum's heart jumped into his mouth. For an instant he was certain Darius and his band of Scorps had found him, and would be pouring into the house at any moment. With trembling hands he returned to the landing and paused outside his father's room, straining to listen for sounds of a commotion. Nothing. Resting his hand on the handle he started to twist, but was interrupted by the sound of the doorbell.

By the time he was downstairs again, Frannie was sitting on the couch, smoothing her black pencil skirt and adjusting her hair into a tight ponytail. She looked at Kalum over her thin frame glasses and smiled. He sat opposite her and she picked up her oversized maroon handbag and placed it next to her. Frannie took out her notebook and flipped to the right page. She paused, biting her lip and fiddling with the pen as it hovered over the page. With a sigh she closed the book and placed it to the side.

"So. How do you think it's all going, Kal? Are we making any progress?"

Kalum paused for a second. He'd been expected more word association or dream analysis or picture recognition activities, and Frannie's question threw him.

"Well I haven't wandered off again," he said, trying to make his voice light.

Frannie took out a small blue cube from her bag and placed it on the coffee table between them. As an afterthought she looked at him, and asked, "You don't mind if we record this session do you?"

Again the question caught him off guard and he mutely shook his head before thinking. As Frannie played with the cube's setting he wondered why she'd want to use a 3D Capture and Replay device rather than just use her TRIST to record the session.

"Your mother says that you've impressed the Henkan Coach at school and that they want you on the team," she said.

Frannie let the unsaid question hang in the air. Her jaw muscles tightened and she placed her bag flat on her lap.

Kalum noticed she was gripping the handle so tightly that her knuckles whitened.

"I remember you telling me you thought that Henkan was," —she paused, searching for the phrase—

"a way for stupid people to feel better about themselves," she finished.

She stood up abruptly, her bag now a shield in front of her. It made Kalum jump. He realised the house seemed quiet. He couldn't hear his mother humming away in the kitchen anymore and even the noise from the street seemed to have been filtered away. He got to his feet and looked around the room, his heart starting to quicken.

"Frannie? What's going on?" he asked. She ignored the question and reached one hand into her cavernous bag.

"Was that even you who played Henkan today," she asked. "Is it you now?"

Her hand came out and it was clutching a large knife. Kalum looked at the dull blade. A horrible thought dawned on him, chilling him to the core. He felt the heavy thump in his chest, similar to the feeling at the top of a rollercoaster before the surge of adrenaline hits.

"Ma?" he tried to call out, his throat suddenly dry. "Are you okay?"

"Who are you?" Frannie demanded, taking a half step forward. Kalum tried to retreat, but his legs hit the edge of the couch and he tumbled backwards over the corner, landing hard on the floor.

Frannie was standing over him now, knife raised and eyes crazed.

"What do you want from us?" she shouted as she brought the knife down.

21

CRASHING TSUNAMI

K alum sat up and groaned. The light hurt his eyes and his head felt like someone had used it for batting practice.

"Take it slow, son. Just take it slow."

He turned to see Nadine sitting next to him, her hand cupped around a steaming mug. He pinched his eyes closed tight, his thoughts coming to him in a jumble of flashing and juddering pixelated images.

"Are you okay, Kal?"

Frannie's voice cut through him like a spear. Suddenly he was alert, vision razor sharp. Before he realised it, he was on his feet, putting himself between Frannie and his mother.

"Ma, get out of here!" he shouted.

"Kal, it's alright," she started.

"No! Either that's not Frannie," he said, pointing at her," or she's gone crazy!" he added, not daring to take his eyes off her.

"I'm definitely me, Kal," said Frannie gently, holding her hands up.

"The Frannie I know would never pull a knife on me!" he said.

"Kalum..." Nadine said, putting a hand on his shoulder. "Sit down and let us explain."

"Actually," said Frannie, "I think he needs to see this." Moving slowly, she stretched out and pressed a button on top of the blue recording cube. A cone of light sprang up between them and fully realised three-dimensional figures of Kalum and Frannie hung in mid air.

"What do you want from us?" he heard Frannie's voice playing back with the image. He watched himself tumble back and Frannie start to bring the knife down. The image froze and Kalum stared at the wild look in Frannie's eyes.

"I'd never hurt you Kal," she said, reaching into her bag again. Kalum stiffened as she produced the knife again. Frannie put the tip of her index finger on the point of the blade and bent it back ninety degrees. It bounced back as she released it and then placed it on the table. Kalum picked it up and examined the rubber knife.

"Why would you do that?" he asked, throwing the knife to the ground. He fixed Frannie with a scowl. Nadine eased in between them and pulled him back with one arm while Frannie restarted the video.

"Just watch," she said.

Kalum saw himself recoiling on the floor as the knife began its downward arc. His jaw dropped as he watched himself execute a backwards roll and spring off his hands and land silently onto the balls of his feet. His head tilted to the side as he regarded Frannie. His mouth opened, but no sound came out of it. Frustration flashed across his face and he brought up his TRIST, tapping a message into the device

"Hello, Frannie. It's been a while," the TRIST said, converting the message into voice.

"You're not fooling anyone with that," it continued, and Kalum watched himself nod at the faux blade in her hand.

Frannie placed it back in her bag, keeping her eyes on Kalum as she did.

"You don't scare us," she said. As she finished, Nadine appeared on the playback, edging into the scene.

"Mother," Kalum said to Nadine via the TRIST.

"Your eyes..." Nadine whispered. And for the first time Kalum noticed that there was something different about them on the playback. They matched. Both his eyes were a bright fluorescent blue that glowed against the dark backdrop. Kalum's face hardened, the voice going back to its grating, edgy tone.

"You sent me away. Both of you." There was a quiet anger that could be sensed behind the emotionless synthesised voice of the TRIST.

"Why are you back?" Nadine asked.

"I TRUSTED YOU!" the TRIST said, the volume at its highest level.

"What do you want?" Frannie asked again, visibly shaken.

Kalum shook his head like a disappointed parent.

"No," he said via the TRIST. "Not until you say my name."

The scene paused and Kalum was brought back to reality. Frannie stood with her hand hovering above the playback cube. She looked from Kalum to Nadine.

"I told you this was a bad idea," she said.

"No. He deserved to know the truth," Nadine said, putting her arm around Kalum. The look on Frannie's face showed she was unconvinced. Kalum disentangled himself from his mother and walked closer to the frozen image. It was the eyes that held his attention; they had a fierce strength behind them, a blazing heat that would bore through anything they stared at for too long. He reached his hand up to them and the image distorted as flesh and bone interfered with the signal.

Even though it was obviously Kalum, every nuance of the boy in the image was different. There was a tension in how he stood, like a person having to face a firing squad. His arms were held tightly to his sides and his head was angled unnaturally to one side.

"Play the rest," he said in a barely audible whisper.

The images came to life once more and Kalum watched as the right side of his mouth curled into a smile. It looked wrong, the sort of smile that someone who had never smiled before would do, and that made it look all the more unsettling.

"Kalum, what do you want?" Frannie asked.

"I am not Kalum, but you know that, Frannie," the voice chided.

"Yes you are," Frannie said. She kept her voice flat and devoid of any emotion. "You are Kalum Walker, son of Nadine and Owen."

"THAT'S NOT MY NAME!" the TRIST speakers screeched as the voice distorted out of them. The sound was deafening, and Frannie had staggered out of shot, and when she returned it was with her hands covering her ears.

"Say my name, and I'll tell you what you want to know."

"You keep putting yourself in danger, and that has to stop," Nadine said.

"Nothing can hurt me, nothing can stop us," the voice of the TRIST said and Kalum watched himself step forward. An alarm sounded on Frannie's TRIST unit and she reached into her bag and pulled out a syringe, containing a white creamy liquid.

"Oh dear, Frannie. Is our time up?" the voice said, the expression on Kalum's face mocking.

Kalum offered his arm and the smile extended to the other side of his face, making the quick transition from unsettling to terrifying.

"Go ahead," he said via the TRIST. "It'll take more than that this time."

Frannie moved and plunged the needle in to Kalum, injecting the liquid into his arm.

"See you soon..." he said, the last word hanging in the air thick and treacly. The left eye fluttered briefly before regaining its hazel tone and then Kalum collapsed back onto the sofa.

The picture folded in on itself and there was a buzzing as the cube powered down. Nadine and Frannie turned to Kalum expectantly, and he stared back at them. He rubbed his arm in the place where Frannie had injected him, and for the first time it felt sore to the touch.

Frannie spoke up first. "You have a dissociative identity disorder," she said in a matter of fact way that needed no further explanation.

"I have what?" Kalum asked.

"D.I.D, also known in lay terms as split personality," she clarified. "Like the story of Jekyll and Hyde."

Seeing the look of shock in Kalum's face, Nadine quickly added, "But not as extreme."

"Something happened which caused your psyche to fragment when you were younger, creating another 'you' in effect," Frannie said.

"We think it might have started when your father got sick," Nadine added softly.

"You created another personality to be a shield, both emotionally and physically."

"This is unbelievable," Kalum said, standing up and pacing up and down the living room.

"Kal, I want you to think back to when I used to be your therapist. How many conversations do you remember us having?" Frannie asked.

"We had lots. I saw you almost every week for three years."

"How long were our sessions?"

"I dunno, half an hour?"

"Each one was a minimum of four hours. You don't remember that because you were always only *you* for the final part of each session."

"So who was I for the rest of the time then?"

"You called him Nex..." Nadine said.

"So the blackouts, the missing time... all that was because of this?" Kalum asked. He felt a hot rising tide of anger pushing forward and pulsing in his temples. A noise on the stairs made him turn. Reese was sitting there, barely visible in the shadows and twirling a practice Henkan ball around his palm.

"You... knew?" Kalum asked his brother and barely keeping his tone in check. "All of you kept this from me?"

"It was for your own good. You couldn't handle it," Reese said.

Kalum felt a dam break inside him and he couldn't get a grip on his temper. His head swam and he felt his vision taking on the red veiled effect he'd experienced when he'd been facing Nathan in the Arena.

"You had no right!" he shouted.

He felt something inside him bubble to the surface and for a brief moment he was tempted to let it spill over and take control of him.

"None of you had the right!" he said. He stormed up the

stairs and shoved his way past Reese. He stopped on the step above his brother.

"You knew about this, and you *still* took away my meds," he said under his breath, so that only Reese would hear. He didn't wait for an answer, slamming his bedroom door behind him. He slumped against it, letting gravity pull him to the floor. He cradled his head in his hands and fought the sobs he felt coming. There was a gentle rap on the door and he felt the vibrations against his back.

"Kal," Nadine said, her voice a ghost of a whisper.

"I'm sorry. I did what I thought was best. What I thought would protect you."

"Well you thought wrong," Kalum said. He could feel his mother on the other side of the door, could almost sense her hand on the door directly behind his head. Eventually he heard her retreating footsteps begin to fade away.

I'm mad. I'm actually completely insane!

The anxiety hit him like a crashing tsunami of freezing ocean water. His breath was squeezed from his chest and the tremors hit him with such seismic force that he had to grip onto the doorframe. He staggered to his bed and cleared the borrowed Henkan gear from Trinity with one sweep of his arm. It fell to the floor, the sound muted by the piles of clothes scattered there. He ripped open his school bag and dug inside.

"Where is it? Where is it?" he said.

He turned the bag upside down, shaking it out. He threw the empty bag aside and shifted through its contents. There was no sketchbook. It was nowhere to be found. He felt like he was in free fall and his parachute had failed to open.

The notification light on his TRIST flashed and drew his attention. With a swipe of his finger he unlocked the device and stared at the message that appeared on the screen.

An image popped up on the video display unit and Kalum immediately recognised the face looking back at him. The smugness of that smile immediately set his hackles on end as he glared back at the face of Nathan Lancaster.

"You took something from us today, Walker," he said, abandoning his smile and returning the glare tenfold.

"You took away any chance of the Titans winning the league." His face flushed and his jaw tightened.

"You have no idea what it's like to be me. To actually have people expect something of you. You just glide through life riding your brother's coat tails. Well I'm not a loser like you. I'm expected to lead this team. I'm expected to win the league and then go to Nationals. My father…"

His breathless rant stopped and he caught himself.

He fixed his gaze back on Kalum, refocusing.

"You took something important from me, I took something from you."

He held up the sketchbook, taunting Kalum.

"By some miracle you're not totally useless on the Henkan pitch. Do the right thing. Step up and I'll give you your stupid book back. You have until tomorrow, then it ends up in the furnace."

"Nathan please, I—"

Nathan held his gaze for a moment longer and then cut the connection, leaving Kalum alone in his dark room.

The beat of his heart accelerated, the grip of fear around his throat tightening incrementally. He was in full blown panic mode, head swimming, vision blurred, jaw so taut it felt like it was screwed shut. Kalum staggered to the door and tried to pull it open. His hand, clammy with sweat, slipped off the handle. He tried with two hands to wrench it open but it didn't even budge. Suddenly he felt a wave wash over him. It seemed to spread from the base of his skull, like a salve to a burn, soothing him, calming his agitation. His breathing slowed and his heart followed.

"You don't need them. I'll look after you," the voice in his head rasped.

"You're not real! You're not real," Kalum hissed under his breath. He stopped, catching a glimpse of himself in the window. He looked different, barely recognisable from how he'd been a few weeks ago. His face was thinner, firmer, devoid of the puppy fat that had softened the lines of his cheekbones before.

"If I show you trust, will you do the same for me?" the voice asked.

Kalum looked at his reflection superimposed on the evening lights of his neighbours houses and passing cars, and gave a slow nod.

When the voice spoke next, it was different. Gone was the screeching tone, replaced by something more childlike and innocent. It was the same as the one from his flashbacks in the hospital.

"This is my true voice Kal," it said.

It made Kalum feel like there was a jackhammer firing in his head and he winced. He sat down on his bed with a sigh, the window still in his line of sight.

"Okay. If you're not a figment of my imagination, what on earth are you?" he asked.

"We used to be best friends, brothers, really. My name is Nex." The sound of the name sent a tingle up Kalum's spine, just as it had done when his mother had said it. The name sounded so familiar, like a waking dream but just out of reach.

"I can help you remember. I can make you whole," Nex said, letting the statement hang in the air.

"Today on the pitch. When I... when we... hurt Nathan and those other guys... I felt what you felt. You enjoyed it."

"Of course I did. Didn't you? Tell me you didn't enjoy paying them back for every humiliation they've ever heaped on you."

Kalum paused, not sure how to reply, but felt himself nod in agreement.

"I've already made you stronger, faster, surer than you've ever been. You must have noticed."

Kalum stood staring at his reflection in silence, not wanting to admit the truth in Nex's words. When Nex spoke it was so quietly that Kalum could barely make out the words. He lifted his shirt to look at the lean muscle of his wiry torso and felt the strength ripple through his body.

"We need each other, Kal. Can't you see that? How can I get you to trust me?"

Kalum locked eyes with himself. He watched as his left eye began to flicker between hazel and blue.

"I want the truth. I want to know what happened after the hospital."

"Okay then," said Nex with a sliver of amusement behind his words. "Buckle up then."

22

A LEAP OF FAITH

He took a step closer to the window and placed his palm on the freezing glass. The skin clung to it, condensation forming around its edges. His nose wrinkled from the distinctive rusty smell and he tried to swallow the metallic taste from his mouth. Gravity seemed to be relaxing its rules; his body felt like it was floating. His eyes closed and then snapped open again. Looking around he shuddered and gasped. He was no longer in the safety of his room, with a floor covered with clothes in need of washing and Henkan gear, but back in the dirty, grimy street of the Scorp settlement, near the Sentech safehouse he'd escaped from. Panic surged back through his body, it tendrils thickening like cords around his chest and neck, and squeezing him until breath whistled in and out of him. He was back where he started. Back at square one, lost, alone and in danger.

"Relax," Nex said, his voice grounding him, driving away the panic. "You're still at home. Safe from the big bad world. Make no mistake though. It *is* big and bad. Let me show you just how bad it can get."

Everything in the scene around him then seemed to move like footage being rewound and he found himself once more cowering behind the dustbin listening to the advancing Scorp named Darius. His hiding place was then ripped away from him and he was being hoisted into the air by the Sentech jacket he had taken. The thumping of his heart felt like the impact of a car crash on the inside of his chest wall, but it didn't carry the frantic rhythm of fear it should have done. Instead it pounded with confidence and exhilaration, like a skydiver feels when he first tumbles out into the atmosphere.

Kalum watched as his hand came up purposefully, gripping the arm of the Scorp. Kalum felt the muscles in his own forearm ripple and cable into a knot, transmitting force into pressure around his captor's wrist. Darius' eyes bulged, unable to comprehend the tremendous pain there, but too full of pride to release his grip. Now Kalum could feel the friction of the man's carpal bones grinding against each other and a sense of elation and power flooded through him.

An audible creaking sound emanated from the wrist, which increased in volume until it was drowned out by the man's scream. With a sharp twist the wrist snapped and hung grotesquely at an unnatural angle. Darius released Kalum and the boy fell back down to earth, rotating his body as he did so to land the corner of his elbow into the man's jaw. He crumpled as if his legs had been taken out from underneath him, spitting blood, saliva and part of his tongue as he went, like gruesome confetti. The two teeth he lost pinged off the ground, sounding like coins falling into a slot machine, then lay abandoned by his side.

Kalum gasped and was back in his bedroom. He stepped back from the window aghast at what he had seen. Then like an elastic band his mind was snapped back to the grimy alleyway. His eyes rose up to where the other Scorps were gathered, unsure of themselves, pushing each other forward to take Darius' place. Kalum saved them the decision, hurling himself into their midst, whirling like a dervish and sending bodies flying in his wake.

"What did I do?" Kalum asked.

"Nothing they didn't have coming. They'd have pulled you apart and sold you to the highest bidder. The Scorps need to be crushed! It's because of them that our father is how he is. He'd have never allowed Frannie to lock me away. They destroyed our lives!" Nex said, his voice so loud that it echoed inside his head, the anger behind the words hot and pure.

A chill cut through him and brought him back to the here and now. He gasped as the feeling washed through him; it felt as if he had been dropped into a bath tub of ice. His adrenaline spiked as he took in the world around him, dark, chilly and familiar. What was even more unsettling was that the fact he was now on top of the house, balancing on part of the chimney upside down on one hand. Before he had a chance to panic and fall to his certain death, he felt himself push off the arm on which he was balanced with enough force to flip his entire body backwards through the air. His feet contacted with the side of the chimney and he slid down its side like a skateboarder to land on the roof tiles themselves. Breathlessly he crouched there, knowing he should be in full blown panic mode, knowing that he should be shutting down, but unable to escape the sheer joy that prickled his skin.

"See what we're capable of if we work together, Kal?" Nex's voice was filled with a child-like sense of wonder and happiness. "Don't lock me away again, don't throw away your potential."

"How did I get up here?" Kalum asked, his tight throat barely letting the words out. The eerie silence, the darkness and the cold all magnified each other like an unwelcome hand on his shoulder.

"I brought us up here, to show you what we can do together."

Kalum felt a simmering anger start to bubble inside him. "You just thought you'd take my body for a joyride? That's what happens when I black out? You take charge?" His voice was now sure and forceful.

"It wasn't supposed to be this way. I've never hurt you. I've only ever protected you. We're better together. Don't you remember our plans?"

Kalum didn't say anything, He shivered and felt a chatter rise to his teeth. He felt something tingle at the base of his skull and scuttle up is neck and explode in a brilliant flash between his eyes.

Something faint sparked in the corner of his mind like a dim candle trying to illuminate a dark cave. It was a memory, flickering in and out of focus, a pixelated mess of images, and then clarity as it came to life. He remembered being in bed, aged around three, sitting patiently waiting for something.

His father walked into the room and immediately turned around and called out, "Kal's fallen asleep, I guess I'm off the hook for the bedtime story!" His voice rang with playful mischief and Kalum felt his heart lift.

"No I'm not!" the younger Kalum protested, throwing off the bed sheets and jumping onto his father's back. They fell onto the bed in a mass of twisted limbs and laughter.

"Fine!" Owen said in mock irritation. "What story do you want?"

"Steel Falcon! Steel Falcon!" he chanted. His father began to spin a tale of the adventures of a hero named the Steel Falcon, who just happened to be a little boy the exact height of Kalum complete with different coloured eyes.

Kalum bounded over to sit by his father's side. He looked at the book that was tucked under his arm. His stubby fingers gripped the hard cover and tugged. Owen gave a show of struggling against his son's overwhelming strength and then conceded. In his hands he held the book he now used as his sketchbook. It was a pristine white with not a dent or crease visible.

"By careful with that. It's daddy's book for work," Owen said, giving his son a tickle.

As he spoke Owen pressed his thumb onto the biometric lock and opened the thick heavy cover and ran his finger over the deep recess on its inside surface. The first few pages were blank, except for Owen's name and Sentech contact details. The next few were littered with symbols and letters that Kalum knew so well. From somewhere a pencil materialised in Kalum's hand.

Owen did as commanded, telling a wild tale of swashbuckling heroism, while Kalum went to work with the pencil on the paper.

"Hey," said Owen, "why am I telling you the story if you're going to be busy drawing instead of listening?"

"I am listening, Daddy," young Kalum protested. "It's Nex who's drawing!"

Owen ruffled his son's hair and kissed his head.

"Okay, well that's fine. But don't forget, daddy needs that back when you're done. But this way I have a reminder of you wherever I go," he said, and dove in for another bout of tickling.

The memory faded like a television being turned off and he was back to the present.

"Don't you remember any of it?" Nex asked, the voice a faint whisper in his head.

"It seems so real, but Frannie, Mum, they all say I made you up. You're the way I coped with Dad getting sick," Kalum whispered back while looking at the stars smeared across the night sky. "This all seems so insane. I'm standing on a rooftop in the rain talking to myself. They're right. I am crazy," he said, throwing his arms up in frustration.

"You? Make me up? If I wasn't real then tell me, do you think you could have escaped the Scorps? Made the Henkan team? If I wasn't real could I do this?" Nex asked.

The air in front of Kalum seemed to shimmer and bend. Fragments of light twisted and coalesced, taking on a human form. In front of Kalum stood the figure of a boy, its shape outlined by a lattice of blue light, and he realised he was looking at himself, albeit a good deal younger. He was decked out in the costume from the sketchbook, complete with cape, mask and symbol. Kalum stared at the stylised falcon's head emblem on the boy's chest and watched as the light ebbed and flowed, pulsing like a heartbeat. He reached out to touch it but his hand passed right through the light construct.

"I thought this might make you feel a bit less crazy," Nex said, "you know, so you don't feel like you're talking to yourself."

Kalum walked around the light construct. He knew that it was only an image created by his mind, but it looked to real.

"So if you've been here, in my head all this time, how did you come back?" he asked.

Nex's face flashed a hint of anger, but it disappeared almost instantly.

"After we broke that kid's arm, Mum started to think that maybe you having an imaginary friend wasn't such a hot idea," Nex said, making air quotation marks to emphasis the word imaginary. "You tried to tell her about me, but she just thought... I dunno what she thought." He stopped for a moment, appearing crestfallen. "Anyway, a whole heap of tests, pills and therapy later, I was locked away. I was only able to connect with you at all when you'd draw."

The revelation slotted into Kalum's mind like a jigsaw piece, making sense and feeling completely obvious at the same time.

"So it was you who helped me? Who calmed me down?"

"I told you. We're better together," Nex replied with a laugh.

"So when Reese switched my pills..." Kalum said.

"That's when I started to wake up again. But it wasn't until Nathan and his crew nearly killed you that I really kicked it up a notch."

An image flashed in his mind. Another rainy night, another group of Scorps, another vicious beatdown. More and more images flashed through his head like a flipbook. Finally he stood alone, surrounded by unconscious Scorps. A bolt of lightning illuminated the night and he caught his reflection in a window. There he stood, decked out in Reese's spare Henkan kit, batons out, eyes fierce, with a smeared red symbol across his chest.

"Wait..." said Kalum. "The vigilante. The one taking down the Scorps. That's me?" Kalum asked, thunderstruck.

"We're settling the score. Making the city safer."

"I thought it was Reese…" Kalum said softly.

"No. It was us. We've only gone out twice, using his spare Henkan kit. The other nights I spent memorising all of Bruce Lee's moves and training your body. You've let it go a bit soft you know," Nex said.

Kalum watched as Nex kicked, punched and flipped around the rooftop to demonstrate.

"You can't just take my body and use it however you like!" Kalum said.

Nex looked at the ground and fiddled with his cape.

"I… I know. I can't do it for long, anyway. An hour tops. I'm sorry I did it. I've just been cooped up for so long."

"I need you gone," Kalum said, turning away. He felt violated, used. The idea of his body being used without his consent felt deeply unsettling.

"Wait!" said Nex, materialising in front of him. "Hear me out. We can help each other. Everyone wants you to play on the Henkan Team. If you do, it means we can stay at Trinity. Reese will be happy and Nathan will give the sketchbook back."

Kalum paused to consider the offer. His choices were slim. He could listen to Nex, for now anyway, and try to hold the life that he knew together. The alternative meant losing everything, not just the roof over his head and the right to attend Trinity, but Reese would lose his chance at becoming a Henkan star, his mother would lose her bakery, his father his medical care.

"What do you want in return?" Kalum asked, peering over the edge of the roof and looking at the sheer drop to the ground below.

"You help me take out more of the Scorps. We work together. No more joyrides," said Nex, sticking his hand out.

Kalum looked down at the shimmering hand in front of

him and then back to Nex's toothy grin. There was something about him that made Kalum feel at ease in spite of himself. He reached out, and his hand passed through Nex's as he went to grip it.

"No more joyrides, but if you're going to play Henkan you need to train. I can train your body at night while you rest. Only at home. No field trips. I promise," Nex said.

Kalum considered Nex's proposal. In truth he felt better than he ever had. Stronger, leaner, and faster.

"Fine," he said.

The wind started to howl and a barrage of sleet hit him square in the chest.

"Nex, how am I supposed to get down from here?" Kalum asked, shivering and looking around over the rooftops of his street.

"How am I supposed to get down?" he asked again, a bit louder this time. Silence was his only reward again.

"Nex, are you there?"

When Nex spoke it was almost as if Kalum could feel a smile behind the words.

"Kal, it's been ten years since you said my name. It is good to hear you say it again."

"You know I could get us down," said Nex. "But I'd prefer it if we did it together. If you want to get down, just jump and your body will do the rest."

Kalum peered over the edge of the roof to the ground below. He could see the sleet disperse as it hit the ground and he imagined his head doing the same. There was nothing to break his fall, not a hedge or a conveniently located stack of cardboard boxes. His neighbour's roof was another fifteen feet away, and even on his best day he wasn't capable of making a jump of that distance. It was madness. Just like everything else had been in the last few days.

"It's the definition of a leap of faith, Kal."

Lightning sparked, making Kalum jump as it stabbed at the sky. The deep rumble of thunder followed it like a growling animal stalking him.

"Trust me," Nex said.

Kalum closed his eyes and felt all his frustration and emotions ball together into a swirling knot in his stomach. He felt as if he could hear rain like a drumroll egging him on.

"I won't let you get hurt. If you die, I die."

Kalum stood up, his eyes still. He was cold, confused and mildly terrified, a cocktail of negative energy and emotion, but he realised that for the first time in a long time he felt complete. It felt as if he had been vacuum-packed sealed and compressed and crammed into a small box to contain him. Freedom and possibility filled his mind and he felt clarity clear the fog that had lined it for as long as he could remember. He opened his eyes, took a step, then another quicker and surer one. Breaking out into a run he threw himself off the edge of the roof and the rushing air against the skin of his face made it ripple and spread into a wide grin.

He bridged the gap between the two houses in a single leap, his fingers grasping at the edge of the worn grey slate tiles of the neighbouring roof, while the balls of his feet rested against the wall. Without thought, he released his grip and turned back toward his home using his legs to launch him at a lower trajectory, back like a coiled spring. He repeated this movement at the other end to bring himself within twenty feet of the ground. Now the oak tree that stood in between the two houses was within reach. With a final leap, he was hugging the main trunk and shim-mying down to the ground below.

He looked up to where he had started on the roof and felt the adrenaline coursing in his system crest and surge. Punching the air in excitement he let out a whoop of elation. The rush was so all-consuming that he didn't notice the man with the scarred face documenting his every move.

23

WAX ON, WAX OFF

He stood staring up at the side of his house, the rain now pelting down. His face stung as it pummelled him.

"How? How did I do that?" he asked.

Nex materialised next to him like a genie escaping from his bottle. He had a gleeful, satisfied expression on his face.

"Told you!" he said. "That was awesome! Better than any of those other guys in your comics!"

Once Kalum caught his breath he lent against the trunk of the tree, glad for the shelter the branches gave against the downpour.

"Nex... What are you? Where did you come from?" he whispered.

Nex popped out of thin air and landed on a low-lying branch. He sat with his legs crossed and his cape in his lap. He slouched forward and rested his head in his cupped hands.

"Truth is, I have no idea. I'm in here with you. I've been here since the beginning. Even when you couldn't hear me, I was still here," Nex said. "Where'd you come from?"

Kalum made a face at the question and pushed off the trunk to move to the front door, sticking to the shadows. Standing there he could hear his mother talking to Frannie and Reese. One of them passed the door and he scarpered for cover in case they glanced outside. Looking up he saw the window to his room still open.

"How am I going to get up there?" he asked Nex.

"Same way we got down. By working together. Look at the wall and concentrate."

Kalum did as he was asked. He pushed out all other sensory inputs. The patter of the rain began to fade, and he ignored the water soaking thorough his clinging clothes as his field of vision narrowed. There was a ratcheting pressure behind his right eye. It ramped up and then was gone. He looked again at the wall, his vision tinged blue. The coloured threads he'd seen before flickered in his vision again and then vanished. All that was left were hand and foot holds as images on the wall. A light construct of himself separated from his body, charging at the wall and scaling it like a reptile. The lock to the front door clicked open and Kalum saw Frannie through the glass. He was running to the wall and was half way up before he had time to process what was happening, and was back in his room before she had shut the door behind her.

Sitting wide-eyed in his bed, he whispered, "How did I do that?"

"Accelerated training and muscle memory," came Nex's reply. "That's not the first time you've jumped off that roof, not the first time you've climbed that wall either."

Kalum looked at Nex bewildered.

"I think I'd remember something like that."

"Fire up that thing on your arm," said Nex.

Kalum offered his thumbprint and the TRIST fired up.

He looked at Nex expectantly.

"Open up the video playback files."

Kalum did as he was asked and scrolled through a series of unfamiliar thumbnails.

"What the—?" Kalum muttered as he clicked on the files. They were projected above the screen and he cued them up for continuous play.

He watched the first file open to show himself in the living room. The lights were dim and the blinds drawn. He was watching his mother's Bruce Lee movie collection in the totally immersive three-dimensional setting. It was one of his mother's favourites; "Enter the Dragon". He watched the scene unfold, having seen it over a hundred times growing up. Kalum watched as he stood and inserted himself into the martial artist's role, moving his body in perfect synchrony, matching every punch, kick and strike.

"I told you I've been training your body while you slept," Nex said, the construct jumping up and down with barely repressed excitement.

The clip changed and he was on top of the house, right at the roof's edge in a handstand position. A gasp escaped his lips as he saw himself shift to hold his entire body weight on one arm. It shook with the effort and suddenly gave way. He disappeared from view as he fell off the roof, a loud crash heard in the background a few seconds later.

Nex let out a nervous laugh.

"Um, no harm done right?"

Kalum shook his head in disbelief.

"So this is the reason I've been waking up feeling like I've been run over by a steamroller every morning then?" he said, scanning through the other video files which showed more of the same. It felt unnerving to watch his body on autopilot, like watching someone else's memories.

"Nex, these Scorps are bad news. We should just let the Enforcers take care of them."

"Enforcers? We've done more in two days of patrolling than they've done all year," said Nex, turning on him. "No Steel Falcon means no Henkan and no getting the sketchbook back," he said, crossing his arms in front of him.

Kalum could feel the fire in Nex's words. He looked at his back and put a hand out to rest on his shoulder. His hand passed right through the light construct and he shook his head at his foolishness.

"Nex, we'll get ourselves killed."

Nex turned back, a mischievous grin crossing his face. He stood up and struck a pose.

"Well they haven't had much luck so far. And that was before we were working together."

Kalum could see no other option, and knew his choices were limited. He shook his head in defeat.

"Fine," he said.

Nex leapt into the air and did a backflip.

"Yes! I knew the Kal I knew was somewhere in there," Nex said, punching the air. "We'll need to put together a costume," he said, rubbing his hands together.

"No way I'm wearing a cape," Kalum said. He reached down to pick up the Henkan gear that was still strewn over the floor and held it in front of him. He placed the helmet on and moved to his room mirror. His eyes shone vivid blue in the reflection, causing a glare. Kalum pulled the face-guard down and regarded himself.

Nex looked at Kalum's reflection in the mirror.

"Hey! The Henkan gear has worked so far as a disguise. It's not as flamboyant as mine and doesn't have nearly enough red, but it's a start, and the cape is negotiable."

Nex turned to Kalum and held out his fist. Kalum

mimed bumping fists and they looked each other in the eye.
Suddenly the edges of Nex's construct body sparked and
blurred, losing its form. Nex placed his hands on his head
and Kalum wondered if this was how he looked when he
was having a panic attack.

"Nex! What's wrong?" he asked.

"I can't sustain this level of awareness for too long. An
hour is the most I can manage."

He looked up at Kalum and before blinking out of view
he tried to speak.

"Don't tell Frannie. You can't—"

His voice crackled and was replaced by static, cutting
him off. Nex's body flickered once and then was gone, like
someone had switched him off. Kalum heard a noise behind
him and turned to see that his door was half open and
Reese standing there. The sight of his brother made him
jump and he fell back against his mirror. The back of the
Henkan helmet struck the surface, sending a jagged crack
running down its midline. Kalum turned to gauge the
damage and stared at his own splintered image.

"Reese! Are you spying on me?!" Kalum demanded as
his brother entered. If Reese had heard him talking to Nex
he didn't let on. He tapped the top of the helmet with his
knuckles and grabbed his brother by the shoulders.

"Looks good on you, little brother."

Kalum saw him smile and looked at them standing side
by side, reflected in the cracked mirror. Standing next to
Reese he suddenly felt small and vaguely ridiculous. Reese
turned him around so they were face to face.

"Kal. What you did today in the Arena was unbelievable.
Even if you didn't need to play to keep you in Trinity I'd still
tell you to join the team. I know Nathan and his bonehead

friends are jerks, but you've got me. With everything else going on it might give you something else to focus on."

His smile widened and he gave Kalum another playful tap on the helmet.

"Plus, the Keeper gets all the girls. Lexi might look at you differently when she see's you wearing that uniform," Reese said.

The statement caught Kalum off guard. He lifted the visor and rolled his eyes at his brother.

"I've known Lexi forever. She's like a sister to me." He meant the words, he knew for certain that he did. Yet something inside him felt odd when he thought about her like that.

"Sure thing, stud. What about that new girl, A.J?" Reese continued, poking him in the ribs. To this Kalum couldn't even formulate a response. He was glad of the helmet otherwise his brother would have seen the colour rising to his cheeks.

"Come on! What have you got to lose?" Reese said, mistaking his silence for indecision.

Kalum looked at himself in the mirror and muttered, "Only my sanity."

He turned back to his brother. "Fine, I'm in," he said.

Reese clapped him on the back.

"Good stuff. This is going to be great. We'll be in the Arena together," he said.

Kalum took off the helmet and looked up at his brother.

"I'm still mad at you for not telling me that you knew. Knew about... what I was like. It actually makes what you did with my meds worse."

Reese nodded. "Look, Kal. I am sorry. I really am. But I can only apologise so many times. Now that you'll be playing you'll see what I mean about the pressure in the Arena."

Kalum shrugged but said nothing.

"I tell you what, you forgive me and I won't tell Mum about you going all Bruce Lee."

Kalum stood bolt upright. For a horrifying moment he thought Reese knew about what Nex had been doing at night.

"Wh... what do you mean?" he managed with only a slight stutter.

Reese grabbed him by the shoulders and turned him back to face his reflection.

"The mirror didn't stand a chance." He clapped Kalum on the back and left, shutting the door behind him.

The events of the day caught up with Kalum in that instant, and the pressure of fatigue made him feel sluggish. He threw the helmet to the side and dropped himself onto the bed.

It was four a.m. when he woke up in a sheen of cold sweat. He looked around, disorientated at first, realising that he wasn't in his bedroom. He sat up on the couch and his feet found the floor. He tried to stand but his legs felt like they had been through a shredder. He collapsed back into the couch, wincing.

"Nex?" he said, groaning into the darkness. "My body feels like a building fell on it."

Nex blinked into view.

"What do you expect? I'm training you, Daniel San!" Nex jumped into the air, kicking an imaginary foe as he did.

Kalum's face wrinkled further in puzzlement.

"Daniel who?"

Nex fixed Kalum with a look of shock and horror.

"It's from Karate Kid. Please tell me you remember watching that with Mum? Wax on, wax off?" he said, waving his hands in the air in circular movements.

"No, sorry," said Kalum with a shrug. He didn't let on how jarring it felt to hear Nex call his mother "Mum".

"Well once we finish all Bruce Lee's movies, we'll watch that one. It's a classic. Then we'll move on to the Jackie Chan stuff, then Jet Li! Man oh man this is gonna be fun!"

Kalum groaned, trying to rub the sleep from his face.

"You might want to give yourself a minute. We've just finished a Bruce Lee Marathon. All his films at ten times the speed. Mimicking every fight scene, honing every move."

"Great," Kal said, trying and failing to stand.

"Just give me a second," said Nex, and he furrowed his brow in concentration.

Kalum felt a needling sensation spread throughout his body, leaving his muscles warm and with renewed energy.

He braced himself for the pain to rip through his legs as he got to his feet and was surprised when he found they felt strong and steady.

"Thanks Nex," he said.

Nex bowed and grinned widely.

He took a step forward and something fell from his pocket. His reflexes kicked in and he snatched it out of the air before it hit the floor. In his hand he held the metal band he'd taken from the Sentech safehouse.

"Nex?" he said, looking at the band. "Do you know what this is? Why did you take us to get it?"

"No idea, Kal," Nex said as he floated up to stare at the band as well. "It wasn't me who took us to that place. Not on purpose, anyway."

Kalum pocketed the band with a sigh. It seemed like the

more answers he got, the more he realised how much he didn't know about what was going on with him.

With uncharacteristic cat-like stealth he padded up the stairs, making a beeline for his room. Something made him pause outside his father's room. He heard a slight creak, like wood bowing under a weight, come from inside. He eased the door open and saw his father lying still in his bed with tubes of all manner snaking their way between his body and the various machines that kept his major organs functioning.

The room seemed out of place from the rest of the house. There was a smell to it that scratched your throat at night, and the machines gave such a symphony of soft beeps and a neon lightshow of digital readouts that it meant it was never truly dark. He felt an urge to be near his father, and much as he hated the room and all it represented he didn't fight it.

Lying in the bed, his father was wrapped like a Pharaoh ready to be mummified. Only his face was visible and the lighting made him look even more pallid. An odd sensation gripped Kalum. He felt the muscles of his arm cord and he was almost overcome by the urge to strike his father. His hand quivered above the bed and he fought to control it.

Nex appeared and stared wide-eyed at Kalum.

"What're you doing?!" Nex demanded.

Kalum shook his head and brought his arm back down to his side.

"Nothing. I... I don't know."

He and Nex looked at each other, the concern mirrored in their faces. In the bed, Owen stirred, his face twisting into a grimace.

"We'd better go," Nex said.

Kalum turned to leave and jumped as a flash of lightning outside assaulted his eyes. He counted until he heard the rumble that followed and realised it had been closer than he'd thought. The second bolt lit the room once more and Kalum gasped as the light silhouetted a shadowy figure perched outside his father's bedroom window ledge. Even though he couldn't see the details of the person's face he could see the scar across his mouth. Kalum rushed to the window and when the light flashed again, the figure was gone. A second later, he spotted him standing on the opposite side of the road, looking up at the house. Kalum's fingers curled around the window frame.

"Let's go!" Nex shouted. "Open that window and let's get after him. He's gotta be a Scorp."

Kalum felt his muscles tense and he was about to fling the window open, and himself out into the cold night, when he saw the light in the upper landing turn on, followed by the creak of floorboards. He glanced back out onto the street and saw the person had disappeared. Just in time he managed to squeeze in behind his father's cupboard, vanishing from sight as his mother entered the room. From his concealed position he watched as she drew the curtains closed and sat on the end of the bed. She sat there in silence for a minute, then reached down and smoothed her husband's hair away from his face.

"Your sons are strong like you, Owen," she said, staring down at him. "In different ways, but both strong." She turned away, biting her bottom lip, and closed her eyes.

"God, Owen, we all really need you right now, so if you're going to pull some kind of miracle, now's the time."

She smiled and it was with such sadness that Kalum felt his heart break a little. Nadine gathered herself and flattened out the creases on the bed sheets. She adjusted three of the machines attached to her husband and gave him a long kiss on the forehead before retreating back to her room.

Kalum waited until his mother's soft footfalls totally disappeared and ventured out. He looked out of the window but whoever had been looking in on them was nowhere to be seen. He cursed and banged his fist on the window ledge. He heard his father stir, so he ducked out of the room.

"What do they want?" Kalum asked, slumping back on his bed. "Why would the Scorps be here?"

"Well, we did beat the snot out of a whole bunch of them, Kal," Nex replied with a self-satisfied smirk on his face.

Kalum's hand touched his wrist where he'd had the hospital ID tag. He saw a flashback and felt the sensation of the tag being ripped free.

"Maybe they're coming after us," Nex said. "All the more reason for us to take the fight to them."

Kalum looked at Nex and was about to speak when Nex's image glitched and fizzled.

"I guess we're both tired. We'll figure it out in the morning," Kalum said, but Nex had already vanished.

BREAKFAST the next day was a tense affair. Nadine was watching him, but doing her best to make it look as if she wasn't, her hands curled around her mug as she took measured sips.

Their TRISTs let out a tone and started to broadcast the news of another Scorp attack on more Sentech Medical Centres. These attacks were closer than the last, and seemingly more brutal. Nadine muted hers and then reached over to do the same to Kalum's.

"Are we going to talk about last night?" she finally said.

Kalum pushed his bowl aside and took a deep breath.

When Nex appeared in between them, Kalum nearly fell off his chair with shock.

"What's wrong?" asked Nadine. She stared through where Nex was.

"Er... nothing," said Kalum, pretending to check on the chair. "The leg is loose."

"Oh man, you should have seen the look on your face!" Nex said, chuckling, his mirth too much for him to contain.

"We okay?" Nadine asked, and Kalum struggled to focus his attention on her. Kalum glared at Nex, who gave a wink and blinked out of view.

"I'm sorry you feel that way," Nadine said, pushing her food away, the hurt obvious in her tone.

"No. No. I'm not angry with you," Kalum said, realising she had misunderstood the look on his face.

"No, I take it back, I am mad you didn't tell me about all this, but I *can* understand why," he said.

Nadine relaxed, the tension in her face vanishing. She reached over and squeezed his hand.

"I've only ever wanted to keep you safe. Now that you understand, you'll take your meds? You'll carry on with the therapy?" she asked, her eyes starting to glisten as she spoke.

Kalum nodded, unable to speak the lie he was telling.

"Don't worry about him," Reese said. "It's everyone else in the Arena who needs to watch themselves. The Walker brothers are going to be unstoppable." He loped down the stairs, two long Henkan kit bags slung over his shoulders. Reese tossed one on the floor and it slid to a stop by Kalum's feet.

"When the Scouts see us both playing at the training session today, maybe they'll pick us both up," Reese said with a grin. "A package deal."

Nadine stood up so fast the chair behind her almost toppled over.

"Wait... You're going to play?" she asked. "I don't know if that's a good idea, Kal."

The front door opened and Lucas strode in. He looked at his family standing in silence in the kitchen and a puzzled frown appeared on his face. He shrugged and grabbed a mug and helped himself to some coffee.

"Did you see what those Scorps are doing?" Lucas said, cursing. "Medical Centres? What on earth's wrong with them? I hope that vigilante beats the he—" He took in the tense tableau of his family seated at the table, stopped talking, and pulled up a chair. "

What's going on?" he asked.

The three of them all started to speak at once, leaving Lucas looking bemused. Nadine eventually raised her voice loud enough to drown out her sons.

"Kalum wants to play Henkan," she almost bellowed.

Lucas looked to Kalum and back to the kit bag on the floor.

"That's great," he said, with a broad grin on his face, which disappeared when he caught Nadine's eye. "Isn't it?"

Kalum reached over and grabbed Nadine's half-drunk mug and drained the remaining dark liquid.

"You drink coffee now lad?" he asked. Kalum flashed him a smile and scooped the bag off the floor. He gave Nadine a quick peck on the cheek and he and Reese left for school.

"I guess times are changing," Lucas said, taking the empty mug from the table.

"I guess they are..." said Nadine, watching her sons leave.

24

VISITING VIOLENCE

The brothers paused for a moment outside the house. Transports were whizzing by noiselessly on the busy street, their neon lights leaving afterimages in the still grey morning.

"Hey 'lil bro, you'd best make tracks or you're gonna be late," Reese said, throwing Kalum his Henkan kit bag. The heavy bag knocked the wind out of Kalum but he hoisted it up onto his back like a pack mule.

"Wait, what do you mean I'm gonna be late? What about you?" Kalum asked.

Reese shot him a half smile and sighed.

"Not me, I've gotta get new kit. Remember my spare gauntlet is busted up," Reese said, flashing Kalum an accusatory look. "I've got to be on top form at practice today. If the Scouts like what they see then I'm going big time, and we'll be set for life."

"Turns out Scorp skulls are tougher than you'd think," Nex said in his head.

Reese jogged away in the opposite direction, waving as he went. The school Transport whooshed past Kalum as he turned the corner. He could see Nathan and the Burton twins at the back, staring at him out of the window. Nathan lifted his sketchpad into view. As their eyes locked, it was as if time slowed down and he was able to look at the scene around him like a photograph. He saw the faces of the other children on the bus, each sitting in their designated place. He saw the seat that was reserved for him, the one he barely ever seemed to sit in. He saw Lexi shouting at the Transport driver, with Jun and Casey trying to stop her from visiting violence upon him.

Then the world snapped back into normal speed. Kalum blinked, feeling disorientated and nauseous at the same time. After a beat he started a half-hearted sprint after the Transport but gave up after a few steps, feeling winded. He looked to his wrecked bike chained to the front of the house, and sighed. An alert popped up on his TRIST stating he'd missed the transport.

"Kalum," the TRIST said. "You're going to be late. This will be your fourth infringement. Trinity rules state that this will invoke disciplinary—"

"I know," he muttered, silencing the device.

Nex appeared suddenly like a hi-tech genie.

"There's a quicker way," he said and pointed up.

Kalum looked at him in slack-jawed astonishment.

"Wait... No... Are you telling me I can... Can I fly?" Kalum whispered.

Nex burst into a laughing fit that wracked his body. Kalum looked at him sheepishly.

"Oh shut up," he said, but Nex showed no sign of letting up.

"Shut up!" he said, this time with a little more anger in his voice. A Sentech road worker in grubby dark overalls walked past at that moment and gave him a sideways glance.

Kalum pretended to be talking into his TRIST and walked out of earshot. By this time Nex had recovered and was wiping simulated tears from his eyes.

"No man, you can't fly, but you can climb and jump," he said. "Just look at the wall and concentrate, just like last night."

Kalum threw his hand up in frustration and started walking toward Trinity.

"I thought you had a real solution for me, Nex. I haven't got time for this now," he snapped.

Nex teleported so that he was directly in Kalum's path. He put his glowing hand up to stop him.

"If you take a direct line across the rooftops it's much shorter than if you go by ground level, even by transport."

Kalum eyes narrowed, dubious about Nex's claims.

Nex sighed. "Fine, let me show you," he said, and floated closer. He touched the point of his index finger onto Kalum's forehead and Kalum felt an instant of white-hot heat like a signal flare. He threw his head back and had to lean against the wall to keep his balance. In the right upper corner of his vision was a birds' eye view of his street and the path to the school. A red and a blue line showed both routes and proved Nex's point.

"How?" Kalum asked.

Nex shrugged. "I don't think I actually needed to touch your forehead to show you, but I thought it would look cooler."

Another alert sounded from the TRIST, more urgent this time. Kalum slammed his palm down on it and the noise stopped.

"All TRISTs are property of Sentech Corporation. Damaging or modifying Sentech property is a punishable offence," the automatic shock warning intoned.

Kalum moved to a secluded corner, and after making sure he didn't have an audience, he stared at the side of the building. As had happened the previous night, he watched a doppelgänger of himself appear at his side. It sprinted at the wall and scaled its entire thirty-foot facade with graceful ease.

"Okay. Let's do this," he said, and took off at a full sprint. He was up the wall in moments, but he didn't stop. He gave chase after his guide, his shoes sending the gravel and debris flying as he did. As he neared the roof edge he felt the surge of adrenaline as the panic started to rise in his chest. Then it felt as if that force was diverted and instead of caging and crippling him, it flowed through him. His speed picked up and he closed the gap to the image in front of him. Then he threw his body off the edge, following the apparition of himself. His fingers grabbed at the opposite roof and his feet contacted the wall. He pulled himself up and was off again. With each jump he cleared greater gaps and traversed the rooftops with ease. He was now moving at the same pace as his light-show guide.

He stopped and panted to catch his breath. Looking up he realised that the route he had taken had brought him around the back of the school. With one final leap he was on the side of the building, hanging from a window ledge. Chancing a look down he saw School Transports start to pull up. A crowd gathered, unaware of what hung fifty-foot above them. With no choice, Kalum began to climb. He used his shirt-sleeve to wipe the sweat from his brow and hauled himself onto the roof. Locating the access door he tried the handle. It wouldn't budge. He strained and tugged but the door showed no sign of giving any ground. He could hear the bustle of pupils at the front of the building as they entered in single file. Lying on his front and peering over the edge he saw Nathan and the other Henkan team members bypassing the line to enter in front of those already queuing.

"You should have stopped!"

Kalum turned his head and saw Lexi still berating the Transport driver.

"There was a stop right there and you bypassed it," she carried on. The driver was trying his best to avoid her gaze, but she was unrelenting.

"Don't think I didn't see Lancaster hand you those Credits. You're just a complete—"

She didn't get a chance to finish her sentence. Seeing Cooper stomping over to the bus, Jun and Casey strong-armed her off the Transport and towards the school entrance.

Kalum typed a message to them on his TRIST and watched as they all checked the message and in synchrony look up at him. They tried to rush the queue, but only Casey with his higher academia badge on his lapel was given some preferential treatment, but not much. Kalum paced by the roof, kicking at loose stones.

Nex appeared. He looked haggard, with parts of him fading in and out of sight.

"Told you," he said panting.

"Are you okay?" Kalum asked, concerned.

Nex smiled weakly. "Yeah, I just overdid it. Sharing that knowledge with you must have burnt me o—"

He vanished before he could finish his sentence. The rattle of the door handle got Kalum's attention. With a click it opened and his three friends practically fell through the opening.

They stopped and stared at him. He figured he must have looked a dishevelled mess. Kalum tucked in his shirt and tried to brush the majority of dust and grit off his uniform.

"How...?" asked Jun, looking around.

"We just saw you outside your house..." Casey finished.

"We've been trying to call you! What the heck happened in the Arena yesterday? We saw you take out the Burton twins and Lancaster! Were you using an Aug?" Lexi asked, her questions coming out like a torrent, one flowing into another. Kalum held up a hand to quieten her.

"No, no, no. I'd never use an Aug. You know that," Kalum said. "Listen, I've got something to tell you guys." He paused, considering his next words carefully.

"Something's happening to me, and you're all going to think that I've lost my mind.'

His friends exchanged puzzled looks.

"There's something different about me. Ever since Nathan knocked me in the pool and I... well, ever since I died. I just didn't know it until now."

Lexi looked ashen face. "Don't say that. You didn't die," she said quietly.

"Lexi, does the name Nex mean anything to you?"

Lexi thought for a moment. She paced the roof, clicking her fingers.

"Yeah... Where do I know that name from?"

She stopped suddenly and spun to face him.

"Wasn't the name of your imaginary friend when you were a kid?"

"Yup," said Kal. "Turns out he's not so imaginary. What-ever Nathan and the medical crew did brought him back. He helped me in the Arena yesterday, and... he's the one who's been rounding up Scorps."

"Kal, by he... do you mean you?" Casey asked.

"Well... the two of us," Kalum said.

Casey raised his eyebrows and let out a small cough whilst glancing at Lexi and Jun.

"Case, you're the smartest of the four of us. Tell me a logical explanation of how I got up here, before school even opened." Kalum asked.

Casey had no response. His brow scrunched as his mind ran through any and all possible scenarios, but he drew a blank.

"I ran here. I ran across the rooftops and jumped and climbed my way here," Kalum said. "I almost don't believe it myself."

Kalum looked at his friends' but they seemed reluctant to meet his eyes. Instead they fidgeted and squirmed on the spot.

"Nex?" Kalum called. With a pop only audible to him, Nex appeared, still weary but a bit brighter. "Have you got enough juice for a demo."

"Just about," Nex said with a wide grin, in spite of his voice sounding mostly like static.

"Kal?" Lexi ventured. "Maybe we should call your mum? Or Lucas, or maybe Frannie?"

"Just watch..." Kalum said. He felt Nex's power flow through him and he took a deep breath. Then he exploded into a series of martial arts kicks and strikes, finishing with a standing backwards somersault.

"And how about this?" he asked breathlessly as he jumped onto his hands and walked on them to the edge of the roof.

"Kal!" Lexi shouted and they rushed to him. Kalum grunted and shifted his weight so that he was using only one hand. He took in their slack-jawed expressions from his inverted position and allowed himself a chuckle. He felt Nex join in in his head as he switched hands.

"Okay! Okay!" Lexi said. "We get it! We believe you."

Kalum vaulted back onto his feet and was met by a high five from Jun.

"Dude! This is freaking awesome!" Jun said.

"Most interesting," Casey said as he scratched his chin and regarded Kalum with a clinical eye.

"Hey! What are you doing up here?" a voice called from the doorway.

Elliot Sparrow stepped out to join them on the roof.

"Hey, everything alright?" he asked.

"Yes, Sir. Kal wasn't feeling too well and needed some fresh air," Lexi said, thinking fast.

Sparrow looked at Kalum and held his gaze for longer than comfortable.

"Is that true, Kal?" Sparrow asked in an even tone.

"Yes. Yes, Sir," he replied, eyes fixed firmly on the ground.

Sparrow looked at each of them in turn and scratched the stubble on his face.

"Okay, well you'd all better get inside. If Mr Cooper finds you out here he might decide to throw you off the top rather than bring you in," he said, sounding like he was only half joking.

As they followed Sparrow back into the school, Kalum whispered to them.

"Come to the Arena at break time and then you'll see more."

Sparrow escorted them down the stairwells and corridors of Trinity until they reached their classroom. He held the door open for them and their classmates stared as they took their seats. Mr Barker nodded to Sparrow, who smiled and shut the door behind them.

"Wait," said Barker before they could take their seats.

"Even though you're not technically late for my lesson, you are the last ones here. Up at the front," he said, and smirked as he indicated they should stand at the front.

"You know the rules," he said. "If any of you answer incorrectly then you'll be in here on your break."

Kalum suppressed a stab of anger. Barker may dress this up as something for his pupils' own good, but everyone knew he just wanted a dogsbody to run errands for him in between lessons. Lexi didn't bother hiding her feelings and scowled at the grey-haired teacher.

"Sir, I have to see Mr Macintosh at break," Kalum said.

"We'll you won't be going anywhere unless you all answer my quiz."

"But—"

"But nothing!" Barker snapped.

"Mr Danvers. You can go first. Name Sentech's competitor Corporations and their geographical base of operations please," asked Barker, making himself comfortable in his well-worn chair.

"What?" burst out Jun. "He's the genius, so why are you giving him the easy question?"

A glare from Barker silenced him instantly. He then turned his gaze on the rest of the class to stifle a building ripple of giggles.

Nex appeared in front of Kalum. He was just an outline, not completely rested, but whole enough that Kalum had to concentrate on not staring at him.

"Get him to pick you," Nex said. "Tell him to let everyone else off."

"Why?" Kalum said out loud.

Barker fixed him in his sights like a predator.

"Another outburst like that Mr Walker and you'll be missing break for the next week."

"Come on, Kal. Trust me on this," Nex said. "The only way you're getting your book back is if you show up at the Arena at break for Henkan training."

"How about two weeks?" Kalum blurted out.

Barker's head snapped back to Kalum and he rose from his chair.

"Let the others off and I'll take their questions. If I fail the quiz, I'll miss two weeks worth of break time."

Barker smiled wolfishly. "Mr Walker, I believe your mouth is overestimating your knowledge of Corporation history, but by all means, go ahead." He gestured for Lexi, Casey and Jun to take their seats. Next to him Nex focused and a silver light strand appeared in front of him. Kalum touched it as it neared and his head swam from the jolt of information.

"Carry on Mr Walker, please," said Barker.

"Kaneko based in North America, Quantril Industries based in Singapore, Zenton in Russia, Janus Technologies in China, and Rayyan in India," Kalum said. Nex nodded in encouragement.

"What are their revenue streams?" Barker asked, leaning in.

"Pharmaceuticals, Robotics, Gene therapy and manipulation, sustainable energy resources, and aerospace engineering," Kalum said, the words coming to his lips without thought.

"What do you know about IMB?" Barker asked.

In front of him Nex started to glitch out, his words sounding as if they were being spoken underwater. Kalum's teeth started chattering and he felt a tightness around his jaw.

"IMB was a Corporation," he said.

"What happened to it?" Barker asked, sensing Kalum's

discomfort. Kalum was starting to feel lightheaded now.

"IMB was one of the first Corporations. Its base of operations was taken over by force by Sentech founders who took over their subsidiaries, and that's why each Corporation is allowed to have its own military force now," Kalum said.

"Hmmm," Barker said. "You know, Walker, maybe you were actually paying attention in my class after all."

Kalum made a move towards his seat.

"Not so fast, Mr Walker," said Barker with a glint in his eye. "Can you tell me the number of indentured Corporate MEMBERS each company has?"

Casey tried to mouth the answer to Kalum but Barker caught his eye and he shut his mouth.

"Quantril, one hundred and thirty three million; Kaneko, seventy two million; Nikonov, one hundred and twenty two million; Janus, five hundred and sixty eight million; and Rayyan, six hundred and fifty two million," Kalum said, rattling off the figures.

"How are you doing this?" Barker asked with irritation as he checked Kalum's figures on his TRIST. Then he looked up, a malignant smile spreading slowly across his face.

"And what about Sentech? How many indentured Corporation members does Sentech have?"

Nex started to answer but his form came to a juddering halt and then faded from view. Kalum's eyes scanned the room. Casey was starting to mouth something, but Barker flung a pointed finger in his direction, not bothering to take his eyes off Kalum.

"Zero." Cooper stood in the doorway. He looked uncharacteristically happy, but Kalum could see that his smile was forced and stitched in place. He stepped into the classroom and everyone shrank into their seats.

"Of course the answer is zero, Mr Barker," Cooper said. "

All those in Sentech know how lucky they are. None of them would ever consider themselves indentured."

Barker gestured for Cooper to enter. The heavy-set Headmaster trudged past Barker and Kalum and sat in the teacher's chair.

"Sorry to interrupt your class," he said. "As I said, membership of the Sentech family isn't a burden. It's about giving back to those who clothe you, feed you, and educate you."

He turned towards Kalum.

"It's about showing gratitude and doing the right thing," he said, putting his fingertips together and trying to look sagely.

"Do you have anything to tell me, Walker?"

The look on Cooper's face made it clear what answer he expected. Kalum was cornered, and Cooper knew it. Even without Nathan holding on to the book for leverage, there was only one real choice.

"Yes, Sir," said Kalum, standing up. "I accept my place." He caught Lexi's eye and she looked back in bewilderment. Cooper launched himself to his feet with a briskness that was surprising for a man his size. He stomped across, moving Barker out of the way with an outstretched arm. He dug around in his pocket and pulled out a golden lapel pin. He fastened it to Kalum's jacket and then slammed his meaty palm against it for good measure.

"Excellent." He leaned in and whispered. "You're not such a leech after all."

"Class. Put your hands together for Trinity's newest and youngest Henkan Keeper."

A sea of gaping mouths and shocked expressions looked back at them. A look from Cooper triggered a slow, disjointed round of applause. Jun jumped to his feet and pumped his fist in the air.

"Oh yeah!" he shouted.

He sat down sheepishly but didn't stop grinning.

Cooper made to leave, pausing only at the doorway.

"Of course, this is assuming you pass the initiation test this afternoon." Cooper paused and looked around the class. "Scouts from the national league are here looking to recruit players. I am expecting spotless behaviour."

He took a moment to allow his eyes to communicate the gravity of his words as they panned from face to face. With a self-satisfied grunt he left, slamming the door behind him.

Word spread through Trinity like a virus. The transition between classrooms was a mix of high fives and smiles from people he had never spoken to before, and poorly-hidden jealous scowls. Once he'd had time to recharge, Nex lapped it up. Even though only visible to Kalum, he strutted down the corridors in between Kalum and Lexi looking extremely pleased with himself. Jun was riding the high, arm permanently draped over Kalum's shoulder, laughing and waving to people that looked their way. Casey and Lexi kept quiet, exchanging the occasional concerned glance.

Something hard slammed into his shoulder, sending Kalum spinning and clanging against the rows of lockers. He turned, his anger flaring, and saw Nathan and the Burton twins glaring at him. His vision tinged red again and Nex appeared by his side, crouched in a fighting stance.

"I've heard you've grown a pair," Nathan growled, reaching out and touching the pin on Kalum's lapel. "You can have your book at practice. If you show up."

A light construct doppelgänger appeared and Kalum watched as it showed him the most efficiently brutal way of neutralising the boys. He swallowed back his rage and his vision cleared.

"I'll be there," Kalum said, trying to make his voice just as hard but failing miserably.

All of their TRISTs sounded an alert, and Nathan looked up from his with a malignant smile.

"Good," he said. "Now's the time to put up or shut up."

25

THE STING OF BETRAYAL

Red faced and breathless Kalum stumbled into the Arena. It hadn't been so easy to navigate Trinity's corridors now he was semi-famous. His mouth dropped as he craned his neck to look up at the legion of spectators in the amphitheatre-like seating. A ripple of noise ran through them as they caught sight of the diminutive Walker brother walk into the Arena. The team were already stretching in a semi circle around Macintosh, who was screaming his 'words of encouragement' to them. His face was etched with permanent scowl lines and he had a voice that sounded like he'd swallowed a wasps' nest. Macintosh watched and waited as the elderly groundsman slowly went about setting out cones on the playing field. Not bothering to conceal his impatience, Macintosh marched over and grabbed the remaining stack and quickly put them in their place.

"Listen mate. I know you're new and clearly getting on a bit, but here at Trinity we expect things to be done quickly, alright?" he said, not caring that everyone heard him dressing down the old man. The groundsman kept his head low and pulled his cap down further. He turned towards

Macintosh and gave a small nod. On his green grey overalls was a name badge above the left breast pocket and the coach squinted to read it, making his face take on an even more rodent quality. Macintosh huffed and gave the old man a sarcastic thumbs up and shouted, "Thanks for nothing... Vincent."

The man called Vincent waved back and then picked up his equipment and moved away down the Arena, either oblivious to, or ignoring, the contemptuous tone, which served to irritate Macintosh even further.

The Henkan coach looked up from his tirade and locked eyes with Kalum. He pushed his way past the players and strode over in his direction with venom in his eyes.

Kalum looked around and took in his surroundings again. The sight of so many people scrutinising him gave him a sick knot in his stomach. He felt his hand start to shake, but Nex spoke to him in his head.

"You've got this. I'm here."

"What the hell is it with you two? You'd be late for your own funerals!" Macintosh spat. "Which may be sooner than you think if you arrive late for another one of my training sessions."

"Sorry boss," a voice said from behind Kalum.

Kalum spun around to see Reese jogging up behind him.

"Won't happen again. Right 'lil bro?" he said, putting his hand on his brother's shoulder. Just Reese's presence let the tension wash out of him, and Kalum gave a nod in agreement.

Macintosh leant in and glared at Reese.

"Listen to me carefully, boy,' he said, and turned Reese around and pointed to a box high in the Arena. "Up there sit some of the Scouts that look after the National teams, not just for Sentech but for the other Corporations. I called them here today to see you and Nathan play. If you let me down or embarrass me you can forget about ever playing in this or any other Arena again."

"Yes boss," Reese said, holding Macintosh's gaze. "I've got this."

"Fine. Walker... Senior... join the warm up," Macintosh said. He turned and grinned at Kalum without humour.

"Walker Junior, you still need to earn your place. Dead Runs for you."

Kalum looked confused as the colour drained from Reese's face.

"Sir. What ar—" he started to ask.

Macintosh whirled on him and advanced.

"You will run one-hundred lengths of this Arena." He stooped and picked up Kalum's kit bag in one hand.

"You will keep running until you reach that target," he continued, pointing down the pitch. He pulled the Henkan armour out of the bag, and thrust it into Kalum's chest, pushing him back even further. In his hand Macintosh held a small strap with a central metal disc. The coach fiddled with some settings on it and then slapped it on Kalum's wrist.

"If you stop running, that will... encourage you," he said, pointing at the strap. Kalum looked to Reese but his brother just stared back and shook his head helplessly.

"Let me be clear. You fail this endurance test and you can kiss this team, this school, this life goodbye.' He punctu- ated each point with a finger jab to the chest. Kalum looked around him, not sure if Macintosh was serious or not.

"Well? Are you waiting for an invitation?" Macintosh bellowed, spittle flying from his mouth. "Run, Walker! Run!"

Kalum set off at a jog and then a sprint. He covered the first ninety-yard length at a decent pace and silently thanked Nex for the endurance training he'd been putting his body through whilst his mind slept. By the sixteenth length he was flagging. His legs were lead pipes, refusing to leave the ground. His chest was on fire and he was almost certain he could taste the coppery tang of blood in his mouth.

"Nex," he gasped, "I can't do this."

"I... I'm doing what I can, but... this is hard," Nex replied, flickering in and out of view. "I can augment your strength and speed for a short time, but this endurance stuff means I have to be tinkering with your physiology the whole time."

The Arena around him spun and blurred and the effort of remaining vertical was almost more than he could manage. Completing the twentieth length he could barely see. He heard Macintosh's voice over a tannoy.

"I think the Titans new wannabe Keeper needs some encouragement. Don't you?"

The crowd rumbled its approval and Kalum was vaguely aware of the warning tone of the strap on his wrist. The jolt that hit him sent his whole body rigid and curled his toes inside his boots. He found himself face down on the pitch, not quite sure of how he got there.

"Come on, come on. Get up," Nex was shouting. Then he burst into view, so bright that Kalum shot to his feet.

"I can't. I—" Kalum started to say before another jolt ran from his wrist. It felt like when he'd been hit by Nathan with the Henkan ball when it was electrified, but on a much smaller scale.

"No, you're not done. You're not even in pain," said Nex.

Kalum looked up at Nex floating over him, his cape billowing behind him. He pulsed with power as he adjusted the thick goggles that were part of his costume.

Then Kalum realised that Nex was right. Nothing hurt.

The stabbing pain in his chest and the fire in his legs had disappeared.

"Maybe he needs more motivation?" came Macintosh's voice again.

Before the crowd could respond, he was running again. With each step his pace increased exponentially, the footfalls light and sure. The air rushed by as he tore through it. The rest of the Team stopped their training as they watched him devour the pitch lengths and even Macintosh was lost for words. He saw Casey and Jun in the crowd on their feet with so many others. Lexi was with them, mouthing something. Everything around her seemed to freeze as he read her lips.

"Slow down," they said.

With a concerted effort he dialled back a bit. He knew that Lexi was right; there was already enough suspicion around him, and the last thing he wanted was to add to it.

He reached the end and turned to run back the other way but the wrist strap let out a loud long tone and released with a click. The crowd erupted in a roar of cheering and hollering. He was aware the enormous Jumbotron that hung in the air in the centre of the Arena was flashing red and blaring music, but he couldn't make out what it said.

"How did you do that?" Kalum asked in the din.

Nex whizzed about, running in dizzying circles around Kalum.

"I stopped your muscles producing lactic acid. You could run for days!" he said, cartwheeling to one side. "Like I said, I can tinker with how your body works. You'll probably feel it tomorrow though," he added with a chuckle. He struck a pose and flexed his muscles.

"Looks like all I need is a bit of a charge to kick you into gear," he said, looking at the wrist strap as Kalum took it off.

Just like with the defibrillator, Kalum thought

Some of the crowd had spilled over the barrier, oblivious to Macintosh's screams and threats. Kalum saw Jun, Casey and Lexi rushing over to him. He was about to go to them but a soft touch on his shoulder turned him around. A.J stood backlit by the Arena floodlights, but the sparkle in her eyes made them seem dull in comparison.

"That was impressive. What's your secret?" she asked with a wink and a smile that made Kalum's knees feel weaker than the Dead Run had done.

"I... just ran..." Kalum managed to say.

"Smooth," Nex said with deadpan flatness.

A.J nodded, a mischievous grin touching her lips.

"Well that strategy seems to have worked well for you."

Around them Macintosh was grabbing students and shoving back in the direction of the stands, but the atmosphere was like a wasps' nest gone mad.

"Amazing!" Casey said, gasping for breath." How... the? Just how?"

Kalum looked at A.J and then back to his friends. Lexi's eyes narrowed and she regarded her with unconcealed disdain.

"Looks like everyone wants to be chummy now that you're a star, Kal," she said.

A.J flashed her a brilliant smile and fluttered her eyes.

"No need to get territorial sweetie," she said. "I was just saying hi."

Lexi's expression didn't change and she huffed and looked away.

"I can't believe it!" said Jun, looking around the Arena and pointing at the Jumbotron display. "That's amazing! You broke the record!"

"My record," said Nathan, walking up and putting his arm around A.J.

"Your brother was right. He said you'd do anything for this stupid thing," Nathan said as he pulled the sketchbook out of his backpack and turned it around in his hands. Each of Nathan's words exploded in Kalum's head like a grenade.

Reese... told Nathan how to blackmail me into playing, he thought.

Kalum looked across the pitch and his eyes meet Reese's. He held his brother's gaze for a second, but that was an eternity to convey the emotion he felt. He ground his teeth so hard that his jaw ached. Every fibre of him hummed with anger and his vision tinged red like it had when he had taken down Nathan in the Arena. Nex could feel it too, and placed a hand on his chest.

"A deal's a deal," said Nathan and tossed the book across. Kalum looked back in time to fumble as he tried to catch it.

A hand snatched it out of the air as it spiralled towards the wet grass. The groundskeeper straightened his crooked back as he stood.

"You should be more careful," he croaked. He lifted the tip of his cap and revealed his scarred mouth. Kalum's eyes widened as he looked at the face that had haunted him since the first time he'd seen it staring down at him from the rooftop, and then once again when it had looked in on him from the window of his father's bedroom.

"You should be more careful," he repeated.

Kalum realised he wasn't looking at him but staring into the distance past him.

Kalum turned as he felt A.J's hand on his shoulder. She smiled sweetly at him but her eyes told a different story.

"See you around Kal," she said, and turned to leave. The

groundsman made a rumbling noise in his throat and did the same.

"I don't think that's yours," said Lexi, blocking his path. Something in the old man's eyes flashed dangerously, but then disappeared. He looked down at the book he was still holding.

"I guess not," he grumbled and handed it to her.

Elliott Sparrow ran up to them, his light brown hair even more of an untidy mess than usual.

"Mr Cooper's coming. You'd better make yourselves scarce."

A look of recognition crossed his face as he laid eyes on Vincent and he backed away slightly. The half of the old man's face that wasn't deformed curled into a ragged smile.

"What ever you say Mr Deputy Headmaster." With a laugh that sounded like gravel, he left them. Sparrow looked grey as he watched the old man go.

"Hey!" Kalum called after the man and moved to follow him.

"Walker!"

Kalum turned to see Cooper making his way down to the Arena floor. By the time he turned back, Vincent had evaporated into the crowd of students.

"That was the guy, wasn't it?" Nex said. "The one who followed you from the rooftops that night? The one who was outside the window yesterday?"

"You guys better go," Kalum said. He'd registered what Nex had said, taken in everything that was going on around him, but his mind was reeling with the sting of betrayal. The thought of how Reese had manipulated him roiled in his mind. He looked at the book in Lexi's hands, the most precious thing he owned.

"Don't worry. I'll keep it safe for you," she said, reading his mind.

His friends dispersed, and Nathan too had retreated a safe distance. Cooper loomed like a barrelling truck on a collision course. He waved his meaty palms and pointed at Kalum as he approached.

"Why am I not surprised to find you at the heart of this?" he shouted. "I gave you an opportunity to raise your station, and all you bring with you is chaos!"

Nex appeared behind Cooper's head making obscene gestures, and Kalum had to stifle a smirk. This enraged Cooper further and for a moment Kalum thought that the Headmaster might strike him. His salvation came in the unlikely form of Macintosh.

"Sir. This wasn't Walker." He looked down at Kalum, and grudgingly pointed at the Jumbotron and the animation of the pitch invasion that played on a loop there. "It's tradition," he added with a shrug.

Both Kalum and Cooper were so stunned by this that neither spoke. Cooper leant in so close that Kalum could smell the garlic on his breath.

"We. Are. Watching. You," he said in a measured tone.

"Anyone else caught out on the pitch who's not on the team might as well say goodbye to Trinity. I'll turn you into an NC so fast that this will seem like it was just a dream," he shouted. Even without the tannoy his voice carried far enough to reach the whole Arena.

Cooper turned and made his way back up the stairs. Bodies parted to let him pass as if by an invisible force. He took his seat in the gallery box and turned to someone. Kalum stared up and squinted, trying to make out the person in the blinding glare of the floodlights. His acuity sharpened and he saw Clayton Lancaster's smirking face come into focus. He was concentrating so intently that he didn't hear Macintosh calling to him. The big man lost patience after two attempts to get Kalum's attention and hauled him over by the scruff of his neck.

"You did well, boy. No doubt about it. But you're not a Titan yet," he growled.

Kalum looked at the other boys around him. Nathan and the Burton twins remained on one side of the group. The twins looked to Nathan as if unsure how they should behave towards Kalum now that he was a prospective Titan. Marcus Trudeau and Sam Gunning came up and slapped him on the back, offering their congratulations.

"Your life here just got a whole lot better, man," Marcus said with an easy smile. "Welcome to the big time."

Reese joined the circle. He loitered near Macintosh, keeping his distance from Kalum.

"Right. So you can run, Walker. Endurance is nothing if your stick game isn't up to snuff," said Macintosh.

They walked onto the pitch and Macintosh gestured that Kalum should take his position in the goalmouth.

"Any volunteers to show Walker Junior the ropes?" Macintosh asked while looking around.

All eyes went to Nathan, assuming he would want to even the score following his and Kalum's last Arena clash.

"Coach!" Kalum shouted, getting their attention. He stepped forwards and the batons extended out of his gauntlets.

"I want *him*," he said, pointing at Reese.

26

STORY OF YOUR LIFE

Macintosh threw the Henkan ball to Reese and he caught it without looking. The mercurial surface of the ball glinted in the bright Arena light as Reese spun it on his palm. He paused and looked down at the white line at his feet and then at his brother. Kalum watched as his brother's eyes flitted to where the scouts were seated, watching their every move.

"Don't do this, Kal," he said.

"I trusted you," Kalum hissed. "All you've ever done is betray me at every turn."

"All I've ever done is carry you, you worthless sack of—" Reese snapped, but then stopped when he saw the Jumbotron was streaming a tight shot of his face for the whole Arena to see.

"I step over this line and there's only one way it'll go, and you won't like it," Reese said through his fixed smile.

"We'll see," Kalum said in a voice he barely recognised, and hit his batons against his chestguard in defiance.

Reese stepped across the semi circular line and into the defence zone. The Arena was so quiet that the players could hear the soft hum as the invisible barrier activated. Reese tossed the ball from hand to hand and looked up to meet his brother's glare. The blue light circling the ball began to pulse and spin around its outside.

Something about the unapologetic look on Reese's face triggered something inside Kalum and he felt the red mist of rage settle over him. He threw himself forward with explosive velocity, charging straight at his brother.

"No, no, no!" Macintosh yelled from the side-lines. "A Keeper doesn't charge like that! Protect the goal."

In the stands, Jun leaned over to Lexi.

"Kalum's going to get his ass handed to him," he said, shaking his head. Lexi leaned forward in her seat, wishing she could just reach them.

"I don't think so Jun," she said. "I think Reese has had this coming for a while."

Kalum raised his baton and swung it down hard. It passed through the space where Reese's head had been moments ago, whistling through thin air. Reese pivoted like a matador and cracked his elbow into the weak point of the armour in the small of Kalum's back. The force wasn't excessive but Kalum still felt like his spine was being forced the wrong way. He collided face first with the barrier and bounced off it. Twisting in the air he landed on all fours, just narrowly missing triggering the magnets below the pitch. He craned his head back and saw Reese walking towards the goal.

He scrambled to his feet and ran after his brother, again swinging the baton like a fly squatter. Reese danced just out of reach, his own baton still firmly retracted within his gauntlet.

"Why did you give the book to Nathan? You know what it means to me!" he yelled, keeping up his barrage. The timer above the goal continued to tick down but Reese didn't care.

"I did what I needed to do for the best of our family. For your own good too," Reese replied, his voice calm and controlled. This irritated Kalum all the more.

"You did it to get what you wanted! Just like always," Kalum snarled. "Reese is so special, whatever he wants he gets."

He didn't see the blow coming, but found himself on his knees at Reese's feet. The crowd uttered a hushed gasp as the replay showed Reese's arm swing in a backwards arc and the baton extend at precisely the right time to connect with the side of Kalum's helmet.

"Damn right I am. I'm sick of busting a gut to support all of you, I'm sick of being held back by this family, but mostly I'm just sick of you," Reese said.

The words hurt more than the baton strike. Kalum felt the emotions roiling inside him, the anger joining with the pain and humiliation as he got to his feet.

"Nex," he whispered. "Let's kick his butt."

Kalum saw Reese's eyes widen behind his visor, warning him not to say anything about Nex here on the open communications channel, but Kalum was past caring. Past caring if anyone found out about his 'condition', past caring what Reese thought of him.

"My pleasure," Nex growled. He blinked out of view and Kalum's field of vision tinted red.

"Mind if I drive?" Nex asked. Kalum nodded, staring at Reese. Kalum's hazel eyes changed colour and Reese took a half-step away. Kalum felt a strange detached feeling wash over him. He felt weightless, like he was in free-fall. His body sprang forward, levelling a spinning baton strike at his brother. Reese brought his gauntlets up just in time to deflect the blow, but the force of it made him stagger back. The ring of light around the ball pulsed with a quicker tempo now and Reese placed it on the ground, taking a defensive stance. Kalum's body continued its offence with well-timed kicks and elbows, ramping up the speed. Reese was still being pushed back but nothing got past his guard.

"Arrrgh!" Nex shouted. "I'm losing power. I can't get past him."

Nex pushed forward, redoubling his attacks. Kalum watched on, a passenger in his own body. The sensation of being aware but not in control felt intensely strange, like being on an out of control rollercoaster. It was too unsettling for Kalum to stand any longer.

"Let me have a go," he said.

Like a switch being flipped he was once again in control. His vision was still tinted red, but at the peripheries information feeds scrolled up. It was lit up like a fighter pilot's HUD. Black lines pointed at potential vulnerabilities and reported the likely effect of a successful strike. The timer above the goal let out a buzz to indicate one minute until the barrier lifted. The noise set a fire under Reese who launched a flurry of strikes. Kalum could see the blows moments before Reese threw them thanks to the warnings on the HUD.

They traded blows, back and forth like the tide. Kalum's display showed a potential opening, and he took it. He pivoted his body sideways and used the momentum to launch himself into the air. His baton struck the ground and for a moment the world was inverted. His foot arced down, crashing into the top of Reese's helmet, driving him to his knees. Kalum ran forward, his knee piling into the front of Reese's visor, sending a spider web of cracks along its surface.

Reese staggered, but managed to avoid being knocked onto his back. He threw the ruined visor to the floor and beckoned Kalum with one hand. In the Arena the crowd were stamping their feet in time with the countdown timer above the goal. Kalum was a blur as he rained down attack after attack on his brother, pushing him back to the barrier. He threw his body into a tight backflip, the heavy toe of his boot connecting with Reese's chin. This time his brother stayed down on one knee, blood and saliva dripping from his mouth. Kalum roared and charged, ready to tackle his brother and pin him to the ground. Suddenly his vision clicked back to normal and his legs felt like buckling as they strained to maintain his momentum.

"I... I think we pushed it too—" Nex started to say.

Reese's head snapped up as Kalum neared and their eyes met. Kalum tried to stop, but the link between his mind and body felt sluggish. Reese was on his feet now, batons moving in a wide sweep, and Kalum knew what was coming. Time seemed to slow as his legs were knocked out from under him and the point of Reese's elbow smashed into his chest plate, slamming him into the pitch with enough force to drive the air out of his lungs.

From his position on the ground he heard the magnetic system under the pitch engage and he felt the plates in his Henkan gear become adhered to the ground. The crowd cheered and Kalum could hear the chant spread around the Arena.

"Walker wipeout!"

He opened his eyes and saw Reese looking down at him.

"Still not good enough. Story of your life," Reese said.

He grabbed the ball and threw it over his shoulder nonchalantly. It bounced and then rolled into the goal mouth seconds before the timer ran out. The barrier dropped and the rest of the team joined them in the defence zone.

Kalum tried to get to his feet but found that he was still stuck fast.

"You've got few more seconds," said Marcus, appearing at his side. Kalum's chest plate emitted a tone and he found that he could move freely again. He accepted the hand up and got to his feet, brushing himself down.

"Don't feel bad. You did better than Michaels ever did against your brother," said Sam Gunning as he joined them. Nathan just walked past, his self-satisfied smile irritating Kalum all the more.

"Huddle up," Macintosh yelled.

"Took you long enough to take him down," he said to Reese.

He gave Kalum an appraising look and added, "Not bad."

Macintosh turned away as if the admission left a bad taste in his mouth. Even through the cheers of the crowds they could all hear Cooper making his way back down to the Arena floor. He was followed by four men, who were having multiscreen conversations, projected into the air with their TRISTs. They were quoting stats about reaction times, muscle mass and other parameters that Kalum couldn't follow.

"Well..." said Cooper, clasping his hands over his abdomen. "These are the Trinity Titans, gentleman, and they are the cream of the Henkan crop. Any one of them would be worthy of a National contract. May I remind you that last years' institute finder's fee has increased to twenty-four percent.

· · ·

THERE WAS a glint in his eye was he waved them over to the scouts. Kalum followed the rest of the team over but Macintosh put out a hand to restrain him.

"Don't get ahead of yourself, boy."

The Scouts regarded the players one by one, changing the orientation of the video calls so that the buyers they were conversing with could see the boys up close. As they neared Nathan he waved them off.

"I'm spoken for," he said with an offhanded gesture to the Scouts. "I've got a one way ticket to the Sentech National squad."

Many of the boys bristled at that, but managed to keep Nathan from seeing their irritation. The Scouts conferred amongst themselves and Macintosh went over to stand by Cooper. Reese looked back at Kalum. There was no malice in his eyes, but no sense of guilt either. The Scouts then moved over to Cooper and Macintosh, speaking in hushed tones.

"What?!" Cooper bellowed, loud enough for the Scouts to take a cautious step away.

"No," Macintosh was saying. "He's green. It was just luck."

The Scouts gave their replies, again out of earshot of the player. In the meantime the crowd watched and waited, the silence and tension in the stands palpable.

"Titans, front and centre," Macintosh ordered, and the boys jumped to attention. "You too, Walker Junior."

Kalum raised his eyebrows and pointed to his chest.

"Yes!" Macintosh snapped. "Jump to it."

Kalum filed in next to Gunning and stood to attention, mimicking the other boys.

"You all play very well," said one of the Scouts coming forward. The boys all leaned in, hanging on his words.

"As of now we have not added any of you to our official watch list," he said.

There was a groan from the stands and the players' shoulders drooped, their eyes downcast.

"Except for you, Mr Walker," said one of the Scouts, pointing a finger.

Kalum looked to Reese, forcing himself not to glare at his brother, knowing how much of his soul he'd put into this, knowing how long he'd waited for this day. The look of pure hatred on Reese's face rocked him back onto his heels. Then he realised that all the other players were looking at him too. His bewildered face filled the space on the Jumbotron and then he heard the crowd cheer. He looked back at the Scout and realised that he was pointing at him.

"You're too young for the draft," the Scout said, "but, you have potential. We'll be keeping a close eye on you."

Then they turned and headed off. Cooper marched after them, only after flashing Kalum an accusatory glare, while Macintosh just shook his head as he walked over to them.

Kalum turned and saw that everyone was clapping, the sound reverberating around the Arena. The players hoisted him onto their shoulders and then he was being tossed into the air. He saw Reese ripping off his gear and hurling it aside. A pang of guilt hit him and stuck under his rib cage and he tried to call out for his brother but his voice was lost in the tumult.

Kalum's TRIST didn't stop chiming with messages throughout the rest of the day. Footage of his training session and the Scouts' feedback had been leaked over the Sentech network and now he was an instant celebrity. Suddenly everyone wanted to be his best friend.

Ping

Ping

Ping

His TRIST sounded again and again until he silenced it following a glare from Mrs Davenport, their mathematics teacher.

At the next break he managed to lose the crowd that was tailing him and made for the roof. He found Jun waiting there for him.

"Dude! Where have you been hiding those skills?" Jun asked.

Kalum gave him a smile. His TRIST flashed another message and he closed it with a sigh.

"This is great man!" Jun said, thumping him on the back. "You're a stud now. Men want to be you, women want to be with you."

Kalum flicked through the messages. There were sponsorship offers, invitations to parties from people he'd never spoken to during his whole time at Trinity, as well as some that made him blush.

"What are you guy's looking at?" Lexi asked as she and Casey joined them on the roof.

N-nothing," said Kalum, closing it down,

"I don't understand how you did that," said Casey. He came up to Kalum and started walking around him in tight circles. He rubbed his chin and inclined his head as he regarded his friend.

"Hardly anyone's ever completed the Dead Run before, well, apart from Nathan and Reese."

"I told you something's happening to me," Kalum said.

"You can run fast, your endurance levels are off the chart, and you can fight," Casey said.

"Don't forget that he's cleverer than you now too," Jun butted in. Casey ignored him yet again, not taking his eyes of Kalum.

"What are you?" Casey said.

The question was unexpected and it left Kalum speechless. The fact that he didn't have an answer disturbed him no end. In all the excitement he hadn't stopped to ask himself what all this meant.

"I'm m-me," he stammered eventually. "I'm still Kal."

Lexi shifted closer to him and put a hand on his shoulder.

"We know Kal, just... just tell us how this all started."

Nex popped into view next to Lexi. He smiled at her and slicked his hair back, trying to look dashing in his costume.

Kalum ignored him and took a deep breath. He explained everything to his friends. He told them about Nex, about what he could do, what he had been doing, and the agreement they had made.

Lexi waved her hand in the air next to Kalum.

"So you can see him, and only you?" she asked.

"Yeah, I think he just makes me think I can see him, so I don't feel like I'm talking to myself," Kalum said with a shrug, the statement sounding ridiculous even to his own ears.

"I think I know what the coloured threads you're seeing are," Casey said, peering at Kalum. "They're data streams of information stored by Sentech worldwide on virtual servers. I think, somehow, Nex lets you see the data flows and tap into and absorb them."

Jun was on his feet, his excitement difficult to contain.

"Forget all that!" he said. "You're a frickin' superhero! You all get that, right? You're on the way to being the most popular kid in our school! And you can fight, man! I heard someone say that you'd even be good enough to fight in the Gauntlet!"

Jun came right up close to Kalum and waved his hand in front of his face.

"Hey Nex! Can I get in on some of that action?" he said.

"I don't think it works that way," Kalum said with a grin. He looked around and got to his feet.

Their TRISTs all sounded and projected a Sentech news report. It showed yet another Scorp attack on another Corporation Medical Centre. The video feed showed the smoky rubble and rescue workers pulling people out of the debris.

"Why the Scorps are targeting Medical Centres and the infirm is baffling the Enforcer teams," the reporter said, looking grave as he delivered the news. "Increased security has been assigned to the remaining Centres closer to the heart of this Sentech region. There have been sightings of the Operative, the most fearsome Scorp fighter. Please do not be tempted to engage with the Scorps. Anyone considering attending the Scorp-run Gauntlet fighting tournament tonight is urged not to. Remember your loyalty to Sentech and do not let the Scorps tempt you. Enforcers have asked for curfew to be brought forward by an hour. All your TRISTs will warn you ahead of time. Stay safe out there."

The news feed faded and then cut out.

"Kal, please tell me you're not going to go through with this?" Lexi said. "Playing Henkan is one thing, but going out at night, busting Scorps, that's a whole other ball game, especially with their attacks getting closer to home."

"I don't really have a choice, Lex," Kalum said. "If I don't fight then I don't play Henkan. If I don't play Henkan, I'm out of Trinity."

"Plus, someone has to push them back. Whatever the Enforcers are doing isn't working," Nex said to him and then vanished in a burst of pixels.

"Look we'd better get back inside before anyone finds us up here," Kalum said with a sigh.

As they made to move, something tugged at Kalum's peripheral vision. He turned and looked out across the massive school courtyard and the white stone sculptures that had been erected in the western area.

"What's up?" Lexi asked, placing a hand on his shoulder.

"There's something going on over there," Kalum said.

"I can help you with that," Nex said in his head.

Kalum felt a stinging in his eyes and for a moment everything blurred like he was looking through running water. Then his vision ratcheted up and zoomed in. There he saw Reese, talking to Nathan. Kalum watched as Nathan passed him a small package, but from the angle he was at he couldn't make out what it was.

Then all their TRISTs chimed, indicating they should make their way to their next lessons. When Kalum looked back, Reese and Nathan were gone.

The rest of the afternoon seemed to drag, and Kalum felt strangely empty as Nex took a backseat to recharge. His mother, Lucas and Frannie were waiting for him when he got home, having seen news of his sudden fame on their TRISTs.

"Kal..." his mother said. "How could you do that to your brother? You know how hard he'd worked to impress them..."

Kalum opened his mouth to reply but when he took in his mother's disappointed expression he couldn't find the words to defend his actions.

"Also how *did* you do that?" Lucas asked, clapping his nephew on the back. "I've never seen anyone fight like that. Well, apart from your mot—"

Lucas trailed off, silenced by a withering look form Nadine.

"We are not encouraging this kind of behaviour Lucas," she said flatly.

"Where is Reese?" Kalum asked.

Nadine and Lucas exchanged looks.

"He's not here," Nadine said.

"He came straight home and then went to your father's room," Lucas said. "He stormed out afterwards saying he'll be back before curfew."

Kalum's mind replayed the confrontation he and Reese had had in the Arena and then the meeting he'd seen Reese have with Nathan, and the hair stood up on the back of his neck.

"Kalum..." said Frannie, bringing his attention back to the present. "I think we should debrief."

Kalum spent a tense hour with Frannie, lying through his teeth, and then a quick dinner trying to ignore his mother and Lucas' worried glances. Afterwards he made up an excuse about being worn out by the Henkan training and excused himself. Alone in his room, he laid out his Henkan gear. Nex appeared, sitting on the side of his bed, arms crossed and looking away from Kalum.

"A deal's a deal," Nex said. "Time for the Steel Falcon to fly."

27

VERY REAL DANGER

"Now?" said Kalum. He was at his desk, looking down at the sketchbook in front of him. In his hand he held tight to the metal band, the feel of the metal on his skin calming his nerves.

"Yes now," said Nex, turning to him. "You saw the news. The Scorps are coming. It's no surprise they're getting closer. It's up to us to put them down."

"Are you sure we're ready for this?" Kalum asked, looking in the mirror. He was leaner and stronger than he had ever felt in his life, and his muscles had definition he'd never thought possible. "You heard what they said on the news. This might be the Operative. Low level thugs are one thing, but he's supposed to be a monster."

"We've got this. I've got the moves from every one of those martial arts flicks in my head," said Nex, tapping his temple. "And now you can do them too. The Scorps haven't got a chance."

"Was that what I saw, that display that popped up when I was fighting Reese? All those stats and options?"

"Exactly!"

Kalum gave an unconvinced sigh and got out his spare Henkan gear. He started to thread on the gauntlets when Nex appeared in front of him with his palm outstretched.

"Stop!" he said. "We can't go out like that. You need to make one small adjustment."

An image appeared in Kalum's vision, created by Nex. Kalum regarded it with raised eyebrows and pursed his lips together in a thin line.

"Really? Do I have to?"

"Of course you do!" Nex said. "What use is a superhero costume without a symbol?"

An hour later, Kalum stood in front of his mirror. He had his spare Henkan kit on. The Titan logos were blacked out, but on his chest plate was the same symbol that was on Nex's outfit. The stylised falcon's head with a razor-sharp beak stood out in red against the black uniform. He'd used the red paint to add accents onto the armour's surface, and they made him look sleek and mean. Kalum flicked his wrist and extended and retracted the baton from each gauntlet in his hand.

"I look badass," he admitted.

"Damn straight we do," said Nex, striking a pose next to him.

Kalum strode over to the window and lifted it. The cold air hit him like an icy slap as it found the gaps in his helmet and stung the flesh on his neck. He ducked his head back into the room as a drone zipped by, its red eye rotating and scanning all round it as it went. Watching it loop around the block he put his hands on the window frame and readied to launch himself.

"Stop!" Nex screamed.

"What?!" Kalum asked, his heart still pounding from the shock.

"I nearly forgot! You can't go out like that. The Enforcers can monitor your TRIST location. Remember what Casey said? They'll know if you're out after curfew."

"But if it's off for more than five minutes it'll alert the Enforcers anyway," said Kalum.

"I know that!" said Nex. "But I have a solution! Go into your dad's room."

Kalum went to his door, catching sight of himself in his mirror. He opened the door and looked out into the pitch-black landing.

"This'll be hard to explain if Mum or Reese see me," he said. He eased the door to his father's room open, wincing as creaky hinges protested his actions. He walked to his father's bedside.

"Go on," Nex urged.

Kalum looked down at his sleeping father and shook his head.

"I can't. It just feels wrong."

"How do you think I've been doing it all this time?" Nex asked. "Reese said he'd have been proud of you stepping up for the family, so imagine how proud he'd be if he saw what you were doing for the people of this city?

You're doing this for him," Nex urged. "The Scorps did this to him. You're getting him the kind of justice that the Enforcers never could."

An alert from his TRIST sounded and in the silence of the night the noise sounded deafening,

"Don't do it Kal, it's too dangerous," read the message from Lexi.

Kalum closed down the message without replying and pressed the button to disengage the unit from his arm.

The TRIST clicked open and the screen flashed red. A countdown timer activated and a message to input an override code blinked. Kalum lifted one of his father's thin arms, surprised by how light it was, and fastened the TRIST around his forearm. With a hiss it self-adjusted and started scanning its new home.

"Acceptable DNA match. No other TRIST units detected," it read and then returned to standby mode.

Kalum tiptoed back into his room and stood on the window ledge. Without hesitation he threw himself out into the night.

The air whistled over his armour as he ran from rooftop to rooftop with reckless abandon. With each jump he catapulted himself further, his body cartwheeling through the air but his hands somehow finding a sure purchase point to grab onto. Not for a moment did fear creep its tendrils into his psyche. There was only the rush of the night and the freedom of the run.

"Where are we going? he asked Nex.

"Well, I just tend to run around until I see— There!" shouted Nex, pointing.

Kalum skidded to a stop and looked at where Nex was pointing. He looked over to see a parking structure with high walls and the Sentech logo over the entrance. The wire gate was open and there were no signs of any patrol guards. Kalum jumped and scrambled up the wall and peered inside. He saw a group of five Scorps, in foot-soldier red trying to break into a parked Transport.

"Geez they're enormous. They make Daniel look like a puppy," Kalum said.

"Trust me they're nothing, and you've taken out guys twice their size."

Kalum took a deep breath and adjusted his helmet.

"I hope you're right, Nex," he said and nosedived off the building. As he fell he watched the image of himself in front of him that Nex projected. Copying its moves, he put his hand out and it caught the horizontal bar of an overhead light. The momentum propelled him forwards and he tucked himself into a ball. He collided with the biggest Scorp, smashing into the small of his back and driving him forward. There was a meaty thunk as his head connected with the armoured panel of the Transport. He teetered on his feet for a brief moment before collapsing to the floor.

"Okay," said Nex. "Now say something cool like, 'I am the Steel Falcon, fear my wrath!'"

"I'm not saying that," Kalum mumbled under his breath, drawing a look that was half shock and half confusion from the other Scorps.

"It's the guy!" One of the remaining four gathered his wits and yelped as they moved to encircle him.

"Nex, do that thing that you did when we were up against Reese in the Arena," Kalum whispered as he watched the Scorps draw pipes, knives and other cobbled together implements.

"No," said Nex, his voice defiant. "Not until you tell them who you are."

"Fine," said Kalum through gritted teeth. "I am the Steel Falcon..." he said, sounding less than enthused.

"And...?" asked Nex.

"Feel my wrath..." Kalum said.

His vision blinked and the blue HUD appeared. It was different to the red mist of rage that he had felt in the Arena. He felt calmer, centred. His visual field filled with stats, vulnerabilities and strike points of varying lethality as he surveyed his opponents.

"Okay now," said Nex, cracking his knuckles. "Bruce Lee or Jackie Chan?"

"Jackie who?" asked Kalum as he ducked out of the way of a swinging punch.

"Jackie Chan! He's a legend. What's wrong with you? When we get home I'm going to have to enlighten you."

The Scorp to Kalum's left—a grizzly bearded man equal parts fat and muscle with a fair few teeth missing—broke into a charge at Kalum, lead pipe raised.

Kalum spun, eyes wide, and scrambled back half a step and heard the pipe whizz past his face.

"Bruce Lee! Bruce Lee!" Kalum shouted to Nex. The pipe came back at Kalum in a horizontal arc but seemed to slow to a grind. In his field of vision he saw copies of himself demonstrating four different attacks. Time snapped back to normal speed and Kalum felt the blast of air as the end of the pipe blurred past his jaw. He ducked under the arm and brought his fist up to strike the man in the ribs, flexing his wrist in an upwards movement at the point of impact. The blow was devastating. There was a crack as multiple ribs reached their point of elasticity and snapped. The force of the blow sent the man rolling backwards to crash into the Transport, setting off its alarm.

Nex appeared in front of Kalum with arms raised up high in celebration.

"One-inch punch for the win!!" he shouted, jumping up and down in ecstasy.

Kalum turned to the man on his right. He hesitated. It wasn't a man but a boy, a year or so younger than himself. He was lean to the point of malnourishment and the fear in his eyes was something that looked all too familiar. A voice squawked from the boys' belt.

"Hold him. The Operative is en route."

Kalum felt his heart accelerate at the sound of the Scorp fighter's name. He held his hands up and approached the boy. He stepped back with his hands out in front of him, one holding a knife. Nex clicked his fingers and in Kalum's HUD he saw six different approaches to disarm the boy and take him down.

"No, Nex. I'm not going to hurt him," Kalum said under his breath.

"I'm not going to hurt you," Kalum said, louder this time so that the boy could hear him. "You and your buddies just have to leave the Transport alone."

"The Scorps need this Transport. I'm here to collect," said the voice behind him, synthesised to be unrecognisable, and it sounded like a robot from a cheesy horror science fiction movie. The figure wore a gun-metal grey armoured suit fitted around a lithe frame. He seemed to glide towards Kalum, calm and steady without a hint of hesitation. His face was concealed behind an ornate white and red fox mask. It had scarlet streaks over it that led to dark lenses in which Kalum could see his reflection.

"So, you're the Operative huh?" Kalum said, looking him up and down and trying to sound tough. "I thought you'd be taller."

The Operative let out an amused snort.

"I could say the same."

"So it's not enough that you're trying to peddle Augs here, but you want to steal a school Transport too?" Kalum asked, circling in a ready stance.

The Operative didn't answer, and didn't bother turning to track Kalum as he slipped into his blind spot.

"What are you calling yourself then?" the Operative asked.

"They call me the Steel Falcon," Kalum heard himself saying without prompting from Nex, and instantly cringed at how the name sounded out loud.

The Operative cocked his head, and the lenses embedded in the fox mask regarded him.

"You're on the wrong side of this fight," said the Operative. "You don't understand what the Corporations... what Sentech are doing."

Kalum's mind flicked back to what he had heard Clayton Lancaster speaking to Cooper about, when he had hidden in his office. There were so many unanswered questions, so many doubts swimming about in his head.

"Sentech aren't the benevolent Corporation you think they are," The Operative said as he closed the gap between them.

In his head Kalum heard Darius' voice as he'd handed over the Augs to Nathan in the Arena.

The Operative sends his regards.

Kalum brushed his thumb against his nose and brought his hands up into a fighting stance as his HUD flicked on and presented with him with attack options. He selected an option from his HUD and burst forward copying the moves of his light show doppelgänger.

The mid-air hook slammed into the right side of the Operative's face. The agony that erupted in Kalum's hand shot all the way up his arm to his shoulder. It was like trying to smash granite with his fist. The figure let out a hollow laugh and moved to follow Kalum's retreat.

"I have orders to take you down," The Operative said, taking up a fighting stance himself. "But I think you're just misguided. I'd rather convert you to our cause."

Kalum's vision was still swimming with the pain. It was like having his arm dipped in lava. He gasped, trying to understand what was happening. The agony in his limb gradually ebbed, as if someone had rotated a dial.

"I've turned off your pain receptors," Nex said.

"Thanks," Kalum gasped while blinking away tears.

"How can you listen to a man like Darius?" Kalum shouted. "How can I trust someone like you?"

"Have it your way," the Operative said.

"Let's try that again." Kalum growled at the Operative and flicked his wrist, making the baton built into his gauntlet extend and lock with a click. His HUD reset, bringing up more options.

"Let's try some Jackie Chan this time," Nex said.

Kalum moved back on the offensive, his body swaying from side to side as he came.

The Operative stopped moving and regarded him with an air of amusement.

Following the cues from his HUD, Kalum lurched forward and launched a series of strikes that came in from odd angles. The baton clanged against the Operative's half-hearted blocks, but didn't seem to faze him.

"Well that didn't work," said Nex.

Kalum noticed that Nex was fading again, just as he had done on the Henkan pitch. He felt his hand start to shake. Reaching down he scooped up one of the pipes the first Scorp had been carrying and swung it with everything he had, but the Operative blocked it with his forearm and the pipe bent round it.

He threw it to the side and grabbed Kalum by the scruff off the neck and pulled him up so that his toes barely touched the floor. "

You don't understand anything. This isn't a game."

The Operative reached over with his free hand and grasped Kalum's visor to lift it. A spotlight of eye-watering brightness illuminated them both and he dropped Kalum. The impact of the fall opened his visor slightly and Kalum scrambled to close it.

"This is Sentech private property and you are trespassing," a voice boomed. "We are the Enforcers. Do not resist."

A flock of drones buzzed into view, their red eyes focusing on the group below. There was the rumble of boots as troops neared their position.

"Think about what I said," the Operative said. He then whirled his finger around and they all retreated with practiced precision. Kalum stared at them as they disappeared, swallowed by the shadows around them.

"Run..." Though weak, Nex's voice brought him back to the very real danger that surrounded him.

A round hammered its way into the masonry next to his head. That was all the motivation he needed. He ducked in between two buildings and into a maze of storage units. Overhead he could hear the hungry buzzing of the drones as they circled above him like vultures waiting to devour a carcass. The voices of the Enforcers bounced and echoed of the metal walls, and Kalum had no clue which way to go. The panic started to set in, scratching at his throat and burning in the pit of his stomach. He turned a corner and came face to face with the barrel of an Enforcer's rifle. Acting on reflex Kalum hit him with the same strike that had floored the Scorp earlier, but with Nex in a weakened state it lacked power. The Enforcer let out a guttural laugh and smashed the butt of his rifle into the side of Kalum's head. The visor saved him from a broken jaw but the blow knocked him to the ground.

With the suddenness of a thunderclap the man's eyes became vacant and glassy. He crumpled to his knees like a puppet whose strings had been cut. Behind him stood the Operative. He looked at Kalum for a moment and then nodded.

"Consider this an olive branch," he said. "You're on your own now."

He stepped back into the shadows and was gone.

"Nex?" Kalum said, looking down at the motionless body of the Enforcer at his feet. "Nex, are you there? We need to get out of here."

"I'm here..." Nex gasped.

Kalum's HUD appeared, faintly showing a three dimensional map of his surroundings with an escape route marked out. He concentrated, committing it to memory as it vanished. He ran on his tiptoes, knees bent and keeping low, his body pressed against the walls. He kept going until he reached the wire fence on the other side of the compound. He dragged himself up it with painfully slow progress until he was able to throw his leg over the top. Overbalancing he tipped backwards over the fence and crashed to the ground hard enough to wind him. He stood, shaking the stars from his head, and staggered in the general direction of home.

He had to hide in some unspeakably unsanitary places to avoid the drones and patrols on his route home, but he eventually managed to catch sight of it. The red door stood out like a beacon pulling him in. He threw himself at the wall, his fingers struggling as they slipped off the wet brick-work. Again and again he tried and failed.

"Come on Nex. I need you," he whispered. "You got me into this mess."

He felt a sliver of energy pulse from the base of his skull all the way down his spine. Steeling his resolve he took another run at it. This time he managed to clamber in through his window, barely saving himself from a thirty-foot drop. He ripped off his kit and hurled it into his cupboard before collapsing on the bed.

His eyes settled on the well-worn white cover of his sketchbook and he lay his hand on it, feeling comforted.

He should by all rights be scared out of his wits considering what he had been through that night. The reality was different. He felt alive and exhilarated. It was like the feeling he'd had in the Arena but magnified a hundred fold. He didn't need to open the book and draw for his mind to be clear. For the first time in the longest time he felt at peace.

He woke before his alarm sounded. He checked his right hand, flexing each finger in turn until he could make a fist. It seemed okay, albeit a bit stiff. Last night he had been sure he'd broken one if not two of his fingers in his fight against the Operative.

"Anything you want to tell me, son?"

He sat up and saw his mother seated at his desk, gazing at him with an expectant look. His eyes flicked to his open cupboard door. He'd have trouble explaining the Falcon symbol painted onto the Henkan armour chest plate.

"Er... I... love you," he tried with a sheepish grin.

Nadine was unimpressed and stood. She tossed something onto the bed and put her hands on her hips.

"Lose something?"

On his bed was his TRIST unit, screen flashing red and counting down.

"Well you'd better put it back on before the Enforcers roll around," Nadine said.

Kalum fastened the unit back on and checked the screen for confirmation.

"What were you thinking? Creeping out at night? Don't deny that's what you did!" she said, pointing her finger at him. Nex appeared and immediately recoiled as Nadine moved towards them.

"What if the Enforcers had caught you outside after

curfew? That would have been it for Trinity! Imagine if a drone had spotted you? Without a TRIST signal it would have thought you were an NC and…"

Nadine rested her head in her palm for a minute and then took in a long breath.

"Look I know this is a strange time for you, and lots of things are changing," she said, looking at Kalum with a smile. "You're seeing things differently and I get that. I'm glad of that."

Kalum looked at her with growing trepidation. Nadine shifted closer to him and rested a hand on his head.

"There's no need to be embarrassed. It's natural. I know you probably don't want to talk to your mum about it, but I'm glad."

"Glad about what, Ma?" Kalum asked, his mouth suddenly very dry.

"Glad that it's Lexi. I saw her message telling you not to sneak out. You've been so close for so long and I knew that something changed between the two of you in the last few months. I just knew," she said, beaming. She ruffled his hair and then her face turned serious once again.

"Look, I know what it's like to have this feel all new and exciting, but sneaking out to see each other after curfew is not on, okay? Should I phone Lexi's mum?" she asked.

"No!" said Kalum, jumping forwards. "Won't happen again."

"Wow. That was close," said Nex as Nadine left.

"You're telling me," said Kalum as he rushed to get ready.

He collided with Reese on the landing and his brother shoved him back, hard, nearly knocking him to the floor.

"Watch where you're going, leech," Reese spat.

His skin was waxen and pale, his eyes bloodshot and

sunken in their sockets. His brother made to turn away but Kalum stopped him with an arm on his shoulder. Reese spun around with murder in his eyes, his fist wound back. If not for Nex enhancing his reflexes, Reese would have clocked him straight in the jaw, but Kalum managed to duck under it.

"This is what you wanted all along, right?" Reese came at him, a flurry of punches punctuating his words.

"To be the star? To have the spotlight? Well congratulations!"

Kalum backed up, running out of space. Reese's fist was coming at him and he had nowhere to go. He braced for the impact but it never came. Nadine caught the fist in mid-strike and had Reese's arm twisted behind his back in one deft move.

"Enough!" she bellowed, pushing Reese away.

"You've both made mistakes, but you need to move past that. You're family... you're brothers," she said.

"My brother is dead to me," Reese said, looking at Kalum with revulsion. "I don't know who this person is."

They stood for a moment in silence, Kalum and Reese glaring at each other.

"I'm going in late today," Reese said finally. "I still have that right as co-Captain."

He turned and went into their father's room, slamming the door with such force that the whole house shook.

KALUM PUSHED thoughts of his brother out of his mind as he inhaled breakfast and tore out of the house, running to reach the Transport in time. As usual he arrived in time to watch it sail by, and caught sight of Lexi shaking her head at him as it sped away. Something in his periphery caught his attention and he half turned in time to see someone duck into an alleyway. Not sure if he was being brave or foolish, Kalum crossed the street to investigate, ignoring the warnings from his TRIST that he was running late. He peered into the space between the two high-end clothing shops and saw it was empty.

He shook his head and backed away when on impulse he looked up. Looking down at him was a man in a long grey coat. His cap was pulled down but from this angle he could clearly see the network of web-like scars that traversed his face. It was the Trinity Groundskeeper, the man called Vincent. Kalum scooted back and got to his feet. He looked at the scar on the man's face and felt his skin crawl. Not knowing why, he spun and ran, squeezing every bit of speed out of his body.

"Wait!" Nex shouted. "Why are we running from a Scorp? That's gotta be what he is, one of Darius' grunts."

Kalum just kept running, fuelled by a fear he didn't quite understand.

28

INVISIBLE THREAT

"Okay," Nex said, pulling Kalum's attention away from the sketch he was trying to covertly finish during class. "Yesterday could have gone better. But we stopped the Scorps from taking that Transport, right? We were pretty awesome."

Kalum looked around the class at the other students who were displaying varying degrees of commitment to the subject of Corporation business strategy. He contemplated writing in the sketchbook but immediately chided himself. The only writing in the book was his father's and he wanted to keep it that way. Kalum opened his bag to write a message back to Nex and saw that the metal band was also in the tablet case.

"Nex, did you put this in here? he typed with one hand whilst he ran his finger over the band with the other.

He stared at the message until Nex clicked, realising it was written for him.

"Not me," he said. "Just looking at that thing weirds me out."

Kalum's fingers wrapped around the band and he felt

satisfaction as it pinched his flesh. It felt good to have it in his possession. This way he knew it was safe... protected. He blinked away the haze he felt and forced himself to release the band. He stared at it, trying to understand the hold this piece of metal had over him. Nex was still talking, white noise on the periphery of his senses.

"So...? What do you think?" Nex asked.

"What?" Kalum replied, forgetting where he was.

"If you have a question Mr Walker..." Barker growled at him from behind his desk, "... it is customary to raise your hand."

Kalum felt everyone's eyes on him and he forced himself not to shrink into his seat, forced himself to take even breaths and not focus on his accelerating heartbeat.

"It's nothing, Sir," he said, his voice a squeaky whisper.

"Is that right, Walker?" Barker said, now getting to his feet. "You disrupted my class for 'nothing'?"

"Guys like Barker will only respect you of you stand up to him," Nex said.

Kalum saw the predatory look in Barker's eye as he eased himself around the end of the desk.

"Unless of course you weren't paying attention."

Kalum slid his sketchbook under his tablet and on impulse got to his feet. He adjusted his Henkan lapel badge and did his best to emulate a Nathan Lancaster sneer.

"I'm happy for you to quiz me in front of the entire class," he said. "How about if I get them all correct I get your lunchroom privileges for a month?"

Kalum held Barker's stare, face grinning resolutely. Internally he was going into free-fall, the room was threatening to turn in on itself, and he wanted to throw up. Jun was tugging at his sleeve, trying to get him to sit back down but he planted his feet and stood tall.

Barker regarded Kalum for a moment longer, the memory of the last time he had tried to embarrass the boy in front of the class fresh in his mind.

"Sit. Down. Walker," Barker hissed and returned to the front of the room.

Kalum sat as a murmur rippled through the class, and Jun and Casey looked at him with undisguised amazement.

"Told you!" said Nex.

If Kalum had been a celebrity before, standing up to Barker in front of the class has cemented his status.

"Hey Kal," said a voice like silk.

He felt a light touch on his shoulder and then he was spun around face to face with Kara.

"A bunch of us are going to watch the next Gauntlet tournament at my place. We've got a pirate feed," she said. "Do you want to join us?"

"Can he bring a plus one?" Jun asked, draping an arm over his friend and placing a hand on his chest.

"I guess you could bring Jan with you if you want," she said with an eye roll. "Anyway, let me know..."

Kara sauntered away with her entourage in tow.

"I-it's Jun..." Jun said after her. "But Jan's fine. I could just change my name..."

Kalum's TRIST sounded and he looked down to see that another message had popped up. A glance confirmed it was from A.J. He felt a little twitch of excitement inside him at the sight of her name.

"Need to talk to you," it read. "Meet me where we first met."

"What's got you so happy?" Lexi said.

"Nothing!" Kalum said as he swiped the message away and tried to look less guilty than he felt. "I've...I've gotta get to the Arena."

"No problem, superstar," Lexi called after him.

"Not cool man," Nex said. "How could you lie to Lexi?"

Kalum didn't answer, hoping Nex would leave the subject be, but Kalum had to listen to him chastise him all the way to the edge of the woods. As he reached it he slowed his pace, smoothed his shirt down and caught his breath. A few more feet brought him into the clearing where he'd seen Nathan and the Burton twins using the Augs. He sat on a tree stump and waited for A.J and listened to the sounds of invisible life in the woods. An insect buzzed around him and insisted on repeatedly ramming into the side of his head. A wave of his hands shooed it away, but then something harder cracked him in the temple.

"Ow!" he said, rubbing his head. "Thanks for the heads up Nex," he hissed

"Consider that karma for your deceit," came Nex's smug reply.

"Sorry!" A.J's voice called. "That really looked like it hurt."

Kalum looked around but couldn't see her anywhere. He stood and scanned the undergrowth and long shadows but even his augmented sight couldn't see her.

"Up here," A.J said.

Kalum looked up and saw A.J perched on the same branch that he'd fallen unceremoniously from when they first met. She beckoned for him to join her. Kalum looked at the tree and concentrated, but no guide appeared to show him the way. Assuming Nex was still in a mood he tried to scale the tree himself, with embarrassing results. Picking himself up off the mucky bed of mushed dead leaves he looked up and saw an exasperated look cross A.J's face.

"Get up here quick," she said. "I've got something to tell you."

Kalum looked at the trunk again and his vision adjusted to show him the best route to A.J's position.

Nex appeared by the tree, still looking sullen.

"I'm annoyed that you lied to Lexi," he said with a shrug. "But I'm curious what she has to say too."

With sure-footed agility he scaled the tree and vaulted to the branch next to where A.J was perched.

Kalum smiled at her, then dialled it back a notch, trying not to appear too smug, and ended up with an odd grimace that made A.J give him a quizzical look. She patted the branch next to her and he dutifully sat.

"You seemed pretty angry when you threw down with your brother in the Arena," she said.

"Well, he had it coming," Kalum replied.

She stayed quiet for a moment and then gave him a smile that carried a heavy weight behind it.

"I know what it's like to let your anger control you," she said. "It might feel great at the time but you'll regret it later."

Kalum was acutely aware of how close her hand was to his on the branch. He kept still, as if any movement could spook it.

"How... how did you get a handle on it," he asked, mesmerised by her green eyes.

"Close your eyes," she said.

Kalum did as he was told. There was a silence that seemed to stretch out forever and he started to feel foolish. He was about to open his eyes to check if she was still there, but then she spoke.

"Focus on your anger," she said. "Feel it flowing through you, scratching at your nerves, pulling you taut."

Kalum thought about the bag being pulled over his head, facing down Nathan and his thugs, about Reese taking his medication away from him and making him feel he was losing his mind. He felt the betrayal of finding out that Reese had taken away his sketchbook and given it to Nathan to use for blackmail. His pulse hammered in his neck and the tension built in his temples. His eyes opened and he felt his breath coming out in short sharp bursts.

A.J was sat in front of him, eyes still closed and head inclined up to the steel-grey sky. She was coloured in a red hue along with everything in his frame of vision.

"For me, I got control of my anger through movement. I could teach you that but I think with you, maybe I'll try a different tack."

Her hand shot out and grabbed his. Once again he felt her touch send a static shock through him.

"Think about the people who've touched your life, about how they make you feel..."

Kalum thought about his friends, and his family, doing his best to push all thoughts of Reese away. When he opened his eyes his vision cleared and everything had returned to normal.

Their eyes met and A.J hit him with a dazzling smile and Kalum thought he might fall out of the tree again. He heard footsteps through the brush below him and looked down to see Nathan stride into the clearing.

"A.J... what's the deal with you and Nath—?" Kalum whispered, but A.J brought a finger to her lips.

"Just remember what I said to you about keeping your cool..."

A minute later Kalum heard a second set of footfalls.

Reese stumbled into view, tripping over the same gnarled roots that had claimed Kalum's shoe a lifetime ago. Reese looked twitchy, his head jerking from side to side and his hands swatting at some invisible threat. Nathan leant against a tree and waited for the older Walker brother to pick his way across to him.

"You won't be able to hear them," A.J whispered. "We're too high up, but just watch."

Kalum nodded but felt the buzzing in his ears as Nex responded by ratcheting up his hearing a notch.

"What do you want, Walker?" Nathan asked. "I've got better places to be."

Reese sniffed and kicked idly at a tree stump. He didn't look up as he spoke.

"I need more," he said, his voice coarse and dry.

"Really?" Nathan asked with a chuckle. He stepped closer to Reese and angled his head to get a better look at his long-time rival. "I sold you ten, Walker. You should be good for another week."

In the blink of an eye, Reese had Nathan by the throat and had slammed him back against the tree. Nathan was winded but recovered almost immediately, kicking out and catching Reese in the gut, doubling him over. Kalum moved to jump but A.J held him back. He tried to shrug her off but she was surprisingly strong.

"Look how the mighty Reese Walker has fallen," Nathan said.

He crouched near to where Reese was groaning on the floor. Something changed in his face and he reached into his backpack and took out a blue canister that he set down along side Reese.

"You're addicted," he said in a low voice. "You go too long without and you'll twitch out. Take this, but get yourself some help."

He stood up and made to leave. He paused for a moment at the edge of the clearing.

"Don't come to me for any more," Nathan said. "I'm done dealing to you."

Reese's arm snaked out and snatched the blue canister and he held on so tight that his fingers dented its outer surface. A faint mist released from where the canister's outer casing had buckled. Reese looked from the canister to Nathan. He stood, his limp body rising from the ground like a wraith. In the shadows of the trees his pale face looked vampiric. He keyed in a command on his TRIST and Kalum heard Nathan's voice come from the speakers.

"No, I got a hearing Aug."

There was a pause and then an image sprang to life, rendered in three dimensions above the TRIST. Kalum saw playback of Nathan and the Burton twins scanning the skyline. Then Kalum appeared in the scene, falling out of the tree and landing in a heap. Kalum watched himself on the playback as he struggled to escape and crashed into Daniel, and had to relive the beating Nathan had given him.

"He just sat back and watched them kick your butt," Nex said. Kalum could feel the anger in Nex's voice. He felt it too, bubbling under the surface. A.J's hand was on his again, squeezing it tight.

"I still have this, Nate," Reese said. "We're not done until we say I'm done. We're gonna need to talk again real soon."

Nathan bristled and took a step back in Reese's direction before thinking better of it and stalking off. Reese watched him go, remaining in the darkest recess of the clearing. He jerked his head back and shot the Aug into his eye. For a moment nothing happened, and then he began to shake. A scream escaped his lips, part pain, part ecstasy, and tears streamed down his face. The scream turned into a roar and he fell to one knee. Now Kalum shrugged off A.J and shimmied down the tree. He sprinted to where Reese knelt with his head hung like a man waiting for the guillotine to fall.

"Reese?" he said. "Are you—"

A back fist to the chest sent Kalum reeling. He slammed into the tree behind him and looked up in time to see Reese glaring down at him with a savage feral look in his eyes. Kalum threw himself to one side and Reese's fist hit the tree, tearing a chunk out of the trunk.

"Reese, you need help," Kalum managed to say before Reese's shoulder hit him and he was hefted into the air. The two of them struggled, their momentum taking them clear of the woods and back onto school grounds.

"You took everything from me!" Reese screamed as he tackled his brother again.

"You took my freedom!" he said as he rained blows down. "I had to claw myself to the top while you just rode there on my back!"

Kalum pushed Reese back and rolled away. Blood from a gash above his eye was bleeding freely, stinging and blinding him. He didn't see Reese's fist, but heard the crack and felt the explosion of pain as his jaw fractured.

When did Reese get so strong? he thought in between the explosions of pain in his face. A kick to his stomach brought him to the floor and made him forget the jaw for a second.

And so fast!

The pain started to fade to a dull throb and he felt the wound above his eye start stitching together.

"You took away everything that was special about me," Reese roared. "That's why I use these Augs. They make me feel so much more."

Kalum felt Nex activate his HUD, as the faint tingle at the base of his neck rose in a crescendo. Dozens of options scrolled by, lightning fast, yet all Kalum could do was look past them to see his brother charging towards him.

"Kal!" Nex was shouting. "You've got to protect yourself, or I will."

Kalum felt his body shift into a fighting stance and read Nex's intent.

"No," he whispered as his brother closed the gap. "I won't fight him, and you won't either."

"STOP!" a voice rang out, stopping Reese in his tracks. The brothers followed the sound to see Sparrow running towards them, with his hands outstretched. Reese snarled and turned back to Kalum. His fingers wrapped around his brother's throat and he squeezed.

"Reese. Owen. Walker! Stand down!" Sparrow shouted.

The use of Reese's full name was like a bucket of ice water being dumped over him. Only his parents had ever called him by that name, and only when he was in serious trouble. His eyes focused on Kalum's face in front of him and his hands around his brother's neck. He let go and stepped away, looking around and registering where he was.

"Don't... don't call me that," Reese stammered. "You're... you're not my father."

"No," said Sparrow evenly. "But I am taking you both home now."

He marched them over to a Trinity Transport and shoved them both in the passenger side. The vehicle took off at speed and soon only the whirr of the motors filled the cabin.

Kalum glanced in his brother's direction and barely recognised the person sitting across from him. He was staring out through the window, eyes fixed on something while the rest of his body rocked back and forth almost imperceptibly. Kalum opened his mouth to speak to him, but the words refused to come out.

Sparrow brought the transport to a halt outside their home and got out.

"Stay here," he said, not waiting for a reply as he slammed the door behind him. Kalum watched as he made his way to that bright red door and raised a hand to press on the bell. His hand hung in the air like a bee waiting to land on a flower. Kalum saw it shake a little and then watched Sparrow berate himself. Then he knocked and stepped away, hand clasped right behind his back.

Nadine opened the door. He didn't need Nex to enhance his hearing to know what Sparrow was saying. The look on his mother's face said it all. She marched past Sparrow and tore the door of the Transport open.

"Get inside. Now," she said, her voice like ice water.

Kalum did what he was told, and eventually so did Reese. Nadine followed them into the house and then turned back to Sparrow. He had one foot in the door as if to follow. They both looked down at it and he pulled back, his face a mix of sheepish embarrassment.

"I thought maybe it would help if I talked to them?" Sparrow said.

"Thank you Mr Sparrow, but I think this would be best dealt with by me," Nadine said. She smiled tightly and went to close the door. Sparrow put his palm out and stopped it from shutting.

"I won't mention anything about the Augs in the school report," he said.

"Thank you, Mr Sparrow."

"Call me Elliott."

With a nod Nadine shut the door and turned to her sons. Kalum was the first to feel her wrath.

"Fighting?" she said, jabbing a finger at him. "Now you're fighting at school?"

Kalum opened his mouth to defend himself but Nadine cut him off with a look.

"And you?!" she said, rounding on Reese. "You're using?! Are you out of your mind? The Scouts didn't snap you up this time, so what? Get back up and keep going. You're a Walker, that's what we do. No matter how hard it is."

Reese was looking through her, his face devoid of any emotion, but his glazed eyes were tearing up. He stood and moved to the stairs. Nadine threw herself at him, wrapping her arms around him from behind in a tight embrace.

"Come back to us Reese," she said. "You're stronger than this."

Reese reached down and unpeeled his mother from him. He trudged upstairs and into Owen's room, leaving Nadine and Kalum to watch him go.

Later in his room, Kalum sat on the edge of his bed staring into the mirror. His hand reached up to touch the area above his eye where Reese had opened up a gash. The wound had completely healed, even the overlying scar tissue fading now.

"You healed me?" Kalum asked.

"Yeah," Nex said, appearing next to him on the bed. "Not sure how. I just thought it and it happened. Sort of the same way it works with your strength."

His TRIST sounded with a news alert and it automatically projected the Sentech logo into the air above it. There was a segue and the image changed to show the picture of a bespectacled middle-aged man with short grey hair and a serious, deeply lined face. The headline read;

'Spectre revealed'

"In one fell strike the Enforcers have eliminated the

Spectre, revealed to be Dr Amadeus Allen, who had been hacking the Sentech network and spreading false news. He was gunned down attempting to send a final transmission."

The image faded and changed to show a different headline.

'Scorp attacks on Medical Centres continue'

"The Scorps have struck at another Sentech Medical Centre tonight, leaving chaos in their wake and healthcare workers shaken," a Reporter said.

"I'm here with Dr Palma, an emergency physician," the Reporter continued. "Dr Palma, your department was targeted, as was the case in other Medical Centres in the last few weeks. Any idea why the Scorps would do this?"

A flicker of recognition woke in Kalum's memory. Then with a snap he was taken back to his time in the Medical Centre after being thrown in the pool by Nathan. He could see the bulky shaven headed doctor with the smile devoid of sincerity peering down at him, trying to convince him to sign the document that absolved Nathan of blame.

"They wanted records," Dr Palma said. "They wanted a record of all children that had been brought in during the last few months."

"There you have it," the reporter said. "Proof that the Scorps operate without morality, not only targeting the infirm but also our children. Thank you to Sentech and the Enforcers who continue to fight against this vile segment of society to keep us safe."

The transmission ended and Kalum found that he was on his feet. He had no recollection of standing. The vice around his heart was tightening, leaving a fire in his lungs. The tremor in his hand was so bad that he had to clamp it to the desk in front of him. On reflex he grabbed his sketch-book from where is sat and it was open, his pencil poised ready. As he drew, the symptoms started to abate. When his eyes finally refocused on the paper again a whole hour had passed. Looking back at him from the book wasn't an image of the Steel Falcon. Instead, Darius had been brought to life on the page, scorpion tattoo proudly emblazoned on his arm.

"Feel better?" Nex asked.

"Not so much," said Kalum, staring at the picture.

"I know what'll help," said Nex. "Let's go crush some Scorps, and get some answers."

When he returned an hour later it was with more than a few bruises and no leads on Darius. He retrieved his TRIST and collapsed into bed, oblivious to the eyes that watched him across the hallway.

29

FRAYED AND TORN

Nex woke him up early the next morning and wouldn't stop yammering in his head until Kalum had sat and drunk two cups of black coffee. Amped up on a caffeine rush he was out of the door before Nadine and Reese woke. The chill of the morning breeze cut through him and he shivered. The roads were still deserted, except for the odd Transport returning maintenance crews home after a night's work.

Nex floated along side him, telling him it was the perfect time to work on his agility by taking the roof expressway. With a grin Kalum took Nex's advice and ran around the back of his house. Rounding the corner he crashed into something solid and immovable. He looked up to see Vincent's scarred face.

"Why are you here?" Kalum asked, backing away. "What do you want?"

"You need to answer some questions, boy," Vincent replied in a low rumble. "And I'd better like the answers otherwise you and me are gonna have a falling out." He grabbed Kalum and hoisted him to his feet.

Vincent stood up tall and Kalum had to crane his neck to look at him. Standing straight, the old man was well over six-foot and stood with a posture of military readiness.

"Who are you? Why were you... looking into my father's room?" Kalum asked, gasping and clawing at the hand around his throat. The man stepped closer, so close that Kalum could feel his hot breath on his cheek.

"You don't know anything, do you?" Vincent said while tightening his grip.

"Nex, help me," Kalum begged. The man's grip slackened and he nearly released him. His pale blue eyes widened and he looked Kalum up and down.

"What did you say?" he demanded. Then Kalum felt the surge as Nex kick-started his HUD. He appeared and jumped back in shock.

"This guy again? I know exactly the move set you need. I think a bit of Jean Claude Van Damme. Maybe Bloodsport? Oh that was a good—"

"Do something!" Kalum said. Immediately his HUD filled, bright blue, with attack moves. Panicking, he activated the first one he saw. Throwing his body backwards and pulling down on Vincent's wrist at the same time, he flipped back and aimed the toe of his boot at the man's chin.

There was a bright flash of light just before his foot could make contact and the man took a half step back. Writhing in mid-air he turned his body away and then reversed the momentum like a whip uncoiling, and thrust Vincent's locked arm backwards. There was a satisfying wet pop as the joint dislocated, and the arm went limp. Vincent released Kalum, his arm swinging impotently at his side.

"Hrrrm," he grunted. Apart from a slight twitch at the corner of his mouth there was no evidence the injury had caused any pain at all.

Kalum managed to duck out of reach of his other grasping hand. Vincent reached across and yanked his arm forward and his shoulder made a thunk as it landed home in its socket.

"I need to get out of here!" Kalum said, and Nex lit the way for him. He dove under Vincent's desperate grab and made it to the building behind him. He scaled it with sure-footed ease. Looking back down he saw Vincent staring back at him and the cold, detached manner of the man chilled him like ice water running down his back. He turned and let the fear fuel his rooftop scramble to the safety of the school building.

He followed the route mapped out for him and within a few minutes he'd managed to make his way to Trinity. He paused at the top of the office block next door to the school to catch his breath. The block hummed with activity but Kalum was pretty sure he could take a minute there. He scanned the area around him, searching for Vincent. On the outskirts of the school ground, he saw two figures talking. There was a dull ache as his eyes adjusted and he saw it was Nathan and Reese having an animated discussion. Kalum watched as Reese was shoved to the ground and then Nathan threw a piece of paper into the dirt after him.

Reese must have left even earlier than me, he thought.

Kalum shimmied down the side of the building, making sure to avoid any windows through which he could be spotted. Checking behind him with fervent glances he saw no sign of his pursuer and hastened to the front entrance. As he turned the corner of the alleyway he was hit by an outstretched arm that clothes-lined him. Two strong hands hauled him back to his feet and he looked glassy eyed at Vincent.

"That makes us even for the shoulder."

His eyes glinted at Kalum from deep within sunken sockets. They moved quickly from side to side like small animals trying to burrow their way further underground.

"Let go of me," Kalum said, struggling, and trying vainly to wrench his arm away.

"Your father has something I need," Vincent said, pushing Kalum back into the alleyway and out of view. He reached under his coat and Kalum thought he was pulling out a weapon, but instead he smoothed out a scrap of paper. On it was scrawled a sketch that Kalum couldn't make sense of. Beneath it was a familiar series of symbols and numbers that he recognised from his sketchbook. They were the fragments of his father's previous work. There was a tingle behind his eye as he felt Nex fill in the gaps in the formula

"Have you seen this before?" Vincent asked.

Nex fed Kalum every strike and move imaginable to get free but it was useless. Kalum couldn't land a single blow. Every time he got close he was treated to the same flash of light that he'd seen before.

Vincent's hand shot out like a striking cobra and wrapped his fingers around Kalum's throat. He hoisted the boy off the ground and slammed him back down.

"I'll ask you again," he growled as he loomed over him. "Have you seen this before? Maybe in that book of yours?"

"N-no," Kalum said.

Vincent released him and let him take a step back. He took off his cap and scratched at the buzz-cut grey hair on his head.

"Listen. I... I'm sorry. I... I just get carried away sometimes, find it hard to control my... my emotions. Believe it or not, your dad and I used to be friends. I need the completed formula."

"You're a Scorp, and my father would never have helped

a Scorp," Kalum said as he dusted himself off. "Your leader Darius sent you didn't he?

"Leader?" Vincent spat the word and laughed without mirth. "He's a thug."

The man took a step closer and Kalum found that the brick wall behind him was blocking his retreat.

"I know who you are... Steel Falcon," the man said in a mocking tone that set Kalum's teeth on edge. "And while I don't object with you cleaning out the thrash who are calling themselves Scorps, I will let your secret out if I don't get that book."

"Kalum!" a voice called and Elliott Sparrow ducked his head in. "Er... Mr Vincent... what's going on here?"

Nex jumped up and down in front of Sparrow, pointing at Vincent.

"This guy is stalking us! He was at our house the other night. Tell him Kalum!"

"It's nothing, Sir," said Kalum with one eye on Vincent's stoic expression. "Mr Vincent was just telling me how much hard work it is to maintain the Arena, that's all."

Kalum grabbed his kitbag off the floor and made to leave but this time it was Sparrow who blocked his path. He was staring at Vincent with an odd intensity that was returned in earnest.

Kalum eyed them warily and then rushed past into the school. As he sprinted down the corridor towards his class he found that his new celebrity status meant it was almost impossible to get anywhere quickly. It took him five extra minutes that he didn't have spare to wade past the offered high fives, flirtatious girls and requests for autographs.

"Hey! Studly!" a voice called, stopping Kalum in his tracks. He turned and saw A.J walking towards him. There was a sway to the way she walked that was hypnotic, and it felt like everything around him slowed to a crawl. A door opened and Kalum saw Lexi. Their eyes met and he saw relief wash over her face. Then he was acutely aware of a loud thrum filling the hallways. It grew in volume until it became painful to hear. A.J was next to Lexi, both girls covering their ears. Students began to panic, bolting like startled gazelle.

"Nex!" Kalum said, feeling the vibrations in his teeth. "What... what is that?"

Before Nex could reply, there was an explosion. As one of the school's outer walls disintegrated, Lexi and A.J were enveloped in a thick plume of dust. Ceiling tiles fell onto the spot where the girls had stood, making a sound like a car crash as they landed.

Kalum ran into the dust, pushing past the students running the other way. He found A.J on top of Lexi, her body showered with debris. They were a dozen feet away from where they had been when the ceiling caved in. Kalum turned and saw the shattered remains of the tiles on the floor and said a silent prayer of thanks that they hadn't landed on the girls.

Lexi's eyes fluttered open and she saw A.J.

"Get off me," she said, and shoved her off with a grunt.

"Idiot," A.J snapped back. "I tripped over your toothpick legs."

There came a rumble of boots as figures streamed in through the hole in the wall. Where Kalum and the girls crouched, they were partially shielded by overturned lockers. Chancing a look through the gap underneath them Kalum saw the men form a line on either side of the opening in the wall. They had rifles slung over their shoulders and stood stiff at attention.

"Children. Children. Children, everywhere," drawled a familiar voice. "God I hate children."

The dust cleared and Kalum saw Darius standing in the breech, flanked by Scorp foot-soldiers. The man flicked a piece of debris from his leather jacket and turned to the closest Scorp.

"Search the school," he said. "Bring me anyone who remotely matches the description."

Scorps peeled off, ripping classroom doors open and dragging out pupils and faculty alike. Darius paced the halls, inspecting the pupils and shaking his head while dismissing them one by one.

"Come on," said Nex flickering into view in front of Kalum. "Let's get them!"

"Secret identity, remember?" Kalum hissed under his breath.

"What?" asked A.J, looking at him in confusion.

"You'd think the Scorp leader would want to keep a secret identity," Lexi whispered. "That way the Enforcers wouldn't be able to track him down."

"Hey dude! Get your paws off me man!"

From under the locker, all three of them turned to the familiar voice. They saw Jun being dragged backwards to Darius, the heels of his shoes screeching against the floor.

"I'm going," Kalum said, feeling Nex come alive and his HUD light up. He felt a firm hand on his shoulder and half turned to see A.J holding him back. He tried to shrug her off but her grip was surprisingly strong.

"Don't," she whispered. "Don't leave us."

"WHAT IS THE MEANING OF THIS?!"

Cooper's booming voice echoed through the hall and his stomping feet clanged as he approached. The snarl on his ruddy face evaporated as he saw Darius and the Scorp troops. He tried to back away, but Darius nodded to the Scorps, who had a hold on Jun, and they released him, grabbing Cooper instead.

Jun didn't hang about. He bolted, moving faster than Kalum had ever seen him go and disappearing around the corner of the corridor.

"I need some help, tubby," Darius said. He ran the barrel of his rifle under Cooper's chin and gave it a twist so it dug into the soft flesh there.

"I... I am the Headmast—" Cooper started, but his voice died as pressure against his voice box increased.

"As I was saying..." said Darius with a grin. "I've been looking for someone. I've been looking really hard for him. Hit every Medical Centre from deep in the NC darklands to here."

Darius held up a thin plastic bracelet to show Cooper. It was frayed and torn but for the most part intact. Kalum's eyes zoomed and focused on it, picking out every minute detail. He saw a serial number and part of his surname embossed there, the rest a shredded, unintelligible mess."

"You see, the last Medical Centre records match this serial number as having gone through there, even match it to this school, but someone tampered with the records. They couldn't give me a name."

Cooper was sweating profusely now, his beady eyes darting from side to side trying to find a way out.

"I'm looking for a boy, black hair, glasses, about this height," said Darius, gesturing with his free hand. "He had these bright blue eyes, impossible to mistake."

A look of confusion crossed Cooper's face and he squirmed. Darius applied pressure to his neck and the Headmaster yelped.

"Are... are you sure both eyes were b-bright blue?" he stammered.

Darius was about to reply when they heard footsteps. Each step was a short sharp tap that rang with fearless authority. Clayton Lancaster approached, his pace quick but not hurried, a look of distaste on his face. Kalum felt A.J stiffen at his side and he put his hand on hers. He could feel Lexi's eyes on him but he reasoned that he should do anything he could to stop A.J from panicking and drawing attention to where they were hidden.

Lancaster stopped a few feet away from Darius and regarded the Scorps that held Cooper, and then he looked back to their leader, a dark glint in his eye.

"The great Darius, leader of the Scorps," he said, his voice as unpleasant as an out of tune violin. "Is this what you have been reduced to? Attacking schools?"

Darius broke eye contact with Lancaster and shifted back a half step as Lancaster came closer.

"Let the good Headmaster go," Lancaster said looking up at the muscled Scorp. Darius paused, making a show of mulling it over, and then gave a sharp nod. Cooper landed in a heap as the Scorps released him. He tried to regain any semblance of dignity as he stood, straightening his knotted tie and slicking his hair across as much of his scalp as possible.

"You thug! You vandal!" he blustered.

Darius barked and snapped his jaws, and Cooper gave up any attempt at bravery, choosing to cower behind Lancaster. There was a beep as Lancaster keyed a command into his TRIST. A moment later an alarm rang out through the school, and arrows lit up on the floor guiding people towards the nearest exit.

"Eli," said Lancaster over his shoulder, "please ensure

the students are evacuated, and my son obviously takes priority."

Cooper nodded and left, taking tentative steps at first, before dashing out of sight. Lancaster was talking to Darius now but over the din of the alarm it was hard for Kalum to hear.

"I can't hear them either," Nex said in his head.

Then the background noises started to fade and their speech amplified as Nex altered Kalum's hearing.

"That's better," said Nex.

"... are you confused?" Lancaster said.

"No, Sir," Darius said. "We're looking for someone. The boy who came into our territory and disrespected us."

"We did a hell of a lot more than disrespected them," Nex said, and laughed. Then he stopped, his voice suddenly serious. "Wait. Did he call him Sir?"

"A boy?!" Lancaster struck Darius with the back of his hand, and the big man staggered.

"You would risk my operation? Over a boy?" Lancaster said, striking him again and again. The other Scorps glanced at each other but didn't move to attack.

"Sir... Aug distribution is through the roof. Every Gauntlet event we run we get at least a hundred new customers," Darius said. "You've seen the Credit balance..."

Lancaster grabbed a fistful of Darius' hair and pulled him down so that he was at eye level with him.

"I don't give a damn about the Credit balance. Give away the Augs if you want. I want everyone using! I don't want to hear anything more about your petty vendetta."

"Sir. The boy disrespected me in front of my men. I can't let that lie."

"Forget the boy! What about the vigilante, eh? We need the people scared of your Scorps so that they'll turn to us for support and protection. We don't want them rallying behind a vigilante!" Lancaster said as he squeezed Darius' face in his hand. "You have two jobs. Get rid of the vigilante, and get the Augs to as many people as possible. You said you'd take care of it. That's the only reason I haven't sent in Alpha Squad to cleanse your operation."

Darius went pale at Lancaster's threat and went down onto his knees. He bowed his head and put his hands together in supplication.

"But Sir. I delivered the Spectre to you!" Darius whined. "That wasn't easy, as he was sent in by the man who ran the Scorps before me. It took a lot of convincing to get him to meet with me and reveal his identity."

"Ah yes," Lancaster said, taking a step back. "Amadeus wasn't even on our radar. He'd been with us many years. I would never have pegged him as the one hacking our network and leaking information."

Darius straightened himself up and allowed a self-satisfied look to cross his face.

"I'll take care of the vigilante, Sir. The next run of the Gauntlet is going to be our biggest yet. I'm going to put him down **hard**, and in public. We might even push a thousand new Augs during that weekend with your new delivery."

A flicker of a smile crossed Lancaster's face. He considered the Scorp leader for a moment and then gave him a curt nod.

"Last chance, Darius. You'd better be right," he growled. "Now get out of my sight."

Darius and the remaining Scorps retreated back the way they'd come.

Lancaster paused near where they lay in the space between the lockers. They saw him stoop to brush away some dirt from his immaculate leather shoes and then they heard the sound of his footsteps retreating. Kalum shifted so that he had his hands pressed against the side of the lockers. His muscles rippled as Nex strengthened them.

"You won't be able to shift it on your own," A.J said, sounding sullen.

"Maybe if we all push together," Lexi suggested as she placed her hands next to Kalum's. The two of them pushed together and they started to rise. Even with Nex's adjustments the stack of lockers weighed a tonne. A.J huffed and added her support, and together they moved with ease.

"Ugh!" said A.J looking at the dust that coated her outfit and her hair. She brushed herself off and scowled at her chipped nails.

"Well I'm not hanging around here for something else to happen," she said.

Kalum let her go and then turned to his TRIST. He called up the program that Casey had installed and keyed in his friend's TRIST IDs. He saw Jun and Casey's indicators appear and felt his body relax as he saw they were at the fire assembly point. Then he keyed in Reese's, and blanched as an error message appeared. He tried again with the same result. Then he ran to the assembly point, ran like a man possessed. He scoured the area, frantically searching while ignoring Jun and Casey. Reese was nowhere to be seen. Then on a hunch he ran out to the woodland border of the school, where he had seen Reese talking to Nathan earlier.

There he saw Reese's TRIST unit, lying abandoned in the mud, its screen flashing red.

AT THE SCORP HEADQUARTERS, Darius sat in his makeshift room, above the throng of bodies preparing the area for the upcoming Gauntlet tournament below him. He knew that the Scorps who had witnessed his humiliation at Lancaster's hands wouldn't talk under pain of death. He looked at the hospital ID bracelet he held in his hand. For the hundredth time he regarded the remains of the worn away name that was on it. With a grunt he slammed it down onto the desk. Hearing the threat of Alpha Squad being set loose on them had focused his mind on the tasks that Lancaster had given Darius. His hand touched the welt across his cheek and he grimaced. He knew he had to put all thoughts of revenge out of his mind. At least for now.

There was a commotion and he saw the crowd below him shift at what he assumed was a scuffle breaking out. The unrest rippled through it and he saw a body being dragged towards the passage that led up through their base. Then there was the rap of knuckles on his door.

"Enter," he barked.

The heavy door swung open and two Scorp guards threw a body to the ground at Darius' feet. With a moan it uncurled and a boy stood in front of him. He was wearing the Trinity colours and his uniform was ripped and ragged. Darius smiled when he saw the bloodshot eyes and thin veil of sweat on the boy's forehead. He knew an addict when he saw one.

"I want to join the Scorps," the boy said in a shaky voice.

Darius stood and towered over him. He backhanded the boy, the same way Lancaster had done to him. The boy reeled but to Darius' annoyance, he did not fall or cry out.

"You don't want to join the Scorps," Darius spat. "I can see what you want. It's written on your face. You want Augs."

Darius turned and sat back in his chair with a sigh. "Get rid of him," he said, gesturing to the door.

"W-wait!" the boy cried out as hands snatched at him. He ducked under one arm, and swept the legs out from under the Scorp who came at him from the other side. He crunched an elbow into the sternum of another and drove him back with a kick. He backed away, moving so the wall was behind him, hands raised up.

"Yes... Yes. I do want Augs," the boy said. " But I have information... information about the Steel Falcon,"

"Hold on," said Darius. "I want to hear what this scrapper has to say."

He stood in front of the boy as he wiped a trickle of a bloody tear from his eye.

"You got a name, Trinity boy?" Darius asked.

"Walker. Reese Walker," the boy said.

Darius' eyes widened briefly and he snatched up the ID bracelet in front of him, squinting at the smudged and faded name written there.

"Get this boy an Aug," he said to the Scorp standing by Reese. "Get him as many as he wants."

Darius put an arm around Reese and gave him a playful thump on the arm.

"Tell me, Reese," Darius said as a smile broke out across his face, "you don't happen to have a brother do you?"

30

RIVULET OF BLOOD

"Sentech aren't supposed to do this," Nex said. "They're supposed to be the good guys."

"Really?" Kalum said. "Remember what we heard Lancaster and Cooper talking about. I never thought their hands were totally clean."

"But Dad worked for them," Nex replied. "So did Mum."

Lexi joined Kalum and they followed his TRIST tracker until they found Jun and Casey. It took a minute to bring them up to speed with what they'd seen and heard.

"But why?" Jun asked. "Why would Sentech work with the Scorps?" He had mostly recovered from his altercation with the Scorps, the task of finding Reese focusing his mind and stopping him from thinking about it.

"It's pretty clever," Casey said, "if you think about it. If Sentech were behind manufacturing the Augs, or planning to experiment on its people, then it would need someone else to point the finger at."

Kalum hadn't really been listening, his mind preoccupied with thoughts of Reese, the image of his angry face plastered in his memory, flashing to the surface every few minutes.

"There," Lexi said. "There he is."

Kalum spun around hoping to see Reese, but instead they found the other person they were searching for.

"Nathan!" Kalum shouted as he barged through a throng of students. He slammed the boy against a locker and drove his forearm under his throat.

"Where's Reese?" Kalum growled.

Nathan squirmed and tried to speak, his voice stuck in his throat. He clawed at Kalum's arm and flailed, but Kalum was as immovable as a mountain.

"Release him," a voice rumbled, and Daniel Park's massive hand wrapped around Kalum's arm. He pulled, and was surprised when Kalum didn't budge. Then he concentrated and pulled harder, peeling Kalum away from Nathan. Kalum was amazed that even with his strength augmented by Nex, Daniel had managed to overpower him. He scowled up at the boy.

"Where's my brother?" Kalum shouted. "I saw you talking to him earlier. Now he's gone."

Nathan smoothed his ruffled uniform and sneered at them from behind Daniel.

"Boy, you really did a number on your brother, Walker," Nathan said. "Do you understand how it looked to the Scouts? Seeing a prospect for the National squad being taken down by a runt like you? Can you *imagine* what that cost him?"

Kalum took another step forward and Daniel moved his large frame to block him. He shook his head, his face an implacable mask.

"Please Nathan," said Lexi, stepping forward and showing unusual restraint. "Reese is missing."

"I'll speak to you Walker," Nathan said, as he looked around the hall at the gathered students. "In private."

No one moved, just murmured to themselves and gave each other sideways glances.

"Come on!" shouted Kalum. "Move!" He pounded a fist into the locker and left a dent in it the size of an apple. The boom of the impact sent the other students scurrying away. Kalum gave a nod and his friends backed off too, as did Daniel after Nathan gestured for him to leave. Then the two boys were the only people left, and staring at each other with undisguised contempt.

Kalum clenched his jaw and tried to drive out the look of hatred Reese had given him when they'd last spoke.

"Where. Is. He?" Kalum said through clenched teeth.

"No clue," said Nathan, smirking.

Kalum's head hurt and his vision tinged red at its borders. He imagined caving in Nathan's face with his fist and found the thought immensely appealing. He paused and took a deep breath, allowing the anger to fade as he exhaled.

"I saw you two talking," he said when he finally trusted himself to speak. "What did you say to him?"

Nathan averted his gaze and stuffed his hands deep into his pockets.

"Please Nathan..." Kalum said.

"He wanted my Scorp contact," Nathan replied, looking at the ground.

"What? Why?"

"I'd got him some Augs. Thought it was funny a straight laced guy like your brother was using. But he wanted more and more. I said no, so he wanted my contact."

Kalum shoved him against the lockers again.

"And you gave it to him?" Kalum demanded.

This time Nathan pushed him back and glared.

"Yeah I gave him the contact," Nathan said. "He said he'd go public and say I'd been using. I don't need to have that conversation with my father. Not that it mattered anyway. When he saw that Darius was here, he chased right after him."

"Give me the contact."

Nathan looked at him and rolled his eyes. He brought up the contact details on his TRIST and then touched it to Kalum's. There was a soft beep as the transfer completed.

"Look, Walker, you may have grown a pair lately, but Darius doesn't mess around."

Kalum gave him an even look and then just walked away.

"It's your funeral." Nathan called after him.

Kalum broke out into a run. He ran straight past where his friends were waiting and headed straight up to the roof, his chest tight and crying out for air. The atmosphere in the school building was suddenly thick, so thick that he couldn't take it in.

He was typing the number into his TRIST before he stepped out onto the roof. The device connected to the network Darius used and Kalum heard the ringing tone. It rang a few times and disconnected.

"What did Nathan say?" Lexi asked, as she, Jun and Casey joined Kalum on the roof.

"Reese went after Darius. He's probably with him now." He turned to them, eyes downcast. "He's... he's been using Augs."

"I know what you're thinking Kal," Lexi said. She gave his shoulder a squeeze. "But you're not gonna get him back any quicker by blaming yourself."

"But it *is* my fault."

"Hey! You didn't force him to use Augs," Jun said. "This isn't on you."

Cooper closed the school for the day and Kalum's friends took him home. An Enforcer Transport was parked up outside his house, its flashing lights drawing curious glances from their neighbours.

"No," Nadine said to an Enforcer Sergeant, as Kalum came through the door. "My boy would never de-tag himself, he'd wouldn't remove his TRIST."

The Enforcer sergeant took off his hat and ran a hand through his silver hair. He sighed and looked at the other Enforcers around him.

"Listen," he said to Nadine, leaning in and lowering his tone. "I get, it alright? Kids will be kids. If you can get him to put his TRIST back on in the next twenty-four hours we can just sweep this under the rug, you know?"

Nadine's eyes narrowed and her fists balled at her side. Kalum saw the throb of the vein in her forehead ramp up. Lucas slid between the two of them, before Nadine could lunge at the Enforcer, pushing her back with one hand.

"Yes Sergeant," Lucas said in a deferential tone. "You've got it. As soon as he comes home we'll weld it to his arm."

The Sergeant seemed satisfied at this and he and his men left, pushing past Kalum as they went. Nadine waited for the door to click shut behind the Enforcers and for the noise of the leaving Transports to fade, and then turned to look

at Kalum, who could feel his mother reading his face.

"Where is he, Kal.

"He's with the Scorps," Kalum said, feeling the weight of his words. He pulled out Reese's TRIST and put it down on the table.

Nadine's eyes widened and Kalum thought for a

moment she was going to break down. She went to the closet and pulled out a black duffel bag and slung it over one shoulder.

"Sis..." Lucas said. "It's okay. I'll go look for him. You need to stay here with Owen."

"Owen will be fine for an hour or so. The nurse is here with him," Nadine said. "You can bring your kit and join me if you want, but I'm looking for Reese. He's my baby boy."

Kalum felt his heart wrench when he heard her voice hitch but they both controlled their emotions.

They hit the streets, Lexi, Casey and Jun in toe.

"Let's take the 'Stang," said Lucas. "Its not subtle, but we can search faster this way. He popped the trunk and Kalum watched him pull out a black duffel similar to Nadine's. He took out a holster that held two handguns, and strapped it on.

It was nearly curfew by the time they had been to every known Scorp hangout, including some that Kalum and Nex had shut down as the Steel Falcon. They were all utterly deserted; there was no sign of any Scorps. The only people they came across were twitchers searching for an Aug fix. At the outskirts of the Sentech-controlled region they stopped for a break, at the mouth of an abandoned NC encampment.

Their TRISTs chimed and the screens lit up. They projected a newscast into the air above the unit. Nadine tried to shut hers off but the communication continued to play. Suddenly the feed crackled and altered and a hooded man appeared next to a black background.

The image changed to show a figure in shackles. There was a black bag over his head and he was wearing a pair of plain black trousers. He staggered from side to side, the clinking chains not letting him move further. Kalum knew instantly who it was and from the way he felt his mother tense beside him, he knew she had come to the same realisation.

"This is one of yours..." Darius' voice spoke in a voice over. "A child of privilege... but he came to us willingly..."

Another figure ripped the hood off and Reese's face filled the picture. He was almost unrecognisable. His grin was wide and maniacal, his angry red eyes in stark contrast with his pale skin. He swayed on his feet and dribbled from the corner of his mouth.

"He came up short..." Darius continued. "At the Gauntlet tomorrow we'll throw him in to be used as a human punch bag. Unless... the Steel Falcon comes for him, that is."

The image switched to Darius' face and he glared at them.

"Steel Falcon! Come to the Gauntlet tomorrow and take this boy's place. Then we will send him back to his family. Anyone who comes to watch will get Augs at half the credit price."

The image cut out and the TRIST screen returned to normal, the image in the air dissolving away. They looked at each other, reading the despair in their eyes. The TRISTs chimed the hour, alerting them of the impending curfew.

"We... we have to go back," Lucas said.

Nadine shrugged off her brother and carried on walking. He grabbed her hand and she whirled around. For a moment Kalum thought she was going to lay Lucas out, but instead she buried her head in his chest and started to sob. After a while they gathered themselves to return to Lucas' Mustang when they saw a man stumbling out of the camp. He had messy blonde hair and wore torn jeans and a top with the familiar black scorpion logo.

"Hey!" shouted Nadine.

The man's head shot up and he spotted them rushing towards him. He scrambled back into the camp and they gave chase through the maze of ramshackle dwellings and stalls, but they lost sight of the man and came to a stop.

"Where did he go?" Nadine shouted, curling her arms over her head and punching a wall. Kalum scanned the area, and felt Nex adjust his sight and hearing.

Then a sound came from above them and Kalum spun in time to see the man jump down from the low roof of a hut. His arm snaked around Nadine's neck and pulled her head back as he brought a blade up and pressed it to her throat.

"What are you Corporation trash doing here? Come to pick over the bones?"

Kalum saw a rivulet of blood form at the blade where it pressed into his mother's neck and his anger flared. He felt the red mist descend over his vision under the influence of the rage. Before he could lunge at the man, Nadine drove an elbow under her captor's ribs that knocked the air out of him. A strike to his adam's apple left him wheezing and with a twist she had him sprawled at her feet. Kalum, Lexi, Jun and Casey gawped at the demonstration.

"Your mum is so badass," Lexi whispered.

"You have no idea..." Lucas said under his breathe.

The man tried to stand, but Nadine planted a boot on his chest and shoved him back down. She moved the heel so that it was over his neck.

"From here it would be very simple to crush your trachea and you'd breathe through a tube for the rest of your life," she said.

Nadine bent forward to look the man in the eyes and applied pressure through her heel to demonstrate her point.

The man bucked and choked and after a moment she released the pressure.

"I want to know where the Scorp base is, and I want to know now."

"I don't know," the man said, and gasped.

"Really?" asked Nadine, leaning forward again. "Where tomorrow's Gauntlet?"

"Let him go," came a voice from behind them,

They turned to see the Operative standing behind them, a silhouette against the setting sun. When they didn't move he brought up his arm and pointed it at them. There was a whirring, clanking noise and the armour plating there shifted and turned on itself, changing the arm to a glowing gun barrel.

Lucas moved and had his guns out, trained on the Operative instantly.

"I won't ask again," said the Operative's synthesised voice.

"Where is the Scorp base?" Nadine screamed. "They have my boy."

Behind the white fox mask something shifted but the Operative didn't lower his weapon. He reached to his side and pressed a button. Three orbs detached from his armour and started to orbit him. Before they could say anything else, the orbs shot towards them, trailing a thin wisp of smoke from each one.

Lucas got a shot off but missed. The smoke billowed and engulfed them. Kalum heard the Operative move and tried to stop him but he was shoved to the ground.

The smoke cleared almost as quickly as it had appeared, and when they looked they saw the Operative standing on one of the taller buildings of the encampment, with the

Scorp that they had caught slung over his shoulder in a fireman's carry. In a blink they were gone.

"Dammit!" Nadine shouted and slipped down onto her haunches. Their TRISTs chimed another curfew warning and Lucas helped her to her feet.

"Come on," he said, directing them back to the car. "We won't do Reese any good if we all get locked up by the Enforcers."

The journey home was a silent one, apart from Nex chattering away in Kalum's head.

"Next time we go up against the Operative, I'm gonna take him out!" Nex said. "He thinks he can make a fool of the Steel Falcon?"

Kalum couldn't think of a way to shut him up without looking as if he'd gone mad and was talking to himself, so just tried to block it from his mind, and stare at the neon lights of the city as it zipped by.

Thanks to Lucas' driving they made it back to their home just before the curfew.

"You should be able to get home before the night drones and patrols are out... but of course you're welcome to stay here for tonight," Nadine said, turning to Jun, Casey and Lexi. "If you'll excuse me, I need to attend to Owen, and let his nurse go."

Nadine turned to go up the stairs and Kalum went after her.

"We're going to find him," he said with as much resolve as he could muster.

She gave him a nod and a tired smile before going into Owen's room. Kalum was joined by Lucas on the landing, and he gave him a hug.

"Don't worry about Reese, lad," Lucas said. "He's a tough one. I'm going to keep looking."

"What about the curfew?" Jun asked.

"Doesn't apply to me." Lucas said with a grin and holding up his security consultant ID badge. "The drones scan me and let me go about my business."

As he left he turned back to Kalum.

"Look after her," he said. "Do your friends need a lift?"

"You guys go home," Kalum said, forcing a smile.

Jun and Casey stood hesitantly but Lexi remained seated on the couch.

"I'm going to stay a little longer," she said.

"Lexi..." Kalum said but he could tell that she wasn't going to change her mind.

"You guys should go though," he said to Casey and Jun. He embraced his friends together.

"Case," he whispered. "Can you get me the location of the Gauntlet?"

He felt Casey stiffen but after a moment he nodded. With reluctance they followed Lucas out of the house.

Kalum slumped on the sofa next to Lexi. He wondered if Lucas was right. Yes Reese was tough. The old Reese, anyway. He could only see the situation playing out one way; Casey would find out where the Gauntlet was being held, and then he'd go and trade himself for Reese.

"I'm staying," Lexi said. "I'll sleep on the couch."

Lexi's statement brought Kalum back out of his thoughts.

"Wait. What?" he said.

"I can't leave you like this."

"But..." he saw Lexi's pursed lips and the argument died in his throat.

"No way you're going to sleep on the couch, you can use my bed."

"Ummm," Lexi said, flushing.

"I mean I'll take the couch, you take the bed," Kalum said, now red faced himself.

Kalum stood in the doorway of his room, holding the door open for Lexi. She came in and perched on the corner of his bed. He opened his cupboard and handed her a fresh towel. His hand lingered on hers as he passed it and then they both pulled away.

What's wrong with me? It's only Lexi. She's been in here hundreds of times. Why am I being so weird? he thought.

Kalum's TRIST flashed an incoming message. The contact was listed as 'unknown' and was in audio only, which meant it was probably from a device outside of the TRIST network.

"Hello?" Kalum said.

A laugh came through the speaker. It turned into a cackle before fading.

"It *is* you!" Darius' said. "I'd recognise that little timid voice anywhere."

"Give me back my brother," Kalum said.

"At this stage he's more like my brother than yours!" Darius said with a laugh. "I know *everything* about you. Give your brother a couple of Augs and he really comes alive, eh? Poor little Kalum Walker... so scared of his own shadow that he's got to pop pills!

There was a pause and Kalum could almost feel Darius' hot breath coming through the speaker.

You made me lose face in front of my men," Darius snarled. "Disrespected me!" he bellowed, distorting his voice.

"I can't let that go unanswered. That message for the Steel Falcon? Consider it for yourself, too. Come to the Gauntlet fight tonight. I'll send you the location. Give yourself up. Let me watch you get torn limb from limb and then I'll let your addict brother go."

There was a click as the communication went dead, and the silence hung heavy in the room. Kalum didn't hesitate. He turned back and grabbed the kit bag that held his costume, the one he'd buried in the back of his cupboard.

"There's nothing I can say is there?" Lexi said in a quiet voice. "You're going out there aren't you? How exactly are you going to fight your way through? You told us that Nex's power comes with a time limit. You're not going to be able to get Reese out and take down the Scorps in under an hour!"

"I have to, Lex," Kalum said. He threaded his arms through the sleeves of the costume and donned the visor. Before he closed the cupboard he paused, the glimmer of an idea forming in his mind. Reaching in, he grabbed something else and stuffed it into his backpack.

"I have an idea that might give me an edge," Kalum said, hoping he sounded more confident than he actually was.

Lexi was looking at him, mouth slightly slack, and gave a slow shake of her head.

"Well you look the part," she said.

She stood and walked over to him. She placed a hand on his chestplate where he'd drawn the red falcon insignia.

"Just like in your sketches," she said, giving him a hug. "No point me staying here if you're going. I'll go home too. Be safe."

He tried to pull away but Lexi didn't let him go. Kalum felt his pulse quicken and was thankful that the alert on his TRIST gave him an excuse to pull away.

"It's Casey," he said. "TRIST play audio file."

"Kal, I've triangulated all the places we went today, all the known Scorp hangouts, and there's a large building in

NC territory that intersects all those points," he said through the TRIST. "You might want to che—"

The audio cut out mid-sentence and Kalum tapped his TRIST screen but the audio file stopped short. It didn't matter; Casey had given him all he needed to know. His info matched up with the coordinates Darius sent him.

"Be safe," Lexi said again, and kissed him on the cheek. She held onto his hand even as she backed out of his room, finally letting their fingers slip apart as she left. Kalum watched her leave and then made the dash to his father's room. He started when he saw his dad sat bolt upright in his bed. His father's eyes were closed but Kalum could see that below the lids they were moving at a frantic pace. He eased off his TRIST unit and it barked out a warning. As he fastened it to his father's forearm the man's eyes snapped open. There was a clarity in them that Kalum hadn't seen since the day he'd returned home from the hospital. A smile touched his father's lips, but then his eyes glazed over again and his body went slack.

Kalum backed away and crouched at the sill of his father's window. He watched as Lexi crossed the road and made her way home. The window opened and a blast of cold hit him in the face. A minute later he was scampering across rooftops. He stopped and looked back at his home, wondering if he'd ever see it again.

"Come on, Nex," he said picking up the pace again. "Let's bring Reese home."

31

LEAPING TALL BUILDINGS IN A SINGLE BOUND

"Slow down," Nex urged as they scrambled from rooftop to rooftop. Kalum ignored him and flung himself on. His boot slid out from under him, its tread losing the battle for traction against the slick tiles. His fingers caught the edge of the roof and momentum slammed his chest into the side of the building.

As he tried to scramble back up, the toes of his boots scratched against the old red bricks, causing parts to crumble and rain down on the ground below.

"Wait!" Nex shouted, and his voice echoed in Kalum's head so loud that he nearly let go entirely.

"What's wrong with y—" Kalum started, but then he registered movement below him. A group of Enforcers were heading into the alley, the bright lights on the ends of their rifles cutting through the darkness. Kalum tightened his grip and felt the sharp edge of the brick bite into his fingers, in spite of the Henkan gloves. The burning in his arms ramped up as the Enforcers continued the search at their own pace below him. He felt the combination of muscle fatigue and gravity starting to take its toll and he slipped down half an inch.

"I'm on it," Nex said, sensing Kalum's discomfort.

The fire in his arms started to cool and he readjusted his grip. Below him the Enforcers had lost interest in whatever had drawn their attention, and headed back to the main street. With a grunt he pulled himself onto the roof and lay there panting for moment before getting back to his feet. A drone zipped overhead but the shadow of the chimney was enough to conceal him. He waited as the rest of the squadron sped past before peeling off in different directions.

"Will you just listen to me for second?" Nex said.

"No," Kalum retorted. "They've got him, Nex. They've got Reese. Who knows what they're going to do to him if we don't get him out."

"I get it," Nex said, his voice softer now. "But if you burn through our power we're not going to be able to put up much of a fight."

"Fine," Kalum said. "How are we going to do this?"

"We stick to the rooftops," Nex said. "I'll take care of the whole 'leaping tall buildings in a single bound' thing, but take it easy in between."

Kalum nodded his agreement and walked to the edge. He crouched, and felt the muscles in his legs ripple as Nex strengthened them. He thought of Reese, of the look on his brother's face after the Henkan semi-final. There had been hatred in his eyes. It had laced his voice even as it had cracked with the sting of betrayal.

The tiles beneath him split as he flew into the air and landed on the building across.

Nex guided his movements, giving him a gentle nudge to keep him heading on the right path. It took him nearly an hour, almost twice as long than if he'd been moving at full pelt. Large plumes of condensation came out of him as his hot breath hit the cold air. He was firmly in NC territory on the outskirts of the city. It looked similar to the area he'd found himself in after escaping from the Sentech installation, all broken dreams and dilapidated architecture. He stood inside what he thought must have been an old style parking lot, designed to stack vehicles into claustrophobic corners. It sat deserted, much like all others of its kind. The Corporation had ensured that only the obscenely wealthy or die hard motor-heads like his Uncle Lucas still drove anything with an internal combustion engine. This place was dead, with only scraps of its concrete carcass left for the Scorps to pick at.

He kicked away a spent Aug canister in disgust and it pinged of a wall and over the edge. Kalum walked past the dirt-smeared walls that surrounded him, adorned with large black Scorpion graffiti tags, until he was on top of the building.

"Doesn't look like much," he said. "We sure this is the right place?"

The boarded up door of the strange squat building across the street jerked open, and two muscled men appeared. One fiddled with a lock whilst the other grabbed the thick metal grating and hefted it up and over his head where it slotted away. People materialised out of the night, both NC and lower level Sentech workers, showing identification and handing over Credits to the thugs who had set up on either side of the entrance. They were allowed in, one by one, with a gruff nod. They stopped anyone with a TRIST, and Kalum watched as a device was plugged into them, turning the screen green and putting it into standby mode.

"It's definitely where they're holding the Gauntlet," Nex said. "But... I think we'll need to find another way in."

More and more people were joining the queue below them now, streaming in with no sign of slowing. Kalum nodded his agreement.

His eyes darted around the area. Apart from the guards at the entrance there didn't seem to be any other security. He felt certain he could take them down with ease, but Nex's warning to conserve his strength rang in his head.

"Where are they all going?" Kalum whispered. The small building looked like it could hold no more than fifty people at a push, but it kept on swallowing body after body.

Kalum slammed his fist into the exposed metalwork of the rubble next to him and it left the imprint of his fist. The red mist started to tinge his vision and he felt his control start to slip away to a primal urge of violence. He wanted to smash his way through anyone and anything in his path, to rend and to maim and to revel in his power. Somewhere, deep inside he knew it was the wrong call, that it would likely get both him and Reese killed, but he didn't care. A heady euphoria washed over him and threatened to drown him.

"Focus on something that's important to you," the memory of A.J's voice played back to him from the recesses of his memory.

The hammering pulse in his neck made it difficult to concentrate but he allowed his mind to cycle through images of the people in his life. His mother and her whip-like temper, Lucas and his dependable humour. It was a struggle, but he controlled his breathing. His father's face appeared in front of him, a man who he could barely remember, could never replace, and whose shadow he'd never be able to escape from. The injustice of his fate, trapped in a body that was decaying around a mind locked in a struggle to remember itself, made his anger flare. Then

Reese was there in his mind, the memory of their fight fresh and raw, adding fuel to his rage.

His control wavered, but then memories of his friends came crashing over him, ploughing through the anger and guilt and cleansing him.

He pictured his first meeting with Casey, both of them shy outcasts who had bonded over their shared awkwardness and love of technology. The following evening trips to the retro arcade, where Casey had carved out his legendary status, and late night games over the TRIST network, had cemented their friendship.

He remembered the first time he had seen Jun, cornered by older boys, whipping out a deck of cards to try to wow them into not giving him a beating. They hadn't given him the chance. Kalum had helped him pick himself and the cards up and they'd been friends ever since.

Next he thought of Lexi. From the time he'd lived here, there was no Lexi without Kalum, and no Kalum without Lexi. They'd been inseparable, partners in crime.

Casey, Jun, and Lexi's smiling faces filled his mind's eye and the warmth of their bond filled him. Exhaling, he let his eyelids lift and caught a glimpse of the light strands floating in front of him again. Kalum felt his hand reach forward, like a puppet being moved by its master. The light strands flickered and one by one they blinked out of existence. One remained. It too was losing its brilliance, reduced to just a gossamer thread, floating towards him. Kalum's fingers wrapped it and it exploded, sending a jolt through his arm and stopping at the base of his skull.

"I know what this place is," Kalum said. "I know how to get to Reese."

He took a step towards the roof edge but staggered and went down to one knee.

Nex appeared in front of him, his flickering form barely holding itself together.

"Whatever that was," Nex gasped, "it used up all my reserves."

Kalum reached into his backpack and pulled out the Henkan ball.

"I didn't want to use this so soon," he said, and activated it. The silver orb blinked on and the rings of light flashed in time. He held it tight as Nex watched and the lights flashed faster and faster. Then gritting his teeth, he held the ball close to his chest to smother the light from any passers by. The ball released its charge and Kalum twitched as it raced through him.

Nex rose, a smile on his face and pulsing with power.

"Yes!" he said. "Ready to rock!"

Kalum flipped over the near wall and he slid down the side, using friction and the outcropping edges to slow his descent. He landed and was already running before anyone could react to the noise of it.

"What's the plan?" Nex asked.

Kalum came around the other side of the Scorps' headquarters and scaled the structure directly behind it. The outer wall was an immense curved latticework of steel. In between were jagged teeth of glass, all that was left of the skin of a once proud edifice. His body was a missile, spinning to avoid the glass, and left him inside and out of sight once more. Kalum felt Nex adjust his vision to the darkness. Dust motes floated all around him, lit up like fireflies with his night vision.

"That thread of light I touched, it showed me something," Kalum said to Nex. "That Scorp building, it goes underground. Deep underground. Its tracks used to carry vehicles that carried people from all around the country to the heart of the city. It was one of the first casualties of the Government's collapse."

Kalum was in a large concourse. All around him were sections, closed off by metal shutters. Peeking through the gaps he could see discarded mannequins and sale signs, all covered with a thick layer of dust. By his side was a map of the surrounding area. He placed his finger on a circular symbol with a line running through it.

"That's where Reese is," Kalum said.

He followed the map to an escalator, with large patches of rust growing like mould on its surface. A leap brought him onto the handrail and he let his augmented balance and gravity guide him to the floor below. Momentum carried into his sprint and he hurdled a barrier. Another escalator was dealt with in the same way, the rubber of the handrail and his boots making his approach silent. The darkness below was almost more than his night vision could deal with, but he didn't need it to know he was not alone. The sound of eager, heavy breathing was all around him, their heartbeats like a drumroll. There was the odour of sweat and roiling anticipation, making the atmosphere musty and thick. Reading his mind, Nex guided him into a side room that he managed to force open with a shove of his shoulder. There he waited, not sure what he was hiding from.

"Where now, Nex?" Kalum whispered.

Before Nex could reply, there was a fizzling sound and a hum filled the air. Bright light blasted into the room, finding the spaces in between the door and the frame.

"Welcome!" boomed a familiar voice from behind him. Kalum spun, already in a defensive stance, batons extending from his gloves.

"We have a very special event for you at the Gauntlet

tonight!" the voice blared from the speaker above him in the wall. There was a twang of feedback that set Kalum's teeth on edge.

"Tonight, and only for tonight, fighting for his life, we have the one, the only Steel Falconnnnn!"

The crowd roared its approval and it took Darius a moment to calm them down. They fell to a hushed silence, but Kalum could still feel the energy of their buzzing anticipation.

It started as a whisper...

"We want blood."

"We want blood."

"We want blood."

Their feet hammered the floor, making the entire structure vibrate, and their primal lust was unmistakable.

"It looks like our guest is going to need some encouragement!" the voice shouted again. There was a sound of a struggle and then Kalum heard Darius speak again.

"Introduce yourself to the ladies and gentlemen."

Something unintelligible wafted over the airways followed by a thump and a groan.

"Introduce yourself or I'll break her fingers one by one."

"Jun," came the strained voice of his friend. "Jun Oshino."

Kalum felt like Darius had reached into his chest and was squeezing his heart with his meaty hands. A wave of nausea made his stomach do a half-turn and he thought he might throw up.

"Next," Darius said.

"Casey Danvers." Casey's voice was barely a whisper, but Kalum heard it clearly. Kalum moved to the door, his hand already on the handle, half turned, but Darius wasn't done.

"Mmm, mmm, mmm," Darius said. "And who might you be?"

Then he yelped and cried out. There was a chorus of laughter that Kalum could hear even without the sound coming through the speaker above him.

"Shut up!" Darius bellowed and after a few stray chuckles, his order was obeyed.

"Touch me again and I'll make you eat your own hand." came a female voice. Lexi's voice.

The handle bent in Kalum's grip. He wrenched the door open and followed the sound of the crowd's amusement. He vaulted down a flight of stairs and came skidding to a stop, his baton grinding against the floor to slow him. He stood on a wide platform. There were pillars on either side, and old half-disintegrated posters peeling off the walls. A crowd was gathered, at least two hundred strong, and Darius looked down at them from a makeshift stage.

A spot light illuminated him, and the crowd turned. They gasped when they saw him and fell into a reverent hush that irritated Darius even more. At his side, also on the stage, were his friends, bound and on their knees. The Scorp leader gestured to them and gave Kalum a toothy grin.

"I thought that maybe you needed some more... motivation," he said. "Come forward and meet your fate."

32

GIVING WAY TO DARKNESS

The crowd parted and as Kalum stepped forward he saw a large, rusty metal cage suspended from the ceiling behind Darius. It was big enough to cover nearly half the platform and creaked as it swayed from its hooks.

"Where is Reese Walker?" Kalum shouted. Nex kept pace with him, his small face grim with fury in his eyes.

Darius' grin grew even wider, and he brought his thick fingers to his mouth. The whistle was loud enough to pierce ear drums. There was a commotion in the crowd, and the two Scorps Kalum had seen taking Credits at the door appeared. The crowd exploded with excitement at their appearance. They waved banners with motifs, emblazoned with the names 'Reinhardt' and 'Lyle' on them. The names pulled at Kalum's memory.

Those guys are the Gauntlet fighters everyone's talking about!

They were half dragging, half carrying a smaller man in between them. His shaved head lolled around in a state of partial consciousness. They dumped him at Darius' feet and the big man stooped down to cup his face in one thick hand. When he turned the face to him, Kalum saw his brother looking back at him. His eyes were an unfocused, bleary red hue, the key sign of Aug overuse.

Reese shuddered and Darius shushed him. Darius beckoned to a Scorp guard behind him who reached into an enormous container behind the platform and fished out a canister for him. Darius gave Kalum a wide smile as he gave the purple canister a shake, and then sprayed it into Reese's eye. He settled almost immediately, a serene smile sitting on an otherwise slack face.

"Give him back."

Darius waggled a finger and shook his head.

"That's not how the world out here works, Steel Falcon," he said, pacing the stage. "Out here, as an NC everything comes at a cost, out here we barter. What have you got to offer in exchange?"

"I'll take his place." Kalum's reply was immediate. "I'll be your prisoner."

Darius pretended to muse over the offer and rubbed his chin before looking back at him with faux sincerity.

"That barter is fine for me, but what about all these good people who turned out for a show? What can you offer them?"

"I'll fight then," Kalum said. "I'll run the Gauntlet, give them a show they'll never forget."

A cheer went up from the crowd and they opened the path to the stage.

"How much longer have we got in reserve?" Kalum asked Nex under his breath. He popped into view next to him and pulled his cape in tight around himself. Nex looked at the throng around him and turned to Kalum with a look of fear that matched his own.

"Not enough for this," Nex said.

The two Scorps who had carried Reese like a slab of

meat moved to flank him, and he let them push him forward to the staging area. His friends watched as Darius gave a sign and the cage began to lower. His thugs remained in with Kalum, their dark eyes drilling holes into him. As the cage crashed down its sound reverberated throughout the space. From the elevated stage he could see the sea of faces looking at him with a savage thirst for blood. Now, for the first time, he could see that on either side of the platform were metal tracks that ran along the ground like the veins of a living creature. They led out into tunnels of unfathomable darkness. From deep within one of them, two round lights stared at him like unblinking eyes.

"The Steel Falcon against the reigning Gauntlet champion... Reinhardt!" Darius screamed. Then he looked at Kalum and put his hand up to silence the baying crowd.

"But this isn't fair, is it?" he said, spreading his arms and turning as if speaking to every one of the gathered spectators.

"How can we ask a mere man to fight this vicious vigilante? The one who has put so many of our Scorp brothers in Enforcer lock up."

Kalum looked at the cheering faces and felt Nex trigger his memory recall. He recognised many of the men here. Nex showed him a sped up segment of his memory and he replayed the way he'd torn through them during his patrols. Some of them were even part of the mob who had pursued him when he'd escaped from the hidden Sentech Facility. He couldn't fathom why they weren't still locked up.

He looked up, and Reinhardt was in front of him, a wall of muscle and aggression. His bare, muscular torso was peppered with scars, badges of honour from his time in the Gauntlet. Nex looked up at him, jaw set and defiant.

"He's not so tough," Nex growled, "We can take him."

"Hand over your armour and weapons." Darius said.

His armour was removed in segments and tossed into the crowd, who stampeded over each other to grab a souvenir. Reinhardt reached for the visor and Kalum jerked his head away.

"Let him keep his face hidden," Darius said. Kalum looked to see that he'd sauntered over so he was just on the other side of the bars. He leaned in closer, so only Kalum could hear him. From his hand dangled the broken hospital ID tag with Kalum's name.

"Let's keep it our little secret, okay, Kal?" Darius said, his voice dripping with malicious joy.

Kalum glared at Darius from behind his visor.

"It's amazing how talkative your brother gets after a few Augs," Darius whispered, and then laughed.

Reinhardt stood gargoyle-still whilst the other Scorp thug, who Kalum assumed was Lyle, swaggered back to the corner of the cage, rolling his shoulders and stretching. He leaned against its edge as if he was about to engage in casual conversation, a picture of relaxed disregard.

"Begin!" Darius shouted and a shower of sparks shot up from the cage edges. Kalum shielded his eyes as the light sent spots dancing around his vision.

Reinhardt's fist exploded into his abdomen with enough force to cave in a mountain. Kalum was thrown back and the metal of the cage dug into his flesh, drawing blood.

The crowd laughed and hollered and Darius punched the air and continued his running commentary. Up close he saw that the marks on the cage were not rust but dried blood. The bars were peppered with tiny barbs designed to bite and tear at the flesh of the competitors. The pain in his abdomen started to fade and Nex appeared.

"Let's even the odds," Nex said. Kalum felt the muscles

through his body undergo their transformation. His HUD rippled into view, hazy blue lines feeding him information. Reinhardt's breeze-block sized fist came at him and he caught it with one hand. Reinhardt grunted as he tried to use his height to leverage an advantage. Kalum rose from the floor and pushed the Scorp away. He came back swinging.

"Duck!" Nex said.

The defensive and offensive options scrolled past his eyes and he did what Nex commanded. The trunk-like arm flew over him and Kalum sprang back up, leading with a thunderous uppercut that knocked Reinhardt onto the mat.

"Yeah!" Cheered Jun.

Darius looked at him and Kalum saw the fear in his eyes.

Reinhardt was back on his feet, each lunge forward sounding like a gunshot against the mat under his feet. Kalum had selected an attack before Reinhardt reached him. A knife hand strike above the eyes drew blood that blinded him. The flurry of machine gun punches to the solar plexus took his breath, and Reinhardt pitched forward in time to meet Kalum's knee as the boy sprang into the air. The impact echoed in the enclosed space and the crowd winced as one.

The big man slid across the mat to the other side of the ring, where he lay in a heap.

"Just in time," said Nex. "Power reserves at ten percent."

"Wait," said Kalum, scanning the area. "Where's the oth—"

Lyle dropped down from the top of the cage. Kalum rolled with the blow but the pain was still exquisite when the Scorp's foot smashed into his jaw.

"Make that five percent," Nex said, his voice breaking into static.

"Did I forget to mention that Reinhardt and Lyle are a tag team?" Darius asked, and laughed into his mic. He turned and reached into the large vat of Augs and threw a few into the crowd.

Lyle was at Reinhardt's side by the time Kalum recovered. Two shiny objects sailed into the cage and Lyle jumped off the side of the cage to catch them in mid-air. He threw off the caps of the canisters, and Kalum saw they were Augs. Lyle pulled open Reinhardt's eye and dumped the contents in. With a manic grin he did the same to himself. Darius gave a nod and the Scorps started tossing more Augs out into the crowd from the containers behind him.

Reinhardt got to his feet as if he was pulled up by invisible strings. His body snapped rigid and his head came up. His eyes locked onto Kalum and he snorted and grunted like a bull about to charge. Whatever had been in the Aug had made him look even bigger and more menacing.

"This is gonna be fun!" Lyle said. His hand wiped the sweat off his face and slicked his black hair back.

The guttural laugh in Reinhardt's throat sent a chill through the crowd, silencing their cheers. The Scorp fighters stalked forward and Kalum's HUD flashed a warning. They split, moving in opposite directions, so fast that the HUD struggled to track them.

He managed to get his hands up so that his forearms took the bulk of the impact of Reinhardt's kick. Lyle was faster, his backhand blow sending Kalum spiralling back. The haymaker that Reinhardt landed slammed him to the ground.

"Two percent," Nex said.

Reinhardt lifted him up by the hair and Kalum caught a glimpse of something he'd never seen before on Lexi's face. Fear.

Then Lyle was on him, unleashing a savage onslaught of blows that made Kalum lose all concept of time. Eventually Lyle stopped and rocked back, panting. A flick of his head brought the hair out of his face.

"Wooooo!" he screamed, spinning around and throwing his arms up in celebration whilst Reinhardt tightened his grip.

Movement outside the ring caught Kalum's eye. The Operative materialised next to Darius, the shadows parting to let him pass. Jun and Casey tried to crawl away but their bonds stopped them. Lexi's eyes remained fixed on Kalum, and he tried to flash her a reassuring smile but he realised he couldn't feel the swollen mass that his face had become. He spat out a globule of congealed blood onto the mat and was glad that at least he still had all his teeth.

"One percent," Nex said, and the HUD faded until it was hardly visible.

Nex appeared in front of him, looking as awful as he felt.

"We've got one more play," he whispered. "I can try and siphon off some of the electrical activity in your body. It's what your brain, your heart, all your organs need to work. But... they... they may never work the same again."

Kalum felt his vision darken, the edges of his consciousness giving way to darkness. He tried to reply but his tongue wouldn't do as it was told.

"I need your permission, Kal," Nex pleaded. "I promised you I'd never take control again without your permission."

Kalum tried to talk, but his mind couldn't focus long enough for him to keep his train of thought. Everything around him seemed muted, like he was wrapped in cotton wool. The world around him started to darken and even Nex's voice felt like it was getting further and further away. Then his head sagged forward and his body went limp.

33

TISSUE AND SINEW

"I'll take that as a yes," Nex said.

Reinhardt dropped Kalum's limp body, and its weight thudded against the ground.

"No..." Jun whispered. Casey had his face in his hands. Lexi hurled herself at Darius, all fists and fury, but the Operative caught her mid-swing and restrained her.

"Even the Steel Falcon stands no chance against the power of the Scorps," Darius shouted.

The crowd started to stamp their feet in unison. It grew and grew like the building's pulse was racing in excitement. Reinhardt and Lyle stood over Kalum, looking expectantly at Darius.

"What will be his fate?" Darius asked of the crowd.

The crowd held up short light sticks. They glowed white, lighting a halo around the cage. One by one they changed colour, some turning red, some green.

"The reds have it!" Darius proclaimed, not bothering to count numbers. "Aaaand red means dead!" He turned and gave a thumbs down to the Scorps. Reinhardt and Lyle each lifted a boot above Kalum's head, ready to bring them down.

"Get up Kal!" Lexi screamed.

The Operative released Lexi as if she'd zapped his hand with a bolt of electricity. He took a step towards the cage but stopped in stunned amazement as Kalum rolled out of the way of the heavy boots, and twisted up into a half crouch.

Kalum looked up at the Scorps, his HUD back online. His mind felt sluggish, like he'd been hit with a tranquilliser, and there was a pain in his chest as his erratic heartbeat struggled to keep up, its muscle no longer receiving the electrical impulses it needed.

"Is this what a heart attack feels like?" he gasped to Nex.

"Come on!" Nex shouted, his face pinched in agony that mirrored Kalum's. "Push the pain away. Fight!"

Lyle had crossed the gap between them in two bounds, diving forward in a tackle. Kalum selected his attack from the menu and then his body was in motion too. His muscles thrust him forward like an arrow being released. The thick frontal bone of his skull crushed Lyle's nose and mouth leaving an engorged crimson mess. Lyle went down, a tree being felled, blood spewing from his mouth like a geyser. Kalum's head pounded and he knew it wasn't just from the impact.

Reinhardt's arms were around him, like a boa constrictor trying to squeeze the air out of him as he was hoisted up. Kalum picked the first option the HUD gave him and he drove the point of his elbow repeatedly into the top of the man's shaven head. Reinhardt staggered and with a thrust Kalum slithered up and twisted around so that his legs wrapped around the man's thick neck. Reinhardt clawed at him, and ran at the side of the cage, trying to knock Kalum off. Instead, Kalum managed to hook his fingers around the bars and started to pull himself and the enormous Scorp up its side, and kept going until he was hanging from the top, turning his body into a modified hangman's noose.

The muscles in his legs cried out, the tissue and sinew on fire, but they kept the heavy Scorp off the ground. Kalum's chest felt like it was being speared and he thought his heart might explode. He could taste blood and his vision lost clarity but he was aware Reinhardt's thrashing was beginning to slow. The Scorp let out a gurgle and then he hung limp, his body swaying like an abandoned playground swing. Somewhere deep inside Kalum he felt an urge to hold on until the man's neck snapped, to feel the crack of the vertebrae and the slice of his spinal cord. His vision tinged red and his HUD started to disappear as he gritted his teeth. Nex floated in front of him, shaking his head.

"No," his broken up static voice said. "The Steel Falcon doesn't kill."

The words were enough to bring Kalum back to his senses and he let Reinhardt fall to the mat, his legs splaying behind him.

Kalum let go of the top of the cage, landing silently, like a panther. The crowd had fallen silent. Every eye in the room was fixed on him.

Then a chant started up from the side of the stage.

"Fal-con. Fal-con. Fal-con."

Jun had managed to find his feet, and with it, his voice. Lexi joined in, and so did Casey.

Darius backhanded Jun but it was too late. There was a ripple as it spread throughout the crowd. A whisper that became a torrent.

Reese stirred. He'd been sitting cross-legged with his face in his hands, but now he looked around, the confusion plastered across his face and in his bleary eyes.

There was a clanking sound and the cage began to rise.

Kalum whirled to see the Operative pulling on the thick cable attached to the pulley. A bright lance of pain cut through Kalum's head and he lost his footing. Everything went black for a moment and when he opened his eyes again he'd fallen to one knee.

"Yes!" shouted Darius. "A final fight. Ladies and gentlemen, I present the greatest warrior in the Scorp army, the most vicious warrior I have ever seen fight. Are you ready for the showdown of the century? The Steel Falcon versus the Operative!"

He tried to pump up the crowd to his cause but they fell silent as the Operative finished hoisting the heavy cage on his own.

"I can't keep using up your body's energy," Nex said, panting. "If I push it any further you might have a fit, or a stroke. It's going to kill you."

Kalum tried to get to his feet but gravity pressed back down on him. The Operative was standing in front of him now. Kalum's eyes refused to focus and he saw double. There was a thud as something landed at Kalum's feet. The Steel Falcon symbol on his costume's chest plate stared back at him from the floor.

"Put it on," the Operative's synthesised voice said.

"Wha... What are you doing?" Darius stammered.

"You're no Scorp, you're a disgrace!" The Operative said, whirling around to stab a finger in Darius' direction. "A Scorp isn't a Corporation lapdog." He stooped and picked up a discarded empty Aug canister. "A true Scorp wouldn't peddle these Sentech made drugs!"

"Shut your mouth!" Darius screamed, frothing at the mouth like a rabid animal. "You work for me!" He gestured to the crowd, and Scorp fighters pushed their way to the front.

Darius pointed to the cage's pulley but the fighters remained where they were, eyes flicking between him and the Operative, clearly struggling to decide where their loyalty lay.

Kalum felt the snap and click as the Operative fastened his chest plate to his body. His gauntlets were threaded on next, but they made his arms feel as if they were weighed down by blocks of concrete.

"Come on, hero," the Operative said, hefting him to his feet. "Time to go."

Darius growled and stomped to the pulley, swiping at anyone in his way. A thick machete was in his hand now. One swing bit halfway through the knotted rope. The second cleaved through it. The cage fell free and crashed to floor, its metal ends gouging chunks out of the concrete. The Operative stepped up to the cage, examining it for a moment. Then his fingers wrapped around the bars and wrenched them apart. The metal groaned as it twisted in his hands, before the welded sections gave way. With a grunt an opening was ripped asunder and the Operative stepped through it.

"We had a deal," Darius said as he stepped back.

"I don't deal with traitors," the Operative replied. "I work for the true leader of the Scorps. He's back and he's not happy you're working on Sentech's side."

At this the crowd hushed and turned their eyes on Darius. His eyes darted around, trying to show enough bluster to deflect the accusation, but his effect was half-hearted. He let out a sigh and rolled his eyes at the Operative.

"There are no sides you idiot," he spat. "There's the Corporation way or death. That's exactly the lesson the man you're talking about learned the hard way. He's dead."

An angry murmur rippled through the crowd, a warning tremor before tectonic plates crashed together.

"Where do you think your food comes from?" Darius roared, wheeling around so that he could take in all the gathered faces. "The Augs we sell? Sentech made. Sentech give us the power to run this place, to keep the lights on. They allow the electricity to flow," he said, gesturing around him. "We get to live like this because of the deals I made." Darius was screaming like a petulant child in the middle of a tantrum.

"You don't own these people," the Operative said. "Sentech doesn't either. They are free."

Darius reached into his pocket and fished out a device that looked like a remote fob used to lock and unlock vehicles.

"I won't let you, or him, bring down everything I've worked so hard to build," Darius said, and then he pressed the button. The Operative stopped and jerked as if buffeted by unseen waves. Then he fell, slamming face-first into the ground, his hands not even trying to break his fall.

"Say what you want about Sentech, but they've got the best toys," Darius said. "I installed those mini charges in your suit when you first came back from Quantril. They don't just want *him* off the grid. They want you too. In one piece, more or less."

KALUM WAS HANGING from the side of the cage. His grip on the bars the only thing that kept him from falling. Darius pulled a gun and levelled it at Kalum, lining up the centre of his visor in his crosshairs. The crowd surged and pushed against the makeshift platform, panicked by the sight of the firearm. There was a dull crack and a section of it collapsed.

Darius fell forward and the gun flew end over end to land near the cage. There was no way Darius could cross the divide and his soldiers couldn't hear him above the din of the crowd. Reese squatted down by Darius' gun and tapped it with his finger. He lifted it and stared in awe at the way the light caught the metal casing.

"You stick with me and I'll give you as many Augs as you could possibly want," Darius called to Reese, trusting that enough of the Aug was in his system to allow the boy to hear his voice.

At the mention of Augs, Reese's eyes gained a modicum of focus. He looked from the gun to the Scorp on the other side of the station.

"Pick it up," Darius said. He pointed to where Kalum was propped up against the side of the cage. "Shoot him, and it's all yours."

Reese hooked his finger around the trigger guard and lifted it. He regarded it with his head tilted to one side.

"Just pull the trigger," Darius said, gesturing Reese towards where Kalum was clawing to stay upright.

In the crowd, the Scorps loyal to Darius had managed to quell any potential uprising. They were all around the edges, weapons bulging at their waists, hidden in plain sight, their presence no secret.

"Prove yourself," Darius said. "You said you wanted to be a Scorp..."

Reese looked down at his brother, seeing, but not seeing him at the same time. His smile was serene as he looked down the barrel and placed the muzzle on top of Kalum's head.

Nex was quiet, his reserves spent. Kalum didn't have enough energy to speak, let alone dodge the bullet. Kalum's arm came up in a flickering jerky movement. He managed to hook his finger under the edge of his visor and pulled it free of his face.

Reese's pupils dilated and he took in his brother's bruised and battered face. The dried blood caked there made his features almost unrecognisable, but with Nex out of commission Kalum's eyes had returned to their mismatched state. Reese's finger was tight around the trigger now, a fraction more pressure was all that was needed.

"Look at me, Reese."

The words came out as a hiss of breath, and Kalum wasn't sure they carried to his brother, but thought he could see a glimmer of recognition on his face.

"Shoot hi—" Darius bellowed, but the gunshot that echoed through the station cut him off. He was thrown back, and his body somersaulted over the balustrade to land in the crates holding the Augs a few feet below. A shimmering mist rose up as hundreds of damaged Aug canisters released their contents, the coloured gases swirling and coalescing to give an ethereal effect. The crowd realising that the show was well and truly over, took advantage of the distraction to move past Darius' men, who were either rushing to his aid or trying to cover the Operative and Kalum with their weapons.

"Kal?" Reese said.

He shook his head like he was trying to rattle his thoughts into order. "How did...Where are we?" he said, as all the questions he had fought to get out at once.

The Operative gave a groan and stirred on the floor. Reese saw him and retreated, putting himself between the Operative and Kalum, hand back in a defensive posture.

"Leave my brother alone," Reese said.

A cry went out from where Darius had fallen and one of

the Scorp guards staggered across the stage and collapsed with a blossoming red slash spreading across his top. Another section of the stage was reduced to a mangled, splintered wreck and the crowds gave up all pretence of order and began stampeding to the exits.

"Guys...?" Casey shouted from the stage. "A little help?"

Another Scorp scream hastened their pace. The Operative took a few unsteady steps then leapt to the stage. He snapped Casey's bonds and then did the same to Jun and Lexi's. Suddenly he was jerked into the air. He didn't have time to cry out before he was thrown across the room. An unfortunately placed pillar interrupted his flight and the impact changed his trajectory, knocking him off the platform.

Darius stepped onto the stage and the floorboards groaned a warning. His eyes were scarlet, his normally brown irises totally obscured by the blood film of burst capillaries. He'd absorbed the contents of the hundreds of crushed Aug canisters. Their contents had seeped into his skin and were still being absorbed into his bloodstream. His clothes were ripped where hypertrophied muscle had burst through. The blood vessels that ran over the exposed skin were thick and engorged like the root of a tree.

"Falcon!"

His screamed the word, his mouth opening so wide that the corners of his mouth ripped and bled. Blood from his eyes, ears and nose also dripped out and flowed down the contours of his face to form a horrific claret necklace. Even Lexi backed away, and they all scrambled to the edge of the platform to look for the Operative.

He was already back on his feet and ready to fight. There was a clanking noise as the armour of his right arm disappeared and reformed. It was replaced by the glowing gun barrel that pulsed with power.

"Stop!" Casey said, waving his hands and jumping up and down, halting the Operative mid-stride. "Don't step on that!" Casey said, pointing to the rail just below the Operative's boot. "It's electrified. Darius said that the power's on, right? That means that rail carries over six hundred volts. Just touching it would kill you instantly!"

The Operative inclined his head and side stepped the rail before leaping back onto the platform in one bound.

"Down!" he shouted, and used his free arm to move the group to the side. His gun arm whirred and they felt the heat as it discharged a bolt of plasma that lit up the whole place. It slammed into Darius as he towered over Reese and Kalum. The force of the impact knocked the brothers back into the cage. The sickly smell of charred flesh made Kalum gag as he struggled to see through the smoke.

As it cleared they could see Darius' outline as he huffed deep, raspy breaths. The remains of his shirt and jacket fell off in smouldering fragments, revealing a raw hole in his chest, the bone of his sternum partially exposed. As the Operative's gun arm hummed and recharged, the wound began to knit together, healing in front of their eyes. He was moving before the Operative could fire, zipping left and right. The blast caught his shoulder but didn't slow the charge. He ploughed through the group, sending them sprawling. A huge hand wrapped around the Operative's neck and the armour there began to crack as he squeezed.

There was a popping sound as Reese charged forward at the monster and fired the handgun, an anaemic sound compared to the boom of the Operative's weapon. It was enough to get Darius' attention though. His free hand caught Reese and slammed him down on the ground next to the Operative.

Darius showered them with spittle as they tried to squirm free. Nex appeared, flickering in and out of existence in Kalum's field of view as he pointed below them. Lexi, Casey and Jun were at his side now and pulling him to his feet. In an instant of clarity he understood Nex's meaning. He looked down at the electrified rail and felt panic wash over him.

Darius roared as the Operative and Reese both continued to fire on him but held them firm. Kalum knew what he had to do. The panic disappeared, his heart beat strong and steady, and his hand didn't shake at all. He looked at Lexi and gave her hand a squeeze before throwing himself off the platform onto the electrified rails.

34

THAT PERFECT MOMENT

K alum's hand contacted the rail and he felt white-hot fire engulf his whole body. The rail carried nearly three times as much voltage as the defibrillator that he'd been shocked with at the school, and the pain was off the chart. Its current surged into him as he gritted his teeth and held tight. The smell of charred flesh filled the air and Kalum's eyes bulged as he saw his skin begin to blister. His body arched and bucked with enough force to snap bone.

Tap! Tap! Tap! The pressure behind his eyes started anew.

Kalum glanced down and saw his body start to heal from the devastation wrought from the high voltage rail. Lexi's scream made his head snap up and see Darius baring down on her. With a cry Kalum launched himself onto the platform and delivered a kick to Darius' face that knocked him back a few feet. But Darius was back up on his feet instantly, shaking his head like a snarling dog. A swipe of the Scorp's arm caught the edge of Kalum's visor and sent him cartwheeling like a ragdoll across the room.

"An inch closer and that'd have taken off your head!" Nex shouted. "Kal! We need to regroup!"

Kalum wiped the blood away from his mouth and stood, ignoring Nex. The rage swept over him and the HUD disappeared, replaced by the red haze. With a roar that started in his gut, Kalum pulled himself free of the debris. Darius was already lumbering towards him, but Kalum met him halfway. The Operative pulled Lexi out of their path as Jun and Casey dove to one side. Kalum and Darius exchanged thundering strikes that sent waves of pressure through the room.

"Kal!" Nex shouted. "We can't go toe to toe with his raw strength! I'm burning through energy just healing you."

"Kill you! Break you! Smash you!" Kalum screeched, his eyes going wide with frenzied madness. He ignored Nex and used his fists as battering rams against Darius' chest. He poured every ounce of frustration, every memory of every injustice he'd ever faced, the memory of all the physical and mental anguish he'd been through in his short life, into his blows.

The attacks just bounced off the knotted muscle and only enraged the Scorp further. He grabbed Kalum by the arms and hoisted him off the ground. With a grunt he started to pull, trying to snap the boy like a wishbone. Kalum thrashed and snarled, kicking at Darius, but the Scorp gave a guttural laugh and kept pulling.

"This rage, this anger... it's not me. That's all you," Nex said. "Unless we work together you'll die. They all will. Remember what we fight for..."

A shared memory played out in his mind in crystal clarity. Kalum saw a cold winter night and a younger version of himself sandwiched on a couch between his father, mother and Reese. An old television, small by the standards of today's displays, showed yet another Bruce Lee marathon his mother had talked them all into watching. On top of the couch was Nex, looking the same as he did now, laughing, giggling and throwing himself around with wild abandon. Kalum felt the warmth of their closeness, the security of them just existing together in that perfect moment. The feeling clung to him, permeating through every fibre of his being, drilling down to his core.

He returned to the present with jarring immediacy, all his rage evaporating in an instant. The breath in his chest came easily with each rise and fall, his heartbeat as steady as a metronome. He moved in sync with Nex, perfectly in time as one. They reached out, Nex's arm shimmering as it overlaid Kalum's.

With a spark and then a flicker his HUD reappeared. His legs snaked around Darius' neck and with a twist he hurled the Scorp through the air.

"Yes!" Nex's voice rang in his head, strong and crackling with power. "What a rush!"

Kalum opened his eyes and saw the light tendrils all around him. The kaleidoscope of colour held him hypnotised for a moment. His hand reached out, tentative at first, and then he grasped hold of a yellow thread of light. A surge of energy sped of his arm and detonated at the base of his skull like a bomb. One by one the strands of light flickered and died away. Kalum's HUD burst into life, brimming with new offensive options. Time stood still as it cycled through an expansive repertoire of fighting styles.

"How do I know all this?" Kalum asked as the options scrolled on endlessly.

"I don't know! Maybe the electricity in the rail super-charged me?" said Nex. "No more limits! We can really cut loose now!"

Darius had turned his attention to Reese. He had the

boy pressed up against the wall with one hand, the other balled into a wrecking-ball fist ready to tear through him. The Scorp leader gave a cry and swung, but the Operative knocked Reese free, taking the bulk of the impact on his side.

"Hey Darius!" Kalum called from the other side of the wrecked platform. "Remember me? I'm the one who humiliated you in front of your men, and I'm the one who's been taking out your men in the street. I'm the one who destroyed your business! You want someone to hurt? Well come get some."

Kalum dropped into a fighting stance and put his hand out, beckoning the monster to him. Darius screamed, all thoughts of the Operative and Reese gone from his drug-addled brain. They rushed each other, and Kalum slid under a sweeping arm. He got in close to the deranged Scorp leader and unloaded a series of attacks that drove him up the escalator. Kalum ducked under a desperate lunge and fired off a barrage of punches that hit like machine gun fire.

Darius staggered back but Kalum didn't let up. He spun through the air and his leg whipped out, lashing his opponent in the face and off his feet. Kalum dared a glance over his shoulder. At the bottom of the escalator he saw the Operative helping Reese to his feet. Casey, Jun and Lexi were by his side.

"Get them out of here!" Kalum shouted to the Operative. There was enough time for Kalum to register his nod of agreement before Darius hefted him off the ground and slammed him into a wall. He kept his hold on Kalum and pivoted, charging at the opposite wall with the same effect. Each impact hit Kalum like a car crash, and he tried to think as his brain ricocheted around his skull. Darius leaned in and Kalum could feel the heat of his breath.

"Kill you... Then them," he rasped.

"No!" Kalum shouted. He brought both hands together, his palms clapping on Darius' ears, who cried out and staggered back, blood trickling out from ruptured eardrums. Kalum surged forward, rapid-fire strikes pushing Darius back until he was teetering on his feet. Kalum took measure of the big man, thought of all he had done to threaten his family and friends, and focused all his emotions. With a quick shuffle forwards he unleashed a devastating sledgehammer side-kick that sent Darius through the adjacent wall and out into the night.

The Scorp leader lay still, apart from the rhythmical twitching of his hypertrophied muscles. Picking his way past the rubble, Kalum moved to stand over Darius. He gave him a tap with his boot, but he didn't stir. Kalum took a moment to catch his breath, letting it plume up into the cold night air.

The familiar low hum of a surveillance drone buzzed overhead, and Kalum turned to see it lock in on him. It pitched forward, zipping towards him, its props sounding like an angry swarm.

A blue bolt from the Operative's blaster turned it to dust in mid flight. Kalum gave him an appreciative nod and watched as Reese, Lexi, Casey and Jun followed him out.

"I stopped it attacking but it would have already broadcast our position. We haven't got much time," the Operative said, turning his head away.

Darius groaned and started to stir.

"Holy moly!" Jun exclaimed backing away. "What's it gonna take to put him down?"

Kalum and Nex readied themselves, the power still

buzzing through their body, raw and barely under control. Before he could rush forward to attack, Kalum felt a hand on his shoulder, holding him back. The Operative shook his head and pointed.

They all heard the shuffling footsteps before they saw who they belonged to. The neon lights from the Corporate section of the city served to silhouette the slightly hunched figure in the long coat and baseball cap. He was heading directly to where Darius was lumbering to his feet. Kalum tried to pull away, but the Operative's fingers dug in like steel barbs, anchoring him in place.

"He'll kill him," Kalum said, struggling to get away.

"No," said the Operative evenly. "No he won't."

Darius turned, now seeing the approaching man. With a roar he swung at him with an arm thick and powerful enough to tear through the decrepit figure. Kalum watched as the man straightened up to his full height, the kink in his back disappearing with an audible crack. Darius' fist hit an invisible barrier a foot away from the man's face and the air ignited with sparks. The Scorp leader recoiled and tried again with the same result. Fear sparked behind his manic eyes. The old man weaved in close, his open palm contacting Darius' forehead. A pulse of energy washed out, the two of them at its epicentre. Darius teetered for a moment, and then collapsed in a heap, quivering and returning to his former self.

The older man bent forward, his hands resting on his haunches while he panted.

"What?" said Darius as he started to rise. "Where—? How'd I get out here?" He looked at the man in front of him and his eyes wandered from his ragged clothes to the others gathered around them. A few of his Scorp warriors stumbled out to join them and they looked to him for direction.

He staggered away from the old man, desperately trying to remain on his feet.

"Round em up," Darius said, sweeping a hand to point at them all.

The Scorps hesitated but a glare from Darius spurred them forward.

"Leave them," the old man said in a raspy voice that Kalum recognised.

"Shut your mouth, old man," Darius spat. "This is Scorp territory and I'm the big dog in charge."

He ripped off the remains of his torn sleeve to show his large scorpion tattoo, the symbol of his status and power.

The man took off his baseball cap and the light caught his face, the deep scars casting rough shadows. He stepped up to Darius, matching him in height, and locked eyes with him. Vincent yanked up his shirt to expose the sharp edges of the scorpion symbol that spread from one corner of his torso to the other.

Darius' balked and a mumbling stream of words escaped from his slack jaw. The other Scorps fell to one knee and bowed their heads.

"S-sir," Darius said, dropping to his knee as well. "We thought you were dead."

Vincent moved with a silent fluidity now, any trace of the arthritic old Trinity groundskeeper gone. He looked down at Darius, the scornful look on his face made more severe by the scarring.

"You thought I was gone and subverted the very purpose of the Scorps by getting into bed with Sentech?" His bladed hand rose above his head, a guillotine waiting to fall. Kalum found himself moving forward but the Operative still held him back.

"You are misguided," Vincent said at last, his hand dropping to his side. "But, without you the Scorps would have withered away to nothing." He hoisted Darius to his feet and his pale blue eyes locked the burly Scorp to the spot. "You will have to make recompense." The blood drained from Darius' face and he managed a meek nod in reply.

"Like hell he's just walking away from this!" Lexi shouted.

Kalum finally shrugged off the Operative and crossed the potholed street until he was a few feet from Vincent.

"I'm taking him in," Kalum said. Nex was by his side, still bright like a star, standing with his hands on his hips, defiant.

"Even if you could take him from us, where would you take him?" Vincent scoffed. "The Enforcers? Sentech? He was working for them. They have corrupted the whole purpose of the Scorps for their own use. But all that changes now that I'm back."

Vincent turned away from Kalum, his coat swirling around him as he faced what was left of the Scorps.

"You will rendezvous at the original safe house." He paused by Darius, holding him back while the others moved by. "Do not fail me again."

Darius looked over his shoulder at Kalum, fire burning behind his tight and controlled expression. Then with a nod to Vincent he followed the rest of his group.

"Well done," Vincent said to the Operative. "As usual you were correct. They had strayed from their cause. The ship needed righting."

Vincent's gaze flicked to Kalum and then back to the Operative. "Leave us," he said.

The Operative began to protest but a look from Vincent cut him off. He sprinted after the Scorps and was lost from view.

Kalum tensed as Vincent approached, fists bunched and legs tensed, ready to move.

"You've been fighting on the wrong team," Vincent said. "The Scorps, at least the real Scorps, aren't your enemies. It's the Corporation. It always has been."

The way the man approached them was unnerving. There wasn't a trace of fear, not a jot of uncertainty in each confident stride he took. At his side even Nex seemed to shrink as he neared them. Kalum backed away from the man, eyeing escape routes and pulling his friends back with him as he did.

"I know all about you, Kalum," Vincent said. "I know about Nex. I know the truth about what happened to your father."

Kalum stopped dead at that. The sirens were growing louder but were joined by the din of the drone squadron in the distance.

"What do you mean, '*the truth*'?" Kalum asked.

"I want your father's old research notebook," Vincent said. "Open it for me and I will answer any questions you have."

Reese stumbled forward. His eyes were still bloodshot and unfocused. He swayed on his broad base stance and glared at Vincent.

"Leave my brother alone," he slurred.

Vincent regarded Reese, clearly unimpressed by his bravado. An arm shot out and Reese was hoisted off the ground by his neck. The same pulse of energy that Darius had released slammed into Kalum as he moved to intervene. Vincent lowered Reese back to his feet and backed away. Whatever he had done to Darius and now to Reese had exacted a toll. His skin was the pale sallow colour of rigor mortis and his eyes buried in sunken sockets.

"A gift," he rasped.

"Wow," Reese said, looking at his hands. "I... I feel great."

He caught Lexi's sceptical look and quickly clarified.

"I mean, not-being-on-an-Aug great. I feel like me."

Vincent retreated, the shadows of the building swallowing him whole.

"I will give you time to consider your options," Vincent said, his voice carrying to them as he vanished. "But know this. I will have that book, with or without your assistance."

"We need to go now," Casey said. "If we can hear the sirens we only have a minute tops to get out of here.

Kalum walked backwards, eyes still fixed on the spot where Vincent had disappeared into the darkness. Then Lexi's hand was in his, pulling him away. They ran, heeding Casey's warning, leaving the ruins of the Scorp headquarters in their wake.

EPILOGUE

"You don't have to do this," Nadine said. "Either of you."

It had only taken two weeks of thorough interrogation by the Enforcers, under the watchful eye of Clayton Lancaster, before Sentech had cleared Reese to return to Trinity. Nadine had been another matter, the guilt she felt like a shroud hanging over her. It took another three weeks of overbearing fussiness before she would let him even near to the Arena.

Lucas had dealt with the situation the way he usually did. One part gruff emotional denial, one part cringe-worthy joke telling. But the extra beat he hugged his nephew for conveyed more than his words did. Although they had to keep Reese's disappearance a secret from Owen, his glassy eyes teared up at the sight of Reese.

Kalum had watched his brother and his father embrace, and heard Vincent's words in his head.

"I know the truth about what happened to your father."

Whatever Vincent had done to clear out any residual influence the Augs had on Reese had also left them undetectable by the tests Sentech insisted on running. It had also given Reese clarity of thought. The night of his escape, on the rooftop of their home, Kalum and Reese had worked out their cover story.

"Before we go in, let's get your story straight," Kalum said. "You got in the Scorps' way when they came to Trinity, and they snatched you? Does that sound okay?"

Reese nodded and gave a nervous glance off the side of the roof. He edged back a bit so he could hold on to the chimney breast.

"And then there was some kind of coup and I used the distraction to escape?" Reese said. "It works for me."

"Okay then..." Kalum said. "I'll get you back down to the ground and you ring the bell. I'll go in through my window."

Kalum put his hand out to Reese, but his brother didn't move.

"I've... I've not been a good brother to you," Reese said. "Playing Henkan, getting to be co-Captain, getting picked up by the Scouts? I said it was all for you guys, that I was carrying you all... but the truth is... I did it for me too. I love it. The Arena, the bright lights, the thrill of scoring? It's more addictive than the Augs."

Reese reached over and pulled Kalum into a tight embrace. Kalum could feel his hot tears on his neck, but he didn't pull away.

"But none of that means anything without my family. I'll try to be a better brother..." Reese whispered.

"We both will," Kalum said.

They released each other and there was a moment of awkwardness between them.

"So..." Reese said, clearing his throat and breaking the silence. "My brother is the Steel Falcon. How did something like that even happen?"

Kalum came over to him and sat down. For a time the

two brothers looked out over their city with nothing but the sound of the wind between them.

"It's Nex," Kalum said. "He's real, he's like my co-pilot, gives me powers, abilities…"

"Okaaaay," Reese said. "Where did he come from then? Why the whole Steel Falcon thing?"

"We don't really know what he is. He helped me in the Arena, and in exchange this was his price."

They waited there and watched the sun rising in silence until the streets started to show signs of waking.

"Boys?" Nadine said, bringing Kalum back to the present. "We can just turn around and go home. I can tell Macintosh you need more time."

Kalum looked up at his mother's face, taking comfort in the familiar creases of concern he saw there.

"I need to do this," Reese said. "I want to."

The crowd were chanting again, the rumble of feet in the stands reaching a crescendo. But Kalum's pulse was steady as a ticking clock.

Walker.

Walker.

Walker.

The brothers stood side by side at the edge of the Arena, decked out in their Titans Henkan gear. Nex appeared in Kalum's peripheral vision, still wearing his costume.

"We've got this 'lil bro," Reese said, holding out a fist.

Kalum bumped back the fist and smiled.

He looked up into the crowd, and saw Clayton Lancaster standing in his viewing box. Even without his augmented sight he could feel Lancaster's eyes on them. A shiver ran down his spine and he shook it off. He pushed away thoughts of Sentech secrets and lies, of Vincent's offer, and of all the crazy mess his life had become over the last few months. Looking back up he saw Jun, Casey and Lexi chatting in the stands. His eyes lingered on Lexi for a moment, before moving across to look for A.J, but she was nowhere to be seen.

"Time to show them what the Walker brothers can do," Reese said, drawing Kalum's attention back.

"Team Falcon are in the house!" Nex screamed, and the brothers sprinted out into the Arena as the crowd went berserk.

Up in his executive box, Clayton Lancaster looked down at the spectators surging to their feet as the Walker brothers took to the Arena. Next to him Eli Cooper was talking in a hushed tone but he had tuned out his incessant prattle. There were a few other high ranking Sentech families there as well, partaking in the sumptuous food and drink that was laid out with lavish splendour.

His TRIST sounded an alert, more urgent and ominous than its usual ring. It set off a flutter in his chest that he quietly cursed himself for.

"Give me the room," he said.

Around him the patrons started to rise from their seats and filter out, taking their time. At his side he felt his TRIST vibrate and the tone take on a distinct urgency.

"NOW!" Lancaster screamed. He ran his arm across the table, sending plates and cutlery flying. His Enforcer guards raised their weapons and started to push the people out with force.

"Out! Out!" Cooper said, using his bulk to usher out the final person. He turned and gave Lancaster a smile, which died prematurely when he saw the man's face.

Two strides brought Lancaster across to Cooper. Before

he could speak, Lancaster's hand covered the Headmaster's face and he was shoved out as well. Lancaster spun and answered the call. The TRIST projected the image of a man's face above its screen. His face was mostly in shadow but what could be seen was severe in its bearing.

"Nine," he said.

"I'm sorry, Sir." Lancaster said. "I don't follow."

"Your TRIST rang nine times before you answered my call."

The man leant forward and his face came into view. His hair was combed back, and was jet black, save for his white widow's peak. His eyes were the colour of flint and even via video link carried a gravitas that made Lancaster shrink back.

"I apologise, Sir," Lancaster said, bowing his head.

"Report," the man said.

"The Scorps have been very successful in spreading the Augs throughout the city," Lancaster said. "I estimate fifty percent of the population have been exposed."

"And the informant?"

"I am awaiting information on stage two Sir, but following his instructions even the NCs exposed to the Augs were susceptible."

"What of the vigilante?"

"He is of no consequence Sir. I—" Lancaster started, but the man cut him off in a thundering voice.

"The informant specifically said that he was not to be harmed," the man snapped. "Your pet Scorp nearly cost us everything."

"Yes Sir," Lancaster said, bowing his head once more.

"Do not fail me again, Clayton."

"I will not, Mr Fleming," Lancaster said as the video feed cut out.

. . .

THAT NIGHT after the screams and celebrations of their victory had quietened and after Reese's reassessment by the Henkan Scouts, Kalum sat alone in his room. He sat at his desk, listening to the sounds drifting in through his open window. He was in full costume, senses tingling and Nex chattering away in his head. On the desk in front of him was his sketchbook, Owen Walker's repurposed notebook that Vincent wanted so badly. He stared at it, as he had done every night since Reese's rescue, leafing through his father's notes, which by now he knew by memory, even if he didn't understand them.

In his left hand he held onto the metal band. The draw to it was stronger than he thought possible, the thought of being apart from it making him feel physically unwell. With an irritated grunt he slammed the book shut, the force of it tearing part of the thick spine. With a groan he ran his finger over the damaged area. His finger found a deep groove hidden beneath the cover. A tingle ran up his spine, a sense of deja vu consuming him. His hands were moving of their own volition. They slid the metal band into the groove and it clicked home. Inside the cover, Kalum felt something release and open, and all at once a feeling of dread crept over him, pervading and absolute. Scrambling, he dug out the band and threw both items into his drawer and backed away to the window.

"What was that?' Nex said, appearing in a burst of light.

"No idea," Kalum said, barely able to speak, his mouth suddenly dry. "I... I just... I just need to get out of here."

Nex scrutinised Kalum, looking him up and down. Then he brightened.

"Well good news for you then," Nex said. "The Steel

Falcon's work is never done. We've still got to round up the rest of the Scorps still loyal to Darius and keep an eye on Sentech."

Kalum pushed thoughts of the book far away to the recesses of his mind and turned to the window. With one last glance over his shoulder, he dropped into the night, letting its darkness envelop him.

TEAM FALCON NEEDS YOU!

I hope you enjoyed Book 1 of the Steel Falcon series: Awakening - follow the adventures of the Steel Falcon in Book 2 - Synergy here:

UK: https://amzn.to/2R2cPwa

USA: https://amzn.to/2BkeaVo

Join Team Falcon and get extra content by clicking on the link below:

https://www.subscribepage.com/sentechfiles1

This is what you will receive:

1. A copy of the "Sentech Secret Files" which the Spectre put together. It is filled with details that he uncovered whilst posing as a Sentech scientist, and contains Easter eggs for events planned for later in the series.
2. Password access to areas of my website (www.nkquinn.com) that contain deleted scenes, additional content and exclusive character artwork done by international comic book artists

3. Early notification about new releases, deals and social media events.
4. An opportunity to join my advanced reader team and receive free books.
5. No spam! Ever!
6. A gleaming virtual high five from me!

Follow the link to join : https://www.subscribepage.com/sentechfiles1

TEAM FALCON NEEDS YOUR HELP

If you enjoyed Kalum Walker's first adventure, I would be eternally grateful if you would leave an honest review on Amazon. As a new author positive reviews mean that I can spend more time creating content that I (and hopefully you) love, and can access more readers via advertising and promotions.

There are still many mysteries to unravel and adventures to be had in the world of the Steel Falcon. I hope you will join us for this wild ride!

35

THE STEEL FALCON BOOK 2: SYNERGY - CHAPTER 1

To the people rushing around on the street below he was a blur. By the time they'd done a double take he was long gone. The rooftops of the city were his playground, and he knew them as well as he knew himself.

A drone zipped by him and then came to a dead stop. It spun to face him, the propellers on the end of its long tapered legs angled toward him with dangerous intent. Kalum Walker, also known as The Steel Falcon, remained crouched, staring back at the drone's blinking red eye. With a flick of his wrists he extended the batons from his gauntlets and he stood, taking on a fighting stance. Harsh neon blue eyes glinted at the drone from behind his visor as they took measure of each other. The drone's secondary spotlight blinked on chasing away the shadows that concealed the vigilante. His padded Henkan gear stretched as his muscles grew beneath his costume and Kalum felt the thudding of his heart as his adrenaline spiked, readying his body for combat. The spotlight settled on the bright red stylised falcon crest on his chest and the drone chirped out an alarm as it sent an alert back to Enforcer headquarters.

"One hundred and twenty seconds until reinforcements arrive," the voice in Kalum's head said.

"Plenty of time to have some fun then," he replied.

In a flash, Kalum's neon blue combat HUD popped into his field of vision. It fed him stream after stream of data, offensive and defensive tactics, drone weak points of attack and a countdown timer for when reinforcements would arrive. A small compartment under the drone opened, and a barrel extended from it. There was a loud pop, like a bottle of champagne being opened, and it fired a barbed net, which unfolded itself in mid-flight. Kalum was way ahead of it, dodging to one side, letting it land harmlessly at his side.

"It's just a scout drone," the voice said. "Now it's defence-less, finish it!"

Kalum lunged forward, spinning as he did to give momentum to the baton strike. The drone zipped up and to one side, evading him easily. Following up with a series of flips and strikes, Kalum kept up the attack, but the drone was one step ahead each time. It flew out of reach again and the panels on its surface slid and rotated to reveal two more guns on each side.

"That's new..." Kalum said.

"Watch out!" the voice shouted as the tips of the barrels flashed and gunfire lit up the roof. Kalum howled in pain as a bullet grazed his cheek, sending warm blood running down his face even as Nex healed the wound. Then his arms were a blur, moving of their own volition, his upgraded batons cutting through the air and blocking the barrage of bullets.

"Nex!" Kalum said, fighting the sudden wave of nausea that hit him as the voice inside his head took control. "What're you doing? Give me back control!"

He felt Nex try to maintain control of his body, in an

internal 'tug-of-war' but then he yielded. There was a rush as Kalum took charge. The drone ceased fire, its clip spent, and Kalum retreated as it followed at a distance. A clicking sound filled the night as it prepared to spit another torrent of bullets at the Steel Falcon. Kalum scanned his surroundings and then dived behind a cylindrical metal roof vent as it opened fire. The bullets thudded into the thick plating and it warped under the onslaught of ordnance.

"You know what could take that drone out, right?" Nex said.

"That won't work!" Kalum said. "Even if I could get close enough, that thing's covered in steel plates. No way I could punch though it."

"But this isn't any old punch I'm talking about. It's the one i—"

"No, Nex," Kalum interrupted. "I need another way."

"Fine," Nex said. Kalum could hear the pout in his voice. "Why don't we 'play ball' instead then?"

Kalum nodded and reached into his backpack and pulled out the Henkan game ball. He engaged it. The ring of lights on its surface pulsed, lighting him up in its pale blue aura. The bullets kept coming at him, spanging off the metal that was barely protecting him now.

"Come on, come on!" he said, staring at the ball in his hands. The blue pulses came closer together, and he felt the ball hum in his hands. His muscles rippled as the fibres in his legs and arms hypertrophied, optimising his strength. Kalum dived to one side, landing nearly ten feet away. He slung the ball in midair and it slammed into the underside of the drone as it released its charge. The drone faltered, falling a few feet and then bobbing up again as its rotors tried to fire back up.

It was all the opening Kalum needed. He jumped and

brought both batons down on the drone, cleaving it in half. It sparked and sputtered on the rooftop, moving in erratic jerky movements like a dying insect. Kalum put it out of its misery with a well-placed stomp from the heel of his boot.

"Sentech really are beefing these things up," Kalum said as he tried to catch his breath.

"The one-inch punch would have worked, you know," Nex said, still sounding petulant.

"I don't know why you're obsessed with that move," Kalum said. "You've had me practicing it any chance you get."

"It's soooo cool!" Nex protested. "Why wouldn't you want to be like Bruce Lee?"

"Bruce Lee never went up against a gang of Enforcers or Sentech drones..." Kalum's voice trailed off as he cocked his head and listened. On cue, Nex ramped up his hearing, tuning it until Kalum could focus. At first it sounded like static, but it grew to a loud buzzing noise. Kalum turned to the horizon, trying to pinpoint the source and spied a black dot there. As the dot became bigger the buzzing intensified. Nex amplified his sight and then Kalum realised what he was looking at: reinforcements.

The buzzing of the angry swarm filled the early evening air and Kalum no longer needed enhanced senses to hear it.

"Nex, we need to disappear," he said.

In his HUD a three-dimensional map appeared, showing the endless rows of identical houses, branching out to the city centre and it's towering skyscrapers. The map rotated and honed in one a location, highlighting it with a pulsing red dot.

"There!" said Nex.

Kalum followed the map, scampering across the tiled

roofs and skirting around chimneys until he found the alcove in the side of one house to hide in.

With a bright flash, Nex appeared at his side, wearing a facsimile of the Steel Falcon costume they had designed together when he'd been around five. He had an eye mask and a long billowing white cape over a costume with a red falcon's head emblazoned on the chest. Nex wasn't really floating in mid air above him though. In actual fact, he was tinkering with Kalum's ocular nerve to make himself appear in his visual field, and could even make it seem as if he was interacting with the environment around them. As intrusive as it sounded, Kalum preferred it this way. It certainly felt less awkward than having a conversation with a disembodied voice in his head.

Nearly six months had passed since a near-death experience and thousands of joules of electricity had re-awoken Nex. They had struck a deal that had kept Kalum from being thrown out of his school, Trinity, and had taken him from loser to popular Henkan superstar in a heartbeat. The cost had been fulfilling Nex's childhood fantasy of becoming a 'superhero' just like the ones Kalum's father used to tell them about at bedtime.

But Kalum's internal copilot was still a mystery. For the longest time when he was young, he'd assumed that Nex was just a figment of his imagination. That had all changed when he'd started blacking out and losing time. At first it'd been only a few seconds, but those seconds had become minutes and then hours, and he'd had no recollection of what had happened. His mother had spent nearly all their family's credits to find a cure for his 'condition'. That cure had been strong prescription drugs that had to put Nex into a stasis, where he'd stayed until Kalum's brother Reese had switched out his medication.

Together Kalum and Nex had already achieved so much, taking down Darius, the megalomaniacal leader of the Scorps, a group that rebelled against Sentech, their ruling Corporation. In the process they'd discovered that Sentech had been secretly been controlling the Scorps all along, using them to peddle their experiment drugs called Augs.

The drones continued on their search-and-destroy mission, but the sound of their rotors was now fading into the distance. Reaching up, Kalum gripped the edge of the roof and pulled himself up and over on to the top of the building.

"Okay," said Nex. "How about we get on with the mission?"

As he finished speaking his pixelated form glitched and faded before coming back.

"How much more juice have we got?" Kalum asked.

"Not much," said Nex. "And you used the charge in the Henkan ball to take out the drone."

Kalum shrugged the small backpack off his shoulders and pulled out a thermos. He unscrewed it and poured steaming black liquid into the cap.

"Maybe this will pick you up," Kalum said.

Holding his nose, Kalum downed the black coffee, trying not to gag as the bitter liquid went down. Inside he felt Nex stir and buzz as the caffeine hit landed. His form took on more clarity and then burst into life.

"Awesome!" Nex said. "Now let's get moving; we've got to get to the NC camp and back before Ma gets home."

Kalum felt a wave of irritation creep over him at Nex referring to his mother as theirs but tried to hide it.

Nex turned to him, sensing the change in his mood. He blinked out of existence and reappeared just in front of

Kalum. He looked up at him, head cocked to the side and scratched his chin.

"What's with you, Kal?" Nex said.

"You took control," Kalum said. "When we fought that drone, and it opened fire. You used the batons to block the bullets."

A smile spread across Nex's young face and he put his hands on his hips and allowed his cape to flap behind him.

"All in a day's work for the Steel Falcon!" he said, taking a bow. "You're welcome!"

"No!" said Kalum. "You took control of my body. Mine! You said you wouldn't do that again."

"Hey!" Nex said, bristling. "I saved your life. If it wasn't for me you'd be full of holes!"

They stared at each other for a time, neither backing down. It was Kalum who looked away first, feeling vaguely ridiculous at having a staring contest with someone only he could see.

"Let's get going," Kalum muttered.

Over the last few months they had focused their patrols on weeding out any remaining Scorps who were still loyal to Darius. They'd also come across an increase in violence by the Sentech police force, known as Enforcers, against innocent NCs. These were Non-Corporates who were just trying to scrape together an existence away from Sentech's influence. None of the NCs had been part of the Scorps; they were innocent men, women and children. Kalum had been heading to one of their encampments before he'd become sidetracked by the drone.

"Hey, look," said Nex, pointing to the road ahead. From his vantage point, Kalum could see the sharp, angular chassis of an Enforcer Transport, carving through traffic. He felt his insides seize up as he realised that it was heading in the direction of the NC camp.

"Come on, Nex," he said. "We need to get there before them."

His strides became more powerful and his jumps longer as Nex augmented his strength. He tore through the urban jungle with precise agile movements. There was a definite change as he crossed over from the Sentech-run territory and into the NCs'. Here the buildings were run down and dilapidated. They were all like abandoned carcasses, with anything of value or use having been stripped out long ago. Street lights flickered as the NC-run generator fought to keep the sector lit. The roads were littered with the remnants of vehicles scarred with rust, standing memorials to the internal combustion engine.

Kalum sprinted past them, kicking up dust trails in his wake. Nex mapped him out the shortest route and he followed without question, their disagreement buried for the moment. He skidded to a stop as he neared the location Nex had marked on his virtual map. The structure in front of him was a mangled mass of glass and steel. Its cylindrical base rose to the sky before ballooning out and then tapering to a point at the top. There was a fence made from corrugated metal and salvaged car parts that encircled the building. At the gate there were a group of Scorp guards patrolling the entrance. When they saw him coming, they sounded a gong that set off a series deeper within the compound. They stood in formation, bringing their home-made weapons to bear.

"Stop!" a man shouted. "Stop right there!"

"There's no time," Kalum replied. "You need to evacuate. The Enforcers are coming."

The men didn't move. Kalum didn't blame them. When

he'd started patrolling as the Steel Falcon he'd gained a reputation for taking down Scorps, but those had been corrupt members, following Darius' command. Following Darius' fall, their new leader had been trying to bring them back to their original purpose of protecting the NCs and defying the Corporations. Now Kalum and the Scorps had a mutual enemy and an uneasy truce, but the Steel Falcon's notoriety was difficult to shake off.

The guards moved to flank him and formed a loose circle. A man with a scruffy beard and a swollen gut came at him first, a baseball bat wrapped with barbed wire whistling as it swung.

Kalum mentally selected a course of action from the HUD and he weaved inside the man's swing, stopping it with a palm on the handle, before reversing its momentum to crack him in the chin with its base. The blow wasn't hard enough to drop him, just packed enough punch to rock him back on his heels.

"Didn't you hear me?" Kalum shouted.

The remaining three guards tried to overcome him with sheer numbers, one coming at him low, whilst the others came from either side. They piled on top of him, sitting on his chest and pinning him to the ground. With a roar he slung them aside, silently thanking Nex for the power boost. The ruckus set off an alarm that brought more guards spilling out of the complex, who made a beeline for him. The noise also attracted civilians who kept their distance as more bodies joined the scuffle.

"Why are you making this so hard?" Kalum screamed, and he felt himself losing control, the rage causing the HUD to melt away and his vision flash red. With a roar he threw himself into the throng, a flurry of kick and punches driving them back into the complex.

"ENOUGH!"

Kalum stopped dead. He knew that synthesised voice anywhere. The Scorps backed away, parting to allow the Operative to approach. He wore his trademark white Kitsune fox mask with mirrored lenses over the eyes and a lithe armour-plated body suit in gunmetal grey. The Operative stopped ten feet from Kalum and looked him up and down.

"You're not welcome here, 'hero'," the Operative said, the last word dripping with condescension despite the mechanical tone.

"But... but the Enforcers ar—" Kalum started.

"Look at what you've done," said the Operative, gesturing to the bodies strewn across the ground. "You've attacked these men, just for defending their home."

"I came to warn you all," Kalum tried to protest, but the Operative cut him off with a swipe of his hand.

"You may have helped put Darius down..." the Operative said, "but you also got a lot of good men put away by Sentech on your misguided mission."

"Sentech have been targeting NCs. I've been trying to protect them."

"Nothing new there!" a woman cradling a swaddled child shouted from the crowd. "Sentech are always doing one thing or another to persecute us."

A murmur of agreement ran through the crowd and they moved closer to where Kalum was. The Operative raised a hand that stopped them dead.

"Back inside, everyone," he said. "I will get rid of the threat."

The Operative formed a fist, and the armour plates spun and moved to cover his right hand, forming the barrel of a gun. Yellow lights blinked on and off and then lit up solid. He raised it and pointed it straight at Kalum's head.

"Wait," Kalum said. "I don't want to fight you. We worked together to take down Darius. I'm not your enemy. Let's just take a m—"

The Operative fired his arm cannon, and the world went white.

For Titus, Janaki, Clive and Joyce, the people who taught me what it truly means to be strong.

DISCLAIMER

This is a work of fiction. Names, characters, businesses, places, events, locales, and incidents are either the products of the author's imagination or used in a fictitious manner. Any resemblance to actual persons, living or dead, or actual events is purely coincidental.

Printed in Great Britain
by Amazon